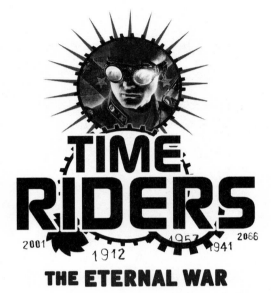

THE ETERNAL WAR

Also by **Alex Scarrow**

TimeRiders
TimeRiders: Day of the Predator
TimeRiders: The Doomsday Code

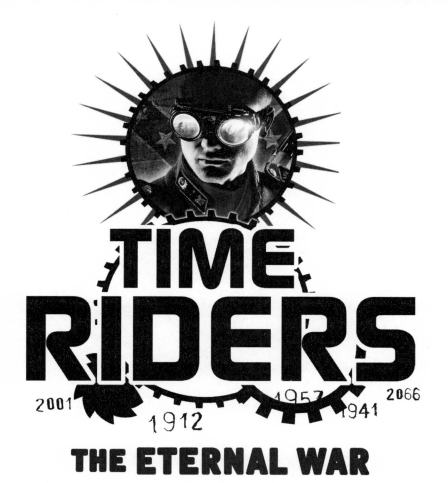

TIME RIDERS

2001 1912 1957 1941 2066

THE ETERNAL WAR

Alex Scarrow

WALKER BOOKS
AN IMPRINT OF BLOOMSBURY
NEW YORK   LONDON   NEW DELHI   SYDNEY

Originally published in Great Britain by the Penguin Group, Puffin Books, in July 2011
First published in the United States of America in May 2013
by Walker Books for Young Readers, an imprint of Bloomsbury Publishing, Inc.
www.bloomsbury.com

For information about permission to reproduce selections from this book, write to
Permissions, Walker BFYR, 175 Fifth Avenue, New York, New York 10010
Bloomsbury books may be purchased for business or promotional use. For information on bulk
purchases please contact Macmillan Corporate and Premium Sales Department at
specialmarkets@macmillan.com

Library of Congress Cataloging-in-Publication Data
Scarrow, Alex.
The eternal war / Alex Scarrow.
p.   cm.   — (TimeRiders)
Summary: A time wave has altered the entire history of the Civil War. Abraham Lincoln
followed Liam into the present from 1831 and now the world is in a dangerous state of
limbo. If the TimeRiders can't return Lincoln to the past, the Civil War will never end.
ISBN 978-0-8027-3481-5 (hardcover) • ISBN 978-0-8027-3482-2 (e-book)
[1. Time travel—Fiction. 2. Lincoln, Abraham, 1809–1865—Fiction. 3. United States—
History—Civil War, 1861–1865—Fiction. 4. Science fiction.] I. Title.
PZ7.S3255Ete 2013   [Fic]—dc23   2012037683

Book design by Donna Mark
Printed and bound in the U.S.A. by Thomson-Shore Inc., Dexter, Michigan
2 4 6 8 10 9 7 5 3 1

Dedicated to the "Secrets Club": Shannon, Wendy, and Rowan . . .
the three other people on planet Earth who know how this tale ends

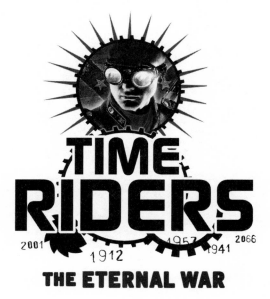

TIME RIDERS

2001   1912   1957 1941   2066

THE ETERNAL WAR

Prologue

2051, New York

Joseph Olivera looked out of the small round window at the flooded cityscape of New Jersey below. The Atlantic was gradually biting chunks out of the east coast of America, leaving tall city blocks emerging in orderly rows from the glistening sea. But ahead of him, where the drop-copter was taking him, he could see Manhattan. The island was still keeping its head above water. Levees built all the way around were going to keep it dry for a decade more, or so the experts were saying.

The copter swooped in over the skyscrapers of Manhattan and headed toward the distinctive convergence of streets that was Times Square. On his left, he spotted Central Park, filled with abandoned cars stacked one atop the other and rusting like a child's forgotten toys.

Joseph cursed his nerves. He was trembling at the prospect of a face-to-face meeting with the enigmatic man—the legend—*Roald Waldstein.*

I will not stutter. I WILL make a good impression. Joseph vowed to himself once again that he wasn't going to stammer as he normally did under pressure. He was going to avoid the tricky words, those that started with a strong "S." Joseph had rehearsed his greeting over and over. It involved no "S" words. He almost sounded normal.

The copter was now circling above the flat roof of the tallest building overlooking Times Square like a dog preparing to settle into its basket. Times Square was a lifeless ghost of itself. He could see pedestrians, one or two electric buses, a lot of places boarded up. The levees may have been holding back the rising sea, but Joseph realized it was a futile endeavor.

This city's dying already.

The copter touched down gently and the pilot shut off the engine, letting the rotors spin themselves out before pulling open the sliding door and gesturing for Joseph to follow him.

"Mr. Walds-s-stein is s-s-staying here?" he asked. "The Marriott Hotel?"

"Mr. Waldstein lives here now. He bought the hotel last year."

The pilot ushered him inside the building and down a cinderblock stairwell to a small foyer, a pair of swinging doors ahead of them.

"Through those doors are his private quarters. He lives alone." The pilot looked at him curiously. "You know, you're very privileged to see him face-to-face. He doesn't do that . . . *ever.*"

"He lives in this hotel all by himself?"

The pilot ignored his question. "A little word about meeting him. He can come across as abrasive and rude. That isn't his intention; he just has no time for small talk."

"O-okay."

"Don't try to flatter him, either. I wouldn't bother telling him he's a genius, or a visionary, or a . . . a wonderful guy. He's heard it all before about a billion times over. You'll just irritate him."

Great; there goes my rehearsed greeting.

"Most important of all, do not discuss the 'incident' with him."

"The . . . incident?"

"Chicago."

Joseph nodded. Of course, he was talking about the Chicago incident, in 2044. The day Waldstein first came to public attention.

"Right . . . Okay." Joseph was trembling.

"Be polite and honest"—the pilot offered him an encouraging

smile—"and you'll do just fine." He pressed an intercom button beside one of the doors. "Mr. Waldstein, I have Dr. Joseph Olivera here for you."

Joseph looked in a small mirror on the wall beside the door. He straightened his tie, patted down a wayward tuft of black hair, and wished he'd done a better job of trimming his dark beard this morning.

A small green light winked on above the double doors. "You can go through," said the pilot.

Joseph pushed the doors inward and his feet clacked off linoleum onto soft carpet.

Daylight flooded from all sides into a circular room. Joseph found himself squinting back at the glare. He could just about make out a head and a pair of shoulders silhouetted against one of the large floor-to-ceiling panels of glass that made up the walls of the penthouse.

Joseph shaded his eyes with one hand as he walked slowly over. "Mr. Walds-s-stein?"

The room was large—forty, perhaps fifty feet in diameter. His eyes beginning to adjust, Joseph noted a bed on one side, a desk, and several cardboard boxes full of papers, but nothing else. A very empty space.

Closer now, he could see a little more detail: the distinctive shock of wavy, wiry, uncontrollable hair, the narrow shoulders.

"It is an honor . . . to meet you, Mr. Waldstein."

The silhouette shifted and turned. He'd been gazing out the window at New York.

"They say Lady Liberty walks on water now."

Joseph had no idea at all what he meant by that. His dumbfounded shrug gave him away.

Waldstein chuckled. "Sorry . . . I confused you. I'm referring to the Statue of Liberty. Liberty Island and the base she stands on are all below sea level." He spread his hands. "So it looks like she's actually walking on water."

"Ahhh," Joseph nodded. "I unders-s-s . . . s . . . s . . . ." Joseph struggled with the infernal word. He felt his cheeks burn hot as he wrestled with the "s" and shook his head angrily.

The word was left unfinished. "I am s-s . . . I apologize. I have a . . . problem with—"

"Stammering?" Waldstein gestured to a chair. "Don't worry about it. It's not important. Take a seat."

Joseph sat down. Waldstein flipped open a folder and flicked through some pages of printed paper. "Dr. *José* Olivera . . ."

"I anglicized my name to 'Joseph,' Mr. Waldstein. It, uh . . . people assume there's a language barrier if your name s-s-sounds foreign." He scratched his chin self-consciously. "I speak in English just as easily as my native . . ."

"Spanish."

Joseph nodded gratefully at being saved the trouble of speaking the word.

"Dr. Joseph Olivera—you're arguably one of the most knowledgeable people in the world on genetically imprinted artificial intelligence."

Be confident, Joseph.

"I am."

"It seems you've done very impressive work for some leading military contractors. Working on genetically engineered combat units being tested right now by the U.S. military?"

"Right."

"And it says here that you are a firm supporter of the anti-time-travel movement?"

"I am."

Waldstein sat forward, his eyes unblinkingly on Joseph's. "I'd like you to tell me why."

Waldstein was testing him.

"Anyone with a s-s-scientific background under-s-stands this. Temporal dis-s-s . . . s . . ." Joseph abandoned the word. He took a breath to steady his nerves, to settle his stammer.

"*Time travel* . . . theory is potentially the most lethal technology ever invented. Theoretically, it has the kinetic energy to be the end of, well . . . of *everything*."

Waldstein said nothing. He obviously wanted to hear more from him.

"I believe, Mr. Waldstein, very much s-so, that there are s-s-some things that should *never* be fooled around with. In the pursuit of knowledge, there are s-some doors that should remain firmly closed. If there is a God . . . *IF* there is a God, then this technology, this knowledge, should be for Him, and Him alone. I believe this."

He paused and realized the next thing he was planning to say would be tremendously stupid. Hadn't that pilot specifically warned him not to mention this?

And now I am going to do just that.

His heart flipped in his chest. "What you did, what happened in Chicago in '44, was very dangerous. But all that you have done s-since that, Mr. Waldstein, has been the right thing. I believe your campaign to prevent further experimentation is all, literally *all*, that s-s-stands between mankind and . . ." Joseph spread his hands as he fumbled to finish. What word to use? What word?

"The end?" Waldstein offered.

Joseph nodded. "Yes, that is it . . . *the end*."

Waldstein was perfectly still, his rheumy eyes giving away absolutely nothing, a tableau of silence that seemed to be lasting forever. Joseph was beginning to wonder whether he'd completely blown it by mentioning Chicago when Waldstein finally stirred.

"Joseph . . . ," he began, "I have a—what shall I call it?—a *project* that I am working on. And I would like you to be a part of it."

"A project?"

Waldstein nodded. "Something that requires *absolute* secrecy. A project that is of *immense* importance."

Joseph's jaw dropped open. "Work with you? I . . . I would be *honored* . . . to . . ." His mouth was flapping uselessly.

"Don't be so quick to accept, Joseph. This is a one-way ticket. *Absolute secrecy*. You would never be able to talk about this project with anyone, *ever*. You will be working with me in complete isolation."

Waldstein's intense gaze was on him, watching him closely, searching his face for the slightest hint of doubt. "Joseph, once you're in on this—*if* I decide I can completely trust you—you must understand that there'll be no walking away."

Joseph wasn't entirely sure what "no walking away" actually meant. An implied threat of some sort? Waldstein was a billionaire, a powerful man. Not someone to cross.

Not that it mattered. Betraying confidences or stealing secrets for a commercial rival was of absolutely no interest at all to Joseph. His passion was his science. A hunger for knowledge.

And this man, Waldstein—the Visionary. The Genius. To have the privilege to meet the legend himself . . . and now the possibility of actually working alongside him. There was never going to be a moment's doubt, not in Dr. Joseph Olivera's mind.

Absolutely no doubt, and yet burning curiosity prodded him to ask one last question. "Is there anything you could tell me, Mr. Waldstein, about this project? The *general* nature of the work, perhaps?"

Waldstein steepled his fingers beneath his chin and closed his eyes in silent contemplation. Joseph took the opportunity to look around the enormous room, glowing from the flood of daylight streaming in through almost three hundred sixty degrees of panoramic spotless glass. This man, with his portfolio of technology patents, was fast on his way to becoming one of the richest men in the country. And yet there was a simplicity to this room and its comforts.

A bed.

A desk.

A couple of chairs.

Nothing else. After all, what more does a true genius want? The mind itself is the palace where all the real treasures, the works of art, the indulgences, exist.

Presently Waldstein lowered his hands and opened his eyes. "The work, Joseph, is really quite simple. It is the business of saving mankind from itself."

Beyond Waldstein's narrow shoulders, Joseph caught a glimpse of the mint-green outline of the Statue of Liberty, so faint that she wavered and undulated in the distance. And, yes, Waldstein was right, she really did look like she was standing directly on the water.

Like Jesus, walking on water.

"So tell me, Joseph, will you help me? Help me save mankind from itself?"

From the first moment he'd stepped into this room and come face-to-face with this brilliant man, there was really only ever going to be one answer Joseph could give.

"Yes."

Chapter 1

2001, New York

Sal stared at it through the grubby shop window.

She was standing outside Weisman's Stage Surplus on a sidewalk filled with bric-a-brac that the owner had allowed to spill outside: an old five-foot cigar-store Indian carved out of mahogany, a treasure chest full of children's dress-up clothes, dusty books stacked in grocer's crates.

It was the store fifteen minutes away from their archway that she'd used to find suitable clothes for Liam, Bob, and Becks's recent mission. That last visit, she hadn't been sure this little place would have what they'd need to go about their business anonymously in the twelfth century. But, surprisingly, among the laden racks of clothes reeking of mothballs and lavender soap, she'd managed to find enough bits and pieces for them to pass unnoticed as three grubby peasants.

A good place to use again, she'd noted as they'd made their way home through the backstreets of Brooklyn with their medieval costumes in plastic bags.

But today she wasn't here looking through the dusty window at the pitiful store display to find something for the others to wear. She was here because of the thing she was looking at now, the thing sitting on the rocking chair just inside the window. A row of stuffed animals and dolls sat side by side on the worn wooden seat like they were posing for a family photo. Several dolls, a clown that would give any child nightmares, an elephant with big ears, a frog with stuffing bursting from a torn seam—and one small sky-blue teddy bear with a single button eye and loose strands of stitching where another button eye must have been once.

"*I know you*," she whispered.

She'd spotted this teddy bear the last time she was here. But with one thing or another distracting her she'd forgotten about it, let it go. Now here she was, drawn to the shop, drawn to gaze at this sad-looking bear. It reminded her of something. A digi-stream show from her time, maybe? A character in an old cartoon? Something, a wisp of a memory that vanished from her mind like a curl of smoke as she reached out to grasp it.

Last night she'd had that dream—no, not dream, *nightmare*—again. The moment the old man—Foster—had pulled her out from certain death to be recruited to the agency. Their apartment building, one of the supertall glass and steel tenement towers that you saw everywhere in Mumbai nowadays, was on fire, and its steel superstructure had been buckling, preparing to collapse in on itself.

Nowadays? She checked herself. She came from 2026. "Nowadays" was where she was based, 2001. Her new home . . . of sorts.

Foster had plucked her from the very last seconds of her life and given her a choice: to work for the agency or join her family and die in the flames of the collapsing building.

Some choice.

Not that she actually got to choose. Dadda had chosen for her, thrusting her toward the old man, Mama screaming and crying to hold her one more time.

Stop it! Stop it!

Sal bit her lip. She didn't need to replay the memory again in her head. It was all still fresh enough, thanks. That awful moment was done, her parents gone, dust, and she was here in New York instead of Mumbai. All done. Or, more accurately, yet to be done. Yet to happen twenty-five years from now.

Yet to happen . . . that at least stole *some* of the sting of losing her parents, of knowing that they died along with everyone else when that tower collapsed. Because—and this was the part that really messed her head up—they were alive right *now*. At this moment in time they were children, *her age*, and they were yet to even meet each other. That was going to happen in twelve years' time, in 2013. They were going to meet at a consumer electronics show in New Delhi. Both their families were going to thoroughly approve of the match, and within the very same year Sal was going to already be a bump growing inside her mama.

And now she was looking at a small blue teddy bear that had absolutely no logical reason to be sitting here in New York in 2001. A bear, *unmistakably the same bear*, that she'd seen her neighbors'—Mr. and Mrs. Chaudhry—youngest boy, Rakesh, always clinging to and slobbering over.

Unmistakably.

The same teddy bear.

It was the very last thing she'd seen from the final second of her old life in 2026: that teddy bear, spinning head over heels into the flames as the floor had suddenly collapsed beneath their feet and the building shuddered in on itself.

Then she'd awoken here in New York, in 2001.

"It's the same . . . I'm sure," she whispered to herself, a confused frown stretching from one brow to the other. Her eyes had never let her down. She saw little things, the tiny details: the way the button eye drooped at an angle, the thread running through only three of the four holes; the bear's pale-blue material threadbare on the left arm but not the right, as if the right had been replaced recently.

The tiny details. Her eyes and her mind were compulsively drawn to those sorts of things. An obsessive habit. She tucked her hair back up behind one ear and leaned forward until her forehead thudded softly against the shop window. She'd always been able to spot the little things that others missed, to see patterns in a seemingly random mess. That's why she'd been so good at playing Pikodu.

"It's the same," she whispered.

How the shadd-yah *is that even possible?*

Her phone suddenly vibrated in the pocket of her jacket. She fished for it and pulled it out.

"Yeah?"

"Did you forget?" Maddy sighed impatiently.

"Forget? What?"

"Today? This morning? Trip to the museum? Remember?"

Sal winced, then bumped her head against the window again. Yes of course, they'd been discussing it last night before turning in. But with her dream—no, *nightmare*—that horrible memory—she'd completely forgotten. She cursed under her breath. "I'm on my way back."

"Meet us there if you want. On the front steps of the museum."

"Right."

"About an hour?"

"Okay."

Sal snapped her cell closed, once again faintly amused at how old-fashioned it looked compared to the T-buds almost everyone back in Mumbai had looped over their ears.

She looked once again at the blue bear. The blue bear that shouldn't be there.

It stared back at her with one button eye, almost challenging her to explain why not.

Chapter 2

2001, New York

Maddy led the five of them through the doors into the Museum of Natural History's main entrance hall. Foster had brought them all here once before, not long after he'd recruited them: Maddy from a doomed plane, moments before it was due to disintegrate midair, and Liam from the sinking *Titanic*. It had been a field trip, a reward for them, a change of scenery. A chance for them to see, to reach out and touch the history they were now responsible for preserving.

Both support units, Bob and Becks, eyed the enormous looming brachiosaurus skeleton stretching along the entrance hall with a detached cool, their silicon minds categorizing the sights, sounds, and smells of the museum as either useful or irrelevant data.

Liam, by contrast, chuckled with delight at seeing the dinosaur once again. A class of elementary schoolkids was clustered around the long, plastic-boulder-covered base on which the skeleton stood, all carrying their activity clipboards, faces craned upward to look at the towering bones, every mouth falling open to form a little "aw" for "awwwwe-some."

Liam nodded a greeting at the old security guard standing beside the visitors' book. "Hey, Sam, how's it going?"

"Huh?" The guard scowled at him, bemused. "Hang on. How do you know my—?"

"It's all right," said Liam, grinning. "We met a long, long time ago, so."

Maddy's eyes rolled behind her glasses. "Oh, grow up, Liam," she whispered, jabbing him in the ribs and steering him away from the guard, who was still regarding them with an expression that was an even split between surly suspicion and genuine confusion.

"Last I heard, we were supposed to be a *top-secret* organization, you know?"

"Aww, he won't remember. I was dressed as one of them Nazi fellas then."

"And the timeline was erased," added Bob helpfully. "The guard will have no memory of the encounter because—"

Maddy raised her hands to shush them. "All right, yes, you're right, Bob." She shook her head. "Let's just generally *try* to be secret, okay? And, while we're at it, Liam, let's try to behave like adults here?"

Liam nodded. "Aye, you're right. Sorry."

"Okay," she sniffed, wiping her nose. She'd picked up a cold from somewhere, probably the dude who'd been hacking and wheezing over the counter at PizzaLand the other night—giving them a little extra unasked-for topping on their pie. She felt like total crud.

"Okay . . . today's about learning a bit more history," she said snottily. "And we can all stand to know a bit more, but it's supposed to be fun too, right? We could all do with some time out of the arch."

"S'right," said Sal.

"And you guys," she said to Bob and Becks. "Split up. I don't want you two support units Bluetoothing binary jibber-jabber to each other all morning. You should use this morning to do some more people-watching. Look and listen, watch how people talk and move and stuff." She glanced up at Bob. "Particularly you, Bob; you still come across a bit stiff and unnatural. You need to learn how to chillax."

Maddy watched Bob's seven-foot frame hunch uncertainly. His thick brow arched and his mouth opened.

Beauty and the beast. He was seven feet tall, three hundred pounds of muscle and bone: a tank in human form. Becks, by contrast, was half a yard shorter, athletic and slight. Yet both had started out, once upon a time, as identical-looking fetuses growing in a tube of murky gunk.

Bob was cocking his head like a dog, puzzling over the term "chillax."

"Never mind." Maddy shook her head. "Just mingle a little, okay?"

Both support units nodded sternly.

"Right," said Maddy, blowing her nose into a hankie. "Okay, meet in the cafe up on the first floor in, say . . . like, two hours?" She tried a weary, flu-ridden smile. "And hey . . . you know, have fun, everyone."

Maddy watched them disperse: Liam drawn toward the entrance to the natural-history hall and the dinosaur dioramas; Sal hovering a moment, undecided, before choosing to go to the History of Native Americans exhibit on the third floor; and Bob and Becks looking like abandoned children for a moment before picking directions at random in which to saunter away.

She watched both go with the oddest feeling of motherly instinct for the pair of them. Bob still moved around with a machinelike gait and stony-faced concentration that made him look like a Neanderthal with an anger-management problem. Becks, meanwhile, moved with ballerina grace; equally lethal a killing machine as Bob, but in an understated way.

Weird. How different they both were: their bodies drawn from the same genetic material, their minds both running the same AI operating system, and yet their experiences, their memories, were varied enough to evolve two very different simulated intelligences. It was kind of like being a parent, Maddy supposed, watching both support units slowly "grow up" and develop different personalities over time.

She watched Becks pace thoughtfully down the hallway, pausing every now and then to study an exhibit more closely.

You really have no idea how important you are, do you, Becks?

The female support unit had data embedded in her silicon brain, a minor sector of her miniature hard drive devoted to holding a secret. Their last crisis had involved locating a medieval document—the Holy Grail, no less—containing an encoded secret that dated from somewhere around the time of Christ. Becks had been able to successfully decode the secret, which, it seemed, had rather annoyingly included a protocol that prevented her from revealing the message she'd managed to decipher. And now, whatever this Big Secret was, it was locked away in a portion of her silicon mind.

Maddy had tried asking her about what was in there, but poor Becks knew nothing; she too was locked out of that portion of her own mind. All she knew was that at some point a "correct condition" would arrive that would unlock the truth.

What Maddy did know was this: whatever truth was lurking in there, it wasn't good news. Not good at all. And it had something to do with a particular word.

Pandora.

Secrets and lies. She hated them. There was never any good that came out of a secret. They were corrosive. Like another one, a secret she was having to keep from Liam and Sal—Liam in particular.

He's dying. Time travel was killing him. Every trip through the portal was corrupting his body's cells, aging him before his time in a far more aggressive, damaging way than the force field that looped them and their old archway field office back around those two days in 2001 that they were stationed in.

She sighed. Even in their eternal two-day bubble world, the same cars, the same pedestrians, the same yellow cabs passing the end of their little backstreet at the same time every day—even in this world frozen into two endlessly looped days, time was passing for them. She'd noticed it, and wondered if Sal and Liam had noticed it too, not that either had said anything to her.

We're all aging.

She could feel it very subtly. It didn't show, not yet, but she could feel it. Maddy had studied her face in the mirror of their bathroom. Stared at her face wondering if she would be able to detect the first faint signs of hairline creases in her skin. But so far, to her relief, no.

As for Sal, she was perhaps a shade taller. After all, measuring the time they'd been in the archway together in a normal way, they must have been living there now for—what—five months?

Was it that long already?

Five months, and like any thirteen-year-old, Sal still had a few more inches of growth left in her. Perhaps, being the youngest of them, the corrosive aging effect of the archway's displacement field would be kindest of all on her, would take the longest to make itself felt.

But Liam . . . *poor, poor Liam*. She could see the signs of accelerated aging in his face even if he hadn't noticed it yet. Or perhaps he chose not to. His jaw and cheeks were less rounded now, longer and leaner. And around his eyes—eyes that always seemed to be wide like saucers with genuine awe at something, or pinched tight midlaughter, chuckling at the oddness of this bizarre life they were living—those eyes . . . eyes that had seen more than any one person should ever hope to see. Around them, in his soft, pale skin, Maddy could see the first traces of age. The very same traces that would one day be the folds of wrinkled skin on Foster's ancient face.

Yes, another freakin' secret.

Liam and the old man who had recruited them were one and the same person. That's what Foster had let slip to her. She couldn't even begin to figure out how that worked. Was Foster a version of Liam from the far future? His older self? Or was he from some other parallel timeline?

Oh God, it made her head hurt thinking about it.

Chapter 3

1831, New Orleans

Abraham Lincoln scowled at the flatboat captain. "But . . . but . . . this is no more than *half* the pay you promised me, sir!"

The captain's grizzled face, buried beneath an unkempt beard, wrinkled up with amusement at the young man's indignant rancor. His eyes glinted under his faded red woollen trapper's hat and he laughed, offering the young man a glimpse of half a dozen tobacco-stained teeth.

"You are too lazy, monsieur. No good to me."

Abraham's jaw hung open. "Curse you, sir! I worked my fair share!"

"*Non . . .*" He shrugged. "You lazy. No good to me. Not very good worker."

"Now, listen here . . ." Abraham balled his fists in frustration, taking a step off the wooden dock onto the bobbing prow of the flatboat, piled high with bundles of beaver pelts. The captain, Jacques, short and stocky, remained unfazed at the young beanpole of a man towering over him.

"You get half; no more," he said calmly.

Abraham felt his temper get the better of him. He reached out and grabbed the collar of the little Frenchman's checked shirt in one big-knuckled fist. "Curse you; I earned—"

The little man was quicker and more agile than his stocky frame would suggest, and with a deft flick of his strong arms he pulled Abraham off balance. He stuck a booted foot behind his heels and shoved him backward.

Abraham pinwheeled with his arms, his feet unable to step back to recover his balance. He toppled over the side of the flatboat and into the Mississippi River, coughing and spluttering his way to the surface of the muddy water to hear the rest of the flatboat crew, half a dozen boys his own age or thereabouts, guffawing with laughter.

Jacques bellowed at them to get back to work, and they resumed tossing the bales of pelts from one to the other onto the busy dock.

Abraham pulled himself, dripping and still spluttering, onto the wooden planks of the dock, his hot temper doused for now by the cool river. He turned to Jacques, the man's broad shoulders shaking with poorly concealed laughter.

"It *ain't fair*, I tell you!" He pushed a tress of sopping dark hair out of his eyes and glared back at the captain. "Hell's teeth, sir—you are even paying a *Negro* more than I!"

Jacques turned to look at the one dark-skinned member of his crew. He shrugged at that. "He a better worker than you, boy."

Abraham realized by the Frenchman's wrinkled, undaunted smile that he was not going to get anywhere with him. "Well, to hell with you, then!" he spat. "Crook! You thieving, piratical parasite!" He moved to the edge of the wooden jetty, standing as tall and defiantly as his six-foot-four-inch frame would let him. "I shall . . . I shall go find other work, then!"

Captain Jacques's bearded smile only widened. "As you wish." He waved a hand at him. "Good luck, *mon ami*. You will need it."

Chapter 4

2001, New York

Liam found himself drawn back to the main hall and the splendid brachiosaurus skeleton erected in the middle of it. He stared up for so long at the graceful arch of vertebrae that comprised its neck that he failed to notice another bustling class of elementary students gather around him, just like the other class, all carrying bright orange activity clipboards. They oohed and ahhed as the others had, craning their necks to look up at the Cretaceous leviathan.

A teacher, or perhaps it was a museum tour guide, was giving the children the vital statistics of the beast, or, as Maddy would say, they were getting a "data-load."

". . . roamed the plains in small family groups of no more than a dozen . . ."

"Well, that's not true," grunted Liam under his breath.

A tiny boy beside him with thick-framed glasses and a buzz cut of blond hair that stuck up like a toothbrush looked up at him curiously.

". . . their green hides, probably as thick as rhinoceros hides, helped to keep them . . ."

"Brown, actually," Liam muttered again. "They were brown."

The boy tugged gently at his shirtsleeve and Liam looked down at him. He whispered something Liam couldn't hear. He squatted down beside the child. "What's that again, fella?"

The boy eyed the guide warily. She was still addressing the assembled children. "I said," he whispered again, "are you a . . . a real dinosaur man?"

Liam laughed softly. He realized the little boy was asking whether he was an expert, a palaeontologist. He stroked his chin thoughtfully for a moment. "Well, now . . . yes, I suppose you could say I am." He whispered softly, pointing up at the towering bones. "I seen these fellas in the flesh, so I have. And I can tell you they're certainly not green."

Behind thick Coke-bottle lenses, the boy's eyes widened. "You . . . you've seen dinosaurs for, like, *real*?"

Liam nodded, his face all of a sudden very serious. "Aye. Went back in a time machine, so I did. Saw all sorts of dinosaurs—including this big beastie." He tapped his nose with his forefinger. "But that's super top secret, young man, all right?"

The boy nodded so vigorously his glasses almost fell off his face.

"I'll tell you something else too: we saw 'em in huge herds. Hundreds of the fellas all together in one place. Incredible sight, so it was." He winked at the boy. "Not small groups like your teacher just said."

"Wow," the boy gasped.

"And, like I said, they were brown, like dust, you see, because there wasn't such a thing as grass back then. They were brown as camouflage against the dirt, not green against grass. See what I mean?"

The boy nodded. "Should I put that down on my activity sheet, mister? Brown?"

Liam glanced down at the boy's clipboard and saw a pop quiz. One of the questions was about the supposed color of their hides.

He nodded. "Sure; put down 'brown.'"

The boy's forehead furrowed with a difficult dilemma. "But . . . um . . . I might not get a point for that."

Liam shrugged. "Aye, maybe so, but at least you'd be *right*, eh?"

He felt a hand on his shoulder and looked up to see Becks standing over them, her hair tied back in a neat ponytail and wearing a plain dark wool sweater that covered the still very visible scar tissue on her left arm.

"Liam, you are aware Maddy would *not* approve of this," she cautioned.

"Ahh; and you see this girl?" whispered Liam to the boy. The boy looked up at her stern expression. "She saw these dinosaurs too. Smacked one of 'em right on the nose, so she did. Actually started a stampede."

"This person does not have security clearance to know about our operations," Becks uttered firmly. "I recommend that you stop."

Liam smiled. "Right, yes . . . of course." He glanced at the boy's clipboard. "Brown, okay?" He shot him a conspiratorial wink and stood up. "What's up, Becks?"

"It is time now," she replied.

"Huh?"

She nodded at a large digital clock above the entrance. It was a couple minutes to eleven. "Time for us to drink coffee."

Chapter 5

1831, New Orleans

Abraham Lincoln staggered across the bar, knocking over several tables along the way, leaving a trail of spilled whiskey and snarled curses behind him as he stepped outside into the evening. The paltry sum of money with which that bloodsucking little French trapper had paid him off was all gone now, tossed down his throat during the afternoon.

The evening was still busy with dock workers hefting bales of hides and pelts off a row of flatboats, little more than rafts made from logs lashed together with a rudimentary shack in the middle. Across the river, he could make out the chimney stacks of several paddle steamers impatiently puffing clouds into the crimson sky. Their several decks were lit by gas lamps. To his whiskey-soaked mind they looked like giant wedding cakes lined with candles floating on the glistening Mississippi. Truly something to behold.

New Orleans was alive and bustling with activity even now, with the sky smearing from afternoon to evening to night. By contrast, back in New Salem, the hearth fires would be burning and the thick log doors battened firmly shut for the night.

This is the place he wanted to be. *Needed* to be. A young man like him with a keen mind and a quick wit could make his fortune right here among all this . . . this . . . *opportunity.* That was it—even the air in New Orleans tasted of opportunity. If a fellow was clever, if he used his mind, he could make his fortune on these streets along this dock. Abraham knew he had the kind of instinct and smarts needed to make himself rich beyond the dreams of a backwoods boy. He just needed that first little chance to get him going. Enough money to get his first enterprise under way.

Not that he knew yet what his first money-making scheme was going to be. And, of course, he'd just spent all the money he had on an ill-tempered afternoon of drinking. Now he was no better than the dozen other drunks tottering up and down the busy thoroughfare: trappers and frontiersmen in tattered deerskins, even one or two Pawnee unused to the bottled white-man's curse, sprawled unconscious amid stacked sacks of grain—and him too, swerving to and fro among businessmen wearing stove-pipe hats and their purse-lipped wives in shawls and bonnets, their bags and possessions behind them on the backs of silent, sullen-faced slaves.

That'll be me one fine day, he mused drunkenly. *A gentleman. A rich, successful businessman. Maybe even a politician someday.* He grinned like a fool as he considered that prospect, stepping off the boardwalk onto the dirt of the busy street, lined with deep ruts carved by the cartwheels of an almost constant stream of heavily laden wagons.

Perhaps even president, one day.

He belched: a long, loud croak that turned heads up and down the thoroughfare. It was, in fact, so satisfyingly loud that he heard the lady in the lace bonnet cry out in disgust. So loud that he didn't hear the thundering of hooves bearing down on him, nor the clatter of beer barrels rolling off the back of the riderless cart, nor the scream from another woman as she realized what was moments away from happening.

Abraham's whiskey-addled mind had just about enough time to process one final thought as the enormous delivery cart careening down

Powder Street behind a team of wild-eyed and terrified horses loomed up behind him—and sadly his last thought wasn't anything noble or profound, nor was it farseeing. It was nothing more than this:

Well now, sir . . . That *was a mighty fine belch.*

Chapter 6

2001, New York

"So, how does Foster look, you mean?" Maddy rephrased Sal's question.

"Yes." Sal nodded. "I mean, is he *really* dying?"

"Foster looks no different than the day he walked out on us." Maddy took a bite of her bagel. Still chewing, she continued. "Not a single day older. Which, of course, he isn't—because for him, every time I go see him in Central Park, it's the *same day* he walked out." She finished chewing and swigged some coffee. "It'll be us who look different to him, I guess. Not the other way around."

"Aye," nodded Liam. "We've been together a while now . . . seems more like an eternity, though."

"Seventy-five cycles," said Bob. "One hundred forty-nine days."

"Five months," added Sal. She looked up at Liam and Maddy. "*Jahulla!* That makes me fourteen now. My birthday was only four months away when I . . . I was supposed to die." She didn't need to elaborate on that. They all knew one another's recruitment tales.

"I missed my fourteenth birthday," she added quietly.

Becks cocked her head, and the appropriate smile for the occasion flashed across her face, as sincere as a screensaver. "Many happy returns, Sal Vikram."

Liam put down the chocolate muffin he'd been peeling out of its paper cup. "Hang on—I've missed my seventeenth birthday!" He reached out and squeezed Sal's hand. "So, a happy birthday to us both, so it is."

"Yeah," she mumbled, "yay for us."

"Uhh, so," Maddy sighed. "This was supposed to be *fun*. Not a freakin' funeral!" She turned to Sal. "We'll get a cake on the way home, put some candles on it, and you can blow 'em out, and . . . and we'll play some party games or something when we get back. How does that sound?"

She nodded, the beginnings of a smile back on her face. "I'd like that."

"Party games?" said Bob. "Please explain how to sub-categorize 'party games' in reference to 'games'."

Maddy shrugged. "They're just stupid games. You don't play to win. You just play because it's funny. Like, I don't know . . . like charades or Guess Who or Twister. The more you mess things up, the more fun it is."

The support units looked at each other, silently discussing how to make sense of that. Maddy chuckled. "Twister, oh man! You two meatbots haven't lived until you've played a game of Twister!"

She realized Sal and Liam were giving her the same bemused look. "Seriously? You guys have never heard of it either?"

Liam pursed his lips. "Is it a bit like chess?"

"What? No!"

"Fidchell? Brandub?"

"Whuh? Never heard of them. No, it's kinda like—"

"Tafl Macrae?"

"No . . . no, nothing like that. It's like—"

"Pog Ma Gwilly?"

"Will you shut up a sec?" she said, exasperated. "I'm trying to explain it." Her eyes suddenly narrowed with suspicion. "Wait a minute, *Pog Ma Gwilly*? You . . . you just made that up, didn't you?"

Liam's good-natured smile widened to a confessional grin.

She was about to reach across the small round table and playfully cuff his ear when she noticed Sal staring far too intently at the cafe's menu card.

"Sal? You okay?"

Her brows were locked firmly together.

Liam tapped her arm. "You that hungry?"

She shook her head slowly. "Thirty-seven items on the menu . . ."

"Uhh . . . all right." Liam looked at Maddy. She shrugged. "Oka-a-y."

"That was a minute ago. Now," Sal continued, "there are only thirty-six." She looked up at them. "Something just vanished off the menu! Just, like, seconds ago."

Liam looked down at the menu card he'd been studying earlier. "Hey—hang on, it's not there anymore."

Maddy leaned over. "What isn't?"

He shook his head. "I was going to order it, and . . . it's, well, it's gone!"

Sal had the menu memorized, almost word for word. "The Lincoln Burger."

"That's the very one!"

"*Beef patty*," she continued, her eyes closed, reciting the missing description. "*With cheese covered in thick barbeque sauce and french fries on the side.*"

"Aye, that's what I was going to order!"

"Sal?" Maddy reached out for her arm. "Did you just feel a time ripple?"

She nodded. "I, uh . . . I think so. I wasn't sure. I thought it was just me feeling sick or something. No breakfast. But then I saw the burger was gone."

They looked at each other in silence for a moment until finally Maddy bit her lip. "We should head back to the arch to heck on this."

The other end of a minute later, the five of them were hurrying down the North American History hall, weaving their way past elbow-high clusters of noisy children, babbling with excitement, clipboards under their arms as they raced from one exhibit case to another on a treasure hunt.

"Could we not get one of them yellow taxis back?" Liam called ahead, his jaw still working hard on the last of his triple-chocolate muffin. "I got a stitch in me side already!"

"Subway," Maddy replied over her shoulder. "It'll be quicker. Come on."

They were near the end of a long glass display case containing mannequins wearing uniforms from the Civil War when Bob's voice boomed down the hall.

"Attention! Maddy! STOP!"

She stopped in her tracks and looked back over her shoulder, along with every last child now frozen midhunt, silent, eyes locked on Bob's towering form. He calmly raised an arm and pointed toward Sal, who was standing beside the glass case staring in at something among the mannequins in Civil War costume.

Maddy quickly made her way through the confused children and elementary school teachers.

"What's the matter, Sal?" she said, drawing up beside her. "What do you see?"

Sal slowly raised her arm and pointed at the back wall of the display, between a mannequin wearing the braided and buttoned dark-blue uniform of a Union general and one wearing a similarly ornate tunic in gray. She was pointing at an oil painting hanging on the back wall.

"And that's changed too," she muttered.

Maddy looked at the face in the painting—the famous painting every schoolkid in America knew by sight. No longer was there that gaunt face, the dark eyes hidden beneath a thunderously brooding brow and the distinctly Mennonite beard. Instead she saw a forgettable-looking balding and portly man with a salt-and-pepper mustache and a rosy, bulbous nose. Beneath the painting was a plaque that read:

President John Bell, 1861–65

"Oh my God!" she said. "Where's President Lincoln?"

Chapter 7

2001, New York

They were back in the archway less than half an hour later, still huffing and puffing after the jog from the Marcy Avenue subway station, Liam whimpering the whole way about his aching side. "I shouldn't have rushed that muffin," he groaned pitifully to himself.

On the screen in front of them, computer-Bob, their field-office AI system, was already spitting out the data pulled in from the external Internet feed.

"He's just vanished from history," said Sal.

"Well, from Civil War history," Maddy replied as she skimmed the dossier being assembled, fact by fact, on the screen. "Nothing in there, nothing at all about him."

"This Lincoln fella was quite important, wasn't he?"

Maddy turned to Liam. "Only the most important figure in the war. The *most* freakin' important. He held the Union together." She saw one of his eyebrows shoot upward, a sign that he didn't have a clue and was hoping she would elaborate. "C'mon, you've been reading up a lot recently, right? Hitting the history books." She glanced at a pile of tomes stacked high beside his bunk bed. "So, please, tell me you know which guys I'm talking about."

Liam frowned for a moment, then grinned. "The Northern fellas; them people in blue."

"Right. Yes. Abraham Lincoln was the president of"—she sighed—
"them people in blue. Otherwise known as the North, the Union. The
point is he kept them together, kept them fighting, led them to victory—
but now he's gone from Civil War history!"

Sal chewed a fingernail absently. "That's going to mean a big wave,
then."

"Uh-huh; five minutes from now we could be looking out at a world
in which the Confederates won." She glanced sideways at Liam. "*Them
fellas in gray.*"

Computer-Bob's dialogue box appeared onscreen.

> **Maddy, I have completed a scan of all the Civil War data
retrieved, and there are no references to Abraham Lincoln in this
time period: 1861 to 1865.**

"Maybe he died," said Sal. "You know—before he should've?"

"Hmm . . . that's a possibility. Okay, then, computer-Bob, look
earlier. Go earlier." She rubbed her eyes, already irritated and red from
her cold. "We have data on him from our own internal historical
database, right?"

> **Of course.**

"So when and where was he born?"

> **February 12, 1809. Hardin County, Kentucky.**

"Do we have a detailed biography? All his movements from
childhood right up to becoming president?"

> **Yes, Maddy. I have detailed files.**

She had a pretty foggy high-school memory of Lincoln. They'd
studied him and the Civil War for a semester. Boring stuff some of the
time, but it got interesting when the country started to pull itself apart
over slavery and the war began.

"He traveled around a bit if I remember correctly, right, Bob?"

> **Correct. His family moved several times. Then when he was a
young adult he left home and—**

She waved her hand at the webcam to stop him. "Okay. All right,
this is what we do." She pushed her glasses back up her nose. "I want

you to search every external database from his birthdate onward. I want you to focus your data-trawling on the places he was supposed to have lived in—Kentucky, wherever else he went. Dig into their newspaper archives; a lot of that old stuff is digitized."

"Hold on." Liam sat back in one of the office chairs, dug his heels into the concrete floor, and pulled himself on squeaking castors closer to her. "The world out there doesn't care a jot for Mr. Lincoln now. He's a Mr. Nobody, right? We're now in a timeline where he never became a famous president. So there wouldn't be detailed biographies an' the like out there on the man, surely?"

"True." Maddy pulled on her lip. "But I remember reading that he was really . . . I don't know, *driven*. He had an uneducated father and grew up poor, if I recall, in a log cabin, and sort of hated all that. Wanted to better himself. So, all right, something's happened, things have changed and he never got to be president, but maybe he managed to become a local mayor or something, or a successful businessman. Something that might have left a small mark on the world."

She looked up at Bob and Becks in hope of a word of support. But both of them were silently blinking: networking with computer-Bob and helping the system with the data shoveling.

"So," she continued, "if he became a local bigwig somewhere, maybe he opened some sort of, I don't know . . . some shopping mall?"

"Shopping mall?"

"Ahh, you know what I mean—*trading post!*" She shook her head irritably. "Or opened some hospital wing, or some charity school for orphaned kids, or made some small-town Independence Day speech or something. The point is, these places all had their own little two-sheet gazette, their own newspaper. And these days all that kind of stuff is up on the net as scanned data."

She turned toward the webcam. "You got that, Bob?"

> **Yes, Maddy, we are already searching.**

"Do you think we'll have any more changes?" asked Liam. "The world doesn't look so different to me. Well, actually, it looks *no* different to me. Maybe that missing burger and the changed painting is all we're going to get?"

Maddy shook her head. "That *can't* be all, Liam. You can't just remove a guy like Lincoln from history and have it amount to no more than a change on a menu. There'll be more changes—" She stopped midsentence. "Just a sec . . ." She dug a hand deep into her jeans and fumbled for something, then pulled out a crinkled ball of paper and quickly unfolded it. Liam recognized it as a five-dollar bill.

"Look! He's still on there!" Maddy said, turning the note around so that Liam and Sal could see Lincoln's face staring out at them with a surly scowl. "There's your answer, Liam," she said. "There'll be more ripples; history hasn't finished fidgeting around to get rid of Lincoln yet."

Fidgeting around? Maddy realized how oddly human that sounded. As if time itself was some curmudgeonly old college professor who grumpily decided to sit down and rewrite the history books.

"This means another someone trying to mess things up, doesn't it?" asked Sal.

Liam nodded. "Another Kramer?"

Maddy shrugged. "Not necessarily another Kramer."

Not long after they'd been recruited, they'd been thrown into the deep end, having to deal with a nut-job from the future who'd thought it would be a great idea to help the Nazis win World War II.

"But if Lincoln's destiny has been messed up," said Liam, "that's changed history. That means—"

"I know," Maddy sniffed. "I know. It means another idiot is fooling around with time travel." She sighed. "All right, so here's our plan: we'll find him out there somewhere. A driven character like Lincoln is going to have made his mark one way or another. He may not have ended up being the president, but a guy like that will have gotten noticed some other way. We find him, and maybe we'll find whoever's just stepped back into the past and changed Lincoln's destiny." She looked at Liam and even managed a laugh; not bad, really, given that she felt like death warmed over.

"And you can tell whatever time-traveling moron it is who's done this that they're in big trouble."

Chapter 8

2001, New York

It took three hours before computer-Bob's dialogue box blinked onto the screen and Becks and Bob stirred from the motionless trance they'd been in. Liam came and shook Maddy awake.

She stared up bleary-eyed at Liam, fumbling for her glasses. "They done?"

"Aye."

"Where's Sal?"

"Viewing. Bob's with her."

"Viewing"—Maddy knew what he meant. Sal was sitting out in the middle of Times Square watching for more subtle ripples of the time wave.

"Any more changes?" she asked, sitting up and swinging her legs wearily over the side.

"Not that Sal or I have noticed."

She shuffled over to the computer desk feeling worse than ever, if that was even possible, despite having managed to grab some quilt time. She squeezed past Becks, still standing like a sentinel, her eyelids flickering and twitching like the wings of a hummingbird.

She slumped down at the desk just as she heard the sounds of their coffee pot bubbling to life. Liam—*bless him*—was making Maddy her wake-up brew. Black, strong, and sickly-sweet.

"Hey, Bob, what have you got for me?"

> Hello, Maddy. We have collated all the data hits for "Abraham Lincoln" dating from February 12, 1809. There are 7,376 data references to the name. Most of these refer to other people of the same name.

"Okay. So can you filter it down to occurrences in places where Lincoln was supposed to have lived?"

> Affirmative. I have done this. There are 109 data entries in relation to the following locations. 1809—Hardin County, Kentucky. 1816—Perry County, Indiana. 1830—Macon County, Illinois. 1831—Coles County, Illinois. 1831—New Salem, Sangamon County, Illinois. 1831—New Orleans. 1836—Springfield, Kentucky. 1846—Washington DC. 1848—Springfield, Kentucky. 1860—Washington DC.

"Right; and some of those hits will be him. Some will be other guys of the same name."

> Affirmative. There is one data entry I calculate to be of particular relevance. Do you wish to see it?

"Yeah, put it up."

One of the monitors on her right suddenly stopped relaying a real-time feed of Wall Street stock values and instead displayed the sepia-colored scan of an old newspaper. She saw the paper's title banner:

The New Orleans Bee. Wednesday, April 6, 1831

"So, which part am I looking at?"

Liam placed a steaming mug of coffee on the desk and settled in a chair beside her.

"Thanks," she wheezed.

> I will enhance the image.

The scanned image zoomed in on a short article at the bottom of the page—no more than half a dozen sentences in print that was almost as faint as a watermark. The magnified image was horribly pixelated, like trying to read words cobbled together out of LEGO bricks.

"Sheesh, can you do anything with the image?" Maddy wrinkled her nose as she squinted at it. "It's just pixel garbage."

> Just a moment. I will alias-average the pixels and apply character analysis. There will be a significant margin of error, which I can attempt to contextually interpret for you.

"Just do what you can, Bob," she said, holding a tissue to her face and blowing her nose noisily into it. "Oh crud, I hate feeling all blocked up and rough," she muttered.

The scanned image blurred, softened, and then hardened again as if a movie projectionist were messing around with the lens. Then a small highlighted green square appeared in the top left-hand corner of the image, grabbing a portion, analyzing it, then moving along and highlighting another portion to the right. Step by step it moved across the image, then stepped down a row and began on the left side once more. On another screen a document opened and words began to appear.

Liam leaned forward and read it aloud.

"Yesterday in the evening a second fatal collision occurred on Powder Street in as many weeks. A delivery cart belonging to Costen Brothers Brewery was responsible for crushing to death in a most horrendous manner a young dockworker. The ravaged body was identified by a flatboat captain as a crewman he had discharged earlier in the afternoon: Abraham Lincoln of New Salem."

There was a little more to the article, an editorial rant about the increasing business of the thoroughfares beside the landing docks and the need for some order to be brought to the chaos of foot and horse traffic sharing the same avenues.

Liam looked at her. "Do you think . . . ?"

She honked again into a handkerchief, shedding shreds of tissue onto the desk. "I fig we definubbly got a winner, Liab," she huffed breathlessly, her blocked nose whistling unpleasantly like a flute.

"Bost definubbly."

Midday in Times Square. Sal sat on her favorite bench, spattered with pigeon droppings and pink globules of discarded gum. Bob sat beside her, taking up the space two other people could easily have used.

"You are different, though Bob. Different from when you were first birthed." She turned to him. "Do you feel different in there—in your mind?" She pointed to his bristly head. Maddy had insisted on shaving his head back down to the scalp the other day. To be fair, she was right: Bob was beginning to look ridiculous. Coarse and dark, his hair should have been weighed down by its length; instead it seemed to perch on his head like a large, spongy muffin. No way he was going to be able to go on missions looking like a seven-foot mushroom.

Bob was giving her question some thought. "I have accumulated large amounts of sensory data. This has altered my operating parameters." He looked down at her. "These are my . . . *memories*."

"Memories, huh?" She smiled. "*Memories*. You sound sort of . . . almost *proud* of them."

He cocked his head. "They are my mission log. They are performance data. They are—"

"You," she finished for him. "They are *you*. They are what make you *you*. That's what my dadda used to say. What makes us who we are is all the things we experience." She reached out and patted one of his thick arms affectionately. "You're so much more now, more than you were, you big lump."

"More than . . . my operating system?"

She nodded. "Does that make you feel proud? Do you feel different?" She shrugged. "Do you even *feel*?"

"I have sense receptors in my dermal layer—"

"No, I mean in your heart—I mean emotions. Do you ever *feel* things? Like 'scared,' or 'happy,' or 'sad'? Things like that?"

He scanned his memories, sorting through trillions of bytes of data:

fleeting images of stormtroopers and giant airships, prison camps and castles, and a million little interactions with Liam O'Connor.

"I have experienced sensations of . . . *attachment.*"

"Attachment? Do you mean affection? What—for Liam?"

"Affirmative. He is my mission operative."

"What about us, me and Maddy? You like us?"

His expressionless gray eyes bore down on her as he sorted through data to find an answer. "I also feel similar sensations for you and Maddy Carter."

She hugged his arm. "Oh, you big *chutiya bakra.*" A thought occurred to her. "What about Becks?"

He frowned. Now there was a challenging question for him to chew on. His eyes blinked as he worked hard for an answer.

Finally he spoke. "She is . . . a part of me. And I am a part of her."

"But do you like her? Do you have 'sensations of attachment' to her? I figure she's like a sister or something."

"Sister?" He considered that for a moment. "A sibling?"

"Yes."

"I will consider the question," he said. She suspected that was probably going to keep him occupied for the rest of the day. Sal shook her head and giggled at him, then hunkered down, cradled her chin in her hands, and resumed watching the world going by.

And then it happened,

Just as she was looking right at it, before her very eyes, the sign above a fast-food restaurant flickered and changed. For a moment she thought she might have been gazing at an LED screen that had finally decided to move on to the next picture on its image list. But it was just a scuffed plastic sign above the glass windows of a fast-food place. One moment it had said Kentucky-Style Fried Chicken, the next it simply read Fast Fried Chicken.

She cursed under her breath, pulled out her cell phone, and dialed Maddy.

"Yeah?"

"I think I just saw a—No, I'm *certain* I just saw another time ripple, Maddy. A small one. You want to know what it was?"

"It's okay, Sal, it's okay. We think we've got it nailed. Abraham Lincoln went and got himself squished by a cart in 1831. You better get yourselves back here, ASAP. If that's another change you just spotted, then maybe the big time wave is coming right on its tail."

"Okay."

She snapped the phone shut and stuffed it back in her pocket. "Back home, Bob." She punched his arm. "Time for us to get busy again."

Chapter 9

2001, New York

"Can I go this time?"

Maddy looked at Sal. "No—that's not your job."

"But I always end up in here. I never get to see anything interesting!"

Maddy shook her head.

"But why?"

"Too dangerous." Maddy mentally winced at that. That was a lame reason. The poor girl had been in almost as much danger here in 2001 as she might have been with Liam in the past. And Sal could see that too.

"Come on, Maddy, it's just as bad here! We've had mutants, soldiers, those weird dinosaur things. You're telling me 'here' is safe?" She shook her head. "That is totally *shadd-yah!*"

Liam and the two units were listening to the argument as they were getting dressed.

Maddy closed her eyes tiredly. She didn't need this. How could she explain to Sal that every trip through a portal could quite possibly strip another year or five off her natural lifespan? That the bombardment of tachyons, the immeasurable forces of chaos space, had a lethal effect on the body: aged it, corrupted it—eventually killed it. How could she explain that to her with Liam just yards away, unaware that soon—far too soon—he was going to be a dying old man?

But then she and Sal were experiencing a milder form of that contamination themselves, living as they did in the archway's resetting temporal bubble, weren't they? Death was coming for all of them one day.

She thought of something her cousin Julian had once said: "We're all dead the moment we're born. Only, some of us get there faster than others." Prophetic, since he died not so long after, lost in the rubble of the World Trade Center's north tower.

"Please!" said Sal. "I want to see some history too!"

We're all dead . . .

At least this wasn't a huge jump. A hundred and seventy years. Nothing, really, in the grand scheme of things, she supposed. The shorter the jump, the less the damage. Their jump to Sunday a while back had probably been little more a dose of poison than the normal Tuesday-night bubble reset. She sighed. Living here in this archway like mole people wasn't really the sort of dream life a person would want to last forever, anyway. One trip into history . . . this trip, a relatively safe trip. Why not?

"All right," she sighed.

Sal yelped and clasped her hands together with excitement.

They had some clothes in the archway that they used to travel back to their "drop point" in 1906 San Francisco. The "drop point" was a stash of support-unit embryos held in suspended animation in the safe-deposit box of a bank that was due to be reduced to rubble and ashes by the infamous and imminent earthquake. With a little customization and by losing the headgear—hat fashion seemed to move along far more quickly than other kinds—the clothes could pass as 1830s outfits. Maddy's corset and skirts might be a size too big for Sal, but nothing that would attract any attention.

Liam was already nearly good to go in his brown jacket and waistcoat; Bob wore a striped linen shirt and scruffy cotton trousers. Becks was almost in the corset.

"Becks, you can stay. Sal's taking your place."

She stopped fussing with the ties at the front. "Is this advisable?"

Maddy shrugged. "It's New Orleans. What's to worry about? Anyway, she's got Bob and Liam with her."

The support unit dutifully nodded and began to undress.

Maddy pointed toward the small archway where their bunks stood. There was a curtain that could be pulled across for a little privacy. "Why don't you do that over there, Becks?"

The last thing she needed was Liam getting all hormonal.

"Sal, you understand this is 1831?"

"Yuh."

Maddy bit her lip. *Crud, this is going to be awkward.*

"This is a time of slavery."

Sal was drinking in the details of the dress and its corset, eager to get her hands on it, to try it on. "Yeah, I know," she replied absently.

"Well . . . your, uh . . . you know, your skin is, like, dark . . ."

Sal looked up at Maddy. "What?"

Maddy shuffled uncomfortably. "I'm just saying you may be treated . . . you may be called . . ."

"I'm not *black*, if that's what you're saying!"

"No, but what I'm trying to—"

"*Shadd-yah!* 'Dark' means I'm African now? You can lump us all together simply because we're not *white*?" Her brow furrowed with irritation. "I'm Indian!" She shook her head and rolled her eyes, then turned to follow Becks over toward the bunks. The curtain swished across the archway behind them.

"I just meant . . . people back then might not make the same distinction," replied Maddy, her voice fading to nothing.

Nice one, Maddy.

"Uh . . . okay," she said, stepping back toward the computers. "Okay, Liam, Bob, the candidate time-stamp is April 5, 1831, and I'm going to drop you in a few hours before the Abraham-squashing incident. The paper said 'evening,' so I guess that means about five or six. You'll arrive at four in the afternoon; I've found a street map of the New Orleans dockside area, circa 1834, which I guess is close enough. We're opening a window in what looks like a warehouse of some kind."

She checked one of the screens. They had a density probe testing the location for obstructions.

"Anything on the density probe, computer-Bob?"

> **Negative. Nothing has passed through the time-stamp location.**

She nodded, satisfied with that. It seemed a quiet enough spot.

"Young Abe Lincoln gets flattened on Powder Street, which, according to the map we've got here, is just a minute or two from your drop location. It's one of the main streets; I'm sure you'll find it easy enough. Just follow the smell of horse poo."

Liam chuckled. Even in 1912—his time—every busy thoroughfare in Cork was dotted with little molehills of manure waiting to be flattened by a cartwheel or eventually scooped up by a street sweeper.

"How do we know which fella to save?" he asked. "I mean, I think I know what he looks like as an old man. A beard and big bushy eyebrows, an' the like. But he's young now, aye? We got a picture of him as a young fella?"

"No, there's none. Not at the age he is now."

"Information," said Bob, flexing inside his shirt. It should have been loose on him, but in fact he barely fit inside it. "Celluloid-based portraits were not in common use at this time, even though photographic technology existed."

"Right," said Maddy. "And at this point in time, no one's gonna think this guy is going to be someone important. He's a total nothing. Not worth a picture." She shrugged. "Well, not yet, anyway."

She glanced at the page of data that computer-Bob had compiled. "What we do know is that he was described as very tall and thin and scruffy." She pointed to a screen showing a JPEG image of Lincoln's presidential portrait. "And check out those freakin' brows; I mean, it looks like he's got a small mouse living above each eye. Even as a young man, that's got to be a feature to look out for, right?"

Bob nodded. "Information: cranial growth variation around the orbital sockets is limited after a human skull reaches maturity, whereas certain other features—nasal cavity and cartilage tissue, soft tissue around the ears, the lower jaw—continue to—"

Maddy waved him silent. "Which means that even as a kid he probably always looked miserable." She wiped her runny nose. "Anyway, just keep your eyes peeled for a large cart loaded with barrels of booze and Costen Brothers Brewery painted on the side. Any tall, miserable-looking idiot looks like he's going to step out in front of it, you grab him. Simple."

Liam lifted his chin to adjust his collar button. "Sounds easy enough, eh, Bob?"

Bob rumbled an acknowledgment.

"How are you doing, Sal?" Maddy called out.

"Almost ready!" Her voice came back brightly through the curtain, Maddy's unintended racial slur already completely forgotten by the sound of it. "It's just a bit big on me."

"I am tightening the corset to its smallest setting to compensate," added Becks.

"Hey!" Maddy frowned. "Don't say it like that. Like I'm a butter-troll or something." She caught her reflection in the plexiglass displacement tube. "*Okay, so I'm not just some skin-and-bones clothes hanger,*" she muttered to herself.

"Completed," said Becks, and pulled the curtain to one side.

Liam held back a gasp, and Maddy found herself nodding approvingly. "Now, that looks better on you than a hoodie, right?"

Sal ran her hands over the corset and skirts. "It feels so weird." She grinned. "I feel like a . . . ugh, *jahulla*! I know this sounds pathetic, but . . . I feel like a *princess.*"

Maddy clapped her hands. "I know—it's kinda cool, isn't it?" She cast a glance at Liam and Bob. "Good; you all look the part. Now undress and bag your clothes. It's a wet departure."

Ten minutes later Liam, Sal, and Bob were treading water in their underwear together in the displacement tube.

"So, a nice, easy mission this time," said Maddy, crouching on the top step of the ladder. "Just find young Abe and grab his collar before he gets himself turned into Lincoln ketchup. You okay in there, Sal?"

She nodded, her teeth chattering. "Guess I'm g-getting a little nervous n-now."

"You'll be fine. Remember, you've done this before. It's no big deal."

"It's the white s-stuff that s-scares m-me . . ."

"Chaos space?" Liam shook his head. "Ahh, you'll be through it in a heartbeat, so you will. Nothing to it."

"Could you h-hold m-my hand?"

Liam nodded. "I s'pose. Sure, if you like."

"Uhh . . . it's probably best if you don't," said Maddy. Her eyes quickly met Liam's, and after a few seconds he nodded. He knew what she was thinking. After all, he was the one who'd seen it up close: fused bodies, bodies turned completely inside out. Very messy. He'd told Maddy about it, but not Sal. It was a grisly detail she didn't really need to hear and, anyway, it only happened rarely. Maddy had no idea what caused it, but when Foster had insisted Liam had to float on his own the first time around—well, there was almost certainly a very good reason for that.

"Works best if you're all floating freely, Sal. But look," she said before Sal could ask why, "you're going together. The other two will be right next to you. And as Liam said, it's, like, a second, no more."

"I'll sing you a ditty," said Liam, "so you'll hear me in there, in the chaos soup."

"There you go." Maddy smiled. "That is, if you can bear to listen to his howling." She started to descend the ladder. "Okay, we should get going, guys. We've been more than lucky with only small ripples so far. Let's not push it."

At the bottom she checked the displacement machine's control panel to confirm it was green right across the board, then called across to Becks. "Punch in a thirty-second countdown."

"Yes, Maddy. Thirty seconds . . . as of now."

"Return window at seven in the evening!" she reminded them. "And, remember, the usual backup windows after that if you miss it!"

She could see Sal's face through the scuffed plastic, wide eyed with growing panic. Beside her, kicking water and still holding on to the top of the tube was Liam, saying something encouraging to her. And then Bob, keeping afloat with strong, powerful kicks. All three of them held Ziploc bags containing their clothes.

"It'll be fun, Sal!" she called out over the increasing hum of the displacement machine. "Enjoy seeing 1831 with your own eyes!"

Sal flashed her an uncertain smile and a wave.

She stepped back into the middle of the floor as Becks's countdown reached ten.

"Okay! Hands off, everyone!" she shouted.

Liam reluctantly let go and began thrashing furiously and ineffectually to keep his head above water. The other two managed to tread water calmly. At five seconds, Maddy bellowed over the rising pitch of the machine for them all to take a breath and duck their heads under the water.

And on "one" they were all completely submerged.

A crescendo of channeled and suddenly released energy merged with the boom of flexing plexiglass, and in the blink of an eye the three of them were gone.

Chapter 10

1831, New Orleans

They were standing on Powder Street nearly an hour before six, watching the dockworkers industriously unloading boats of all different sizes while horse-drawn carts clattered up the busy thoroughfare. Although that snippet of digitally archived news from a long-dead New Orleans newspaper had claimed the event had occurred "in the evening," it would be foolish to assume that meant for certain it happened after 6 p.m. Liam told them that in *his* time people still generally didn't wear watches. Time was less specific. You'd arrange to meet someone in the afternoon, not "at 2:35 p.m." as he noticed most modern New Yorkers seemed to do.

"Just keep looking," said Liam, craning his neck to look up and down the busy street. "He's a tall, grumpy-looking fella."

"Affirmative."

Sal nodded. But it was far too easy to be distracted by the sights and sounds around her.

Nothing can prepare you for what it's like, Sal—actually standing in the middle of a piece of history. That's what Maddy had told her after her trip to 1906 San Francisco. And she was right.

She and Dadda had once gone to a technology expo while they'd been in Shanghai for one of her Pikodu tournaments. One of the last, as it happened; international relations between China and India were beginning to chill then—a sign of the troubled times ahead. At the expo she had tried out a prototype of a thing they were calling a Reality Hat. It looked like a shower cap with marbles stuck all over it. She'd put it on and almost instantly found herself smelling things, hearing things that weren't there, and then finally seeing herself in a Roman street. Of course nothing was quite right. The scene was computer generated; very realistic, but still there were little jerks in the animation here and there that gave it away. The visuals, the smells, and the sounds were being transmitted into her head, stimulating her senses. She had been stunned by how convincing an experience it had been.

But standing here, now, in history for real . . . the Reality Hat seemed like a shallow experience by comparison.

"Hold your horses," muttered Liam. "Look at that fella over there." He pointed along the street on the far side. Bob and Sal turned to look. Across the thoroughfare they could make out a tall, thin man in a scruffy, threadbare coat and a battered felt hat jammed thoughtlessly askew over a mop of dark, unruly hair. He had emerged from a tavern, clearly the worse for wear. He stood, or, more accurately, swayed, outside the door, surveying the busy street in front of him.

"Jayzus . . . he's had a few!" Liam turned to Bob. "Do you think that's our fella?"

Bob's eyes narrowed for a moment. "I have an approximate height match."

"And he does look a bit like the Lincoln in the painting," said Sal.

He certainly had the thunderous scowl and the dark, brooding eyes hooded by brows that all but hid them in the fading light of the afternoon.

"Right, good enough for me," said Liam. "Let's go grab him before he does something foolish."

Liam hopped off the storefront porch they'd been standing on. He waited until there was a gap in the horse-drawn traffic before leading them cautiously across the muddy street.

Lincoln hitched up the trousers that hung loose around his waist. He should have spent his money on some decent food, not on liquor. He shrugged at that. He could find something to steal to eat. The docks were an easy place to forage for food; there was usually a dropped sack here or there. He could always work for a cooked meal even if he couldn't find paid work. A man might find himself sleeping under the stars here in New Orleans, but he'd never find himself starving.

Lincoln belched, a real howler that turned heads up and down the street and solicited tsks and muttered disgust from a portly gentleman and his sour-faced wife as they walked past him.

He tipped his hat and grinned at them before congratulating himself on a world-class burp. He ambled drunkenly into the street, his long legs feeling as unstable beneath him as a pair of stilts.

He was just about to take another stride forward when he felt something grasp the back of his coat collar, and suddenly he found himself lurching backward and landing heavily on the ground.

It took him several moments to comprehend the fact that he was lying on his back in the dirt, looking up at salmon-pink clouds lit by the setting sun between three silhouetted heads peering curiously down at him.

"What in tarnation! Who the . . . ?" he started to blurt.

"Mr. Lincoln?" asked one of them—an Irishman, by the sound of his accent.

Lincoln groggily struggled to get himself up onto his elbows. "Now, who . . . who ishhh the infernal f-fool of a halfwit who . . ."

"Are you Abraham Lincoln?"

Lincoln's eyes struggled to focus on the face that had said that. "And . . . and who the d-devil . . . wishes . . . wishes to know?"

A much deeper voice rumbled, "Please confirm your name."

Lincoln's eyebrows arched as he took in the sight of Bob. "Good g-grief, ssshir . . . are you a man or a . . . some s-species of a grizzly bear?"

"*Shadd-yah!* Liam, check out the mess that wagon's making!"

"Jay-zus! That's a pretty pickle. C'mon, let's get him up," said the Irish voice. He felt a strong pair of hands grab him roughly.

"I . . . AM . . . FERPECTLY . . . I mean, p . . . puh . . . *PER-FECTLY* . . . capable of shhhtanding up by my . . . by myself. Yesh . . . indeedy. Now *UNHAND* me D-DIRECTLY!"

He felt the hands release him. Slowly, with a lot more effort than he'd originally thought it would require, he managed to pull himself back onto his wobbling legs. The twilight world of New Orleans was spinning around him like a cartwheel. And those three faces, none of which he could quite focus on, still seemed to be looking at him.

"Are you all right?" The Irish voice again.

"I AM FINE!" Lincoln bellowed hoarsely. "FINE AS A . . . a . . . a . . . FINE as a goat in a briar patch! Fine as an OIL PAINTING!" He managed a grin. "Ah'm asssh FIT . . . asssh . . . a . . . a . . ."

"As a . . . ?"

He opened his mouth. He was thinking of saying "horse." But instead what came out was something that sounded a little like "bleurghhh."

The last thing he heard before the world spun onto its side and he passed out was someone saying, "Oh, gross, all over my shoes; charming."

Chapter II

1831, New Orleans

"... *he's a pitiful sight, so he is.*"

It was completely dark now. Lincoln could hear the gentle lapping of the Mississippi against the hull of a boat nearby, and somewhere deep inside his throbbing mind he figured out that he was slumped along the docks somewhere. The sky above was clear and the moon floated high among the stars, casting a surprisingly strong silver light across the river and the city, now finally settled and still for the night.

"*You think he'll be okay if we just leave him here like this?*"

"*He'll be fine, I'm sure. He's a big boy.*"

The voices were speaking quietly, not quite whispering, but almost.

"*Well now, since we missed both our return windows, we've got all of tomorrow to wander around and explore New Orleans.*" A pause. "*So, Sal: what do you make of 1831?*"

"*Totally bindaas! It's so real! But it feels unreal too. Do you know what I mean? Like, I can't really be back here.*" That particular voice, the female voice, had an odd accent. Lincoln couldn't quite place it. He'd once met a Welshman who'd had a similar, singsong way of talking.

"*Aye, I still have to pinch myself. Sometimes I wake up on me bunk still thinking I'm in 1912, in the steward's quarters, and that all this time-travel nonsense has been a dream.*"

"*Me too.*"

A pause.

"*So, do you want to see if we can find rooms somewhere to sleep?*"

"*I'm too excited to sleep.*"

"*We can walk around a bit. Or wait here until sunup and explore. Bob, how long until the return window opens?*"

A deep voice. "*The twenty-four-hour window will open at four. The time is now six minutes past one in the morning. You have fourteen hours and fifty-four minutes until the portal opens in the Jenkins and Proctor warehouse.*"

"*Well . . . I could stand a walk. It's a warm night. It's nice to be out of the archway for once.*"

Lincoln heard movement and closed his eyes. A moment later he felt a gentle nudge, the grain sack beneath him shifting, and the warm breath of someone leaning over his face.

"*He still asleep?*"

"*Dead to the world, I think.*"

A chuckle. "*Jahulla, it's hard to imagine this drunk being the president of the United States, isn't it?*"

"*He's still got a while to sort himself out, so he has.*"

"*Information: the American Civil War begins in April 1861.*"

"*Well, there you go: he's got exactly thirty years to sort himself out. Loads of time.*"

A pause. "*What do you think, Bob? You suppose we've patched up history?*"

"*The target person is alive. History data files show that he will embark on a career as a lawyer in the next few years, then go into politics.*"

"*Lawyer? Shadd-yah! You're joking!*"

"*Negative. Not joking.*"

A pause.

"*Hmm . . . I could imagine him as a lawyer. He's got the temperament. Argumentative, so he is. Anyway . . .*" He heard a footstep. "*Come on,*

Sal, let's go and explore New Orleans while we've got the chance. He'll be fine. We should leave before he wakes up. With a bit of luck he won't even remember us."

Movement again. Lincoln heard the swish and rustle of cotton skirts, then the receding sound of footfalls down the wooden planks of the dockside. He opened his eyes once more and watched the three dark shapes: one a giant of a man, another a slender young man, and the third a young woman. His mind was still foggy from the whiskey he'd been drinking earlier in the afternoon; foggy, but still able to function. In the last couple of minutes he'd heard enough to make a feebler-minded person than him question their very sanity.

1912 . . . time travel . . . ?

As a boy, Lincoln had once discussed such an absurd idea with a friend: what if a man could speed up the turning of a clock? Or slow it? Or stop it? Or even wind it back the wrong way? What if a man could walk in days past? Meet great men from history and talk to them? An absurd idea. A fanciful notion for their imaginative young minds. Yet here it seemed to be, the very idea he and his childhood friend had playfully considered while resting in the branches of a sycamore tree.

Is this possible?

Perhaps in some far-off future time—1912, for example—it could be possible. The ingenuity of man appeared to know no bounds. Every year it seemed a new device was being invented, new knowledge of how God's Earth functioned uncovered. Who knows what science men would be wielding like magic in the year 1912?

He eased himself into a sitting position. His head pounded as if some small gold prospector was at work in there with a rock hammer.

And what was it the much deeper voice had said? That he would be a lawyer? And one day . . . did the girl actually say it? Did she actually say the word "president"?

He felt a shudder of excitement course through him, blowing away the cobwebs of his hangover.

President?

If that were true, really true, if those three strangers did actually come from a time beyond his own and could know such things, know his destiny . . . then they would know how it would be possible that a poor fellow like him would one day lead this country as its president.

His skittering mind reached out further. Perhaps there was an even greater goal, a greater destiny for him than a life in politics. He realized it would be a far greater thing to be the only man from 1831 to visit the future, to actually see with his own eyes all the wonderful devices on air, sea, and land that man's ingenuity could create. He imagined the cities of this time full of towers of glistening crystal that prodded the very heavens.

I would truly like to see this future . . .

Chapter 12

2001, New York

Maddy sat with her feet up on the computer desk, her sneakers resting on a stack of pizza boxes. She watched the monitor in front of her, a looping display of tragedy unfolding in painfully endless repetition.

The flickering, shaky camcorder footage of a passenger plane swooping low over the skyscrapers of Manhattan . . . and in those precious heartbeats of time before it finally crashes into the side of the north tower . . . a hope? Even though you know what happens, isn't there always that fleeting moment of hope, the possibility that it might actually miss this time? That it just flies between them? That Julian and nearly three thousand other people might return home that day and tell their families of the near miss that terrified them all for a few moments?

But the footage never changes.

She watched it in slow motion. It ended, as it always did, with an orange fireball, a quickly growing pillar of black smoke, and a million sheets of paper raining down like confetti, like snow, onto the streets of Manhattan.

Maddy remembered that day as if it was yesterday. She'd been nine. An ashen-faced teacher's assistant had burst into her classroom at school and blurted out the news. The television set in the corner had been switched on, and there it was, the smoldering north tower. She remembered her teacher sobbing, and other girls in her class following suit.

Or maybe there was a chance that this world, with its subtly altered reality—no President Lincoln—was going to be different enough to allow American Airlines Flight 11 to take off and arrive at its destination, and no one was going to die tomorrow. It had only been one tiny ripple of change so far, but, not for the first time, she wondered how nice it would be to preserve an alternate world changed just enough to spare Julian and three thousand others their lives.

"Maddy?"

She looked up at Becks, standing beside her. "Huh? Hey, Becks."

"I have finished."

Maddy had given her the task of checking on the growth tubes in the back. There were six fetuses hanging in that awful, murky, smelly growth solution, being fed a mixture of nutrients that kept them in stasis. None of them would grow any larger until they activated the growth mode and cut the mix with steroids. As long as they had power feeding the tubes, the fetuses—future Bobs and Becks—took care of themselves. Although, occasionally, the filters needed to be pulled out, cleared of gunk, and put back in. A horrible job. Even worse, Maddy mused, than pulling rotting hair and skin and whatever else was in there from a blocked drain. Even worse, if it was possible, than emptying their chemical toilet.

"All of the growth tubes are performing optimally," she said drily. "All the in-vitro clone candidates are fine."

"Good."

"Do you wish me to make you some coffee?"

Maddy could still smell gunk on Becks's hands. "Uhh . . . no, that's okay." She picked up a remote control and switched one of the monitors to show a cable channel. *Sesame Street* was on. She recognized it as an old episode she'd seen too many times over the years. But, of course, here in 2001, for every kid just coming in from school and watching it now, it was a brand-new episode.

And one of those kids is—was—me.

She had to be out there, right now: a nine-year-old Madelaine

Carter, sitting in the kitchen having an after-school bowl of Captain Crunch, most probably watching the very same episode. And Mom, sitting at the kitchen table beside her, asking her about her day and Maddy grunting answers back.

What she wouldn't give to just grab her coat and wallet, walk out of the arch, and take the first flight from JFK to Boston. What she wouldn't give to walk through the front yard and onto the porch and ring the doorbell. To say, "Hi, Mom," when she opened the front door. "I'm your little girl, all grown up. How's tricks?"

Most of all, what she wouldn't give to step in past her mom, cross the hall into the kitchen, and hunker down in front of that little girl, with her frizzy hair tied in a ponytail, her hands dirty, her jeans scuffed from playing soccer with the boys.

"Hey there, Maddy, wanna know who I am?"

Becks sat down beside her. She silently studied Maddy's face, before cocking her head curiously. "Maddy Carter. Why are you crying?"

"Huh?" Maddy shook her head, her mind once again back in the archway, her eyes once more on the screen, watching Bert and Ernie argue over who ate the last chocolate-chip cookie in the jar.

"Dirt," she mumbled. "Dirt in my eye." She rubbed her eyes dry under her glasses. "Becks?"

"Yes, Maddy?"

"You recall our last conversation with Foster?"

"When we went to Central Park?"

"That's right."

That's where she could find him, same time, same day. For him, a moment that passed once; for her, looping back in their forty-eight-hour bubble, it could be a repeated encounter out there in the park, beside the duck pond.

"I recall your conversation with Foster."

"You remember we asked you when you could unlock that data—the decoded message in the Grail?"

"Yes, Maddy, I remember that."

"You replied—"

"The data would be unlocked when it is the end."

"Yes—'the end.' What did you mean by that?"

Becks cocked her head to the other side. "It is the only answer the protocol permits me to offer."

"But what do you think it means? What is it referring to? The end of *what*?"

Becks shrugged. "I have no data on that."

"The end of . . . me? You? The agency? The world?"

The support unit's gray eyes locked on Maddy's. "I repeat, I have no data to interpret the message."

"Is there no way we could dig that hard drive out of your head and access that locked part of it? Scan it somehow? Siphon the data?"

Becks studied her coolly.

"No offense, Becks—but hacking open your skull and digging out your brain seems like the only way we're going to find out what 'the end' actually means."

"Tampering with my onboard computer would trigger the self-destruct mechanism. There is no viable way to bypass this protocol. The information will be revealed to you when certain conditions are met."

"But you don't even know what those 'conditions' are!"

"I will know when it happens," she replied calmly. "Then you will know the contents of the message."

Maddy shook her head with frustration. "Argghh . . . you're so annoying!"

"I apologize."

She sighed. "Go make yourself useful. Make some toast or something."

"Yes, Maddy." Becks turned obediently and headed toward their kitchen area.

"And wash your hands first!" Maddy called after her.

Maddy settled back into her chair and watched the world outside through her bank of monitors—the subtly changed world that now no longer recognized the name Abraham Lincoln.

Secrets and freakin' lies.

She resumed her little daydream of going home, seeing Mom, seeing herself, and kissing all this insane nonsense good-bye.

Chapter 13

1831, New Orleans

The Jenkins and Proctor warehouse was quiet. Around them casks of wine and canvas sacks of cornmeal were piled high. Outside through the wooden-slat walls they could hear the voices of several dozen men, the bray of a pony, the smack of heavy oatmeal bags being dropped onto the docks, the far-off toot of a steamboat; the life of the day indulging in one last surge of activity before the sky lost its sun.

Sal sat on a pile of sacks, exhausted from hours on her feet, but exhilarated by the world she'd witnessed.

"Information: three minutes until the twenty-four-hour window is due to open."

Liam got to his feet and checked over the top of a stack of cargo to make sure, once again, that they were alone in the storehouse. "I do hope our friend Mr. Lincoln has sobered up."

They'd checked back where they'd left him earlier this morning. He was gone. Not that they were surprised. The docks were a busy place from dawn to dusk, and more than likely he'd crawled away in search of somewhere quieter to nurse his hangover.

"Ah, well," said Liam, "we'll soon know if all's better when we get back."

"Maybe he isn't so important to history after all," said Sal. "I mean, it was only a little change we saw, wasn't it? Maybe that's all that's going to happen."

Bob retrieved data. "Historical accounts from the unaltered historical database indicate his strong leadership and the announcement of the Emancipation Proclamation in 1863 were critical to the North winning the war."

"The whuh?"

Bob turned his gaze to Sal. "The Emancipation Proclamation was an executive order by President Lincoln that all slaves were to be given their liberty. It was an order enacted in the third year of the war and applied only to some of the—"

"*Shadd-yah!*" said Sal. "*Third* year of the war?"

"Affirmative."

"But are you saying for the first three years the North had slaves too?"

"Affirmative. There were slaves in the Union states."

"But . . . I thought that war was all about slavery. That it *started* because of slavery!" said Sal. "The North—the blue soldiers—were fighting to end it, and the South—the gray ones—wanted to keep it."

"There are a number of listed reasons for the war. Slavery was considered a secondary or contributory issue at the beginning of the war, but became a primary issue toward the end."

Liam sat down on a bag next to Sal. "I've been reading up on the Civil War. I remember this; some historians said this Proclamation was a tactical decision to weaken the South. It was designed to cause unrest. But, more important than that, the British government was sort of thinking of coming to help the Confederate South . . ."

"Why?"

"Because they saw the North, the Union, as a growing threat. They were becoming too rich, too powerful. Becoming too big for their britches. Threatening British dominance. The British government thought it might be better if America was divided, so they wanted to help the Southern states, the Confederates, split off and form their very own nation. That's right, isn't it, Bob?"

Bob shrugged. "I have some conflicting data files on this. Historians disagree."

"But here was the problem, Sal: the British people were against the idea of slavery. So it wasn't going to be easy for the government to convince their people to go along with helping the South. And this fella, President Lincoln, was a smart chap. He realized that if this war's *headlining* issue was slavery, if the British people could see more clearly that one side, the North side, was totally against it—then there was no way they'd let their government support the slave masters in the South."

He shrugged. "It was the right thing—what's the word . . . the *moral* thing to do, to free all the slaves," said Liam. "But, the way I see it, it was also very clever, like a chess move. To make sure the Confederates didn't have Britain come into the war on their side."

Sal shook her head. "I thought it was much simpler than that. Right versus wrong."

Liam hunched his shoulders. "Wars are never about right and wrong. Always seems to be they end up being about power . . . money . . . something both sides want for themselves."

"Information: I am detecting the density probe."

Liam got up wearily from the sacks of cornmeal. They'd been walking through the early hours of the morning and most of the day, and his legs ached. He turned and offered Sal a hand. "Ma'am?"

She was struggling with the layers of linen and cotton petticoats and the tightly laced bodice as she tried to get to her feet.

"Whuh?" she said, looking at his hand, utterly bemused. "What do you want?"

He sighed, grasped one of her gloved hands, and yanked her to her feet. "Jayyyz, don't gentlemen offer ladies a polite hand anymore in your time?"

She shook her head. "Uhh, no, not really. I'd probably run if a stranger reached out for me like that."

"One minute left until extraction," said Bob.

Liam suddenly snapped his fingers. "We're probably going to have to come back here again, once we're sure history's been corrected."

Sal looked at him. "Really? Why?"

"Liam is correct," said Bob. "The distillery wagon represents altered history—"

"And we'll need to trace it back and find just who caused them horses to bolt." Liam looked at Bob. "We should've followed it up last night, right after saving Lincoln." Liam cursed, frustrated with himself for having been so dense. "Why didn't you suggest that, Bob?"

"It was not a stated mission priority."

Liam cursed again. "We'll need to come back again and see where that wagon came from, find out what spooked them horses." He fumed in silence for a moment. "Jay-zus, that was stupid of me."

They waited for the window, listening to the bustling activity outside. Bob counted down the last ten seconds, and then, with a puff of air that sent Sal's bonnet fluttering, the shimmering orb of displaced time hovered darkly in front of them. Sal took a final look around the storage shed, savoring for one last time the smells of woodsmoke, leather, and horse manure.

"I enjoyed my trip," she said, a little wistfully. "I wish . . . ," she started to say, but didn't finish. She didn't need to; Liam knew exactly what she was going to say.

I wish we could stay.

He nodded to let her know he felt the same. "Best get going," he said finally.

"Good-bye, 1831," she said, then reluctantly stepped through.

Liam looked up at Bob. "Well, better get back home, then."

Bob nodded. "Correct."

They stepped into the displacement window one after the other.

2001, New York

A moment later Liam emerged from the milky void into the archway to see the three girls standing beside the computer desk, awaiting his arrival.

"Hey-ho!" he chirped as he strode toward them. "World saved, yet again!"

Bob emerged from the portal behind him with a heavy grunt as his feet found the firm concrete.

"Stand clear!" said Maddy as she turned to the desk to instruct computer-Bob to close the portal.

Liam stepped toward Maddy. "Me an' Bob need to go back again, Maddy. We didn't manage to . . ." He stopped. Sal's eyes had gone suddenly wide, a white-gloved hand raised to her mouth.

"What's up?"

Behind him, the crackling burr of energy around the portal suddenly ceased as it snapped out of existence, and the archway resumed its normal quiet hum of computers and the fizz of fluorescent lights sending a cool, clinical glow down from above.

"GOOD GOD! WHAT IS THIS DEVILRY?"

Liam spun on his heel to see a tall young man crouched and cowering in panic and confusion in the middle of the floor, eyes as wide and terrified as a bull's in an abattoir.

"Oh, great," sighed Liam.

Chapter 14

2001, New York

The man recoiled fearfully at the sight of Bob, taking several quick steps away from him. "WHAT IS THIS P-PLACE?" he bellowed anxiously, his eyes darting from one of them to the next.

It was Maddy who reacted first. She took several steps forward. "Liam? Is that . . . ? Oh crud, that's not . . . ?"

"Yes, I'm afraid it is, Mads. It's Lincoln."

Her jaw hung slack. "Oh my God!" She advanced slowly. "Mr. Lincoln? Abraham Lincoln?"

Lincoln's manic eyes settled on her. His shaggy eyebrows scowled, covering his fear with suspicion. "You . . . you *know me*, ma'am?"

Maddy nodded. She even offered him something that looked like a polite curtsy. "Yes, Mr. Lincoln. Yes we do."

Lincoln's voice softened from an outraged courthouse bellow to something quieter and altogether more agreeable. "Then, please, ma'am, tell me where in tarnation I have suddenly ended up." He looked around the brick archway. "Just a moment ago I was in the Jenkins storehouse." His eyes fell on Liam. "Listening to you, sir, and your two friends talking about things incomprehensible to me."

Liam cursed his carelessness. "Jay-zus, he must have been following us!"

Lincoln carried on. "And then I saw that . . . that round *doorway* appear out of—" Lincoln's deep growl of a voice became a breathless whisper and his mouth snapped open and shut like a fish caught on a hook. "It arrived out of nothing! Like smoke, like . . . like a vision of angels. Like . . ."

Sal chuckled at that.

"Fool that I am, I dared to step through." He glanced at Liam. "To follow you through, sir, through the . . . that . . . that doorway, to find myself in a . . . an unearthly *whiteness!*" He scratched anxiously at the thick bristles of his beard. "Then I find myself here—in this strange place!"

Maddy took another step forward, now only a yard from him. "You can relax, Mr. Lincoln. Please . . . it's all right, it's okay. You're perfectly safe here."

Lincoln studied her in suspicious silence for a moment. "You, ma'am. You sound less foreign to me than the others." He nodded at Bob. "Particularly that ugly ox of a man there. Good God! If I had a dog as ugly, I'd shave its posterior and teach it to walk backward!"

Lincoln chortled drunkenly at his own joke.

Maddy shook her head. *He's been drinking.*

"Now you, ma'am," he said, eyeing Maddy warily, "you have the sound of New England in your voice."

"Boston," she replied. "I'm from Boston."

Lincoln nodded slowly. "And I trust you have a name?"

"Maddy. Maddy Carter." She offered her hand to him. "We mean you no harm; in fact, we came back in time to save you."

For several moments he regarded her hand as if it were a snarling dog ready to snap at his fingers. "*Save* me?"

She nodded. "You nearly stepped right in front of a speeding wagon."

"Aye. It was Bob here," said Liam, slapping the support unit's meaty shoulder, "who yanked you back out of the way. Do you not remember?"

Lincoln remembered that. Remembered being winded and lying on his back. But then it was all a confusing mixture of things he might or might not have seen or heard. The only thing he'd been sure of was the whispered conversation in the dark of the dockside. The mention of his name. The mention of a destiny. The mention of the Jenkins warehouse and the specific time of some mysterious rendezvous.

"Yes, perhaps I do remember something of that," uttered Lincoln. He cocked a bushy eyebrow and narrowed his eyes as he struggled to make some sense of his whiskey-soaked recollection. "A big, fast wagon? Barrels on it . . . was it?"

Liam nodded. "Aye. A brewery wagon. The horses were running wild, so they were."

"There, you see?" said Maddy. "Liam and the others went back to save you."

"Back?" Lincoln nodded. "That's some of what I heard these three say to each other. Back . . . they came *back in time?*"

Maddy shot a look of irritation at Liam and Sal. Careless talk. They should've been much more cautious in what they were saying and where they were saying it.

"Yes, Mr. Lincoln," she admitted. "Yes; they actually came back in time."

Lincoln's scowl vanished and was replaced in an instant with a smile that looked horrifically out of place beneath his dark, brooding eyes. "INCREDIBLE!" He suddenly grasped her hand firmly and shook it. "Most incredible!" He let her hand go and advanced toward the others.

"Sir!" he said, reaching out for one of Bob's large paws. "Sir! As unsettlingly strange as you look, I am indebted to you for saving my life as you did!" Lincoln's energetic voice filled the archway as he pumped Bob's arm furiously.

Bob looked at Liam for help.

"Just say 'no problem,' Bob."

"No problem," he rumbled.

"And you, sir!" Lincoln greeted Liam. "You, sir, I suspect, by the way you talk, are from Ireland!"

"Cork, Ireland, aye. Liam O'Connor, at your service."

"A pleasure to make your acquaintance, Mr. O'Connor!"

He let Liam's hand go and then graciously bowed in front of Sal, taking a gloved hand and kissing it. "Young madam!"

Sal giggled as if his kiss had tickled. "I'm Saleena Vikram. Uhh . . . just call me Sal."

He glanced at Becks, reaching for her hand. She eyed him distrustfully as he grasped it and then, as he was about to kiss it, he hesitated, taken aback by the livid ribs and swirls of scar tissue running across her hand and forearm, all the way up to her elbow. He quickly released his tight grasp.

"You . . . you have been in a fire. I am sorry. I hope I haven't hurt you, ma'am?"

"I am called Becks," she said coolly. She looked up at Maddy, who offered her a subtle nod. "Yes, that's right, a fire. But I am all better now."

He nodded politely. Finally he turned back to Maddy. "And you, Miss Carter, I presume you lead this small and remarkable group of mysterious heroes and heroines?"

She shrugged self-consciously. "I muddle through somehow I guess, Mr. Lincoln."

He stood back, hands on hips, to study them all. "Quite remarkable," he muttered again. "And am I to truly believe that I am standing in a time that is in my *future*?"

"Yes," said Maddy.

Lincoln looked at the row of computer monitors on the desk, displaying different news feeds from around the world. "And those pictures—those *moving* pictures, they are of this time?"

"Yes; live cable-news feeds," she replied, realizing as she said it that there was little in that answer he would understand.

He leaned forward, studying the monitors closely one after the other. "Remarkable. Like . . . like little windows looking out upon every corner of this world of . . ." His words died as he pulled in a gasp.

"Good Lord!" he yelled, stepping toward the monitor on the end.

"These buildings! Are they as giant as they appear?" he said, pointing at one screen. Maddy turned around. On one screen MSNBC was doing a news story on Wall Street. There was some stock footage of Manhattan's skyscrapers taken from a news helicopter.

"Oh, yeah; that's New York. Where we are right now."

"New York, you say?" Lincoln bent over the messy desk, peering closely at the monitor. "*That* is New York! *Remarkable!*"

Liam gently nudged Maddy as Lincoln's gaze wandered from screen to screen, muttering with ever-increasing incredulity.

"Are we not causing contamination here, Maddy?" he whispered. "I mean he has to go back, so . . . to be the president of the Union states?"

"Yes, you're right," she replied.

"Surely we can't send him back to his time knowing about all this?"

She cursed quietly. "He already knows too much. I need to think what we're—"

"GOOD GOD!" Lincoln suddenly exclaimed. "A DISASTER!"

"What now?" Maddy pulled away from Liam and rushed forward. "What is it?"

Lincoln's pointed finger was shaking. "A *calamity*, Miss Carter, a calamity, I tell you! Right there through this window! Look!"

She followed his wide-eyed gaze and saw that he was watching the looping footage of tomorrow's trade towers disaster.

"No . . . no, see, relax, this isn't *live*." She shook her head, wondering how she was going to explain the difference between *live* footage and *recorded* footage to a man who'd never seen a moving image before.

"Are there people living in that structure? That tall tower?" He turned to her. "In what city is that explosion happening?"

"New York."

"Tarnation! You mean *here*? This very place?" Lincoln turned to the others. "Is this future of yours in the middle of some *war*?"

Maddy shrugged. "Well, sort of . . ."

"Then we must join the fight!" Lincoln turned and rushed into the gloom toward the far end of the archway.

"Mr. Lincoln!" called Maddy. There was no answer. But she could hear the corrugated-iron shutters rattling under the impact of his fists. "Oh crud; he's a real pain," she groaned, and made her way across the floor to join him.

"Mr. Lincoln?"

"Where is the door, Miss Carter? We must *join this fight* and defend our—"

"Mr. Lincoln, will you please calm down!" She pressed the green button to one side of the shutter door, and with the whine of the motor and the clank of chains, it lifted, spilling evening light across the archway's floor through the slowly widening crack.

"There's no war going on right now! No invasion of America!"

"But I saw it just then, Miss Carter, with my own eyes! A *vast explosion!*"

"It's just an image of something that's *going* to happen. That's all. Nothing you need to get all upset about! Okay? Look—everything's fine outside right now!"

The shutter rattled to a halt. For a moment she was unsure whether to show Lincoln the world outside. The more details he learned of the future, the more contaminated his mind was going to be. For an anonymous man with little or no influence on history, that might be an acceptable contamination. But for a man destined to be president . . . ? Well, like she'd said, he already knew too much. A little more wasn't going to make any difference either way.

"Take a look. Everything's just fine."

She gently ushered Lincoln forward, stepping into the cobbled alley. She grabbed his shoulders and turned him to his left, so that he faced the end of their backstreet and the dirty, garbage-strewn dock beyond. Above them, the Williamsburg Bridge swept across the East River toward the glowing lights of Manhattan. It boomed and rumbled as a train went over, drowning out the honks of bridge-borne traffic above and the distant wail of a police siren.

"See? Nothing's going on. There's no war!"

"God help me! This . . . is quite . . . rem—"

"Let me guess. Remarkable?" she finished for him.

Lincoln didn't reply. Instead she heard a gurgling sound. She turned in time to see Lincoln's eyes rolling drunkenly back until she could see only the whites. His head lolled to one side; his body slackened like a rag doll, but remained upright and standing. It was then that she noticed the thick fingers of Bob's hand around Lincoln's throat.

"My God! You just *killed* him! You just snapped Abraham Lincoln's neck!"

"Negative," said Bob. "He is unharmed and unconscious. I have compressed a nerve cluster in his neck."

Sal, Liam, and Becks emerged into the flickering amber lamplight of the backstreet. "I'm sorry. It was my suggestion," said Liam. "I gave Bob the order to do that."

Maddy looked anxiously at Lincoln's body slumped in Bob's arms. "You sure he's not . . . you know, *dead?*"

"He will be fine," said Becks. "Information: he will experience only some bruising and some minor swelling."

Maddy pulled on her bottom lip for a moment, then finally nodded. "Okay . . . yeah, in that case, good idea, Liam. With any luck he'll wake up back in New Orleans thinking this was all some sort of a drunken dream. He'll blame it on the whiskey." She stepped back inside the arch. "Quick, let's get the displacement machine charged up before he comes to."

Chapter 15

2001, New York

It took ten minutes to get three-quarters of the LEDs on the charge display lit up. Maddy was certain that was going to be enough. She only needed to send Bob, Liam, and the unconscious form of Lincoln back to 1831. She turned around to check that Bob and Sal were still keeping an eye on the man, curled up on one of the armchairs.

"How is he?"

"Still out," replied Sal, looking up from something she was reading on the table.

"Okay, computer-Bob, we'll use the same drop-location data as the last trip. Punch them in to just before they rescued Lincoln from that wagon."

> Affirmative, Maddy.

"When he wakes up, he'll think he passed out right outside that inn you mentioned, Liam."

"Right. Then me an' Bob need to sniff out what caused that wagon to go hammer and tongs."

"You got it." She turned to the webcam. "Oh, and get a density probe running."

The last thing they needed was a dockworker witnessing the arrival of Lincoln and heralding him as some kind of prophet from God.

> Density probe is activated.

Liam was standing beside her. "He's a character, that Lincoln fella."

"A regular firebrand," she said. "Too much energy for his own good, like a freakin' toddler on a sugar rush." She pulled up the density-probe display bar and nodded with satisfaction that nothing so far had stepped through their drop space. "If he'd been alive in my time, I guess he'd make a pretty good children's TV show host—except for the fact that he'd scare the kids with that unibrow."

Liam laughed. He got the gist of that. "Still; I suppose it's energy like that that makes a poor farmer's son a president?"

She nodded. "I guess so. I'd like to think that—"

The MSNBC news feed flickered. Both of them caught the sudden change out of the corners of their eyes: the news reporter standing outside the White House and reporting on President Bush's sliding approval ratings had been wearing a pale blue shirt and a black tie—now all of a sudden he was wearing a white shirt with a dark red tie.

"Did you see that?" said Maddy.

More than the shirt and tie, his skin a second ago had been a coffee color, but now it was white. The same face, the same dark, slicked-back hair, but the skin had lightened a tone, as if some studio engineer had adjusted the contrast setting on the camera.

Maddy turned in her chair. "Sal . . . I think we just had another wave. Bigger one, this time."

Sal was on her feet. "I'll go look outside." They'd left the five-dollar bill just outside the shutter, hidden beneath a discarded McDonald's wrapper. On one side was the Abraham Lincoln image. She wondered if this time wave would have wiped his face off the bill and replaced it with another scowling president.

Maddy turned back to Liam. "Okay, I think we need to put Abe back pretty fast." She winced at the sight of the empty plexiglass tube. It would take too long to fill it up again. "You guys are going back dry." She looked at Liam, still wearing his morning coat and cravat, and Bob, still dressed like a dockworker. "And you're still all dressed right, so we're good to go."

The noise of the shutter cranking up echoed across to them. Sal stepped outside into the evening. "Looks the same!" she called in. "Manhattan's still there!"

Maddy sniffed and wiped her nose. "Well, that's something, then."

"*Jahulla!*" Sal came rushing back in.

"What?"

She ran over to the computer desk. "Look! See?" She spread the five-dollar bill out on the desk. Lincoln's face was gone, and, just as Maddy had expected, in his place was another elder statesman with muttonchop sideburns and a joyless frown.

Becks joined them, looking down at the note. "Lincoln's presence has been completely removed from this timeline."

Maddy nodded. "No Lincoln Memorial in Washington, then, or—"

"STOP!" Bob's voice suddenly boomed. They all turned just in time to see the heels of Bob's boots disappear out of sight through the open shutter door and out into the alley. Becks responded immediately and sprinted across the archway to join him.

Liam looked at the armchair where Lincoln had been slumped unconscious just moments ago. "He's only gone and done a bleedin' runner!"

Lincoln's long legs carried him swiftly down the cobbled backstreet, the soles of his boots slapping the ground like an audience applauding his death-defying escape into the darkness.

Behind him, two dozen yards and no more, he could hear the heavier footfall of that giant of a man moving with unbelievable agility. Lincoln was a fast runner; as a boy in Coles County, Illinois, he had won every race with his friends—legs like a stallion, his father used to say.

The busy end of the street opened up in front of him. He could see mesmerizing lights of all kinds and all colors: lights on horseless carriages, lights down the sides of buildings, distant winking lights far up in the sky.

He passed a large, barrel-sized bucket of rotting garbage and yanked at it. In his wake he heard it fall, spilling a small avalanche of stinking refuse across the cobblestones. He chanced a glance over his shoulder just in time to see the giant man slip in the rotten mush and lose his footing.

"Ha haaaa!" Lincoln yelled triumphantly as his pounding feet now found firm pavement, and instinctively he turned left onto the busier street, resolving not to allow the bewildering sights of the future to tempt him to hesitate and lose his hard-earned lead on his pursuer.

But even with his sprinter's legs carrying him quickly away from those mysterious travelers in time, who quite clearly were intent on taking him back to his hopeless, backbreaking dead-end life in New Orleans, his mind continued to spin like a yarn wheel at the incredible sights and smells and sounds all around him.

This is the future of America, he told himself. *The future, the future, the future*, his feet slapping the sidewalk to the rhythm of his mantra. He felt as excited as a dog with two tails.

This is the future! And, by Jove, I think I like the look of it!

Chapter 16

2001, New York

"Oh, come on—you've gotta be kidding!" Maddy slammed her hand on the desk, exasperated. "You lost him? Both of you? You actually lost him?"

Becks and Bob stood side by side, both still gasping from the aborted pursuit.

"Abraham Lincoln is very fast," said Becks, a hint of shame in her voice.

"Yes, and you—and numb-nuts here—are both supposed to be superhumans! You know? Superstrong? Superfast? That kinda thing?"

"His sudden departure was not something that could be predicted," muttered Bob, like a scolded schoolboy. "He appeared to be unconscious."

"Perhaps he was faking it?" said Sal. "Listening to what we were saying?"

Liam nodded. "And didn't fancy going back home."

"Well, duh," sighed Maddy, removing her glasses and pinching the bridge of her nose. "You think?"

Liam missed the sarcasm in her voice. "Yup, that's what I think."

"Oh crud." She slumped down in one of the office chairs. "So how are we going to find him now? He could be anywhere in New York."

The five of them stood in a silent tableau for a while. In the background, several TV stations quietly babbled the evening news to themselves.

"Why are we so completely terrible?" Maddy muttered rhetorically. "Super-secret time-travel-prevention agency? I'll tell you what we are: a freakin' joke. That's us. Three clueless kids and a couple of trained monkeys." She leaned back in her chair, closed her eyes, and started massaging away an emerging migraine with the tips of her fingers.

"Well, to look at it this way," said Liam after a pause, "he's a tall, mouthy fella, wearing clothes from the last century. Someone's going to notice him soon enough."

"And your point is?"

Liam shrugged. "He might cause a scene and end up on one of them news stations?"

"Or get himself arrested," added Sal. "A weirdo like that."

Maddy shook her head irritably. "This is New York, Sal. It's all weirdos."

"But he's got a mouth on him, so he has," said Liam. "I fancy that'll land him in trouble with a policeman soon enough."

An attitude. He has that, all right.

Maddy suddenly opened her eyes. "Oh God! And he'll lead the police right here! Right to our door!"

"Information: we can establish an unencrypted, open link to the NYPD incident-report database," said Bob.

"We could monitor this and respond to any relevant communications traffic," added Becks quickly. The pair of them were like two chastised children, both desperately seeking to redeem themselves.

Maddy sat forward, the chair creaking with the sudden lurch of movement. "Okay, yeah, that's . . . that's something we can do."

She turned toward the computer monitors and saw that computer-Bob was already in the process of establishing a link to the New York Police Department's computer system.

"Good boy, computer-Bob." She turned back to the others. "And maybe we'll find him anyway, right? I mean, he's got no money, so he can't get a cab or a bus or a train. And he isn't going to get a room anywhere looking the way he does. The thing is . . . where might he head?"

"Over the bridge," said Sal. "Toward Manhattan . . . toward the bright lights."

Liam nodded. "It's what I would've done on me first night. You just want to see all that up close."

"Yeah . . ." Maddy pursed her lips thoughtfully. "He really did seem to like the big buildings. Okay, then, here's what we do. We'll split up and search for him. Bob and Sal, you two head over the bridge and go north up Bowery, Fourth Avenue, and Broadway toward Times Square. Liam and Becks, you head down toward Wall Street. Those are the two glowiest, shiniest parts of town, right? Hopefully, he'll make like a big dumb moth and head to one of those two places. If we're lucky."

She fumbled among the detritus and garbage on the desk and found what she was looking for. She tossed Liam and Sal a cell phone each. "I'll monitor the police call-ins here. If we get a likely candidate, I'll dial it in."

Liam frowned. "'Dial it in'?"

"Call you! On the phone—the thing in your hand! I'll call you on that!"

"Ahh." He nodded. "Right you are."

"So, is that clear, everyone?"

Four nodding heads.

"And, Sal, Liam, Bob: get changed back into your normal clothes. Quick as you can. You look like a convention of Quakers or something."

Chapter 17

2001, New York

Lincoln stood gaping in awe at the confusion of blinking, fizzing, flickering multicolored lights, the neon signs in Chinese, the pedestrian crossings blinking WALK and DON'T WALK, the cars and cabs looking to his eyes like impossible devices that shouldn't be able to move on their own without the aid of horses in front—and yet they did.

His ears were filled with a riot of alien sounds, sounds he couldn't possibly make sense of: a rhythmic pounding that spilled out of the back of a vehicle as it rolled past him, a noise so deep he felt his chest shuddering in synchronicity; the sidewalks and streets filled with people speaking languages from all over the world, so it seemed, every one of them holding slim and shiny pebble-shaped contraptions to their ears and talking into them or alternately looking intently at their tiny, glowing surfaces.

Languages, so many of them, but the most perplexing ones were those he had an inkling were some form of unidentifiable English. He could make sense of fleeting bits and pieces, phrases shouted out from one side of the street to the other, peppered with words he couldn't begin to try to decipher.

It was awe at first, and pride, that almost had him crying. Pride that his nation, his fellow Americans, ambitious and brave men and women, pioneers, adventurers, and entrepreneurs all of them, would one day build something so magnificently, toweringly spectacular and ingenious and colorful as this incredible city of glowing cathedrals.

"Hell's bells and *tarnation!*" he gasped out loud. Even *his* thunderous voice was lost amid the bustling din of Chinatown. "This is a truly remarkable place!" He shook his head with utter incredulity. "Truly *remarkable!*"

It was then that a short woman standing directly in front of him said something.

He cupped an ear, realizing she was talking to him. "I beg your pardon, ma'am?"

She looked to him to be Oriental and giggled shyly as she spoke. He bent down low, almost doubling over to hear her better.

"It is very noisy, ma'am. Pray you might speak a little louder."

She spoke again. "Like yoo hat very much!"

"My hat?" He self-consciously touched the brim of his battered felt-topper. "Why, thank you!"

Then without warning the woman whipped an object out from her handbag. It glistened gun-metal gray, square like a tinderbox, with one glassy eye that glinted dully at him.

"Ma'am? What, may I ask, are you—?"

She pulled the small device up to her face and said, "You smile now, please?"

A blinding flash of light suddenly exploded from the object and Lincoln staggered back, screaming in abject terror, quite certain the device was some sort of weapon and that he'd been shot at.

He collided with someone else, and a moment later they were in a tangle of limbs on the ground.

"What you doin', fool?"

A young, dark-skinned face glowered from beneath the peak of a spotlessly white cap emblazoned with an NY.

Lincoln grimaced awkwardly, patting himself down to make sure he wasn't bleeding from the Chinese woman's "gunshot."

"My apologies, I . . . I must have . . . I thought . . ."

The young black man angrily pushed Lincoln's gangly legs off him. He uttered a stream of words Lincoln couldn't begin to fathom.

"As I said, I am sorry. I thought I had been shot by a . . . a small woman with a . . . well, with some curious weapon."

The young man looked at him as he got up, dusting himself off. He shook his head in half irritation, half bemusement. "You wanna watch yourself."

Lincoln looked at the young man and noticed a ragged tear along the knee of his pale denim trousers.

"Good Lord! I appear to have ripped your clothes! I beg your pardon."

"Huh? What? No, hey . . . that's jus' meant to be like—"

Lincoln shook his head, looking the man up and down. "I have some small coin on me. You must allow me to at least recompense—"

"No, hey, that's fine," waved the young man. "Jus' watch out next time, a'ight?"

"No, I insist," said Lincoln, digging into his own threadbare trousers. "Where's your master? I'll give the money to hi—"

"Hey! What did you just say?"

Lincoln froze, cocking an eyebrow. "Ahh! I see! My mistake, young man. You must be a freed Negro, then?"

🕐

Both police officers heard the call on the squad car's radio.

"*We got a disturbance, corner of Mott and Canal Streets. Caller said we got a pair of guys tangling like fighting dogs.*"

Bill picked up the mic. "Okay, we got it; we're just around the corner." He stubbed his cigarette out, put his cap on, and straightened the peak in the driver's side mirror. "Damn. Fun's startin' early tonight."

"Ain't that right," Jim replied, tossing the uneaten half of his corned-beef sandwich back into its paper bag and stuffing it into the car door's side pocket. The beef was going to be cold by the time he got back to it, and the mustard all soaked up into the bread.

Great.

He turned on the siren and took the next left. "And sheesh, it's only Monday, fer cryin' out loud."

Bill chuckled in his seat as the squad car sped down the busy street, the siren clearing a gap between both lanes of sluggish traffic.

Chapter 18

2001, New York

"See anything?"

Becks shook her head. "I see no one who matches his description or similar."

Liam shrugged his shoulders. "To be honest, I can't imagine us spotting anyone *similar*. He's an odd-looking fella, so he is."

Although he seemed to Liam to be an utterly peculiar individual— one moment manic and excitable as a child, the next curmudgeonly and as bad-tempered as a mule—there was something about Lincoln that he found vaguely likeable. Perhaps it was because he seemed so *honest*. His over-the-top mannerisms, his loud voice, his thoroughly expressive face, seemed utterly incapable of masking whatever happened to be going through his mind. Lincoln appeared to be one of those people completely incapable of deceit.

Or, as Liam's Auntie Doe used to say, "the poor fella wears his heart on his sleeve."

He recalled one of the other boys on the *Titanic* being a bit like that, one of the junior stewards. Liam remembered thinking the fellow wasn't going to last long on the ship. Too ready with a muttered curse if he failed to get tipped. The chief steward said he was a bad penny. Trouble. Certainly not the kind of young man they wanted wearing a White Star uniform.

Liam gazed at the winking lights of the traffic backed up at an intersection and wondered if that boy was one of the lucky few who'd made it off the ship alive to be picked up later by the SS *Carpathia*.

🕐

> **Maddy?**

"Yes?" she groaned. Her cold had chosen the last half hour to get worse. Her head was pounding, her throat was rough, her arms felt like she'd been bench-pressing hundred-pound weights, and her legs ached as though they'd run a marathon.

> **There has just been an incident logged on the New York Police Department's intranet system that I calculate to have a high relevancy factor.**

She pulled her chair along the table to face the webcam. "What have you got?"

> **"19:31 hours. Disturbance on corner of Mott and Canal Streets. One male, Caucasian, approximate age 22. Possibly a vagrant. Booked using probable alias—Abraham Lincoln."**

"Oh boy—we got him! What's he done now?"

> **Data entry originates from the 5th Precinct police station.**

"Any idea where that is?"

> **Just a moment; searching.**

She snatched her inhaler off the desk and took a wheezy gasp from it; asthma *and* a cold—no, strike that, *flu*—oh, *and* a whole pile of unwelcome stress on top of that. She wondered how much punishment her frail body was supposed to be able to take.

> **19 Elizabeth Street.**

Sal and Bob were probably closer. She dialed Sal's number.

"Sal?"

"Yes?"

"We've got ourselves a winner. He's gotten himself arrested already!"

"Surprise, surprise."

"He's being held at the precinct station over on Elizabeth Street. No more than five minutes from you, I think."

"You want Bob to go in and break him out or something?"

"God, no! That'll kick up a mess we can do without. No, just go in and ask about him. Doesn't sound like he's done anything *too* serious. Say he's your eccentric cousin or something and you're there to take him home and give him a good talking to." She shrugged. "We might get lucky and have them release him into your care."

"Okay, I'll give it a try."

Maddy hung up, settled back in her chair, and blew her nose into a hankie before dialing Liam. It took him about two dozen rings before he finally answered.

"Ah, so you managed to figure out how to answer it, then, Liam?"

"Aye. Them silly little buttons on the front all look the same to me, so they do."

Her patient, long-suffering sigh rustled down the phone line before she proceeded to explain as quickly as she could where Lincoln was and that he and Becks had best come home to the arch. She figured Sal wasn't going to have much luck talking the police into releasing Lincoln. Chances were they'd probably let him out first thing tomorrow morning with a verbal warning if he hadn't done anything too bad, or on bail if he had.

She hung up and aimed a hang-dog look at the webcam. "Can I go get some bunk-time now, do you think, Bob?"

> **Recommendation: minimum four hours' sleep. You are not functioning to your full ability. You look like total *chudyah*.**

Maddy smiled, surprised and a little impressed with computer-Bob. "Sal's been teaching you more naughty words, hasn't she?"

> **Affirmative.**

Chapter 19

2001, New York

"What're you doing, Jim?"

His friend looked up from the computer terminal and rolled his eyes. He'd undone the top button of his NYPD uniform shirt and rolled his sleeves up. Jim looked like a man who'd already punched out and gone home. Only, of course, he hadn't.

"That fruitcake we picked up earlier in Chinatown just generated a bunch of paperwork for me."

Bill slumped down in his chair, facing Jim over their desks. "What's he done now? I thought we were holding him overnight with a caution."

Jim scratched his nose with a pen, then ran a hand through his buzz-cut blond hair. "Stupid idiot went and said some crazy stuff about the Twin Towers comin' down. Said they was goin' to explode." He sighed. "Which means, with the FBI's Threat Alert System on amber, fer crissakes"—he shrugged—"I gotta go log it all in."

"Of course," Bill said as he shook his head, "he said a whole bunch of other crazy stuff too. What was it?"

Jim chuckled. "Oh, you mean that he's gonna be the president one day, and that he's been transported through time from 1830-whatever by a bunch of time-travelin' kids?"

Bill nodded. "And that name? Like something out of the Bible.

Abraham Landon?" He checked the screen in front of him. "*Lincoln . . .* Abraham no-middle-name Lincoln."

They looked at each other for a moment before Jim finally spoke. "*Stupid* name, huh? You see us ever havin' a president with a dumb-soundin' name like that?"

Bill shook his head. "Not with that funny way he talks. Like a southern gentleman . . . like a pastor, a firebrand preacher or somethin'. Know what I mean? Tell you what, though, man, I can almost believe the crazy son-of-a-gun just stepped out of the Wild West."

Jim looked up at him. "What? You trying to say he *isn't* a crazy loon who needs lockin' up in a room with no hard edges?"

Bill snorted. "Nope, I'm sayin' he could make a nice buck doin' Crazy Preacher-o-grams."

"Yeah, right—like that's the first thing you're gonna order for your pal's bachelor party, huh?"

"Come on, man, finish up; let some FBI pencil-neck figure it out."

Jim nodded, pecking out a few more words on the keyboard before finally slapping a heavy hand on the desk. "Done!"

Bill grinned. "One for the road, my man?"

"A beer? Sure. But just the one. Don't wanna—"

"*Don't wanna keep yer mamma up,*" parroted Bill with a well-worn smile. Same lame old line. "Problem with you, Jim, ol' buddy, is you need to come up with some new one-liners."

"Yeah? Or what? You gonna go find some other dumb sucker to partner up with?"

They weaved their way out of the deserted precinct office, all cubicles and desks piled high with paperwork.

"Now, you know me better than that, Jim; you an' me, we're like an ol' married couple."

"Gross," Jim muttered as he grabbed his coat. "Now I got a *goddarn* picture in my head that's gonna give me nightmares tonight."

Chapter 20

2001, New York

The sound of the cell door being unlocked and wrenched open roused Lincoln from his sleep. Bleary eyed, he blinked back the glare of morning light spilling in through the window and looked up from the bunk at three men in dark suits crowding into the cell and staring down at him.

"Abraham Lincoln?"

He rubbed his tired eyes and lifted himself off the pillow onto one elbow. "Yes, that is I."

"You will come with us, please," said a dry, emotionless voice.

Lincoln pulled himself up to a seated position and swung his legs off the bunk. His bare feet touched the cold floor. "Gentlemen," he started, "I have done nothing to deserve being incarcerated like this! Being treated like a—"

"Sir, you will put on your shoes and come with us now."

Lincoln's face clouded with anger. "I will do *no such thing*, sir! Not until I receive, at the very least, an apology for—"

"All right," said one of the suits, his lips barely moving. "Cuff this scumbag."

The other two fell on him like a ton of bricks, pinning him down on the bunk as he squirmed and thrashed beneath their weight.

"THIS IS AN OUTRAGE!" he barked. "HOW DARE YOU—"

"Save it for later, pal," grunted one of the men lying on top of him, fumbling for Lincoln's wrists. "You're in a world of hurt, buddy," said the other. "You filthy, murdering, terrorist sc—!"

"Agent Belling, best keep your feelings to yourself, son. While you're on FBI time, I expect a certain level of professionalism."

"Sorry, sir."

"Now, get him up."

Between them the two men hefted Lincoln off the bunk and turned him to face the third.

"THIS IS A TRAVESTY—"

"I'd advise you to keep your mouth firmly shut, Mr. Lincoln. Emotions are running *very* high this morning, and the last thing my boys and I need to hear coming out of your mouth right now is a whole lot of *attitude*."

"I INSIST YOU TELL ME—"

"Last night you were logged making a claim that the World Trade Center was coming down this morning."

Lincoln frowned. "Those two tall towers? Yes, I—"

"A few minutes ago a second plane just collided with the other tower." The FBI agent's jaw clenched. "You're either a prophet or a terrorist. Either way, we've got a whole bunch of questions for you."

He stepped backward from the cell into the corridor. The other two men shuffled out of the cell with Lincoln wedged between them. "You've just been signed over to FBI custody." The man smiled coolly. "Your sorry, murdering, terrorist, scumbag butt is ours now."

🕐

Maddy turned to the others, standing together on the sidewalk outside the precinct station. "All right, it's half past nine. I guess there'll be some police clerical staff at their desks by now who can sign a release form for us."

She looked at Liam, Sal, Bob, and Becks. "So, Liam, you come with me. The rest of you, just . . . just stay here."

"But what if they won't let him go?" asked Liam. He opened his mouth again and was about to point to both support units, Bob reaching inside the raincoat he was wearing to pull Foster's old shotgun from the waistband of his trousers, clearly eager to bring the thing out of retirement and use it once again.

"No! We're not shooting this place up! I said that already. If they say no, then we'll just have to figure something else out." She pointed up at the sky, where a solitary column of dark smoke arced across the cloudless sky. "See that? Everyone's watching the news. Everyone's watching 9-11 unfold. People are angry and very, very frightened—and that includes the cops. As far as they know, right now, this could be the first of a whole wave of terrorist attacks."

She took a fluttering breath. Nervous. "The last thing we want to do this morning is kick up a disturbance, okay?"

Liam shrugged. "All right."

She reached out and grabbed his arm. "Come on."

They climbed a couple of steps off the sidewalk and crossed a small forecourt that would normally have been filled with patrol cars and police bikes. Pretty much all of them were out this morning. Crowd control. Panic control.

They stepped in through swinging doors; ahead of them was a counter and a thick panel of plexiglass behind which two female uniformed officers and several plainclothes officers stood, all of them staring at a small portable TV perched on the corner of one of the desks beyond.

Maddy stepped up and wrapped her knuckles lightly on the barrier. "Excuse me?"

Maybe they heard, maybe they didn't.

"Excuse me!"

One of the women in uniform managed to tear herself away from the screen. Maddy could see her eyes were red with tears. "Oh my

God," she whispered to Maddy, as if they were old friends, "it's awful, isn't it?"

Maddy nodded. Right now, she felt disconnected from the disaster slowly developing at the south end of Manhattan, but she certainly remembered the emotions all around her back at school, when they, like these police officers, had sat and gasped and cried as they watched the flames climbing the sides of both the north and south towers.

"We're here to collect our . . . uh . . . well, our cousin. He was brought in last night and cautioned, I think."

The woman on the far side sniffed and dabbed at her eyes. "Right . . . yes . . ." She seemed a little relieved to have something to put her mind to. "Gonna need a name, please."

"Madelaine Carter. And this is Liam O'Connor."

"No, I need the name of the arrested."

"Oh, right—it's Abraham Lincoln."

The woman nodded and pulled out a clipboard with a computer-generated event log clipped to it. "Lemmesee, lemmesee . . ." Her finger ran down the printed page. "Abraham Lincoln? A D&D." She looked up at them. "Drunk and disorderly. Looks like he was booked in at ten fifteen last night."

"That's him," sighed Liam. "He, uh . . . he does like a drink every now and then."

"Gets him into all kinds of trouble," added Maddy.

"We're going to give him a good telling off, so we are." Liam shook his head sternly. "I wouldn't want to be him when we get the fool home."

The woman nodded absently. She picked out a reference number and began entering it into a computer. "Going to need you to sign a release form. Are either of you members of his immediate fam—" She stopped dead, her mouth hanging open, her eyes on the screen. "It says the FBI came for him this morning." The policewoman looked up at them. "You just missed him. We transferred jurisdiction to them about ten minutes ago."

Maddy swallowed nervously. *That doesn't sound good.*

The policewoman stared uncertainly up at Maddy and Liam, a look of growing suspicion in her eyes. "I . . . uh . . . you say you *know* this Abraham Lincoln? You're *associates* of his?"

Associates? That made them sound like . . . *criminals.*

"We're, like, family . . . sort of," she said with a faltering smile. "Uh, is there a problem?"

The policewoman ignored her question. "Just one moment." She turned away from them and hurried across the front office to where the others were gathered, still staring at the small TV set.

"Liam . . . something's really wrong," hissed Maddy.

The woman was saying something to the others, then suddenly all five heads turned from the TV to look their way.

Oh crud.

"I think we should leave," said Maddy.

"I think you're right."

Liam waved his hand and called out to them. "Hey, you know what, fellas, we'll come back another time! I can, uhh . . . I can see you're all rather busy!" He backed up a few steps from the counter and the plexiglass shield.

"Stay right where you are!" called one of the plainclothes officers, his hand reaching under his jacket.

"Oh crud!" hissed Maddy.

Sal stood between both support units outside on the sidewalk, feeling strangely conspicuous. She noticed the same eerie stillness here as she'd seen on countless occasions in Times Square: people standing motionless, gazing up at the sky, most of them with a cell phone to one ear, sharing these moments of horror with a loved one somewhere else in the city. Even some cars were still, stopped at intersections even though they had a green light, their driver's side doors open or windows wound down to better see the thick pall of smoke filling the sky.

With all eyes tilted upward, it was only Sal—who had seen the 9/11 sky far too many times already—who noticed the black van smoothly rolling out of the precinct's forecourt. As it turned left at the intersection and rolled past them, she thought she caught a glimpse of a familiar bearded face through the barred window in the back of the van.

"Uh? Was that . . . ?"

Becks looked down. "What is it, Sal?"

"That van . . ." She pointed.

Becks followed her finger. "The black van? Registration Washington BLL 443."

"Yeah, I thought I just saw . . ." Her uncertain voice faded to nothing as the van calmly weaved its way through the stopped traffic, took a right, and disappeared from view.

Liam grabbed hold of Maddy's hand and turned and ran out through the swinging doors.

Outside on the sidewalk, Sal and the other two looked up.

"Maddy!" called Sal. "I think . . . we think we just saw Abraham being driven away in a—" She stopped. "Hey, what's up?"

Maddy grasped her shoulder, struggling to fill her wheezing lungs with air.

"Maddy? You all right?"

"We"—*wheeze*—"we . . . got a new plan!"

"What is it?"

At that moment the double glass doors of the precinct swung open and several uniformed police officers emerged, hands resting on their gun holsters, looking around at the passing foot traffic on the sidewalk.

"Run!"

Chapter 21

2001, en route to Quantico, Virginia

Lincoln glowered at his three captors in silence for the better part of an hour. The horseless vehicle they were traveling in was uncomfortable and bare. There were no windows that he could see out of clearly, and the occasional lurching motion was beginning to make him feel sick. He had no idea how long they had sat like this, a man to either side of him and one sitting opposite, returning his glare through round, wire-framed glasses with cool professional contempt.

To his left a hatch suddenly snapped open, revealing wire mesh and two more men in a cabin in front. Lincoln had the distinct impression that he was seeing the drivers, the operators, of this curious vehicle.

"Agent Mead, sir!"

The man who had been silently staring at Lincoln turned and slid up the bench opposite. "What is it?"

"Message from the New York field office, sir . . ." The man's voice was hesitant.

"Well? What is it?"

What the man muttered, Lincoln couldn't make out. But for the first time he thought he saw a flicker of emotion on the bespectacled man's face. The conversation was quick, and the trapdoor snapped shut immediately after. The man moved back down the bench to stare at

Lincoln once more. His jaw was grinding away, his lips pressed tightly together, the knuckles bulging on his fists as he silently clenched and flexed them. Finally, in a voice clogged with emotion, he spoke.

"Jesus." He shook his head. "God knows how many innocent civilians just died. One thousand? Five thousand? Ten thousand? We may never know."

"What's happened, sir?" asked the agent to Lincoln's left.

"They came down."

Both agents cursed.

"North and south, both of them, the whole damned thing—gone!"

Lincoln frowned for a moment, and then realized the man was talking about those two magnificently tall buildings he'd seen exploding back in that brick archway. "The two straight towers are completely destroyed now?"

Lincoln could see the man with the spectacles wanted so much to throw a punch at him, but was doing his best to contain that urge. Nonetheless, he decided it was worth another attempt to explain his bizarre circumstances.

"Now, you must listen here, sir. I told those two *rude* gentlemen last night all about this! I was trying to explain to the foolish ignoramuses that I have somehow managed to travel in time—"

"I'd shut up if I were you."

"Good God, sir! This is a *free country*!" Lincoln sighed angrily. "I have a right to speak my mind, sir!"

"Right now, no, you don't."

"Do you know who I am, sir?"

"Sure, I know who you are. You're some whack-job terrorist. Some messed-up fanatic who believes in killing innocent civilians to make some sort of screwed-up point!"

Lincoln leaned forward and narrowed his eyes. "Now you *will* hear me, sir. I shall be president of this country one day, and—"

The man wearing glasses moved with incredible speed, and Lincoln found himself doubled over, gasping for breath, winded by a blow to his solar plexus. He tried his best not to vomit on the metal floor between his feet.

"Agent Belling, you saw what just happened, didn't you?"

"Yes, sir. The vehicle lurched violently and the detainee fell on your fist, sir."

"Precisely."

Lincoln looked up at them. "*What?* No! That man just punched me!"

"Like I said, *Abraham*," said Agent Mead, "it's probably best if you shut up right now."

Chapter 22

2001, New York

"He must have blabbed about 9-11," said Maddy. "He must have said something about the Twin Towers being blown to pieces when he was arrested last night." She looked at the others, then pointed to one of the computer screens. "He saw it all on there, didn't he?"

"It is logical that with foreknowledge of the event, the authorities will think he is involved," said Becks.

"Exactly! I remember when 9-11 happened there were arrests all over the country, you know? Like, within hours of it all happening! If the FBI just whisked him away somewhere in the back of a van, then they must believe he's a terrorist. That he's involved in 9-11 somehow."

"But if he's also telling them he's Abraham Lincoln," said Sal, "maybe they'll just think he's a total loon and let him go."

"Information: this is an altered timeline," said Bob.

Maddy nodded. "Exactly; Bob's right. It's a timeline, remember, where there was no famous Abraham Lincoln. He can tell them till he's blue in the face that he's *the* Abraham Lincoln. It won't mean a freakin' thing to anyone!"

She got up from her armchair and paced up and down the length of the kitchen table. "We've got to figure out where they're taking him and snatch him back before we get another time wave coming along. The next change could be a big one. We need to find him quickly."

"What's the FBI?" asked Liam.

"The Federal Bureau of Investigation," said Maddy. "Special police, if you like. They investigate terrorists and criminals. In fact, they're like *extra*-special police."

"Like Scotland Yard?"

Maddy shrugged. "I guess."

Liam nodded. "All right, then—do they have a place they work from? Like us, like our archway? A base?"

"Washington DC, I think," replied Maddy quickly. "That's where FBI headquarters is, if I remember *The X-Files* correctly."

"The X . . . ?"

"An old TV show—it's not important," she replied. "Look, that's got to be where they're taking him. That's what happened in the aftermath of 9-11. I remember reading about the FBI rounding up every suspicious-looking character they could, processing them, and holding them until the camp at Guantanamo Bay was up and running a few months later and ready to take them."

She turned to Becks. "Can you get computer-Bob to put together a data package on the FBI and their HQ—layout, location, that kind of thing? Also any information on the suspects rounded up after 9-11— where exactly they were held?"

"Yes, Maddy."

She turned to the others. "It doesn't seem like we've got a lot of options. I can't think of anything else we can do. We need to make our way down to the FBI's HQ and . . ." She looked up at Bob. "And if worse comes to worst, Bob, you're going to have to do your one-man-army thing and bust him out for us."

"That will require extreme violence," said Bob. "I will need more weapons."

Maddy nodded. "Oh, you can be sure of that. This is going to get messy."

"Where did you say this FBI place was?" asked Liam.

"Washington. You've already made that trip, Liam. Remember?"

Liam frowned for a moment, then recalled. "Aye." He and Bob had traveled by truck from Washington to New York through a very different America back in 1956—an America overrun by Nazis.

"We're going to need a car, then," said Sal.

"A car, and some big guns for Bob." Liam glanced up at the support unit and grinned. "He does like rather big guns."

"Affirmative."

Maddy planted her hands on the table. "And we need to get going soon; I mean, like, in the next hour."

"Who's going?" asked Sal. "We can't all go, can we? Doesn't someone have to stay here?"

Maddy nodded. Sal was right. Somebody needed to stay here to coordinate the opening of a return window.

"Well, obviously you need to stay, Mads," said Liam. "We need you here to organize it all. Bob, Becks, and I can do this. The pair of 'em are an army between them, more than a match for anyone, so they are."

"Let me come with you," said Sal.

Liam shook his head. "It'll be dangerous. You'd best be staying here."

"I'm always here! I'm always *safe*—I never get to do anything!" She turned to Maddy, looking for support. "This time, please—let me do something more than just watching for things!"

"Liam's right, Sal," Said Maddy. "There may be shots fired if they have to—"

"I should be dead anyway, right?" said Sal. "All of us should be! I should have been burned to death in Mumbai with my family. But I'm here now. So every day is an extra. Every day is *bonus time*. And what's the point if all I ever do is sit here and do nothing useful?"

"You *are* useful, Sal. You're *very* useful. You're our early warning system!" said Maddy.

"I want to do more!" Sal folded her arms. "I *need* to do more."

Maddy gazed down at the wooden table in silence, then glanced at the time on her wristwatch. It was past twelve o'clock. Throughout today, things across America were going to happen quickly. Right now, somewhere in the panicking corridors of power, a FEMA-directed order was being issued to suspend all airplane flights across the entire nation. President Bush was in Air Force One in a holding pattern, escorted by two F-16 fighter jets. The Pentagon was on fire. Vice President Dick Cheney was sitting out the unfolding crisis in the Presidential Emergency Operations Center in the basement of the White House.

And Abraham Lincoln was—if Sal was right, if she *had* seen him in the back of that black van—undoubtedly being taken down to the FBI's headquarters in Washington to be interrogated. He was probably already on the interstate, heading south through New Jersey.

"Okay . . . ," she said, "Okay, this is what we're doing. No need to drive down there. We're going to open a window down there, right now, right outside the entrance to the FBI's place. Not a *time* jump, just a *location* jump."

She looked across the archway toward the computer desk. Becks was standing beside it, motionless, engaged in a silent Bluetooth conversation with computer-Bob. "Just as soon as we've got information on the layout and some coordinates we can use." She turned back to look at the others.

"Liam, you and Bob and, okay, you too, Sal, you're going down there to watch the traffic going in. If you spot him, if you actually see this black van with Lincoln looking out the back window and think there's an opportunity to snatch him, then you go for it, okay?"

The three of them nodded.

"Meanwhile, me and Becks and computer-Bob, we need to pool data. We need to get every piece of information we can on how all the terror suspects were moved around in the first week after today: where they're being held, how they're moved, and so on." She shrugged. "If you guys miss him, then we're going to need to build up a picture of where all the suspects are being held today. If we lose him, if we let the trail grow too cold, we may never find him again. I hate to think where that's going to take us. I suspect we're lucky that history's only tweaked itself so far." She pulled out a handkerchief and blew her nose noisily.

"Sheesh . . . and God knows how long that's going to last."

Chapter 23

2001, New York

Half an hour later, Bob, Liam, and Sal stood in the middle of the archway's floor, just outside a faint hand-drawn circle of chalk, four feet in diameter. Within the circle the concrete floor was gone—or, more accurately, scooped out, leaving a shallow crater as if an impossibly large bowling ball had been dropped from the ceiling.

Maddy hated the sight of it. They'd refilled the small crater multiple times; she'd even bought a cheap throw rug to cover it. But several times now they'd had to open a portal in the middle of the archway—"going dry" was their term for it. "Going dry" because there hadn't been enough time to fill the displacement tube with water.

"Now, let's see . . ." Maddy looked at her watch. "It's nearly twelve thirty now. If the FBI grabbed Lincoln just after nine thirty, and it's, what, a three- or four-hour drive down Interstate 95 south into Virginia?"

"Correct," said Becks. "That would be my calculation."

"So I've set the coordinates for the exit ramp off Interstate 95 that leads to the grounds of the FBI Academy at Quantico. It's a pretty discreet, quiet spot. Russell Road. There's a checkpoint where every vehicle has to slow down and stop; you gotta show some ID and stuff. That's maybe the best place for you guys to keep watch."

She hunched over the desk and tapped at the keyboard as she spoke. "I'm not bumping you backward or forward in time—it's just a straight spatial transposition. You should get to that checkpoint before the van arrives." She glanced back at Sal. "If, that is, you're absolutely *sure* you saw Lincoln in the back of it."

Sal's hesitant nod wasn't entirely reassuring.

"Okay, then." She clicked the mouse on a dialogue box and punched in a one-minute countdown.

"What about a return window?" asked Liam. "Do we not need to agree on a—"

Maddy rolled her eyes. "See the mysterious contraption Sal's holding?"

Liam turned to look at her. She grinned as she held out her hand, her cell phone sitting on her palm.

"Just gimme a call, okay? And I'll bring you right back home. No need for funky fossils or ancient parchments this time."

"Oh." Liam looked sheepish. "Right . . . yes, of course."

"And look, Bob, if that van looks like it's full of SWAT guys wearing Kevlar vests and packing big guns, then don't be a dummy. You may be a tough brute, but you're not invincible."

"I will operate within acceptable risk parameters."

She looked at Liam. "It's your decision to make, okay? If you feel it's too dangerous, then we can figure out something else. At the very least we'll know *where* they're holding him and we can work out some other plan of action."

"Aye."

"Okay . . . so, everyone good to go?" She checked the screen. "Twenty seconds." The displacement machine's hum began to rise in pitch and volume.

"Careful, guys, all right? Particularly you, Sal. Let the boys do their work."

Sal sucked in a tremulous breath, clearly excited by the prospect of doing something more proactive than sitting there and intently watching the world for subtle changes. "I will."

A draft swept across the archway, sending candy wrappers flying and pizza boxes shifting across the desk. Before them a shimmering sphere of daylight suddenly pulsed into existence.

"See you soon," Maddy called above the hum of energy.

Sal waved her hand as Liam took the first step into the portal.

Maddy watched him vanish, followed a moment later by Sal, gritting her teeth and wincing as she stepped in, and then finally Bob.

"Close the window, please."

Computer-Bob obliged, and the spherical field collapsed into a single point and vanished.

She sat down beside Becks, facing the dim glow of a row of monitors, all of them showing news feeds from different channels, a variety of live-footage angles of the same thing: the smoldering ruins of the World Trade Center and the dust-covered, ghostly faces of a thousand firemen, paramedics, and police officers staring in stunned silence.

A frozen tableau.

The only movement seemed to be the still-fluttering sheets of paper circling restlessly in the sky like a flock of birds taking flight to seek a new home.

Chapter 24

2001, Quantico, Virginia

Liam, Bob, and Sal squatted down amid the tall grass beneath the shadow of a red cedar tree. At the bottom of the freshly mowed sloping lawn was a single-lane road winding its way anonymously through the woods toward the grounds of the FBI academy.

Fifty yards in front of them, a small outbuilding—all scuffed plastic windows and corrugated iron—housed a pair of security guards. Both of them were staring at the glow of a TV on a desk inside. Where the three of them were crouching at the edge of the tree line, on a normal day, they would probably have been spotted by now. But today both of the guards were glued to their television set. A brass band could've marched past and they wouldn't have noticed.

"Bob?" said Liam. "If that van does turn up and I give you the order to go and rescue Mr. Lincoln, what's your plan?"

Bob's eyes narrowed in consideration for a moment. "Incapacitate the vehicle first. Then incapacitate any armed guards, and proceed with extracting the target from the van."

"We want to get our fella out of there unharmed, so we do."

"Affirmative," he grunted. "I will assess the threat of harm to Lincoln and proceed only if the percentage is favorable."

"But you're not going to kill those guards in that hut, are you?" asked Sal, looking at them. "They're just old men."

Bob frowned at her. "If they are obstructions to the mission objective, they will be valid targets."

"Just give 'em one of your battle roars, Bob," said Liam. He nudged Sal gently. "You should hear him." He'd seen men recoil from it before. A fleeting recollection filled his mind: the front few ranks of an army of veteran knights and grim-faced mercenaries had faltered, albeit for a moment, at the monstrous sight of Bob standing astride a mound of rubble at the base of the breached wall of Nottingham. That heartbeat moment before the clash of arms, the thundering of thousands of boots, the jangling of a million rings of chain mail, the rising crescendo of every charging man screaming a noise of hate mixed with fear . . . but, above all that, there'd been the deep bellow of Bob's roar, like some sort of grizzly bear calling from one valley to the next.

"That'll scare the bejayzus out of them two poor fellas. They'll take off like rabbits, so they will."

"My size can be intimidating," said Bob matter-of-factly. "That is a factor that works in my favor."

"Make a scary face, Bob," said Liam. "Something really *gnarly*."

"Scary face?"

"Yeah; sort of like your angry face, but much more so."

Bob pulled up a file from his memory. His brows suddenly rumpled and joined into the menacing ridge of a unibrow. His thick horse-lips pulled back to reveal a row of teeth that looked like they could stamp holes through sheet metal.

"You remind me of a big, bad-tempered dog that's had its chew toy taken away," said Sal.

Liam shrugged. "Perhaps, but would you hold your ground with a face like that bearing down on you?"

Actually, she imagined, she probably wouldn't.

The three of them were silent for a while, the only sounds the restful far-off hiss of interstate traffic, the muted burbling of the TV set, and the chirping turf-war calls of jays and thrushes in the thick branches above them.

"So tell me—I'm interested: are you happy with how today has gone?"

Lincoln looked up from his feet at Agent Mead sitting opposite.

"Is that what makes your day? Hmm? Killing innocent American civilians?"

Lincoln's jaw set. "I *am* an American, sir."

"Oh yeah? But, what? You don't like the way America is? Is that it? This is your way of changing it *for the better*, is it?"

"I have no knowledge of your two towers or who it is that has decided to destroy them."

"Right," said the agent sarcastically. "You're still going with the 'I've come from another time' story."

"That is the fact of the matter, sir. Yes."

The agent shrugged. "So then, let's run with the ball, shall we?"

"Run with the ball?"

"Why don't you tell me your time-travel tale again."

"It is no fiction, sir! I live in the year 1831."

"1831, eh? I bet this is all pretty weird then, huh?"

Lincoln sensed the man was mocking him. "Of course," he answered drily. "As it would be to you if you had traveled across one hundred seventy years of time."

"So you must think it's pretty far out, huh? Spacey? Futuristic?"

The other two men were quietly laughing along with their boss.

"Well, since you ask, I think this world is decidedly rude. What I have seen of it."

"Rude?" The agent shook his head. "That's priceless." He grinned, amused by that. "Go on; you're *almost* convincing."

Lincoln was happy to. "Although what I have seen of its constructions and devices are quite beyond my comprehension, I do see clearly it is an amoral, selfish world."

"Really?"

"Quite so, sir. And lazy. Why is it that everyone is so fat?"

The van leaned into a turn and then began to slow down.

"Ah, looks like we're nearly there," said the agent. He smiled coldly at Lincoln. "The next bunch of fellas who'll be asking you questions aren't going to be quite so indulgent, Abraham. Soon you're going to be thinking of us as the *nice* guys, trust me."

Through the partition at the front they could hear the driver talking to someone, a crisp, professional exchange.

"You're going to vanish into a dark cell somewhere, Abraham. Every day of the rest of your life is going to be extremely unpleasant. And while all that's going on, I want you to think long and hard about what you and your terrorist buddies have done. All the innocent people you've wiped out today."

There was the muffled sound of a voice raised in a challenge, and a moment later the *crack* of a handgun.

"What the—?"

They heard a loud thud against the van, making the whole vehicle rock and a side panel bulge inward. All three agents began to fumble inside their jackets for their weapons.

The rear door of the van was suddenly wrenched open, spilling blinding daylight inside. Lincoln looked up, his eyes narrowed against the glare, and recognized the outline of the giant he'd seen in the archway yesterday.

The men in suits had their guns out, aimed, and were all shouting in unison at the giant man to raise his hands when, as one, they simply stopped.

"Jumping Jeezus—what in God's name is THAT?" gasped Agent Mead.

The giant man paused and turned around to look at what they were staring at.

Finally Lincoln did the same. Looking out of the back of the van, he saw it for himself: an impossible sky.

Chapter 25

2001, Quantico, Virginia

Liam and Sal stood up together and emerged from beneath the low branches of the cedar tree to get a better look at the rapidly advancing wall of reality, chasing its way toward them across the Virginian countryside.

At first it looked like a whole continental shelf was filling the blue sky, as if the earth's crust had split and one half of North America was sliding across and engulfing the other. But it wasn't solid; it churned and changed like a liquid as it raced toward them. Like brewing storm-cloud formations filmed and then played in fast forward.

In among the looming darkness faint watermarks of fleeting possibility appeared: fantastic buildings that had never been, twisted creatures that had no place on *this* earth, and a sea of tormented faces—lives glimpsed momentarily, people who could have been, but never would be.

"Oh boy," gulped Liam. "It's going to be a big one, right?"

Sal nodded. "Yes . . . a big one."

Then it was upon them, the slam of a tornado moment. A maelstrom of thrashing energy and darkness. Liam kept his eyes open, absolutely determined to witness it all, this being his first time seeing a time wave up close, being outside the archway and seeing for himself what reality replacing reality actually looked like. In the few seconds of it he thought he glimpsed a Roman soldier morph into something half-human, half-mechanical; the screaming, tormented face of a newborn baby become a girl, a woman, an old woman, then a decaying skull—a complete life lived in no more than a second.

Then it had passed over them.

Liam turned to watch it go, a twisting, undulating, serpentine ribbon of black receding across the sky away from them like a freight train.

"Jay-zus . . ." Breath failed him. He sucked in a lungful and tried again. "Jay-zus-Mary-'n'-Joseph! Did you . . . did you ever see anything like that?" he gasped. He looked beside him. Sal was on the ground, all of a sudden kneeling amid rows of shin-high stalks of something: a harvested crop of wheat or corn, maybe.

Liam helped her up.

"That . . . was . . . incredible!" He grinned manically at her.

Sal looked around. "This is *very* different, Liam."

Liam hadn't even bothered to take in the new reality yet; his mind was still on the infinite possibilities he'd glimpsed in the time wave. He turned around to look where Bob and the van and the guard hut had been only moments ago.

They were in a large rolling field. The woodland behind them was gone. Fifty yards away, he was relieved to see Bob standing perfectly still, nonchalantly studying the new world around them, and then, a moment later, the tousled hair of Lincoln's head emerging from the stalks as he began to sit up.

"Come on," said Liam. They wandered over toward Bob and Lincoln, who was on his feet now. He saw Liam approaching.

"That . . . that storm? That hurricane we . . . we . . ."

"Aye." Liam nodded. "That's the sort of thing you get when you remove something from history that shouldn't be removed."

"You . . . you are talking about *me*, are you not?"

"Aye."

Lincoln looked around at the field, wide eyed. "I . . . Are you telling me, sir, that *I* make *this much* difference to the world?"

"So it seems."

"Good God!"

"Liam," said Bob quietly.

"I cannot conceive of . . . of . . ." Lincoln continued to bluster. "Of anything I might do in my life that could so alter a world as much as this!" He looked down at his big hands. "What could these do that could change a world so?"

"Liam," said Bob again, his eyes on the sky.

"Yeah," said Sal. "Liam . . ." Her eyes were on the same thing as Bob's. She patted his arm insistently as a shadow fell across the field. Liam turned around and looked up.

"Oh . . . ," was all that came out of his mouth.

Lincoln managed more. "GOD'S TEETH!" he boomed. "What in tarnation is *that?*"

A gigantic boiler hung in the sky, slowly drifting across the fields. It was perhaps three or four hundred feet long. The afternoon sun glinted warmly on its copperplated side. Slung beneath it was what appeared to be a building of some sort: a confusion of pipes and chimneys, silos, ladders, and gantries, round portholes and hatch-like doorways on several floors. It seemed to be held beneath the copper behemoth by four immense crane-like arms, suspending the building like a mother cradling a child.

They watched it slowly drift above them, across their field of ragged stalks to another field rolling over a hill in front of them. It moved silently, with no roar of engines—just the sound of wind rustling through the gaps in the "building" hanging beneath, thrumming cables, and clinking chains, loose and swinging.

Eventually it began to settle down to earth a quarter of a mile away from them.

As it neared the ground, the large crane arms hissed steam from their "elbows" and gently flexed, lowering the building between them to the ground. It settled on thick stilts that adjusted to the uneven tilt with the audible hiss and thud of compressed air until it was level.

"*Shadd-yah!* Now *that*"—Sal nodded—"is really, really cool."

The enormous airship rose slowly, its arms retracting to leave the building standing free in the middle of the field. After a few moments they began to see some activity. A large door opened and a wide ramp emerged, extending down to the ground. Then finally, something that looked vaguely familiar to Liam: a tractor belching steam rumbled out on caterpillar tracks and down the ramp, followed by another, and another, and finally a stream of figures.

The building's chimney stacks started puffing tendrils of smoke, and they heard the clunk and whir of machinery starting up in the field.

"It's a portable farm! That's what it is!" Liam laughed. "A bleedin' pick-me-up-and-put-me-down farm!"

Lincoln shaded his eyes with a hand. "Am I to presume such a fantastic construction as this is not normal to *your* time?"

"This *is* our time, Mr. Lincoln," said Sal. "Just a very different version of it. Everything's changed."

"Yet we did not?" Lincoln looked confused. "How is that?"

"It's because none of us should be here now anyway, right?" Liam looked at Bob.

"Correct. None of you should be alive in, or be part of, 2001, therefore you are not affected by the causal change of the time wave."

Liam looked at the slowly rising airship. "I think it might be advisable for us to find somewhere to hide until we know exactly what sort of a world we're in right now. Everyone agree?"

Heads nodded.

Liam looked around and spotted what appeared to be a derelict barn on the far side of the already harvested field. "Off we go, then," he said.

Sal glanced one more time at the ascending sky vessel. She noticed it was segmented, and as it gracefully achieved altitude, its segments began to stretch and spread, gradually telescoping along its length until it looked like a sleek antique submarine.

"Come on, Sal!" Liam called after her.

She looked once more at the recently deposited building; to her eyes it looked more like a factory than a farm. And the small figures descending the ramp, emerging into the field, disappearing into the distant crop of wheat or barley or whatever it was—there was something peculiar about the way they moved, a shuffling inelegant gait that made them look strangely top-heavy and apelike.

"Sal?"

"I'm coming . . . I'm coming."

Chapter 26

2001, New York

Maddy rocked on her heels. Then, for a moment, she was actually *airborne*, everything on the desk in front of her hovering an inch above the surface for less than a heartbeat. She reached out for the corner of the desk to keep her balance as the whole archway lurched, then convulsed with the bone-shaking impact of something hard beneath them.

Beneath?

Showers of grit and cement dust cascaded down from the roof, while dozens of bricks clattered to the floor and exploded in clouds of redbrick powder.

"Oh my God—was that an earthquake?"

The computer monitors and the archway's lights flickered out in unison, and from the back room Maddy heard the deafening crash of what sounded like a significant chunk of the archway roof collapsing.

In the dark she winced at the sounds of damage and chaos going on around her, wondering if the entire Williamsburg Bridge was going to come crumbling down on her like a house of cards.

The rumbling outside that had preceded the quake faded away, and finally it was quiet except for the patter of grit still trickling down from the loosened bricks above them.

"Becks? You okay?"

"Affirmative," her voice came out of the darkness.

Maddy fumbled with her hands along the desk, feeling empty soda cans, pens, pads . . . finally finding her inhaler. She took a pull on it and it rattled and wheezed, giving up its medication and easing the tightness of her throat.

"My God . . . I thought that was a wave."

"I believe it was," replied Becks. Her voice was farther away now, on the other side of the arch.

Maddy's legs bumped gently against one of the office chairs, she sat down in it gratefully. "It's never felt like *that* before, though."

She could hear Becks fiddling with something. "There is no power feed to the shutter motor."

Maddy looked around the pitch black. She couldn't even see any standby-mode LEDs. *No power at all.* The generator in the back room should have fired up by now. She should have heard the rhythmic thudding already. Instead, nothing.

"Do you wish for me to open the shutter?" asked Becks.

Her heart skipped a beat at the thought of checking the state of the world outside. Given that moment of freefall and the horrendous crash a second later, she wasn't sure what to expect out there. Still, sitting here in the dark and clutching her inhaler wasn't going to achieve much.

"Yes. Go ahead."

She heard the handle being cranked and the clack of chains, and then after a few seconds her eyes picked out a faint ribbon of light along the bottom of the entryway. As it widened and brightened, a pall of muted daylight spread across into the archway, and her heart sank as she saw their floor littered with rubble and shattered brick. A deep crack ran across it—a palm's width at its widest, exposing old pipes and dusty stress cables.

She suspected the bridge's entire support stanchion was structurally unstable. Perhaps even so damaged that if they ever got out of this fix and returned to normality, they might need to find a new home.

The thought unnerved her more than anything. She realized she'd grown accustomed to this place. It was the anchor, this grubby dungeon, when all around them was a swirling sea of chaos; it was the one constant. In all the crises they'd been through together thus far, there had always been *here*—this archway, this desk, this chair—in which to hide, lick their wounds, and come up with a solution.

Maddy got up and picked her way across the floor toward the widening ribbon of light. Outside she could make out fallen brickwork and rubble, with weeds poking through.

It reminded her of Kramer's apocalypse. Maybe history had somehow managed to double back to that other alternate world, a nightmare landscape of irradiated ruins and those pitiful mutated creatures who had once been human.

She stood beside Becks.

"That's high enough," she whispered. If there were unspeakable horrors outside ready to attack them, then she didn't want the shutter door wide open.

She chewed her lip anxiously. "I'm not sure I wanna see this one."

Becks said nothing, her eyes gray, noncommittal, impassive. Waiting for Maddy to issue her orders.

"Okay; no point in me being all girly, right?" she mumbled before ducking down, squeezing under the shutter, and emerging outside. Still squatting on her haunches, she got her first glimpse.

"Oh, sweet Jesus . . ."

Becks stooped down low and joined her outside. Together they slowly stood up to get a better view of the world around them.

New York was barely recognizable. The Williamsburg Bridge above them ended in a twisted mass of cables, railway lines, and fragmented asphalt that angled down into the East River. It looked like it was a casualty of war from some time ago.

They were perched at an awkward angle at the bottom of a large, shallow crater. She took a few tentative steps up the side and looked out over the uneven lip.

Halfway across the East River she could see the stumps of the bridge's midway support stanchions. On the far side, swathed in a thin mist, Manhattan looked like a moonscape of gray rubble, punctuated with the barely standing skeletons of bombed-out buildings, like a dozen hands' worth of broken fingers pointing accusingly at the sky.

A long time ago, a *lifetime* ago it seemed now, Maddy used to play a computer game called *Call of Duty*, a World War II shooter. One of the better multiplayer levels had been set amid the ruins of Stalingrad, a twisting maze of gutted, half-collapsed buildings, craters, and blown-open cellars. What she was staring at now was pretty much just that.

She turned to look at the state of things on their side of the river. Brooklyn was almost equally unrecognizable. Although the devastation seemed one degree less total on this side of the river, all the buildings were gutted skeletons—shattered, artillery- or bomb-damaged, and blackened with soot. There were, however, some almost complete frames of buildings still standing. A factory to their right, across a pockmarked and cratered quay, had no roof, but at least it still had four complete walls lined with empty window frames, scarred, splintered, and gouged by shrapnel and gunfire.

"It's a war zone," said Maddy.

Becks joined her and nodded. "Affirmative. There is extensive evidence of prolonged war."

Maddy looked at her. "No kidding."

"Look!" said Becks, pointing up at the sky.

Maddy followed her finger and saw through a haze of fog that seemed to fill the whole sky like a low-hanging autumn mist the ghostly outline of several large shapes that moved slowly and purposefully together like a pod of whales.

"What the hell are those?"

"Aircraft?"

"Too slow for airplanes," said Maddy. "And too large. They look like balloons or zeppelins of some kind."

They watched the faint shapes maneuver, their profiles long and nautically slender, topped by an irregular outline of stacked protrusions that made them look eerily like battleships.

Then Maddy caught a strobing flicker of light on the ground, a distant flash through the haze that momentarily revealed the broken-teeth outlines of faraway bomb-damaged buildings. A moment later they heard the faint percussive *thump* of explosions.

"Sounds like someplace is being bombed," whispered Maddy.

"It is a war that is still in progress," said Becks.

Maddy looked across the river at the ruins of Manhattan. The hazy air over there was momentarily clear, and she was able to see a little more detail. She caught some movement, a glint of metal from something that looked like a gun turret slowly rotating on an artillery platform. In among all the chaos of gutted skyscrapers, knotted and rusting support cables, sagging floors, and slopes of rubble and dust she thought she detected the regular, ordered geometry of pillboxes and bunkers.

She turned her back on the river and Manhattan to look northeast toward Brooklyn and Queens, or what was left of it. Across warehouses with collapsed roofs and twisted industrial cranes no good to anyone now, beyond low apartment buildings that were pockmarked and deserted, she thought she also saw the telltale signs of an entrenched front line.

"Great," she muttered. "Just great."

"What is it, Madelaine?"

"That's a front line over the river, and on this side, over there, that looks like another front line. Which, of course, makes where we're standing . . . no-man's-land."

Their pitiful archway was half-buried at the bottom of this large crater.

It looked like it was an *old* crater, from an older war. It was bisected by a shallow trough lined with sandbags in places, and almost completely filled in in others. Abandoned trenches. Abandoned some time ago, by the look of them; an old battle line left to slowly fade away.

She wondered who the soldiers hunkered down in the rubble of Manhattan were. She turned to look at the signs of defense structures amid the shattered industrial ruins of Brooklyn and wondered who was dug in there. Not that it mattered.

We don't want to be stuck here.

She glanced back at the archway, looking like a pile of bricks salvaged from some old tenement that had been pulled down to be replaced with something else; a mound of broken masonry at the edge of a construction site. She supposed back inside—while it was still managing to hold itself up—the news wasn't going to be any better. Sensitive equipment, computers, motherboards—how any of that could have survived that impact . . .

"We'd better go back inside and see if anything's working," she said eventually.

Chapter 27

2001, New York

Colonel William Devereau could feel the vibrations of the distant bombing raid through the floor. It felt like they were giving the front line farther north, up near Queens, a pounding. They liked to do that every few days. A reminder that they had air superiority and could deliver destruction to any stretch of the line that they chose.

Not that it achieved a great deal.

Their carpet bombing would create another hundred new craters, shift rubble around from one place to another, and maybe inflict a few dozen casualties, but that was about it. All the way along the New York sector, they were dug in deep as ticks. The damage was psychological, if anything.

Devereau pulled out a crumpled packet of cigarettes: Gitanes, French made. They were as bitter as bile, but far better than the American-made lung-shredders. He lit up, took a pull, and hacked a gob of thick phlegm onto the floor. He might have bothered to quit smoking except for the fact that, statistically speaking, a sniper's bullet or a sky-navy bomb would probably get him first anyway.

Quicker than cancer.

He took this morning's high-command communiqué and slit open the sealed envelope with the tip of his bayonet. His French was just about passable. He could read it, even if he struggled to speak it. A page of telegraphed pronouncements; the usual garbage. The war was going well, the Sheridan-DeGrise Line, running from the Atlantic west across America, was holding true. The troops were to be congratulated and told keep up the good work.

Devereau balled up the communiqué and tossed it onto his small desk. Few of the troops spoke a word of French anyway; he could just as well tell them anything he wanted. French was the language of high echelons of command. The Union's generals were almost entirely imported: mostly well-connected, Paris-based sons of billionaires who wanted to carve out a few years of military glory for themselves before settling down to a cozy life back in mainland Europe.

The troops, on the other hand, the poor wretches cowering in their bunkers right now and hoping today's bombing raid wasn't going to drift farther south, were all local boys, from Michigan, Pennsylvania, New York State, Ohio. Sons of soldiers, *grandsons* of soldiers, who'd held the line here for the Union for the last hundred and thirty-odd years.

He laughed dryly at that. Once upon a time it was the Union of Northern American States. But not anymore. The "Union" by name, perhaps, but no longer run by American generals and presidents.

He sighed. Long ago he'd given up trying to explain to the men under his command that the French and their other European allies weren't over here bankrolling this war for them, for their dream of a united nation of free men. They were doing it for all their own reasons. *Political* reasons, *complicated* reasons, that were hard to explain to young men who could barely read and write.

Anyway, careless talk like that about their French benefactors could end up with him smoking one of these Gitanes in front of a hastily assembled firing squad.

Ah well, do your duty, come what may. *Fais ce que dois, advienne que pourra.*

On the wall of his small bunker room, damp concrete sweated in patches. Among the patches hung an old sepia photograph in a wooden frame. A collector's item now.

Devereau stood in front of it and studied the row of generals in camp chairs smiling for the photographer as they held their ceremonial sabers to one side. Generals from the old, old times, the very first period of the Civil War—all of them proud sons of America: Meade, Sherman, Grant, Hancock, all thick whiskers and proud smiles beneath their soft felt hats.

A soldier could fight and die for men like that. For a cause like that—a united America. For freedom. He shook his head sadly. But not for *this*, not for what this stale war had become: generation after generation of American boys dying on one side for the French . . .

The room vibrated from the sonic boom of far-off ordnance.

. . . and on the other side for the *British*.

Chapter 28

2001, Quantico, Virginia

The inside of the derelict barn smelled of compost, the afternoon light spearing in between the loose wooden slats and catching sluggish airborne motes of dust.

"Here, this'll do us for now," said Liam, catching his breath.

Lincoln sat down on a desiccated bale of hay. "Young lady," he began, still out of breath himself, "and gentlemen . . . we meet again, for the third time to my counting." He frowned. "Liam. Liam O'Connor? If memory serves me?"

"Aye."

"Please, now—please tell me my timely escape from that under-bridge dungeon of yours is not the cause of all this . . . this *alteration*?"

Liam laughed desperately. "I'm afraid it's that, and your untimely jumping into our window home from New Orleans, Mr. Lincoln. That's what's caused this, all right. A bit reckless and . . . not too clever of you, truth be told."

"You have become a timeline anachronism," rumbled Bob. "Until you are safely returned to your original time-stamp, history will remain contaminated and this timeline will persist."

Sal handed him a worn smile. "You've been a very naughty boy."

"So it would seem." Lincoln looked down somberly at his feet. "I believe I owe you all an apology."

Liam, getting warm inside the barn, unzipped and took off his jacket and one of a bunch of hooded sweatshirts branded with various sports team names that Sal had purchased for him from Walmart some time ago. He wore them without knowing—or particularly caring—who the Yankees, Red Sox, or Bulls were.

"Bob, what do you suggest we do now?"

"Recommendation: we should remain here for the moment, Liam, and await a tachyon signal. They know our location. Madelaine will attempt to open a return window for us."

"If she can," said Liam.

Bob nodded. "Correct. If she can."

Lincoln looked up. "Your time-traveling machinery is broken?"

"The displacement machine requires a lot of power, so it does. We draw it in from the city's supply," Liam said, unfastening the buttons of his waistcoat. "If New York has changed and we're not getting any energy, then we have a bit of a problem."

"We have a generator, though," said Sal.

"Aye. For what good the thing does."

"Maddy will be running it by now," she replied. "It just takes a little while to charge up the machine."

"This is only a *positional* translation," said Bob. "The energy requirement for the return portal will be small. I estimate only three percent of capacity charge would be required."

Sal peered out between the wooden slats. "There, then; shouldn't be too long for us to wait."

"What if this 'portal' of yours *does not* appear?" asked Lincoln. "What then? Are we stuck in this place?"

"*Jahulla.*" Sal made a face. "Are you always this pessimistic?"

He shrugged. "No woodsman ever felled a tree by smiling like a fool at it."

Liam pursed his lips. "Very poetic." He joined Sal in looking out at the distant farm-cum-refinery and the fleet of smoke-belching tractors and combines buzzing around in the field. The first of the vehicles was returning up the ramp and into the cavernous dark entrance of some sort of delivery bay with a payload of harvested crop. It reminded him, bizarrely, of termites feeding their queen. He shuddered at the unpleasant comparison.

"If Maddy's got technical problems on her end . . . ," he began.

Jay-zus, now, when does she ever not?

". . . then I suppose we'll not be getting a portal back home," Liam finished.

"Hold on!" said Sal. "It's worth a try, I guess." She pulled the cell phone out of the pouch of her hoodie, flipped it open, selected Maddy's phone on speed dial, and held it up to her ear. A moment later, she shook her head. "No signal."

Liam looked back outside, up at the sky—blue and cloudless, just like the *normal* September 11 had been. The sun had dipped past midday an hour ago and glinted with a bronze warmth off the hull of the airborne vessel hovering several miles away, still looking impossibly large.

"If there's nothing from Maddy by the time it gets dark, it means she's got problems. No power, most likely." He shrugged his shoulders. "Which means we've got good news and bad news."

Sal turned to look at him. "Bad news first, Liam. You should always do bad news first."

"All right: the bad news is it means we're walking home. The good news is that if Maddy's got no power, the archway field won't be on, which means it won't reset without us." He looked at Bob. "I suggest tonight we start making our way northeast, back to New York. What do you think?"

"Affirmative. That is a valid plan. If we maintain a direct route back to New York, I will be able to detect any narrow-beam tachyon signal she might attempt to send."

"Tonight? *Night*, sir?" said Lincoln. "Why on earth would you want to choose the *night* to walk home? It's when all manner of scoundrels and thieves emerge for their nefarious purposes."

Liam continued to study the distant airborne object. "I don't know about you, but I'm a little nervous about all that stuff out there. That's pretty advanced technology, isn't it, Bob?"

The support unit joined him beside the wall of the barn and peered out. "The airborne vessel may be using lighter-than-air technology."

"You mean . . . like a balloon? Like them Nazi airships?"

"Affirmative. The ground vehicles appear to be using conventional combustion-engine technology. Comparable to the normal timeline." He turned to Liam. "With closer inspection we could determine more precisely what technology levels exist in this alternate timeline."

"Uhh . . . how about we *don't* make a closer inspection?" Liam slapped Bob gently on his back. "Nice idea an' all, Bob, but to be entirely honest, I'd rather we just made our way back home as quickly and as quietly as we can."

"I agree," said Sal. She was going to say something about being a little perturbed by the workers she'd glimpsed emerging from the refinery and shuffling down the ramp. They were barely more than dots at that distance, but there had been something unsettling, almost inhuman, about the way they moved.

"Nighttime I suggest, Mr. Lincoln," said Liam. "Given these people have big floaty air vessels, we'd be far more easily spotted in the day."

"Nighttime," Lincoln grumbled. "Well now, Mr. O'Connor, we shall just have to hope this is a safer world by night than my . . . home—place—time . . ." He shrugged the end of the sentence away. He was still struggling with the terminology of time travel.

"Oh, I wouldn't worry too much," said Sal. "We've got Big Bad Bob. He'll look after us."

"Affirmative. I am a support unit. Your safety, Mr. Lincoln, is a primary mission parameter. You are to be safely escorted to the New York field office, and from there returned to 1831."

"Anyway"—Sal forced a cheery smile—"I'm sure Maddy's going to get things up and running and open that portal any time now, right, Liam?"

He tried to wear the same breezy optimism on his face, but it didn't take. Instead he cocked a skeptical eyebrow at her. "I presume you're talking about some *other* team there, Sal, right?"

"Huh? Why?"

"Well, to be sure, and I'd hate to think I sound as grumpy as our lanky new friend here, but"—he shrugged—"it never bleedin' well seems to go quite that smoothly for *us*."

Chapter 29

2001. New York

Maddy stared, heartbroken, at the small mound of debris in the back room. A portion of the ceiling had completely collapsed. Through a jagged hole in the brickwork above she could see shards of sunlight poking through. The bricks had cascaded down onto two of the growth tubes, shattering the plastic and spilling the protein solution and fetuses onto the floor. There was nothing that could be done for either of the growth candidates—one of each, a baby Bob and a baby Becks; they were quite dead.

"Oh God . . . oh no, this is awful."

Their relatively new generator was damaged as well, the casing battered and dented. A panel on one side had been knocked away and dangled from the frayed remains of several cables.

All the damage had been caused when the archway had appeared in this alternate reality, hovering several feet above the ground where the crater was. The whole archway had dropped by almost a yard. Enough of a shock for the old brickwork, held together by crumbling cement, prayer, and gravity, that it had failed them.

"I have evaluated the damage, Madelaine," said Becks. "The general structure of the archway is severely compromised."

Maddy nodded silently.

"The generator is not functional at the moment, although it is possible that I might be able to repair it. I will need to first dig away the bricks to assess the level of damage." Becks pointed to the shattered tubes. "Those two tubes cannot be repaired. The other three growth tubes are undamaged; however, the fetuses inside them will be viable for only another forty-eight hours without power."

"It just gets better and better," Maddy replied. The sound of her voice scared her. It was small, defeated, barely more than a whisper.

Becks looked at her, missing the irony entirely. "No. There is worse news, Madelaine."

Maddy nodded at Becks to go on.

"The tachyon transmission array is completely destroyed."

Maddy cursed under her breath. The transmission array was an important piece of equipment, a relatively small but efficiently crafted signal transfer dish that had sat quietly in the far corner of the back room and, until now, never had warranted her specific attention. It did its job, and had never required any maintenance. The only reason she knew of its existence at all was because she'd recently—out of sheer boredom—read through a manifest of the technical components in the archway.

But now there it was, smashed to bits, nothing more than a twisted mesh of fine wires and shattered eggshell silicon.

Maddy had an idea what that meant. "We can't signal Bob, can we?"

"Correct. More importantly, even if we had an adequate source of electricity, we will be unable to open or close any displacement windows."

Those words failed to fully register with her.

"What did you say?"

"We use the same array to target signals as we do to target tachyon stream pulses to open a portal, Madelaine. Without the transmission array, we are completely unable to open any portals. We are unable to operate in any meaningful way. This field office is no longer able to function."

Maddy felt her legs wobble and give way, and before she knew it she was slumped on her knees amid the piles of red bricks and cement powder. Tears streamed uncontrollably down her dust-covered face, leaving clean tracks on her cheeks in their wake.

"Madelaine? Are you okay?"

"No, not really," Maddy blubbered. She buried her face in her hands.

Bricks shifted and slid as Becks stepped carefully around and squatted down in front of her. She reached out and gently pulled one of Maddy's hands away from her face. For a moment she studied Maddy's eyes, screwed up behind her glasses, red and puffy.

"Why are you crying?" she asked softly, almost tenderly.

Maddy sniffed and wiped her cheeks with the back of her hand. "What the hell else am I going to do? We're totally screwed. We're finished this time. Might as well just . . . I don't know, just curl up and . . . and . . ."

"That is not a sensible course of action, Madelaine."

Maddy looked at her. Becks was impassive and calm, almost childlike in the way she was squatting on the bricks, like some wartime child having a tea party with her broken dolls amid the rubble of her own home, oblivious to her fate.

"Don't you see, Becks? We're all done here. We're *finished.*"

She stood up and clattered her way slowly across the bricks toward the doorway leading back into the main arch. She left Becks still squatting on her haunches, patiently awaiting further instructions.

"Madelaine?"

Maddy looked around the mess of the archway. The airborne dust that had filled the place half an hour ago had now settled, leaving a pale coating of powder on everything.

"Madelaine?" Becks called again from the back room. Her voice, normally so commanding, surprisingly deep for her feminine frame, right now sounded almost like the forlorn bleating of a lost lamb.

Maddy made her way across the floor, over the wide crack in the concrete, and ducked under the open shutter to look out again at the gray ruins of New York. Smudges of smoke marked the horizon to the north—Queens—where the bombing raid had taken place earlier. And the salmon-pink sun, now setting behind the tortured skeletons of Manhattan's once fine and proud buildings, cast dappled paintbrush strokes of meager warmth across no-man's-land—the only color on this colorless landscape.

Becks's faint voice echoed out of the archway after her once more. "Madelaine! What are my orders?"

She ignored the support unit, leaving her sitting in the gathering darkness among the bricks, abandoned like an orphaned child.

"Madelaine?"

One step in front of the other in the gathering twilight, each one easier than the last. She realized that she could leave. Walk away from it all. Walk away from the responsibilities she'd never asked for, walk away from secrets she didn't ask to know about. If all their field office was now was a crumbling archway and a bunch of machines that didn't work anymore, what difference would it make if she stayed or left?

I can just go.

She turned her back on the East River, Manhattan, and the sun setting beyond, and faced northeast toward the ruins of Brooklyn, toward Boston . . .

Home.

Perhaps even in this alternate timeline the same people had met, fallen in love, and made the same babies as before and somewhere northeast of here, in her home city, there was a little girl with glasses and frizzy strawberry-blond hair who liked playing around with her father's computers more than playing with Barbie dolls. Perhaps that home was there. Perhaps her mom and dad were the same two people and she could explain to them who she was, get them to understand that she was their daughter, only ten years older. For them it would be like having an older sister for their only child. A sister who could understand her in a way no normal sister could: a mentor, a guide, a friend.

Her faltering steps across the rubble-strewn landscape quickened.

A part of her argued the case that she still had responsibilities and obligations here. Liam and Sal, they too were stuck in this . . . whatever this world was. But what could she do for them? Sit on her bunk and wait for them in the dark? Wait until some bombing raid came along and gave this portion of the city another pounding?

Maddy shook the nagging voice away. She really hadn't needed Becks to catalog how complete and catastrophic the damage was to their equipment.

In the absence of a plan, or anything left of their field office for which she had to be responsible, there was only one small voice that made sense. A childlike voice.

I want to go home.

Chapter 30

2001, somewhere in Virginia

The man looked down at them, surprised. "*New York!* You wan' go New York?"

"That's right," said Liam.

"You craz-ee." He shook his head. "I take you far as Dead City. No more. I goin' west—New Pittsburgh, maybe Cleveland. You should go west too."

"Dead City?"

The man shrugged and said something to his wife sitting beside him in the odd-looking vehicle's front cabin. He turned back to Liam. "Yuh—Dead City, you know? Ol' times use' to be call' *Baltimore?*"

It was dark, and Liam could only see the side of the man's face, lit by the lantern swinging in the fresh breeze. He read the expression as friendly bemusement.

"You and your friends sit in back with chickens. I take you north some way." The one eye Liam could see glinted in the lantern's amber light; it was locked suspiciously on him. "You no trouble?"

Liam spread his hands, then turned to make sure Bob had tucked the shotgun away out of sight. "I promise you, sir, we'll be no trouble." He glanced at the side of the man's vehicle. It reminded him of a traditional Romany caravan; every surface seemed to be lavishly decorated with intricately carved designs, and down along the side a multitude of hooks protruded, from which pots and pans and other kitchen miscellany rattled and clanged softly as the gentle breeze stirred the ears of corn to either side of the empty road.

"We'll just be in the back, then," said Liam, "keeping your chickens company."

The man nodded, satisfied with that, then turned to his wife and began chattering to her. She didn't seem quite so pleased to have passengers come aboard.

They made their way to the back of the caravan. It rattled and vibrated from the idling engine beneath, which intermittently spat clouds of vapor out between the spokes of its six wide, wooden cartwheels.

Liam pulled open a wire-mesh gate at the rear and stepped inside to see a cramped space almost completely filled with carefully stacked household possessions. The rest of them followed suit, the vehicle lurching as Bob finally pulled himself up inside and slammed the mesh door behind him. There was just about room for the four of them to huddle on the floor, shoulders rubbing shoulders and legs pulled up in front of them.

With a cough and a splutter the vehicle lurched forward, and a thousand different objects around them began to squeak and rattle and clank. It might not be the most comfortable ride for them, but at least it was taking them in the right direction—north, toward New York.

So far there had been nothing from Maddy. No portal, no message. Not a good sign.

Liam was thinking of something interesting to say when, with a flutter of dislodged feathers, a rooster emerged from behind a wobbling cupboard and settled on top of Bob's head.

"Oh, sorry," said Liam. "I actually thought he was, uh . . . you know, *joking* about having chickens in the back."

Bob swiped a big hand at the bird, and it scrambled and flapped around the enclosed space for a full minute before finally, tentatively, returning to roost on Bob's head again.

"No place like home," offered Liam.

Bob stared indignantly back at him.

"You, sir, look about as happy as a clam at high tide."

Bob switched to stare indignantly at Lincoln.

"It suits you," said Sal, affectionately patting his arm.

Chapter 31

2001, somewhere in Virginia

As dawn started to make its mark on the horizon, the man deposited them at a junction of roads: one of them heading west, the other continuing north. He warned Liam once again that heading north to New York was "no good."

"Why? What's going on in New York?"

The question caused the man to cock his head curiously. "You serious?" He didn't wait for Liam to answer. "You been 'sleep all your life? The city . . . it all gone now. New York, it just big ruin."

"A ruin? What's up with it?" He turned around to the others, standing beside him on the shoulder of the road. Sal's eyes were wide, her face ashen.

"How you not know this?" the man asked, incredulous.

"Well, we've . . . been away, a long time." Liam's answer sounded lame, and the man shrugged a "whatever," as if to acknowledge that the answer maybe wasn't his business.

"The war, it stay there. It never move on. Been there forever."

"War?" Lincoln took a step closer. "Great Scott! Did you say 'war,' sir?"

The man leaned back in his cabin, wary of the tall man's belligerent face. "Yeah . . . you not know of war?"

"No, sir! A war between *who*, man? Tell me!"

Liam rested a hand on Lincoln's shoulder. "Easy there, fella."

The man's wife muttered something into his ear and he nodded, firing up the engine on his carriage. It coughed and clattered noisily before settling down to a noisy chug. He was clearly getting a little nervous about these crazies he'd picked up and deposited here at this crossroads in the middle of nowhere.

"Please!" said Liam. "Don't go yet. We need to know more!"

"I tell you this; it not safe. North, fighting there never stop. You should go west." He pointed east across the rolling fields of barley. "East no good too . . . Dead City, maybe twenty-five mile that way. Poison. No good for you health."

He shrugged an apology as his wife tugged insistently on his arm. "We go now." The carriage's large wheels rolled forward onto the road as a cloud of acrid smoke erupted through the spokes.

Liam coughed and waved it out of his face. As it gradually cleared, he watched the carriage clatter, rattle, and chug its way along the road heading toward New Pittsburgh—or at least that was what the hand-painted sign at the junction indicated.

They watched until the carriage was just a faint twinkle of swinging lanterns in the distance.

"I suppose we should find somewhere to hide before it gets too light," said Liam. He looked around. On either side of the roads heading north, south, and west, as far as his eyes could see in the gray light of dawn, was nothing but shoulder-high stalks of barley swaying gently and whispering in the breeze.

They followed the single-lane road heading north. Only a dozen vehicles passed them by, most of them ramshackle carriages, carrying families and their worldly possessions stacked high.

One vehicle in particular sounded different enough as it approached for Bob to suggest they hide. And they did, crouching in the field amid the barley as the vehicle drew nearer, came into view, and eventually rolled slowly past them.

Sal exchanged a glance with Liam.

The vehicle was military, "tank" being perhaps the most appropriate word to describe it. It looked almost comically top heavy, with the approximate proportions of a small terraced house. The top "floor" was a large gun turret that looked like it probably rotated, from which protruded three short-barreled cannons. At the very top a hatch was open, and they could see a tired-looking army officer in a crimson tunic and white sash smoking a pipe and gazing out across the rolling fields.

The bottom floor of the tank was a mass of iron plating and rivets flanked on either side by caterpillar tracks that ground noisily along the paved road. The tracks wound around a large solid-iron rear wheel and a much smaller spoked wheel at the front. Between the wheels on each side, a miniature side-cannon protruded.

As it slowly passed them by, Sal got a glance at the rear of the tank's bulky chassis. Iron-plated shutters were open, revealing three panes of glass, like the bay window of a suburban house. Through them she could see, by the muted amber light of a gas lamp, half a dozen soldiers gathered around a table, having breakfast by the look of it, and bunk beds stacked three high.

They watched the enormous vehicle trundling its way northward. The rumble of its engine and the squeak and groan of the caterpillar tracks continued to hang in the air long after they'd lost sight of it in the pallid light of dawn.

Liam looked at the others. "That looked like a gentleman's club on wheels."

🕐

An hour later, just after the sun had breached the horizon, they finally came across a smaller, potholed lane that branched off the road and led into what appeared to be a deserted hamlet.

They soon found themselves in a town square overgrown with weeds. The buildings surrounding it were boarded up and derelict. Over every ground-floor window wooden slats had been nailed in place—years ago, by the sun-bleached look of them.

"A ghost town," said Sal.

"Aye."

Bob strode toward the door of the nearest building, a chapel. Its timber walls were flecked with white paint here and there, but most of it was the dull pale gray of weathered wood.

"Information," his baritone voice rumbled as he reached out a hand to hold down the frayed and curled corner of a notice nailed to the chapel's door. The others joined him as he read out the faint printed words on the tattered page.

"Notice of clearance: this settlement has been evacuated in accordance with the War Appropriations Act. It is illegal to enter, occupy, and/or make use of these properties, which are scheduled to be cleared and used as additional farmland in due course."

"It's an old notice," said Sal, pointing at a date in the corner. "See? June fifth, 1985."

"Been deserted for, what? . . ." Liam frowned as he struggled to do the math.

"Sixteen years," said Bob.

"Right."

"I'm thirsty, Liam," said Sal.

He realized he was also thirsty. The cool of dawn was soon going to become the cloying warmth of a September morning. They needed to find some drinking water. "I suggest we look around and see if this ghost town has a well or a rainwater tank or a spring or something."

The sun was warming the sides of the old buildings, casting long, cool shadows in their wake across weed-strewn front lawns. He could see the remnants of lives lived here: a swing dangling from a rusting A-frame; a mailbox on top of a post nailed to a picket fence, inside it the dried twigs of some bird's abandoned nest; a clothesline with the tattered threads of laundry still pegged to it, flapping gently.

Liam suspected that the people living here sixteen years ago must have been evicted with little or no warning.

Feeling a pang of guilt—he didn't know why—he swung a kick at the chapel's wooden door. It creaked, but failed to give.

"Let me," said Bob, casually thrusting one shoulder against it. The door didn't even bother trying to argue with him; it cracked, then surrendered and rattled inward.

"Right," said Liam, rubbing his sore toe, "let's see what we can find."

Chapter 32

2001, New York

Maddy realized that she must have been lost in some sort of a daze. The night had passed without her really even being aware of it. She vaguely remembered settling down in the corner of some bomb-damaged warehouse, gathering her knees to her chest for a little warmth, and crying. She must have fallen asleep at some point, and now it wasn't daylight that had woken her up—it was someone's boot, roughly kicking her side.

"Hey, wakey, wakey."

She looked up to see two men staring down at her. Soldiers, by the look of them. They both wore something that approximated a uniform: dark blue, almost black tunics; belts; buckles; pouches; and cloth slouch caps. She blinked back at the brightness, then reached for her glasses and wiped dust from them.

"Come on, sweetheart," one of them said. His face seemed to be mostly beard beneath the peak of his cap. "Gonna have to take you in, girl. Colonel's gonna want to talk to you." He offered her a hand.

"I'm sorry—am I . . . am I in the wrong place or something?"

"Wrong place?" Beardy-face laughed. "Hell, girl, the whole darned sector's the wrong place."

She let him pull her up. "I'm sorry . . . I don't . . ." She looked at him. Beneath his hat, his skin was dark, his cheeks speckled with gray stubble. "Am I in trouble?"

"You're a civilian in a frontline Union defense zone." He shrugged. "If the colonel thinks yer a Southern spy, you gonna be in a whole *world* o' trouble, girl."

"S'right," said the other soldier, pale as cigarette ash and surely only a couple of years older than Sal. "Had us a spy through this way coupla months back, didn't we, Sarge?"

"Uh-huh," replied the black soldier. "Weren't no girl, though." He studied her suspiciously. "Either them Southern boys're gettin' clever, or they gettin' desperate."

"I'm not a spy," said Maddy. "I'm just . . ." She realized she had no answer that wasn't going to sound utterly unconvincing. "I'm just . . . *lost*," she said finally.

"Well"—he pursed his lips—"guess we'll be lettin' Colonel Devereau be the judge a' that, huh? Come on now, miss."

The two soldiers led her through the bombed-out ruins onto a street temporarily cleared of rubble. She looked up at a warm morning sky spotted with pink clouds, and for a moment savored the warmth of the sun on her face.

"You ain't gonna run on me, are you, miss?" asked the young one. "We gotta shoot at yous if ya do, see?"

"Hey now, Ray—she look to you like she gonna run?"

Maddy shook her head wearily. She wouldn't know where to run even if she had the will to do so. "I'll be a good girl," she said quietly. "I promise. What's your name, by the way?"

The man looked surprised at the question. "You lookin' for introductions?"

She nodded. "I'm Maddy."

He laughed. "Well, since you insist on bein' so formal an' all. Name's Sergeant Freeman, an' this young drainpipe is Private Ray Calder."

"Fellas just call me Ray," grinned the young man.

Colonel Devereau sat down to enjoy his mug of coffee. A rare treat: *real* coffee beans shipped in from some far-off exotic country. He was just beginning to conjure up the swaying palm trees and golden beaches and turquoise lagoons of some distant tropical French colony in his mind's eye, stirred by the aroma of the strong black brew in his chipped enamel mug, when his adjutant knocked on the bunker's metal door. The door rang like a tuning fork.

"Yes?" he sighed. The door creaked heavily open.

"Sorry to interrupt, sir. Patrol in sector five picked up a non-combatant. A girl, sir."

"A girl?" He made a face. "She out there in the corridor?"

"Yes, sir."

He sighed. *Of course . . .*

He waved a tired hand. "Bring her in, then."

He picked up his mug again and held it beneath his nose, enjoying the smoky aroma once more, while outside he heard orders being barked down the concrete passage. A moment later the girl in question stepped over the lip of the doorway.

She was a sorry sight: a bespectacled child, thin, pale, and grubby. She was wearing what he would consider to be workman's trousers— faded blue canvas. And her top was a smudged white shirt with no buttons, loops, or any sign of feminine embellishments of lace or ribbon, just a printed word: "Intel."

"Take a seat," he said.

She stepped forward and slumped onto the wooden chair in front of his desk. Very unladylike in her posture.

"So, are you going to give me your *real* name? Or am I going to get your *spy* name?"

"Maddy," she said. "Madelaine Carter. It's my real name."

He shrugged. "Okay. There's a start, then . . . *Maddy*." He took his first tentative sip, testing the hot coffee with a top lip covered in drooping bristles.

Maddy looked up at him, her eyes narrowing as she studied him silently. "You and your men are dressed up like *Civil War* soldiers. Like, from the 1860s or something. Except"—she shook her head—"I don't see any muskets. Your soldiers have weird-looking assault rifles."

Devereau laughed. "Good God . . . *Civil War!* That's a very old-fashioned term you're using, young lady. *Civil War?* This war hasn't been called that in well over a century."

She frowned, puzzled. "You're telling me that this . . . this is the *same* war?"

It was Devereau's turn to look perplexed. "You're *asking* me that, young lady?" he said, pulling on the handle of his mustache. "As if . . . you actually don't know?"

"Yes."

He sipped his coffee, swilling the rich bitter taste around his mouth. "So, I presume this is how you were instructed to behave, then, if you got caught? Hmm? To act the fool? To appear insane?"

"You don't know the half of it." She laughed bitterly. "Maybe I am."

"Well"—he put down his mug and spread his hands—"why don't you tell me 'the half of it,' as you say?"

"You'll only think I'm completely crazy, or lying." She shrugged. "Because I'm not from this world, see? I'm from another world. Another time, really." She shook her head. "What's the point? You're not going to believe anything that comes out of my mouth, right?"

He stroked his beard in silent contemplation for a full minute. "Here's the thing: if I were sending you to spy on the South, I'd dress you anonymously. I'd pick someone who looked and behaved normally. You, on the other hand, young lady, are neither." He pointed a finger at her shirt. "And it seems very foolish to me to be putting that badge on the front of you. It would be a bit like a thief wearing an I AM A BURGLAR sign around his neck."

She looked down at her sweatshirt. "Intel?" She smiled. "Oh, you think it's short for 'intelligence,' right?"

He returned her smile. "Indeed. Military intelligence. You might just as well have put the word 'spy' on your shirt."

"Intel, they're a manufacturer of silicon chips," she said. "In *my* world."

He frowned.

"Silicon chips? You know, like in computers?"

"'Computers'? What is one of those?"

"Are you serious?"

They sat in silence for a while. Outside the colonel's bunker, a muted clunking of metal on metal could be heard, machinery starting up somewhere in the subterranean nest of rooms and passageways.

"Well, now," said Devereau, sipping his cooling coffee. "I'm halfway to believing, Miss Carter, that you're *not* a spy, or, at the very least, if you are one, you're not a very good one. And that might just spare you from going in front of a firing squad."

Her jaw dropped a little. "Firing squad?"

"Ahh, I see that seems to have focused your mind a little. Yes, I have ordered men to be executed, an unpleasant and occasionally necessary part of being a frontline commander."

"I . . . uhh . . . look, I'm not a spy! God, no! That's . . . that's not me . . . I—"

"Actually, you needn't be alarmed. I suspected as much. You really are far too odd, young lady. However, I think it would be a good idea if you start telling me—"

"Time traveler!" Maddy blurted out. "I'm a time traveler! I travel through time!" Then she winced at how ridiculous that must sound to him.

Devereau could have laughed at her ingeniously novel reply. But he felt like seeing how well thought-out her outburst was. "Indeed? Now, is this the same idea as is used in that famous work, *The Time Machine*?"

"*The Time Machine*?" Maddy's mind raced. Yes, that old book had been written in 1895—the *correct* 1895, that is. Perhaps even in this corrupted timeline the same author, H. G. Wells, could have been inspired to write the very same, or a very similar, book?

"Yes!" she replied. "Yes—the technology exists to move backward and forward through time. Well"—she shrugged—"it *will*. In the year 2044 they'll figure out a way to do it."

Devereau nodded patiently. "And, let me see, you're expecting me to believe you are from the year 2044, I take it?"

"From the future, yes. But actually, I work in 2001. But not *this* 2001, if you see what I mean. A very different one."

She was confusing him.

"See, this is wrong. It's *all* wrong! This . . . this . . . room, that ruined New York outside, this war! It's all wrong. It shouldn't be like this!"

"Oh? How should it be?"

Maddy leaned forward. "Your side won! It won over a hundred thirty years ago! The North beat the South! America became one big nation. It became the world's most powerful nation! Do you know that this nation even managed to *send a man to the moon*?"

"Miss Carter"—he smiled wryly—"you'll never know how much I'd love to believe a fanciful story like that, but—"

"It's true! Honest to God, it's—"

"This nation is a mongrel nation, and that's all it'll ever be. Too busy fighting itself, state against state, brother against brother. And now"—Devereau lowered his voice to a more cautious level—"and now we're all but governed by France and Europe; and the Southern Confederacy is little more than a colony of Great Britain."

"No," she said, shaking her head. "No. You're so wrong! *This* is wrong! There's a correct history, a way it should go. And in the *correct* history, the North wins in 1865. And do you know why? Do you know *how* it wins?"

"Go on."

"Because it made the issue of slavery—abolishing slaves—a war aim. It decided to make that the main reason for the war. And it worked!"

"Slavery?" He shook his head. "There's no slavery. There hasn't been since, well now . . . since 1871, when the South signed an alliance with Britain's King Edward VII."

"The South, the Confederates, don't have slaves?"

"Of course not."

"Then . . . then why are you guys fighting each other?"

He shrugged. "It's a question I ask myself every day." Devereau sighed. "Truth is, we're pawns of the British and the French. We're fighting their war for them."

"My God . . . this is so wrong. This is all because of Lincoln."

"Lincoln?"

"A man named Abraham Lincoln. He was your president when the Civil War started."

Devereau shook his head. "There's never been a President Lincoln—"

"Not in this timeline, no. But in mine—in *correct* history—it was *his* idea to make it about slavery! He's the reason the North won the war!"

Devereau stroked his beard. "Now, what a lovely idea that would be." He looked at her. "Timeline? What is that?"

"It's, uh, sheesh, it's really hard to explain. It's the way events in history go. They happen in one way or another. We call each possible way in which a history happens a 'timeline.' We have a machine that can transport you from one timeline to another." Maddy smiled. "You know, in *my* timeline, this war ended in 1865. The North won, and the states came together again. The United States would go on to do some incredible things . . ." She held herself back from saying *and some bad things.*

Devereau looked down at the battered enamel mug in his hands and sighed the deep wistful sigh of someone who wished he could share in this fantasy, could actually believe that it had a shred of truth to it.

"You know," she said, "I can prove all of this to you. I really can."

He looked up at her. "And how could you possibly do that?"

"I've got things I can show you."

The girl, this Madelaine Carter, supposedly from another time, another place, had walked into this room five minutes ago with a listless, almost defeated way about her. But now it seemed she'd found a spark of something inside; something infectious. Something he longed to feel himself.

"What things?"

She grinned. "How would you like to see my time machine?"

Chapter 33

2001, New York

Becks righted the aluminum shelving unit that had been knocked over by the falling bricks. She picked up loops of cable on spindles, dusty old motherboards, a box of electrical components, and electronic gadgets and gizmos brought back to 2001, all stamped with the W. G. Systems logo.

She set these things back on their shelves, neat and orderly, just as they had been before the archway had landed in this timeline with a crash.

She found the broom behind the cracked plexiglass displacement tube and began methodically sweeping the fractured and uneven concrete floor, pushing the fallen bricks and mortar into a pile in the middle. She moved the broom with a rhythmic rasp in the darkness, her eyes adjusted to the faintest glimmer of moonlight that found its way through the cracks in the archway ceiling.

Her eyes dilated in the dark and registered little. They were glazed over. From the outside, she looked for all intents and purposes like someone in a deep state of shock. Traumatized. A lost soul seeking solace in the simple task of cleaning up.

But inside her head, the silicon-wafer computer hummed with activity, lines of code chasing each other in tireless loops as she tried desperately to make sense of the situation she was now in.

Alone.

Maddy was gone. There was no strategist. There was no team. There was not even a field office anymore. This dark hole was nothing but dust-covered secondhand furniture, an old high-school desk, and a row of computers that more than likely were never going to work again.

[DATA]

She shook her head. She didn't want to acknowledge the data.

[DATA]

She closed a silicon-synaptic data gate, not wanting the machine code to tell her what she already suspected. That somehow this was all her fault. That she had provided inadequate information or, worse, *inaccurate* information to Madelaine Carter, causing her to make an erroneous judgment call. That the team was no longer operational.

She and Bob had both failed to apprehend the target: Abraham Lincoln. She realized that was perhaps the first in a string of errors that had led them to this point. And now she was here sweeping bricks in the dark.

[DATA]

The stream of hexadecimal data found another way through the myriad circuits to get her attention.

[Assessment: end-of-run condition = TRUE]

End-of-run Protocol

1. **Extract hard drives from system computers. Destroy**
2. **Retrieve tachyon phase accelerator and displacement attenuation boards from displacement machine. Destroy**
3. **Self-terminate**

The protocol left no vital technology behind; all the rest, the computers, the growth tubes in the back, the generator, even the rest of the displacement machine, used circuitry that could be assembled from components bought from any electronics store. The question was, was this really an end-of-run condition?

She looked around at the dark corners of the archway. Her memory spooled a million different moments from the last few months of stored data:

The first time she'd made a hot drink for Maddy and added coffee granules, tea leaves, *and* hot chocolate powder, not realizing the hot drink was meant to be just one of those, not all of them.

The time Liam had gotten her and Bob to play *Mario Kart* on the Nintendo and they'd spent seven hours straight playing on the machine, beating Liam to last place every race.

The first time she felt something that was more than the code of her operating system or her AI plug-in. In the prehistoric past, a moment of . . . affection? When Liam had told her that she wasn't a mistaken addition to the team. That she'd done well. That the team should have two support units in it. A Bob and a Becks.

Sal teaching her swearwords in Hindi and Mumbai street slang. She had a whole database of curses and insults she could hurl, making her sound as convincing as any other rickshaw driver in the down-town smog.

She even had her "borrowed" memories as Bob. They felt almost as real as her own: duplicated video and sound files of Bob observing the assassination of President John F. Kennedy from the Dallas book depository; Bob making the choice to search every internment camp in the Washington area to find and save Liam.

Hadn't Bob changed a mission priority then? Actually decided his own mission priority? Rewritten code?

She stopped sweeping and stood statue-still in the dark, the broom still held tightly in her hands. Her internal clock passed the better part of an hour with her frozen like that, before finally a string of characters broke the deadlock.

[Assessment: end-of-run condition = FALSE]

She stirred, looking up from the floor.

Mission Priority
1. Damage assessment, recovery analysis
2. Locate and retrieve Strategist Madelaine Carter

Chapter 34

2001, somewhere in Virginia

"I'm going to read you what I found," said Liam. He shuffled closer to the fire in the middle of the room.

After exploring the deserted hamlet, they had decided to settle in the kitchen of a farmhouse. Aside from the chapel, it was the largest building around. They found a pantry full of old, dust-covered cans of food. Everything else in there had long since perished or been scavenged by rats or wild animals.

Now, as the afternoon sun waned and a cool wind began to whip up over a decade's worth of dead leaves, they had a fire going in a rusting brazier as Sal, Lincoln, and Liam hungrily spooned mouthfuls of a tepid, tasteless stew.

Liam put down his bowl and picked up the old dog-eared notebook he'd found in what had clearly once been a young boy's bedroom. The brittle pages were covered with the untidy pencil scribbles of Liam's handwriting.

He looked up at Sal and Lincoln, both eager to hear the notes he'd made from the study they'd come across in the farmhouse, lined with shelves full of books and magazines and stacks of old newspapers tied up with twine. Bob, meanwhile, stood in the corner of the kitchen, the shotgun nestled in his thick arms, looking out through a grimy window across a backyard full of weeds.

"Now, we know in *correct* history the Civil War ended in 1865." At least Liam did—he'd been reading up on that period of history a few weeks ago. He'd surprised himself with how much information was still in his head. Better memory than he thought he had. "The deciding battle of the war was the Battle of Gettysburg. In correct history, the Confederates lost that battle badly and the Army of Southern Virginia under General Lee never really recovered. Well . . ." He looked down at his notes and flipped through a couple of pages. "Well, in *this* timeline, it seems they managed to win. The Union Army retreated back to Washington in disarray. And"—he looked up at Lincoln— "President *John Bell*'s government made a hasty retreat north to New York to make that city the new seat of government."

"You are implying that President Bell, that man . . . should have been me?"

"Yup."

Liam returned to his notes. "So, after the Union defeat at Gettysburg, Great Britain finally came out in *open* support of the Confederate South."

"So they were *already* on the South's side?" asked Sal.

Liam shrugged. "Kind of. Not openly, though—just helping a little, discreetly."

"Why discreetly?"

"Slavery. The British public were appalled by it. They'd demanded its abolition at home years earlier. And because the South still used slaves, Britain couldn't bring themselves to fully support them. But, on the other hand, the British felt threatened by the growing industrial power and influence of the North, the Union.

"All that changed when, after Gettysburg, the British made an offer to Jefferson Davis—"

"And who's this Jefferson Davis?" asked Lincoln.

"The Confederate's president. The offer was a clever one . . ." Liam fumbled through the pages of notes he'd made this afternoon and finally found the paragraph he was looking for.

"To announce the first measures of 'a post-slavery economic reformation.'"

Lincoln's eyes widened. "Good God! An end to slavery in the south?"

"The beginning of the end. It was enough of a gesture," said Liam, "for the British public to allow their government to openly ally with the South."

"And this Confederate President Davis went on to put an end to slavery?"

Liam nodded. "So it seems. There was an uproar among all the slave owners in the South, of course. But then when convoys of British ships stuffed with money and food and weapons started arriving, I suppose the poor common people of the South figured out that maybe supporting the arguments of the rich slaveholders wasn't doing them any favors!"

"In 1865," Liam said, looking down at his notes, "Davis announced the Freedom Act. It made it a crime for one man to be owned by another. There were still many who claimed that by doing this the Southern states' economy would completely crash. That freed slaves would kill their former masters and run riot in the streets."

Lincoln raised a shaggy eyebrow. "And did they?"

"No." Liam shook his head. By then, British money and troops and supplies were flooding in. The Confederacy held together, and the freeing of slaves was not the end of the world for them, as they'd feared."

Sal leaned forward. "So go on."

"The year after, in the North, President Bell made a similar announcement, the Proclamation of Liberty, which looks like it was almost a word-for-word copy of the South's one. But it was enough of a gesture to encourage the French and several other European nations to put their support behind the North." Liam looked up from his exercise book. "And from that point onward the war wasn't about slavery anymore, because both sides of the struggle had turned their backs on it."

He put his notes down, reached for his bowl of stew, and hungrily spooned in a mouthful.

"So, is that as far as you got?" asked Sal.

He nodded, his mouth full. "I'mnnn goinnnnn to mmmeeeed sommme mooore 'ater ommm," he sputtered, juice dribbling down his chin.

Lincoln gazed into the flames in front of him. "I have, I must admit, not dwelled a great deal on the notion of slavery. Just that it is the way of things. The order of things. That a white man is better suited to spend his time on matters of the mind, a black man to be merely a beast of burden. Just like a farmyard, every beast has its particular role to—"

"*Chuddah!*" Sal's jaw hung open. "How could you actually *believe* something like that?"

Lincoln stroked his bearded chin thoughtfully. "It is a commonly held perception. After all, it is white men with their superior technology who enslaved black men. Is history not the story of more *advanced* races and civilizations conquering other—"

"Oh, right! Does that make *me* a beast of burden?" she said sharply. "Because my skin's brown?"

"On the contrary." He shrugged casually and offered her a well-intended smile. "Despite your brown skin—being a half Negro?—it seems quite clear to me that you are in fact a very bright child. I—"

Liam winced at Lincoln's choice of words.

"Ughh! I don't have to listen to this!" Sal placed her bowl of stew on the floor and stood up. "People like you don't exist in my time! It may not be such a great time, but at least we don't have to listen to . . . to ignorant *pinchudda* like that!" She turned away and stormed out of the kitchen.

Lincoln looked at Liam, perplexed. "What is the matter with the girl?"

"The way you said what you said. It . . . well, it could've come out sounding better."

Lincoln's brow lowered into a dark scowl as his gaze returned to the fire. "I meant praise by what I said."

Liam finished his stew and set his bowl down. "We should all get some sleep if we're to get going again tonight." He got up. "Bob, how long have we got until it's dark?"

"Four hours and fifty-two minutes, Liam."

"All right, will you wake us up then?"

"Affirmative."

Liam headed out of the kitchen's back door into the weed-strewn yard to find Sal sitting on a squeaking swing.

"You all right?'

"He's a racist!"

Liam stood beside the swing's frame, resting his hand on its paint-flecked surface, feeling its unsteady sway. "He's from 1831. That's the way people spoke and thought back then. They didn't know any better. He didn't mean anything nasty by it."

She shook her head. "I've never been . . . never had something like that said to me before!" She looked up at him. "I feel like he's just *trashed* me . . . my parents . . . everyone I've ever known, just by saying what he said. Judging people by the color of their skin!"

"I think he was trying to be kind."

"*Kind?! Jahulla . . .*"

Liam shrugged. "Ah well, I've been mistaken for Welsh before, would you believe? I've heard many a silly Englishman lump us Irish north and south Welsh—and Scottish—even, together in the same pot. Imagine that?"

And many an Irishman confused the Chinese with Japanese, he mused. *Quite probably many a Chineseman confused Turks with Persians; and many a Persian confused Celts with Saxons.*

He reached out and squeezed her hand. "Come on, Sal. Let's go back inside. We need to get a little rest, so we do, before we start out tonight."

Chapter 35

2001, New York

"You realize, young lady, that this is the dead zone?" said Colonel Devereau.

She stopped and turned. "Dead zone?"

He pointed across the landscape of ruins leading down toward the East River. Beyond the river's smooth, dark water lay the skeleton of Manhattan. "We're just about within range of their snipers. One of them might try to take a potshot if he's bored enough."

"*What?*" Maddy ducked down to the ground, her bound hands crossed over her head. Neither Devereau nor any of the other soldiers moved. A murmur of laughter rippled up and down the patrol line as they watched her fidgeting on her haunches.

"Relax," he said. "It's well beyond accurate range. All the same . . ."

He took off his forage cap, reached to his side, unclipped a rifle with an attached bayonet, popped the hat on the tip, and raised his arm, sweeping the hat slowly in a figure eight.

"What are you doing?" hissed Maddy. "You're attracting attention!"

"Indeed; I'm signaling the enemy."

Maddy looked up at him as he stepped forward across the rubble, up onto the top of the low uneven wall of loose bricks. In the stillness, broken only by the tidal lapping of poisoned water nearby, she expected a shot to ring out and this reckless officer to drop, headless, like a butcher's carcass.

Across the river, her eyes picked out faint movement, the glint of metal.

"There," he said, stepping down. "They'll spread the word on their side. We should be safe from potshots for a while."

"But"—she got to her feet—"that's the *enemy*, isn't it?"

"I know the colonel over there. Pleasant-enough fellow."

"You know him?"

He sighed. "We've been staring over this wretched river at each other for years. Decades, actually. We meet once a year for Thanksgiving." He turned to his men. "Don't we, Sergeant Freeman?"

She recognized the bearded man who'd found her earlier this morning. "Yes, sir."

"A chance for the boys on both sides to let their hair down." Devereau pulled up some binoculars and inspected the Southern lines briefly. "In fact, a couple of years ago, East River froze right over; the boys had a snowball fight."

"Whupped 'em good, too," said Sergeant Freeman, grinning.

"Indeed we did." He lowered his binoculars. "A good day," he added wistfully. He turned to her. "Now then, you say your 'base' is here somewhere. And this miraculous time-traveling device of yours?"

She heard the barely concealed amusement in his voice.

He's humoring himself. For a moment she wondered what her fate was going to be if she failed to convince him that the broken machinery in the archway was what she said it was.

And what about Becks? Presumably she was still sitting inside awaiting further orders, or perhaps she was nearby, watching them even now. She wondered how the support unit would act once she spotted Maddy, cuffed and being led toward the archway by men with weapons.

"It's around here somewhere," she said, looking across the wasteland toward the collapsed remains of the Williamsburg Bridge. That was her only way of orienting herself, the only landmark she could recognize. "Not too far from the supports of that bridge over there."

"Right."

"I have a . . . a friend over there, though."

Devereau looked at her sternly. "You're not alone?"

"Look, she's not a spy either."

"Is she armed?"

Maddy shook her head. "No . . . no weapons, but she . . . well . . . she can be *dangerous*."

Devereau seemed amused by that. "Twenty men; I think between us we can handle an unarmed woman."

"No, really," said Maddy. "Trust me, she's really nothing like me. She, well, she can be kind of deadly. I should call out to her first. Let her know it's okay."

The colonel eyed her suspiciously for a moment.

"I won't call for her to run or anything, I promise."

He stroked his beard thoughtfully. "All right, then. But, to make it perfectly clear, if I hear anything come out of your mouth that sounds like a code word or a warning, I shall be inclined to shoot you."

"Right. I promise." She cupped her hands around her mouth. "BECKS!" Her croaky voice echoed off the shattered corner wall of a nearby warehouse; it bounced and reverberated through the maze of rubble and half-standing buildings, through dead Brooklyn, fading slowly like the memory of a dream. Finally, there was only the mournful whisper of a breeze causing a window shutter somewhere to clap insistently against a rotten frame.

"It's Maddy! Are you there?"

Her voice faded.

"It's okay—*I'm* okay . . . these soldiers aren't going to hurt me!"

Nothing but the far-off clatter of the shutter and the tidal hiss and draw of the languid East River lapping at the nearby shore.

"It appears that this friend of yours has abandoned you," said Devereau.

Maddy shook her head. "No, she wouldn't do that. She's out there somewhere," she said, pointing toward the ruins of the bridge. "There's this big shallow crater over there somewhere, and our archway's at the bottom of it. If we go a bit closer . . . ?"

It was then that a solitary sound caused Devereau's men to drop to their knees and raise their rifles: the clatter of a loose slate tile sliding down a mound of rubble. Then silence once more.

"Becks?" Maddy called out again. "Is that you?"

The men were looking in all directions, up and around at the broken walls and exposed half floors of gutted buildings, perfect positions from which a sniper could pick them all off. She heard some of them cocking their guns, the click of safeties coming off.

"*Becks?* You there?"

The stillness was broken by another sound of movement, the direction of the source confused by echoes bouncing off the pockmarked walls of the buildings to either side of them.

"*Why did you leave me?*" a voice echoed across the stillness. The colonel and his men were turning, looking around nervously—here, there, everywhere—trying to determine where the voice had come from. It sounded almost sexless. Neutral. Unwelcoming. Almost hostile.

"Becks? Where are you?"

"*Your departure was . . . inappropriate.*"

"I . . . I'm sorry, I just . . . I don't know what happened, Becks. I freaked out, I guess."

A long silence.

"Becks?" Her cry faded to nothing, leaving Maddy with an unsettling thought flitting around in her head.

Becks doesn't sound right. She sounds different. Her voice, normally so clinical, so reassuringly logical, seemed to carry the hint of human emotion in it. Anger? Resentment? She'd never heard those things in Becks's voice before.

"Becks? Please . . . come out!" She glanced at the soldiers; all of them, it seemed, were fingering their triggers anxiously.

She's spooking them.

"Please! Tell your men not to shoot if she comes out," said Maddy to Devereau. "She won't hurt anyone. I'll instruct her not to."

"Instruct her?" Devereau's eyes narrowed. "You make her sound like a guard dog."

She ignored him. "Becks! Please! Come out slowly! These soldiers aren't going to hurt you or me. They're not a threat!"

A few moments later the fading echo of her voice was answered by the sound of clattering rubble, and then Becks's face emerged from the gloom in the corner of a bombed-out basement to their right.

"There!" shouted one of the soldiers, and a moment later the air was split by the crack of two rapid-fire shots. A plume of cement dust exploded from a cinderblock beside Becks's head as she clambered out of the darkness into the pallid daylight.

Sergeant Freeman immediately bellowed a cease-fire.

She stepped forward down a slope of rubble toward them, unperturbed by the near miss, her cool, gray eyes on Maddy alone.

"Raise your hands where we can see them!" barked Devereau.

Becks approached slowly until she was no more than half a dozen yards from them, then stopped, calmly evaluating the threat level of the soldiers for a moment.

"Becks!" said Maddy. "It's fine! These guys are friendly—just show them your empty hands!"

Becks slowly raised her arms and opened her hands to show her palms, then turned her attention back to Maddy, cocking her head curiously. "Why did you leave me?"

She seemed to need an answer, as if nothing more could be discussed until the question was answered satisfactorily. Maddy could imagine that the software in her head was stuck in a loop of code, running over and over in an infinite circle, unable to escape until it had some relevant data to process.

Best be honest with her.

"I . . . I just wanted to go home. I . . ."

"Information: you are not permitted to leave the agency."

"Come on, Becks, cut me some slack here! You said everything was all smashed up, didn't you?"

Becks nodded. "Affirmative."

"Well!" Maddy shrugged. "So, I suppose I figured . . . I thought our team was all finished. That's why I—"

"A mission is still in progress." Becks's gaze flickered across to Devereau and then back to her. "And there is still a time contamination event that must be corrected, Maddy."

"Yeah? And how are we supposed to do that, huh? Some other team's going to have to sort this one out, because we're totally freakin' ruined, aren't we?"

"Negative."

"What?"

"I have now made a complete evaluation of the damage. I can affect adequate repairs, if we are able to secure suitably adaptable components." She looked at Maddy with an expression that almost looked like a plea. "I must have new orders, Madelaine. What are your instructions?"

Maddy stepped forward, reaching out for the support unit and grasping Becks's scarred left hand tentatively with both of hers. She squeezed gently. "I'm so sorry," she whispered.

Maybe it was in her mind, maybe it was just wishful thinking, but she thought she felt Becks return the gesture with the slightest squeeze.

"Let's go back to the arch, Becks. You can show me what we need to do to fix it up." She turned and nodded at Devereau and his men. "I think these guys might be able to help us out."

"Affirmative."

Chapter 36

2001, somewhere in Virginia

Liam was shaken roughly awake. By the slanted stripes of bloodred dusk stealing in through the slatted windows, he could see it was Sal tugging on his arm.

"What . . . *what?*" he muttered irritably.

"Some weird dwarf just ran in and stole Bob's gun!"

"What?" He took a moment to digest that. It sounded like the tail end of some bizarre dream. "What did you just say?"

"A dwarf—or maybe it was a child." It sounded like she wasn't sure this wasn't a dream either. "It happened so fast. I was talking to Bob, and this *thing* just ran into the kitchen, grabbed the shotgun, and ran out again."

"Thing?" Liam sat up on the creaking sofa. "Where's Bob?"

"He ran out after him to get it back."

Good thing, too—it was the only weapon they had between them. Apart from Bob himself, that is. He shook away the last tendrils of sleep and stepped through the kitchen, where Lincoln's long frame was sprawled across the table, still fast asleep. The back door was wide open.

"He went out the back?"

Sal nodded.

Liam stood in the doorway. He could hear the fast-receding rustle and thrash of movement across the cornfield at the end of the weed-infested lawn. In the failing light he could just make out where Bob had entered the field, leaving a wake of broken and flattened cornstalks.

"He'll get it back, I'm sure," said Liam. "He's fast."

"I hope so."

The setting sun was no more than a golden sliver trembling on the horizon, the flesh-pink clouds combed out across the sky directly above it like cotton candy.

"We'll make a move as soon as he gets back," said Liam. "Grab as many cans as we can carry, and—"

"Liam," whispered Sal.

"What?"

"Do you see that?"

"See what?"

"There." She pointed down the yard toward the edge of the field. He saw nothing but the dark parting of flattened stalks in the chest-high wall of gently swaying corn.

"What? I can't see any"—Then all of a sudden he did. Dark shapes, slowly emerging from the field and stepping into the backyard.

"Hey! Who's that out there?" Liam called.

The shapes moved carefully toward them, low shadows blending in with the tufts of weeds and the darkness of the ground.

Jay-zus.

Liam dragged Sal back inside the kitchen and slammed the door shut. The noise roused Lincoln from his slumber. "Curse you! I was sleeping!" he snarled.

"What are they?" whimpered Sal.

"I don't know, to be sure . . . but—"

The door suddenly lurched on its hinges, rattling from an impact. A splintered crack ran down the middle of it.

"What the devil is going on here?" roared Lincoln, still bleary eyed with sleep.

"*Chuddah!*" Sal gasped. "The window!"

Liam turned to see hands fumbling at it. No, not hands . . . not quite. They looked peculiar, but they were moving, scrabbling, scratching too quickly to identify what it was that looked so odd about them. The grime-covered glass suddenly shattered as something was lobbed through it.

"Out! Out!" Liam barked, pushing Sal ahead of him and dragging Lincoln out of his chair. They tumbled together from the kitchen into the dark hallway beyond.

He slammed the door closed behind him. It would swing *into* the hall, which meant they could lean things against it to prevent it from being opened.

"Block this! We need to barricade it!"

They looked around desperately, and Lincoln gestured to a tall grandfather clock. Liam nodded. He and Sal helped him drag it across the dust-covered floor and tilted it back to lean against the kitchen door with a clumsy thud. It chimed noisily in protest at the rough treatment.

They could hear the back door being battered and finally giving way to swing inward; the bark of wooden chair legs bumping and scraping; the clatter of things knocked over, falling, shattering, and rolling across the floor.

"Th-they're inside!" whispered Sal.

A moment later the door they and the grandfather clock were pressing their weight against shuddered under a huge impact, as if someone—or *something*—on the far side was wielding a mallet.

Lincoln cursed. "Who the devil is this?"

"I don't know . . . I don't know!"

"Not *people*," hissed Sal. "They're not *human!*"

To their right along the dark hallway that led to the front of the farmhouse, the handle of the front door rattled as something tested it. Liam turned to see a hairline seam of crimson twilight glowing between the bottom of the door and the doorstep. It flickered with movement as God knows how many shapes began to gather outside.

"GO AWAY!" Sal screamed.

A crash against the front door, and Liam saw a sliver of light in the middle of the oak panel.

That won't hold for long.

Stairs. He remembered there was a staircase in this hallway, leading up to the first floor.

"Over there—the stairs, we need to go up!"

"Are you insane, sir?" snarled Lincoln. "We shall be trapped with nowhere to go!"

"Doesn't matter—Bob will be back soon. He'll sort them out."

"He is but one man! There sounds like no less than an army of men out there!"

"They're not *human*," Sal said again.

The front door shuddered violently under the impact of another heavy blow, and a second bloodred crack joined the first. Not a hairline thread this time, but a ragged gash.

"Upstairs! Now! It's our only chance!"

"Okay—yes—come on!" Sal nodded quickly.

"Damn you, sir! I will not run like a yard dog. Find me a weapon and I shall—"

"For cryin' out loud," snapped Liam, "what is it with you? Do you *want* to die?"

Lincoln's face was thunder. "I am no coward, sir! I shall stand and fight!"

"Well, I am," said Sal. "So can we go, *please?*"

They suddenly heard the clatter of falling grit on the floor beside their feet. They turned to look where it had come from and saw what appeared to be a jagged red eye on the plaster wall beside the kitchen door.

"Huh?"

It blinked. Or, more precisely, it flickered.

"'Tis a hole," said Lincoln.

A small fist punched through the plasterboard and broke off a shard of plaster, which crumbled to the floor with a hiss of cascading powder and grit. Another small, dull spot of dusk-red appeared beside it. And another.

"Oh Jay-zus wept! They're breaking up the bleedin' wall!"

Lincoln pursed his lips. "Perhaps then, we should . . . as you suggested . . . ?"

"Run? Come on!"

The kitchen door bulged and cracked from a heavy blow, and the grandfather clock lurched with a tuneless jangle of chimes. The three of them scrambled down the hall past the front door, yielding again under yet another hammer blow. A strip of wood clattered to the floor, and through the fresh gap Liam thought he caught a glimpse of something that resembled a face, wide and flat, with pinhole-small black eyes, and a hole—a *hole*?—for a nose.

What are these things? Demons?

"Up! UP!" he screamed at Sal and Lincoln. "GO UP!"

The front door was looking horribly fragile now, a spiderweb of cracks and gashes that flickered and widened with each shuddering blow.

Liam followed them up the wooden stairs, stumbling more than once in the darkness. Sal was waiting for him on the landing at the top. "Which way, Liam? *Which way?*"

"Either! *Just go!*"

Behind him, down the stairs, he heard a splintering crack, either the kitchen or the front door finally giving way. He could hear Sal still there in front of him, hopping uncertainly from one foot to the other, and Lincoln beside her, panting heavily.

"*GO!*" Liam screamed.

Sal fumbled along the dark landing, hands patting and feeling the wall in front of her for a door to open.

Liam heard the grandfather clock collapse onto the floor, filling the house with a jangling chime.

They're through!

He turned away from the stairs as he heard feet scratching—clawing?—on the wooden floor and a bizarre humming. Almost like human voices, but humming as if the things down there—whatever they were—were somehow gagged.

He turned and started into the dark, patting the damp, peeling walls with his hands to feel his way. "Sal!" he hissed.

He realized too late that she and Lincoln had turned right at the top of the stairs, and he'd gone left. The darkness was filled with the sounds of feet scrambling and scratching up the stairs behind him and that unsettling humming sound, which was more like a gagged snarl now than a hum.

His hands found a recess, a doorframe, and finally a handle. He grabbed it with both hands and pushed the door open, and was met with the faintest bloom of ruddy light from the very last blush of dusk. It seeped in through a small, dusty attic window.

Liam shut the door behind him, stumbling over boxes of soft things, perhaps toys or clothes. The room must have been used for storage; the roof was low, with a thick wooden beam running the length of it. He ran across to the tiny window, ducking under the beam, to fiddle with the latch to open it. Behind him he heard the tap and scrape of feet and claws, muted snarling and labored breathing, then the crash of a fist on a door and the splintering crack of old, dry wood giving way.

And then his blood chilled. He heard Sal scream, muffled by a door farther down the landing. He realized as he fumbled with the latch of the window that their pursuers had chosen to follow Sal and Lincoln and not him.

Crashing and splintering again. The things were ferociously hammering on it, tearing Sal's door to pieces. Liam hesitated. He'd planned to open the tiny window and squeeze himself through, perhaps to hide outside on the roof. But . . .

Sal screamed again.

But those things were going to get her.

Liam cursed under his breath. "Ahh, Jay-zus . . . !"

His hands fumbled for something, *anything*, to use as a weapon, frantically patting the floor around him while he listened to the struggle down the hallway: Lincoln bellowing curses, Sal screaming, horrible mewing sounds from those creatures, things being knocked over, blows being landed, the scrape and thud of feet on boards.

"Come on . . . *Come on!*" he hissed. He heard Sal desperately pleading, and Lincoln's baritone voice raised to an enraged roar. The sound of a violent struggle. He had to admit it—Lincoln had mettle. That obnoxious, loud-mouthed, long-limbed idiot sounded like he was putting up a fight with just his bare fists. Going down fighting.

Liam's fingers touched a pole of some sort. He felt his way down it to a thicket of coarse fibers. A brush or broom of some kind.

Ah, stuff it; good enough.

He picked it up and charged across the small attic room toward the doorway. Failing to remember the low beam.

Failing to duck.

Chapter 37

2001, New York

Colonel Devereau and Sergeant Freeman crouched down and shined their flashlights under the half-open corrugated-iron shutter door into the dark space beyond.

"This is it?" he said. He sounded disappointed. "This is your time machine?"

By the subdued tone of his voice, Maddy wondered whether he actually really *had* wanted to believe what she'd told him was true. It would make persuading him, and gaining his help, a great deal easier if he did.

She knelt down and looked inside. The archway appeared to be in a lot better shape than it had been in yesterday. Becks must have spent the night fixing things up; she'd swept away the fallen bricks and mortar, straightened up the shelves that had collapsed, and cleaned the general mess inside. Apart from the gaping crack running across their floor and the jagged holes in the roof, it looked almost normal except, that is, for the fact that it was utterly dark.

"We have no power," said Maddy. "Our generator was totally trashed when we, uh, landed here."

Devereau shoved the shutter a little higher, and it clacked noisily. The men of his platoon ducked inside, and another half dozen flashlights snapped on and began sweeping the archway, picking out details here and there.

"Negative, Madelaine," said Becks. "The generator works. I was able to affect a temporary repair. I will go switch it on."

Becks stepped inside and made her way briskly toward the sliding door leading into the back room. She was lost in the darkness.

"Hey! Miss!" snapped Sergeant Freeman, swinging his rifle off his shoulder. "Where 'n hell you think you're goin'?"

Becks turned to look at him as his light danced across her face and said calmly: "To turn the power on, of course."

"It's through that far door," said Maddy. "There's a storage room back there. That's where our generator is."

Devereau shrugged. They'd walked once around this odd construction. It reminded him of a termite mound: a large, badly assembled hummock made entirely of crumbling bricks. There was presumably no place inside for this other girl—Becks—to run or hide. "Better follow her back there, Sergeant," he said to Freeman.

They headed through the opening to the back room, and a moment later Maddy sighed with relief at the reassuring sound of the generator chugging to life.

The archway's fluorescent lights flickered, then winked on in unison.

Devereau cursed. He reached out toward the shutter door and yanked on it. "Gimme a hand," he said to a young soldier. Together they wrestled it down until it clattered and bounced against the floor.

"We're right in the middle of the dead zone!" said Devereau. "The last thing we want to do is get the attention of their sky navy with a careless show of lights!"

"Oh . . . yeah." Maddy nodded an apology.

The computer monitors were on, all of them showing the system slowly booting up. Becks emerged, Freeman with her.

"There was damage to the fuel tank," said Becks. "We have lost a significant portion of our reserves." She approached Maddy and Devereau. "We will need more fuel, Madelaine."

"To recharge the displacement machine?"

"Affirmative."

"But wait! What's the point? You said the tachyon transmission array was—"

"I believe it may be possible to acquire analogous transmission technology and reconfigure it to channel tachyon particles—"

"Excuse me!" Devereau made a face. "Can you two stop talking whatever gibberish that is for a moment?"

They both looked at him.

"All right, now; I suppose I'm more than halfway toward believing the pair of you aren't Southern spies." He pulled out his packet of Gitanes and lit one, hacking up a gob of discolored phlegm onto the floor as he did so.

"Do you mind?" said Maddy testily. "That's disgusting."

He ignored her. "But you, miss—both of you, actually—have got yourselves *a lot* of explaining yet to do if you don't want to find yourself chained up in a federal military prison." He pulled on his cigarette and blew a cloud of rancid smoke into the air between them. Maddy wrinkled her nose at the stench.

"A *hell* of a lot of explaining," he added.

Becks was silent, a guarded expression on her face.

Maddy shrugged. "Sure, why not? You might as well hear it all . . . *everything.*" She turned to Becks, expecting her to sound a note of caution. "After all, this timeline isn't supposed to exist. None of it; not this war, not these soldiers." She smiled candidly at him. "Not even you, Colonel Devereau."

"I should not . . . *exist?*" His voice was midway between incredulity and anger.

"Not the way you are. Not like this."

He frowned and jutted his bearded chin indignantly. "Ma'am, I happen to like the way I am, if it's all the same to you!"

"Look." Maddy sighed. "It's really complicated. I guess I'd better explain to you all about how time travel works." She nodded toward their threadbare armchairs. "Want to go grab a seat? This could take us a while."

Chapter 38

2001, somewhere in Virginia

Bob's single-minded pursuit of the small creature that had boldly dashed into the farmhouse kitchen and stolen their one firearm from right under his nose was getting him nowhere.

He was standing in a field of corn. It was too dark now for his eyes to pick out the broken stalks suggesting which way the creature had fled. He was four hundred yards away from the farmhouse, the light was failing, and a warning was flashing in his mind.

[Tactical error]

He was about to process that into an analysis tree when he first heard the shouting and banging drifting across the silently swaying field of corn from the farmhouse.

Several conclusions presented themselves:

1. **The childlike creature is not alone**
2. **The gun being stolen was a distraction**
3. **The others are in danger**

He bounded back through the corn, keeping to the path of flattened stalks he'd already made. Ahead of him, the noises grew more distinct, more frantic. From the sound of it he determined the struggle was coming from inside the house somewhere, and as he drew closer he could see that the back door through which he'd rushed only minutes ago was nothing more than a splintered frame swinging gently on bent hinges.

He heard a high-pitched scream and identified the voice as Sal's. Something inside his head twitched; not the silicon wafer but the small wrinkled nugget of flesh, the brain the size of a rat's with which it had a synaptic-wire link. As he bounded across the overgrown backyard, his mind was drawing up a shortlist of candidate words to describe what he felt.

Guilt (90% relevance)
Shame (56% relevance)
Anger (10% relevance)

He'd been fooled, lured out into the field so that the others were left entirely alone, vulnerable. No gun between them. No support unit to protect them.

He crashed through the remains of the swinging back door, knocking it off its hinges. The kitchen looked as if a tornado had passed through it; everything that could be dislodged or broken had been. The wall was a mess of plaster dust and fist-sized holes, revealing the wooden slats of support posts. The door into the hallway looked just like the back door—smashed to splinters.

"LIAM!" Bob bellowed into the house.

He heard nothing now. The sound of struggling and screaming had ended at some point in the last thirty seconds.

"SALEENA!" he tried again, stepping into the hallway, his eyes adjusting to the gloom.

He could see scratch- and scrape-marks across the floor, along the walls . . . up the stairs. Quickly, urgently, he clambered up them, the old wooden steps groaning and creaking under the burden of his weight.

He turned right at the top of the stairs. A door at the end, scratched, battered, and split with a deep crack down the middle, hung wide open. In the room beyond he could see the frame of a bed on its side, an overturned chair. A last stand had taken place there. No bodies, though. Gone.

In the space of only minutes, seconds, the humans it was his duty to protect had been snatched away from him.

He took another few steps into the room and saw more signs of the struggle. A chair leg, wrenched from its seat, perhaps used as a club. One end of it was spattered with blood—black in this waning dusk. There were splashes and dots of it on the pale walls.

The logical part of his mind berated him with a simple message.

[Mission status: FAIL]

The organic part was prepared to express its assessment of the situation with a flood of feelings he was unable, or unwilling, to find appropriate labels for right now. He backed out of the room and slumped against the wall of the landing, sliding down until he was a hunched mass of dejected muscle at the bottom of it.

"You have failed," his deep voice rumbled softly, like a boiler switching on, a subway train passing through a subterranean tunnel.

"You failed," he said again, this time with a slight tremble in his voice. He supposed, if Becks had been here, she would have found that intriguing, impressive even, that his voice was unintentionally conveying an emotion.

The computer in his skull was nagging him to make judgment calls on a growing list of new mission-priority suggestions: to continue making his way northeast to New York? After all, Madelaine Carter was still there and still needed protecting. To attempt to locate the bodies of Liam O'Connor, Saleena Vikram, and Abraham Lincoln? Because there was always the chance, the possibility, one or more of them might still be alive.

To self-terminate . . . out of sheer shame. Perhaps his AI was now unreliable, faulty. He had made a poor judgment that had resulted in this. It had been an all-too-obvious ploy to lure him outside.

Unconsciously he balled a giant fist, angry with himself for being so . . . *stupid*. Perhaps another support unit uploaded with freshly installed software and not burdened with many months' worth of memories of kinship, adventures, jokes even, would do a far more efficient job than he.

He was giving self-termination some serious thought, even though the software was advising him strongly that it was an illogical conclusion and achieved nothing useful, when he heard the scrape of a footfall beside him. He turned quickly to look along the almost pitch-black landing, ready to tear something, *someone*, apart limb from limb, for no other reason than mere revenge.

And he saw Liam standing there, wide eyed, exhibiting post-traumatic stress behavioral indicators.

He was in shock.

"LIAM O'CONNOR!" Bob's voice boomed.

Liam took a shuffling step forward, clutching his head. "Bob . . . Jeez, I . . . don't know what . . . I just . . ."

Bob lurched to his feet and closed the gap between them, and before his computer brain could cringe with disapproval, distaste, and embarrassment at the behavior of its host body, Bob's huge, muscular arms were wrapped around Liam's narrow frame and squeezing him hard.

"You are alive!" he rumbled unnecessarily.

"Bob . . . I think they took Sal . . . and Lincoln."

"They are alive?"

Liam was struggling to breathe, his nose and mouth crushed against the wall of Bob's sweaty shoulder. He pushed the support unit back, and Bob loosened his hug.

"I think so. I think they took them—"

His words were suddenly drowned out by a deafening roar that made the landing, the whole farmhouse, vibrate like the head of a snare drum.

White light flashed into the building, dazzlingly bright, finding holes and cracks in the ceiling above them, sending pin-sharp blades of light down onto them that swept across their skin, across the wooden floor.

The light came from above; the roar too. Directly above them. They tumbled down the stairs before either of them had discussed whether it might be a good idea to actually remain hidden somewhere inside. They stepped through the shattered remains of the front door and out onto the porch, looking up at the brilliant white light. Liam shaded his eyes; it was as intense and uncomfortable as looking directly at the sun. A false dawn of artificial sunlight trained down on them.

"*What is it?*" he all but screamed. He couldn't even hear himself, let alone whether Bob managed to answer.

An icy blast of air swept down on them, and he felt something cold and wet settle on his cheeks. In the light he could see a million white fluffy flakes of something slowly descending, swirling in the downdraft, seesawing like feathers, like ash from a forest fire. But they were neither.

My God—it's snowing!

That's exactly what it was.

Snow?

The deafening roar that had filled the air, making talking, even shouting, an utterly pointless endeavor for the better part of the last minute, suddenly ceased. It left them in a silence filled only by Liam's rasping breath and the soft whisper of snow settling on the ground around them.

"What the . . . ?" muttered Liam, feeling more and more flakes landing on his upturned face, on the back of the hand shading his eyes.

The blinding light swept off Liam and Bob and back onto the farmhouse, then across the other buildings in the small rural hamlet, like a probing eye trying to make quick sense of the scene.

Liam tracked the thick beam of the spotlight all the way up into a dark and completely starless sky. He thought he was looking at a dense bank of snow-laden clouds above them; that might be the best explanation for the unseasonal and surprising arrival of snow. But then a row of smaller lights suddenly appeared, a row of spotlights trained upward, casting fans of light across a smooth, burnished copper hull.

His mouth was useless, slack and open and doing little more than making a gurgling note of surprise.

Chapter 39

2001, New York

Colonel Bill Devereau stared at the images on the computer screens: a slide show of pictures pulled by computer-Bob off the system's database at Maddy's request. Photographs of New York, busy and vibrant. Times Square packed with yellow cabs and tourists, a giant billboard with Shrek's green face leering out over milling pedestrians. A cowboy in underpants and Stetson and boots busking with an acoustic guitar, surrounded by grinning girls. A picture of the Spice Girls posing together in front of the Empire State Building.

"My God!" he whispered.

A picture of Lady Liberty, mint-green and undamaged by bombs and small-arms fire, standing proud and tall, holding aloft her beacon of hope.

"I forgot what she looked like," he said.

"Is the statue damaged in this timeline, Colonel Devereau?" asked Becks.

"Bill," he said softly. "I guess you two ladies can call me Bill."

"Affirmative, Bill."

He shook his head sadly. "She's no more than a rusting stump. Bombed by the South back in 1926 during the Second Siege of New York. They blew her up . . . then used Liberty Island to deploy several artillery batteries. From there they pounded Manhattan to rubble."

"Where—*when*—we come from, Bill," said Maddy, "I mean, it's today's date, September twelfth, 2001, the very same date, but it's a very different time. Anyway"—she waved her hand, dismissing the point—"the thing is, in our time New York's all there in one piece." She smiled sadly. *Well, sort of.* She decided there was no point mentioning the Twin Towers to him. It would only complicate things.

He drew his eyes away from the slide show of images. They glistened with moisture, tears he was determined not to shed in front of the girls—and more importantly, in front of his own men. "This is . . . *this* is really how our world should be?"

"Yes."

He looked back at the nearest monitor to see an image of President Bush and Prime Minister Blair standing side by side behind lecterns, addressing an audience of the press. Then the image switched to one of Homer Simpson strangling Bart Simpson.

"And you, and all these devices of yours"—he nodded at the tall rack of circuit boards to their left, the displacement machine, and the large empty plexiglass tube—"this technology of yours could change my world to how it appears on these . . . what do you call them?"

"Computer monitors."

"These *computer monitors* of yours?"

She nodded. "This war should've ended in 1865. That's how history is supposed to go."

He stroked the thatch of dark bristles on his cheek, deep in thought. "This really is quite a story you are asking me to believe."

Maddy sniffed. "Well, it's the truth. Although, sometimes, you know, I wish it wasn't."

Devereau pulled on his beard with a gloved hand. "And you say this technology, this 'time displacing' device, can send you to any time?"

"And any place, too, yeah."

Devereau noticed Sergeant Freeman out of the corner of his eye, standing nearby and just as bewitched by the slide show of images. "What are you thinking, Sergeant Freeman?"

The old NCO shook his head. "Seen a lot of things in my time, sir. Perhaps too many things. But this . . ." He hunted down the right words to express what he was thinking. "These . . . these here pictures, if they are what this city, what this nation was *supposed* to be, then I guess I gotta wonder how the hell we been stupid enough to end up makin' this mess of a world we all livin' in."

Devereau nodded thoughtfully.

"If we can fix our machine, we can change it back," said Maddy. "It would cause a time wave that would correct everything. You'd all live very different lives. Be very different people." She wondered whether she ought to add that some of them might not even exist. A different century and a half of history would mean very different family trees for some of these men.

"And the thing is," she added, "none of you would have a memory of this war, because, well . . ." She shrugged. "Because it will have never taken place."

Sergeant Freeman nodded. "I say amen to that."

Devereau adjusted the collar of his tunic. "And what, pray tell, is a 'time wave'?"

"A vibration through space-time that leaves behind it a recalibration of reality," replied Becks.

"A wave of reality overwriting reality," added Maddy.

Devereau frowned. "I would become someone else?"

"Correct, Bill," said Becks. "Everything and everyone is recalibrated."

His eyes narrowed. "Then surely my allowing you to alter history would be like . . . well, not to put too fine a point on it, ladies, it would be like killing myself."

Maddy pursed her lips. He was, of course, right, in a sense. A time wave would erase Devereau and everyone else, and in its wake leave other versions of themselves or, quite possibly in many cases, leave absolutely no version of them at all.

She looked back at the slide show. There were plenty of things wrong with the 2001 she and Becks had come from, but it had to be better than this war-torn hell. She could see Devereau's eyes, and Freeman's too, eyes that glistened with a deep melancholy. After all, she guessed they were both men who had spent most of their lives living in concrete bunkers and staring across the rubble and the river at men just like themselves.

These images on the screen were a beacon of hope; of what could have been.

"Something else I should explain to you," said Maddy. "There's no guarantee this reality is stable; that it will hold. Things are unbalanced right now, and somewhere at some quantum dimensional level reality is sort of 'considering' whether this timeline is stable enough to stick with, or whether it needs to adjust itself again."

"Adjust itself? What do you mean?"

"Another time wave could just as easily come along and wipe this reality away and replace it with something *far* worse."

Devereau frowned. "Worse?"

"Okay . . ." She gave it a moment's thought. "For example, a world in which the South has already *won* this war."

"Good God! A victory for the Anglo-Confederacy?"

"Or much much worse," she added.

"Worse!" He stiffened. "Worse than that?"

"Oh yeah." She nodded. "Trust me, Bill. You ought to see some of the crazy stuff we've seen. It would turn your hair white."

Chapter 40

2001, somewhere in Virginia

In stunned silence Liam watched the enormous vessel that had loomed above the farmhouse settle lightly onto the ground, jets venting blasts of ice-cold nitrogen gas, filling the air around them with an arctic mist and a blizzard of snowflakes. From within the swirling fog he heard the heavy clanking of chains and winches, and finally the thud of something smacking the ground heavily. A moment later he heard the clatter of horseshoes on metal, the throaty snort of horses, and men's voices softly calming them.

Soon, something began to emerge from the mist.

Bob shifted position, preparing himself to defend Liam.

"Easy there, big fella," whispered Liam, and patted Bob's side.

He could just about make out several dozen bulky four-legged beasts—but they certainly weren't horses, as he'd first thought. They seemed to be heavy up front, by the look of their faint silhouettes, with much more slender hindquarters. He squinted into the mist and the dancing flakes of snow, beginning to thin now as the venting jets ceased.

He heard an *ooof* of exertion from someone and the soft thud of boots on the ground. A figure was approaching them.

"Uh? Hello over there?" The figure drew close enough for Liam to see it was a man in a well-tailored army uniform.

"Ahh . . . there you are!"

He drew up in front of them, a trim man in his late twenties. Beneath the pointed peak of his white pith helmet Liam could see a clean-shaven face with a friendly smile spread across features that seemed artfully chiseled specifically to melt the hearts of women. He was wearing a sharp crimson tunic with brass buttons that led down to an equipment belt cinched tightly around his waist.

"Best not to run, gents," he said, and offered a hand in a crisp white glove. "Captain Ewan McManus. Third Company, Fourth Battalion, Black Watch Regiment."

Liam offered his hand. "Uh . . . hello."

"I suspect you chaps have just had a nasty run-in, haven't you?" He cocked his head. "Some bother, was it?"

Liam nodded. The last few moments of shock, confusion, dismay, and bewilderment were beginning to blow away like the thinning mist around them. He remembered Sal was out there, perhaps nearby still.

"Yes! Oh Jay-zus! They took our friend. They . . ." He was saying "they" but he didn't have the slightest idea what "they" were.

"Dammit! That's not good news." Captain McManus grimaced. "You're saying they've taken captives?"

"Yes! She's just a young girl, a child, really! And another one, a man. They were here just minutes ago . . . minutes ago!"

"I know," said McManus. "We've been on their trail. Animals. We think it's these ones. They raided a farm town about a dozen miles west of here earlier this afternoon. Awful mess. A bloodbath. Killed the lot of them. Women, children."

The officer turned around and cupped his mouth. "White Bear, up here, please!"

Over the man's shoulder Liam could see a platoon of soldiers in similar tall helmets and red tunics sitting astride those beasts that he had yet to actually identify. One of the men hastily dismounted and hurried forward to join them. He had long black hair in braids and dark skin dotted with faint smallpox scars.

"Chief?"

"White Bear's our tracker. He's a Mohawk. Absolutely the very best," assured McManus. He turned to the Indian. "Get me a heading. We're going to follow them on the ground. All right?"

"*Dah.*" White Bear nodded and trotted off toward the farmhouse.

"I suspect they're heading northeast toward Dead City. That's where others of their kind have gone in the past. We'll do our best to catch them before they get there."

"What are they?" asked Liam.

The officer looked at him, surprised. "You don't know?"

He shook his head. "No. I thought they were . . ." He didn't know where to begin. *Monsters? Demons?* He ended up offering a confused shrug. "Me and Bob . . . we're sort of new here."

McManus looked up at Bob, acknowledging him for the first time. "Good grief, you're a big chap!" He turned back to Liam. "Jolly big, isn't he?"

Liam nodded impatiently—like he needed to be told that. "Those things? Those creatures?"

"Well, now; yes, I suppose you must have at least *read* about this in the papers. That we're using some more experimental types of genics to work on the plantations over here." He shook his head. "*The Evening Times* and the other newspapers were ranting about that when we were shipping out from London. We've had simple-minded eugenics working in factories and farms back home for ages, but these recent innovations—the dextrous hands with thumbs, and the larger brains; awfully clever stuff, if you ask me—well, that's become a heated issue. They don't like it, the idea of genics being smart enough to change the oil on an auto-locomotion engine, or being able to write their name." McManus looked at them. "But you must know about that, of course?"

Liam nodded convincingly. "Sure . . . yeah, of course."

"So," the officer continued, "we're trying out these more advanced types over here in the southern states. Generally the smarter genics are really jolly good. Very impressive, actually. But we do get problems every now and then. They can go off occasionally and turn exceedingly nasty."

The officer suddenly shook his head with disgust at himself. "I'm sorry, awfully rude of me; I didn't manage to get your names."

"I'm Liam, Liam O'Connor. And the big fella here is Bob."

McManus offered Bob his hand. "Pleased to meet you, Bob and Liam. Now look: we're going to try to run these genics down before they get to the city's outskirts. We'll do what we can to get your friends back, but—I'm not going to tell you a lie—they can be very unpredictable."

"What do you mean?" asked Liam.

McManus shook his head. "They can be gentle, tender, loving even. Then without any warning at all, without any reason, they can turn on you. Be quite deadly, in fact. There's no knowing what sets them off." He looked at the trickle of drying blood running down from Liam's temple and gestured at the gigantic vessel looming over them. "There's a regimental surgeon aboard the ship. I suggest you go aboard and let him have a look at you. And we shall go and—"

Liam shook his head. "No—I need to find her! Please! I have to come along!"

Bob nodded. "Affirmative. Enough time has already been wasted. We cannot lose them."

The officer looked at them both, silently.

"She's my *sister*," said Liam finally, desperately. He tossed a quick glance at Bob. "Both of our . . . sister. Isn't she?"

Bob acknowledged that with an unconvincing nod. "Yes. We are . . . *family*."

"Your sister?" McManus frowned circumspectly. "Hmm; I shouldn't really do this, allow civilians along." He stroked his chin. "But . . . well, yes . . . missing family, you want to do all that you can to find them, don't you?"

Liam nodded. "We won't get in your way. We just want to find her! And our friend."

McManus summoned one of his men. "Sergeant Cope? These two civvies shall be joining us. Clear some saddle space for them, will you?"

The sergeant, eyes dark beneath the brim of his helmet, and the rest of his face lost behind a large walrus mustache, nodded briskly. "Right you are, sir!"

McManus turned back to Liam and Bob. "You've ridden a huff?"

"*Huff?*"

"A huffalo?" He shook his head. "Not to worry, you'll be riding rear-saddle." He glanced at Bob. "Going to need to pick a jolly big one for you, though."

At that moment the Indian tracker, White Bear, emerged from the farmhouse and jogged across to Captain McManus.

"Northeast." He gestured past the building toward the gravel road on which Liam and the others had entered the hamlet earlier that day. "The tracks go that way."

"How many do you think, White Bear?"

"Fifty. Maybe more. Many different ones. Some big. Some small." He glanced quickly at Liam and Bob, then back at his commanding officer. "Only one human track. Man, I think."

Liam looked alarmed, and the young officer raised a hand to calm him. "That may just mean they're carrying your sister. To move along faster, you see?" McManus turned to his men. "Platoon! Ready your mounts!" And then he tugged something down from the side of his helmet, a padded leather pouch that settled over his ear. From that he pulled out a thick telescopic brass arm that curved around his jawline and ended in a brass mouthpiece.

He tapped it once. "Captain McManus to duty officer. We have some very reliable tracks down here. We're going to follow them on foot."

He nodded to a response coming through his earpiece. "Right you are; we'll call you if we need you."

He smiled at Liam. "Ready?"

"Yes! We need to go now, before we lose them!"

The officer nodded over toward the two huffs that had had rear saddles cleared of field equipment. "Of course. Let's find your friend and that sister of yours."

Chapter 4I

2001, somewhere in Virginia

They moved silently through the darkness across the seemingly endless cornfield. Sal was bouncing uncomfortably over the shoulder of
some huge, lumbering beast. She might have said "man," but she'd
only caught the briefest glimpse of it. It stood on two legs and had
two arms, that much she knew, and that was about as much of a
comparison as she could make to a human.

The group of them—"pack" seemed like a better word—moved
swiftly through the corn stalks, leaves and cobs swiping at her face.
She tried to call out to Lincoln, not sure whether he too was somewhere
among the pack—behind her, or ahead maybe, draped like her over
the meaty shoulder of one of these things. But a hand, the oddest-
shaped hand she'd ever seen—two fat fingers as big as eggplants and
a thumb like a squash—clumsily smothered her mouth, mashing her
lips painfully against her teeth.

It seemed like almost an hour before the group emerged from the
edge of the field and hesitated by the side of a road—the very same
road, she suspected, they'd been driven along earlier.

It was fully dark now, and a nearly full moon had emerged into
the sky to bathe the night a quicksilver blue. Upside-down, she could
see these creatures more clearly. They were all humanlike insofar as

they stood erect on legs and their arms swung free. But their size and shape varied immensely. She saw that about a dozen of them were as large as the one carrying her. They teetered on small legs, incredibly top-heavy, with a muscle mass that put Bob to shame. They reminded her vaguely of silverback gorillas, except there wasn't a single hair on them. Bald from head to toe, skin pale, almost translucent in the moonlight.

Their heads didn't look anything like a gorilla's head either: loaf-shaped skulls, smaller than a regular adult human's skull, with tiny, almost delicate faces. Eyes so small they almost looked like pinholes. Beneath those, a gash. No nose, just an open flap of flesh, a hole. And beneath the non-nose, a simple lipless slit for a mouth.

Sal twisted her head and saw others, much smaller, more agile-looking. They had slender torsos with narrow ribcages that reminded her of salamanders. She noticed their hands were the same kind: two fingers and an opposable thumb. But these were long and thin with bony knuckles and fingernails that were more like claws. Their heads were similar, but the eyes were much bigger. She glimpsed all-black eyes, wide and round, that blinked in the moonlight like those of an owl.

She saw one of a third type, the smallest, the size of a child, with a head disproportionately large. It must have been that one who had burst into the kitchen and stolen the shotgun. She wondered where that gun was, whether this creature had dispensed with it, not knowing what it was or how to make use of it.

Are they that stupid?

She suspected not. They'd cleverly outflanked them in the farmhouse, bottling them up in the hallway. At the very least they seemed to know a house tended to have a back door *and* a front door.

This smallest creature, the "child," had the same hand configuration, but the two fingers and the thumb looked completely human. The hands could easily have been those of some factory worker who'd lost the little finger and ring finger of both hands in some unfortunate industrial accident. Its face looked odd in the light; she thought she saw some scarring around its lipless mouth.

One other thing she noticed about all these creatures, the last observation she made before the brute carrying her began to lope forward and her vision blurred as her head bounced and bumped against his muscular chest, was that every one of them was completely naked except for a solitary item of clothing. One of the "apes" had a lady's straw sunhat on its head, the strap tucked under its chin to hold it on. Another had a threadbare scarf wrapped around its neck. One of the "salamanders" even had a lady's polka-dot summer dress on, far too large for its narrow frame.

They looked like children playing dress-up, children who'd raided their mother's wardrobe and each taken a single item they liked.

The creatures trotted silently along the asphalt road, cautiously watching both ways for signs of an approaching vehicle, and looking up into the starry sky with wide, fearful eyes. They padded several hundred yards up the road. Finally, after a small noise from the "child"—some sort of instruction—the pack of creatures flitted quickly across both lanes and into the enormous field on the far side. The stalks here were shorter, with pommel-like heads of something fluffy that batted against her face as they lumbered through.

Running beside her, she caught a glimpse of another "ape." Stretched over his shoulders was the dark shape of Lincoln's long, limp body. His head bumped up and down lifelessly against the other creature's bulging chest, and for a moment she was afraid the man was dead, that she was all alone with these freaks. But then Lincoln flinched at a bump and spat a curse at his ape. A big three-fingered fist smacked the back of his head to shut him up. Lincoln snarled indignantly, cursed, and struggled with the creature, landing ineffectual punches on its enormous shoulder, a heaving, powerful, elliptical bulge of muscle tissue that flexed and wobbled beneath ghost-pale skin as it continued to barge forward with all the grace of a rhino, oblivious to Lincoln's pitiful and futile attempt to fight back.

Sal closed her eyes, relieved he was still alive. Relieved she wasn't alone, and desperately hoping these creatures were leaving a trail that Bob and Liam would be able to follow.

Chapter 42

2001, New York

"All right, then, young lady," said Devereau. He puffed out a foul-smelling cloud of cigarette smoke that Maddy wafted away from her face with a gentle wave of her hand. The colonel didn't seem to notice that. "You'll have whatever help I can offer you. But I'll bet we have nothing of your sort of technology in our bunkers."

"Thank you."

He shrugged. "If these gadgets, contraptions, and devices of yours do what you say they'll do, then perhaps it should be us thanking you . . ." He hesitated, frowned, and then slapped a hand over his tired eyes and shook his head. "But yes—no! Arghh! The logic of this time travel is confusing." He sighed. "Of course, if you're successful and change history back to *your* version of events, I wouldn't know any different, would I? We would know nothing of . . . of what has been done?"

Maddy nodded.

"Affirmative," said Becks.

"Good God, this time-traveling nonsense plays the devil with your mind," he muttered. "I should think it must drive you to insanity dwelling on such things all the time."

"It gives me a headache," Maddy conceded. "But I think I'm beginning to get the hang of it now."

It was dark in the archway. The generator had been turned off to conserve what fuel was left in the tank, and the glow of a candle flickered across Maddy's messy desk, reflected in the dark screens of the computer monitors. Outside the archway she could hear Devereau's men talking in whispers, could see the glow of their cigarettes in the night as they kept watch for the Southern sky navy.

"So . . . this traveling through time; what is it for you, Miss Carter, a profession?" He wheezed a smoker's laugh. "A hobby, is it?"

Maddy looked down at the mess across her desk, caught in the dancing glow of the candlelight.

"More like a duty, really," she replied. "Not one I chose, exactly. It just sort of happened, ended up being me and a couple of other poor suckers who have to do it."

"And you, Miss Becks? What about you?"

Becks looked at Maddy questioningly.

"Hell, why not?" Maddy smiled casually. "Go ahead, you might as well tell him the truth about what you are. None of it's going to make any difference when—*if*—we can fix this mess."

Becks nodded slowly. "That is true, Madelaine."

"*What* you are?" Devereau looked confused. "You said 'what' just then, didn't you? Not 'who'?"

"I am a support unit," said Becks. "That is to say, an artificially engineered life form. My organic frame has been genetically edited and designed for combat and reconnaissance roles by a military DNA-software contractor."

"She's also a real barrel of laughs," added Maddy.

Becks frowned, disgruntled at that. "I *have* developed basic humor files."

"'Genetic'?" said Devereau. "Is that the word you just used?"
Becks nodded. "Yes."

Devereau stroked his beard. "The Anglo-Confederates have been experimenting with a similar-sounding invention. 'Eugenology' I believe they call it, playing with the bricks and mortar of nature itself. Playing in God's very own laboratory. Is this a similar thing to what you just said?"

"Affirmative. The manipulation of genetic data. Altering the growth instruction code of stem cells to produce an organic life-form that meets specified criteria. In my case, I have physical strength that is approximately four hundred percent greater than a normal female of similar build. I also have a hyper-reactive immune system capable of repairing extreme body damage."

"Which means you can shoot her and she'll pretty much just shrug it off like a bee sting." Maddy took her glasses off and rubbed her tired eyes. "Although that doesn't stop her kvetching about it."

"I *can* feel pain. That is necessary damage feedback data," said Becks. She looked at Maddy. "'Kvetching'? What does this word mean?"

Maddy shook her head. "Complaining. Don't worry about it; I was trying to be funny."

Becks cocked her head momentarily and filed something. She turned back to Devereau. "It is possible to destroy this body," she continued. "It is possible for the immune system to be overwhelmed. If too much blood is lost, for instance, this body's organs would systemically fail like those of a normal human body."

Devereau seemed to draw back from her into his chair, putting a few inches more space between himself and Becks. He eyed her warily. "The South has experimented with eugenic creatures on the battlefield before. They've been fooling around with that ungodly science for the last thirty years. Twenty-three years ago at the Battle of Preston Peak, when our boys were making a push along the Sheridan-Saint Germain section of the front line, they put an experimental company of those devils on the battlefield." Devereau shook his head, recalling old headlines. "The press at the time called them 'The Almost-Men'."

He ran a hand through his dark hair, threaded with silver-gray at the temples. "It was a massacre. The rumors of the time, the stories in the press, were truly horrendous. Three thousand men holding the town of Preston Peak, most of them recent draftees from the state of Ohio. Just boys, really. We lost every last one of them. When the North counterattacked with a tank regiment and steam-walkers and retook the town, they found only parts of bodies."

He tossed his Gitane onto the floor and crushed it with the heel of his boot. "They found a . . ." He looked at Maddy. "This isn't very nice, Miss Carter."

"Well, you've already started," she replied uncertainly. "You might as well go on."

"As you wish. They found a body mounted on a wooden crossbar. A head, arms, torso, legs, all from different men. As if these creatures had been mocking man, parodying the Southern science, trying to make their very own creature. The soldiers entering the town found very few of the creatures alive; they'd turned on each other, as if killing every human in the town hadn't been enough. But before doing that they'd turned on the Southern officers who'd been assigned to lead them. Trust me, Miss Carter, you *really* wouldn't want to hear what they did to them."

Maddy looked at his face. "No, I guess you're probably right."

"Since then, they haven't experimented with *military* eugenic units. But we know they have eugenic workers. Hundreds—thousands—of them working the plantations. They must have a better understanding these days of how to control them, how to design obedience into their minds."

"In my time, that's basically the same technology as genetic engineering." Maddy looked out the open shutter at the moonlit ruins of Brooklyn. "You know, when we arrived here, I didn't think things looked that, you know, *advanced* in this timeline."

"Scientific development is not necessarily symmetrical," replied Becks.

She nodded. Becks was right. War, in this case a permanent state of war, seemed to have had the effect of accelerating some sciences and slowing others. For example, those bombers, the South's sky navy that Bill had mentioned, seemed to be using a lighter-than-air technology far more advanced than was available in the normal 2001—while, on the other hand, it seemed that there was no sign of any computer technology, or if there was technology, it was rudimentary.

"The Anglo-Confederates have invested much in these modern sciences," said Devereau. "The British seem to have access to the finest scientific minds, the most advanced laboratories, and, of course, they certainly have the money."

Maddy made a face. "Well, they're not doing so great in our time."

"I find that difficult to believe." He laughed drily. "The British Empire encompasses half the world." Devereau fiddled with the frayed cuff of his uniform tunic. "Whereas our government"—he lowered his voice—"useless self-serving politicians, all of them, rely on technology that is decades old. Tanks and steam-walkers that stall and fail in the middle of a battle. Rotor-flyers that drop out of the sky at the first touch of a bullet. But," he sighed, "so long as the Union High Command has an endless supply of men to throw into the meat grinder, so long as this cursed eternal war remains a stalemate, there are businessmen, industrialists, and weapons manufacturers who remain powerful, and very rich."

Maddy noticed that his voice had become almost a whisper. "You wouldn't say those things in front of your men, would you?"

He shrugged. "I suspect they all feel the same cynicism I do. But it would take only one of them to report my words to the High Command, and I would be facing a firing squad. So"—he offered her a fatalistic smile—"I keep my grumblings to myself and do my job, and hold my part of the front line."

His tone changed, and his expression became a little more hopeful. "So tell me, then, what piece of mysterious machinery is it that you need to fix this time-traveling device of yours?"

Chapter 43

2001, somewhere in Virginia

"*What?* Did he just say we lost them?" Liam swung a leg over the saddle of the huff and dropped down onto the ground. The creature—half buffalo, half horse—snorted irritably at his sudden ungainly dismount.

Captain McManus nodded. "Yes, it seems we have. Clever creatures, these ones. They split up, and one group left a dead-end trail for us to follow."

White Bear, on his haunches studying footprints in the hard soil, nodded. He looked up at them. "They're very smart." He shook his head, disgusted with himself. "Tricked me."

McManus patted the Indian's shoulder. "It's okay, White Bear. We'll pick their trail up again in the morning."

Liam stepped forward. "You can't stop now!"

"Yes, we can—and we should. We've lost them. We'll end up spending the night chasing shadows and have nothing to show for it come sunrise."

"But . . . they're going to get away! Please! We have to—"

"We'll make camp here. At first light"—he tapped the earpiece in his helmet—"I'm calling in the regimental carrier. We'll have some more hooves and boots on the ground. I assure you, we're going to find them."

"Find them?" Liam's voice rose, angry and exasperated. "But you've just lost them!"

"On the contrary, Mr. O'Connor, I'm almost certain they're headed that way," he said, pointing to the horizon. "I'd say it's less than ten miles from here."

"What is?"

"Dead City, what used to be known as Baltimore. We've had genics go rogue on us before; that's where they tend to head. They know we prefer to steer clear."

"Why?"

"Surely you know?" He shook his head. "Good God, where exactly have you spent your entire life, Mr. O'Connor?"

"I just . . . I . . ." Liam shrugged. "A priory. Kirklees Priory."

"Ah, Catholic, are you?"

"Aye, something like that." Liam nodded impatiently. "What's wrong with this city?"

"The North poisoned it with virals. Killed thousands of innocent civilians with Hapsburg's disease. I know it's been nearly twenty years since then, but they say the rats and wild dogs carry the spores. You really wouldn't want to go in there if you can help it. That's why the feral genics use it as a refuge."

"I'll go in! Me and Bob, we'll go—"

McManus patted his shoulder reassuringly. "Don't worry. If that's where they've gone, and I suspect it is, I shall be taking a company in there to flush those vermin out. My boys are all inoculated against Hapsburg's. We'll find them, all right. Now, if you don't mind, matters to attend to . . ." McManus turned away from Liam and began issuing orders to his walrus-faced sergeant, who barked them out again in a parade-ground voice. The platoon dismounted and began to make preparations to camp for the night.

Bob joined Liam. "McManus is tactically correct with this decision, Liam."

"But"—Liam balled his fists—"she's out there. She needs us!"

"Both of them are. It is our mission priority to retrieve them *both*."

Bob was right, of course. They needed Lincoln to be alive too, if they had any hope of putting history back where it belonged.

Bob tried a reassuring wink. "I calculate a high degree of certainty that we will retrieve them unharmed."

Liam looked up at the support unit and realized he was doing his best to be supportive. Even though his mind was little more than looping strings of computer code, somewhere inside his coconut computer head was a friend, reaching out and trying to help.

"Yeah . . . maybe you're right, you big ape."

Chapter 44

2001, somewhere in Virginia

The tea was good; strong and steaming. Liam gulped it down despite the heat scorching his throat. He hadn't realized just how thirsty he was.

A brazier glowed in the middle of the field—a harvested field, rows of severed stalks flattened by army boots and the hoofs of two dozen one-ton huffalos, now tethered together in a surly huddle of muscle and hide, lowing and snorting.

Four soldiers stood guard, staring out into the darkness. The rest of the platoon was wrapped in thick woollen ponchos. Most of them, used to the rigors of army life, were taking full advantage of the few hours of dark left and were already fast asleep.

Captain McManus reached for the pot hanging from a metal frame over the glowing coals in the brazier. He topped off Liam's enamel mug.

"Thank you."

"My favorite time of the day," said McManus as he sipped his tea. "The few hours before dawn. There's a wonderful tone to the sky just before sunrise. Especially in such places as Asia Minor." He shrugged. "Afghanistan . . . very nice. The sky's almost a vanilla color before dawn."

"It's almost always a gray dawn in Cork," said Liam.

"Ahh, now." McManus grinned and wagged a finger. "I *knew* there was a slice of Irish in your accent, Liam O'Connor. Just couldn't quite place it."

"Well, some of it's rubbed off. Recently, I've been living—sort of—with a girl from Boston." He shrugged. "And a girl from India."

McManus looked at him curiously. "If you don't mind me saying, you really are the strangest fellow I've met in a good long time."

Liam hunched his shoulders. "You don't know the half of it."

"You seem, I don't know—you may laugh at this—you seem to me like a Rip van Winkle. As if you've slept all your life. How is it that you seem to know so little of world affairs? Do you not read the papers?"

"Like I said, me and Bob, we've been away in a priory. On our own. Me mother died recently, so we came home to care for Sal. And, well, the three of us finally decided to . . . uh . . . to see some of the world together, you know?"

"Well, you haven't chosen the best place in the world to start your travels, Liam. The war here may have ground to a halt in recent years, but . . ." McManus looked cautiously around before continuing in a slightly lowered voice. "There are rumors flying around that that's going to change."

Liam perked up, his eyes off the smoldering coals. "What do you mean?"

McManus stroked his smooth chin. "It's no big secret, Liam. This particular war is losing popular support back home. The British people are weary of it. War. It's all anyone in Britain has known." McManus, warmed by the brazier, unbuttoned his tunic collar. "We have so many different wars going on at the moment, you understand? We're fighting separatists in northern India, bandit militias in our African colonies, tribal war-bands in Afghanistan and Persia. I can't tell you how many dusty little backwaters my men and I have seen action in."

He shook his head sadly, his eyes lost in the glowing embers. "And it's always the same brutality, the same mindless cruelty. One tribe of savages hacking the next to pieces. And always, *always*, it's the women and children who die first. I . . . I've seen things, Liam, some truly horrible things."

Liam regarded the young officer's face, saw eyes that all of a sudden looked far older than they should. "You sound like you've seen more than enough fighting."

McManus shrugged. "I can fight any number of battles. I can stand on a battlefield alongside my men and stare down another army," he smiled. "I'm a soldier, that's what I'm trained for. But . . ."

"But?"

"But it's the evil, it's the sheer, cold hate I see in our colonies, Liam . . . the *savagery*. They're not even fighting *us* half the time; they're too busy settling old tribal scores. Odd, isn't it? You'd think the people in these far places would unite together to fight the British redcoats. But they don't . . ." His words trailed off into silence, and for a while they listened to the wheezing and snoring of two dozen men asleep on the field.

"I do sometimes wonder why we bother to keep this empire of ours. Why we're there. It's not like these places *want* the law and order we try to bring to them. They seem to relish their barbarity, what they do to each other. You can't *educate* these people." He shook his head. "It's a nasty situation."

"Aye, well, I find it's usually because some rich and powerful fella somewhere's making money out of the nasty situation." He shrugged. "That's probably why you and your men are all over the place."

McManus shrugged. "Perhaps. There's always money to be made in a war zone." He finished his tea. "I do wonder why we're in all these blasted places. When I lose men and have to write home to their mothers or wives about how they died courageously for a good cause . . ."

"You wonder what that good cause is?"

"Yes." He nodded. "You know, a part of me says our boys should all return home and leave these savages to it. If hacking each other to pieces is what they want, then who are we to impose our ways on them?

But then . . . then I remind myself that the ones who end up suffering the most are the children. When you see it for yourself, Liam—when you've seen what I've seen, it's hard to walk away."

"But is it not wrong that you're there in the first place?" Liam raised an eyebrow. "There were plenty fellows I knew who didn't have much good to say about the British."

"For good or bad, we're in the situation we're in, and the truth of it is, Liam, we're beginning to lose control of our colonies. We need more boots on the ground in Africa, in Asia Minor, in the Far East, and we can afford fewer boots on the ground over here."

"Does that mean . . ." Liam looked at him. "Does that mean your side's about to surrender?"

McManus looked at him pointedly. His silence was weighted.

"So, hold on . . ." Liam had heard some of the men earlier this evening muttering something about their regiment's hasty redeployment to America. "That's why you're over here—to *finish* the war?"

McManus's head tilted in the slightest of nods. "Our men are stretched far too thinly. I believe this particular war is one our government wants to be done with once and for all." He ran a hand through his blond hair, pushing a stray lock from his chiseled face.

"A final push by the South—and then, I suspect, a hastily negotiated peace."

Chapter 45

2001, New York

"I'm not so sure this is such a good idea," said Maddy. The boat bobbed gently on the river's tidal waves, its steam engine puffing smoke and coughing as it powered a churning paddle wheel at the rear.

"We'll be just fine," said Devereau. "I know Colonel Wainwright; he won't order his men to shoot at us while we're under a white flag."

Maddy looked up at the rag fluttering from the small boat's masthead. She wished the thing was bigger and somewhat cleaner—whiter and more noticeable. It looked more like a loose, flapping sail than it did a flag of truce.

Now two-thirds of the way across the East River, she could see the Southern front line in more detail: trenches of reinforced concrete and bunkers with viewing slits from which protruded the long, thick barrels of fixed artillery. She could make out individual faces moving among the structures, and a growing buzz of activity as they drew closer.

"They're going to blast us out of the water," she muttered.

Becks was beside her. "We have been within effective range for the last five minutes." She turned to Maddy. "And they have not fired."

"Well, I guess I'll take that as a good sign, then." Maddy grinned anxiously.

"Affirmative."

The boat finally approached a wooden jetty protruding past a graveyard of rusting and rotting hulls of long-sunk vessels lying beached on the silted banks of the river.

The pilot reversed the engine, churning water noisily behind them and slowing the boat as a couple of soldiers waited at the prow to hop over the side onto the end of the jetty.

"I just hope this isn't mistaken for some sort of amphibious invasion," Maddy found herself muttering under her breath.

"Negative," said Becks. "There are too few troops for this to be an effective assault."

Maddy sighed. "Duh, really?"

The boat thudded gently against the pier, and the two soldiers dropped onto the creaking wooden planks, quickly securing a line to a mooring post.

Devereau stepped down onto the wooden planks. "Allow me," he said, offering a hand to Maddy as she prepared to jump down to join him.

"Oh, what a gentleman!" She grasped hold of his hand gratefully. "Thank you."

Becks was next. Devereau offered her his hand.

"I will not be needing assistance," she said, casually leaping down with a heavy thud of firmly planted sneakers.

"Obviously you don't." Devereau shrugged. "Sergeant Freeman?"

"Yes, sir?"

"You and half a dozen men come along with us. The rest stay on the launch."

Maddy looked around and shivered. The morning was still fresh and cool, the clear September sky stained a beautiful salmon pink by the rising sun.

"Don't be nervous, Madelaine," said Becks. "I am with you."

She grasped the support unit's hand. "I'm fine," she lied. "Just a little cold, that's all."

Devereau joined them.

"What happens now?" asked Maddy.

Her question was answered with movement. At the far end of the jetty, a welcoming committee had assembled. She saw a dozen men in uniforms remarkably similar in design to those of Devereau and his men, only a dusty gray instead of a dark blue. Leading an escort of armed men was an officer in his late thirties, sporting a dark beard like Colonel Devereau, only trimmed in a way that reminded Maddy of some jaunty, laughing cavalier.

A dozen yards short of them he stopped. With a theatrical flourish, he whipped off his felt slouch hat to reveal long sandy hair and bowed like an actor taking a curtain call.

"Colonel Devereau! What a pleasant surprise!" he smiled. "Unless I've completely lost track of the date, it's quite a few weeks yet until Thanksgiving, is it not?"

"Colonel Wainwright." Devereau stepped forward and extended his hand. "Indeed. I'm not over here to share our annual bottle of sherry."

Wainwright shrugged. "More's the pity."

Devereau gestured toward Maddy and Becks. "I have with me a couple of . . . ladies, who are, shall I say . . . in need of some assistance."

Wainwright raised an eyebrow. "Assistance?"

"Yes." Devereau took a step closer to the Southern colonel. "James"—he lowered his voice for Wainwright alone to hear—"they have an intriguing tale to tell. Very, very intriguing."

"Something for my ears alone, is it, Bill?"

"Indeed."

"Important, I assume?"

"Very."

Wainwright thoughtfully stroked his cheek for a moment. "We shall have to be discreet, old friend; I've got *visitors* in this sector."

"British?"

He nodded. "Top brass; a routine inspection of our defense network going on in the sector next to mine." He grinned. "I suspect they might take a dim view of my consorting with the enemy."

"Then perhaps we shouldn't waste any time standing out here."

"Right." He looked past Devereau. "Ladies! Pleasure to make your acquaintance! Bill, why don't you come with me? As it happens, I've just put some rather decent coffee on."

Devereau allowed Maddy to take the lead in explaining her situation, with Becks clarifying the finer technical points every now and then—technical points as wasted on the Southern colonel as they'd been on the Northern one.

Wainwright sat poker-faced through half an hour, with a courteously tolerant expression on his face. Like a friendly old man listening to a child's tall tale.

Maddy finished and sipped her cold coffee.

"Well . . . that is a devil of a thing," Wainwright said eventually. He looked at Colonel Devereau. "William? What do you make of this?"

"I would happily have locked her up and considered her to be one of your spies had she not shown me glimpses of her world."

The Southern colonel's tawny eyebrows rose with curiosity.

Devereau tapped the shoulder bag Maddy had cradled in her lap. "Show him the things you've brought along."

Maddy nodded, then dipped into the bag and pulled out a copy of *Wired* magazine. "I buy them occasionally. This is September's issue." There was a stack of magazines by her bunk, issues of gadget and game magazines. Every few days since being recruited, she felt compelled to go out and buy magazines to read in order to feel somehow still in touch with the world. God help her, she even had a few of those awful gossip magazines with nothing but pictures of drunken celebrities stumbling out of nightclubs and limos.

Wainwright flipped through the glossy pages of special-effects shots for forthcoming movies. Maddy pulled out another, a *National Geographic*. "This is better," she said. "More pictures of the real world, not just movies."

"'Movies'?"

"Like the news-o-tropes, James," said Devereau. "Moving images with sound."

"Ah," grunted Wainwright as he reached for the magazine Maddy was holding out. He flipped through more pages, pausing on a photograph depicting the space shuttle *Discovery* launching from its pad in Cape Canaveral. And another showing the Earth from space.

Wainwright looked up at Maddy. "You are telling me this is true? That men . . . have stepped off this world?"

"Oh yes! In fact, men have stepped on the moon." She smiled. "And that's pretty old news in my time. Happened back in 1969."

Wainwright shook his head suspiciously at pictures of the International Space Station being bolted together by a man wearing an impossibly bulky suit of what looked to him like white linen. Skeptical.

"This is . . . quite a story." He stroked his bearded chin. "I certainly would like to believe a world like this exists." He offered Maddy a wistful smile. "I would want to believe that, but these pictures . . . they could be the work of the Union's propaganda division, Bill."

Devereau laughed. "You think my High Command could be this inventive? The fools can barely organize food shipments for my men."

Wainwright shrugged. That much was true.

"Well . . . I've got this too." Maddy pulled out her iPhone. She switched it on and turned the glowing screen to face the colonel.

He jerked in his seat, one boot inadvertently kicking the table and spilling slops of coffee. "Good heavens! What in God's name is that?"

"Just a cell phone," she said. "A bit like a field radio, I guess."

He gazed wide-eyed at the screen.

"You've got radios, right?" she asked. Wainwright looked at her. "Wireless communicators?"

Devereau had assured her that the South had far better battlefield-communications equipment than his regiment, who still relied on telephone-cable technology decades old and prone to going down after the frequent Southern bombing raids.

"Yes . . . yes, of course." Wainwright reached a gloved hand out to touch her iPhone. "Such an incredibly small device."

"Oh, and it does a bunch of other stuff too. Plays music. Wanna hear some?"

His eyes glistened in the gloom of the bunker. He nodded.

She tapped the screen, and a moment later the phone's small speaker played a scratchy beat and a few garbled words of hip-hop.

Both Wainwright and Devereau made remarkably similar faces: something halfway between a wince of disgust and a polite smile of pity.

"This really is *music*, you say? Music from your time?" asked Wainwright.

Maddy turned it off and offered them an apologetic shrug. "Well . . . not everything is an improvement, I guess." She handed the iPhone to him. Wainwright was quiet for a few moments as he stroked the glowing screen in silent wonder.

"James . . . ," said Devereau. "You and I, our men, could be living our lives in *that* world, not this one." He leaned forward, his bayonet scabbard tapping a chair leg. "This girl's country is America. But it's a different America. It's a whole nation, a united nation, not a shattered and broken one. Our men, our people, have their own flag, their own government!"

"Bill." Wainwright raised a hand to politely hush his friend. He stared at the iPhone in silence, caressing its smooth screen. "This . . . this seems to me to be technology far in advance of even that of the British."

"It *is*," said Maddy. "It's everywhere in my time. Every kid has one. Well, almost every kid."

He looked at her. "This is a child's thing?"

"Oh yeah—well, not a toy, but, you know, kids can use them."

He turned to Devereau, his expression a question. "Bill?"

"I've seen other things, James. These ladies arrived out of nowhere, right in the middle of our old, abandoned lines by the river. They have machines, devices. You really should inspect them."

"This . . . what this girl is saying, this is for real?"

"I believe it to be." Devereau nodded. "There is no other explanation for these pictures, for that device you are holding in your hands."

Wainwright once more gazed at the screen, at the colorful icons of the apps.

"James, if she's right, if there really is another America, it would no longer be a broken battlefield. There'd be no British and French fighting each other on our soil . . . spilling American blood." Devereau tapped a finger on a magazine page, on the image of the space shuttle launching. "Americans achieved that, James. Not British. Not French. *Americans.*"

Wainwright looked up at him. His eyes narrowed. "There was a dream once, old friend, wasn't there?"

Devereau nodded. "A nation of the free. Yes—there was a dream."

He passed the phone back over the table to Maddy. "And you say your time-traveling machine can change everything to how it appears in these pictures?"

"Yes."

Wainwright slowly nodded, thoughtfully weighing up all that she'd brought to show him. "Well, then—what is it you need from me?"

Becks leaned forward across the table. "An axial feed parabolic radio antenna."

"Excuse me?"

"A satellite dish?" said Maddy. Both colonels looked at her as if she was speaking Hebrew. "A radio dish?"

"Ah . . ." Devereau raised a finger. "I think they may mean a communications saucer."

Maddy nodded. "Yup; that sounds like what we're after."

Chapter 46

2001, Dead City

Sal grunted in pain as the creature finally dumped her unceremoniously on the ground. She looked around at the dark place and saw nothing but a few faint glints of daylight. But she could hear plenty: grunts and groans, the gasp of dozens breathing heavily, the rancid odor of stale sweat.

A match suddenly flared in the darkness, and she saw she was in the coal cellar of some building along with the entire pack of these strange creatures. The match lit the end of a thick candle, already well used, sheathed in drips and rivulets of hardened wax. In the steady glow she watched the creatures. Some of them settled themselves on beds of scrap cloth and threadbare mattresses, and she realized that this must be their . . . *lair*, for want of a better word. Some of the creatures had no bed or nest to settle on. She noticed that the small childlike creature seemed to be organizing something, distributing scraps of cloth to those without something on which to rest. She heard hushed mutterings and grunts as it pointed and gestured to make itself understood to half a dozen of the salamander-like creatures. They seemed uncertain of their surroundings, and frightened.

They're new to this group. She supposed this pack must have picked them up on a foray out of—

Her blood ran cold.

Dead City.

That's what this place was, wasn't it? She'd caught glimpses, turning her head away from the creature's sweat-soaked shoulder, fleeting glimpses of the outskirts of a deserted town, weeds chest high, saplings growing in the middle of cracked asphalt roads, long ago broken into a crazy quilt by Mother Nature. The sun coming up, casting shadows from tall brick buildings lined with windows fogged by grime and algae, nubs of moss emerging from cracked wooden window frames.

She'd caught sight of old storefronts and signs, faded and flaking: McKenzie's Hardware Store, Russell and Barton's Candy and Confectionery, Ma Jackson's Fried Chicken. Signs that swung lifelessly above smashed windows and the hollow shells of rooms beyond, long ago picked clean of anything useful or edible.

Dead City. Hadn't that traveling man warned them not to stray any closer?

"Miss Vikram." She turned her head at the sound of the whispered voice, and saw, to her relief, Lincoln lying on the pile of coals beside her.

"*Jahulla!*" she hissed, surprised at how pleased she was to see him. "Are you okay?"

His wiry hair was clotted with dried blood. "One of those infernal big ones walloped me hard in that farmhouse. I must have been knocked senseless for a while."

"I think we're in that Dead City that the man said we shouldn't go near."

Lincoln nodded. "I believe we are."

"I'm frightened," she said.

"Me too." Lincoln swallowed. "Do you have an idea what these creatures are?"

She shook her head. If she believed in the things her parents had once believed in—in Shiva, in Brahma and his four heads, and Vishnu with all his arms—all that crazy stuff, perhaps she might have allowed herself to think they were something supernatural, something evil.

"Spawn of hell?" whispered Lincoln. "Demons? Do you think we died, and this is the very first layer of the underworld?"

She looked at him, incredulous. "Why? Do you think that?"

He winced as he fumbled at the lump on his head. "These are not any creatures of Earth I have ever seen."

Their whispered conversation had attracted the attention of the "child." It stopped organizing the others and wandered over toward them with an awkward gait that looked like an uncomfortable approximation of a person walking. As if it was making a conscious effort to appear more human.

Sal and Lincoln instantly stopped speaking and looked up at it from the pile of coals they were lying on. She could see it more easily now, even if it was just by candlelight. It was no more than four feet tall, slender and narrow-shouldered. Its head was loaf-shaped like the others, but, in proportion to its meager body, much larger.

The creature squatted down, a position that looked more comfortable for it to settle into, and cocked its oversized head curiously at them. Its eyes were bigger than those on the apelike things that had carried her and Lincoln, bigger and more childlike. But it was the mouth that drew her attention. There were no lips, just a jagged, uneven line of scarred, ribbed, and bumpy flesh. As if some careless, or perhaps drunk, sculptor had fashioned them as an afterthought from lumpy clay.

Sal, surprised she hadn't spotted it before, noticed that the creature had a dark bow tie around its thin neck. It looked almost comical, and reminded her again of children playing dress-up. If she wasn't so terrified of what these creatures were going to do to her and Lincoln, she might have thought this thing actually looked almost cute.

"I . . . I'm . . . Sal," she whispered. "M-my name . . . is . . . S-Sal." She pointed at Lincoln. "And he is . . . A-Abraham."

It cocked its head again, its eyes—all black like a rodent's—narrowed, and faint frown lines appeared on its featureless pale skin. The gash of a mouth flexed unpleasantly.

"Shal?"

"Saleena," she said again. "M-my full name . . . is Saleena."

"Shaleena?" it repeated carefully.

"No, it's *Ssss*-aleena."

"Thatsh what I shaid. Shaleena?"

She realized its malformed mouth was producing a lisp. She nodded. "That's right, then."

It looked at Lincoln. "Ay-bra-ham?" it pronounced carefully.

He nodded.

The creature looked down at them for a full minute in thoughtful silence, then finally its lips rippled and flexed.

"My name ish . . . Shixty-one."

My name is Sixty-one?

"That'sh what my name *ushed* to be." The creature's lips moved in a way that Sal interpreted as a possible smile, although with the twisted, jagged lines of its "lips," the twitch of movement could have meant anything.

"I changed my name. It'sh Shamuel now."

She shot a quick glance at Lincoln. *Did he just say Samuel?*

She looked at it again. "Your name . . . did you s-say y-your name is *Samuel*?"

It nodded. There was a hint of childlike pride in that gesture, she thought. Like a little boy showing his teacher that he can actually tie his own shoelaces now.

"That'sh exshactly right." It smiled again. "Shamuel'sh the name."

Chapter 47

2001, outside Dead City

Captain Ewan McManus studied the city skyline through binoculars. "Marvelous," he muttered without any real enthusiasm. He lowered the binoculars, his eyes squinting beneath the peak of his helmet.

"Are you saying they went in there?" asked Liam. "That's the Dead City you were talking about last night, right?"

McManus nodded. "The very same."

White Bear was beside them. He'd just returned from scouting ahead. "Tracks lead into the city," he said. "Many more tracks, go into the city."

"As I suspected." He tucked the binoculars back into a pouch on his belt. "This area's been plagued by runaway eugenics. They raid for food, sometimes just for fun. And that's where they scurry back to."

"I also see a human track—small, light, maybe girl," said White Bear, looking at Liam. "Your sister? She walks. Maybe eugenic needs to rest awhile, *dah*?"

"Oh Jay-zus! Thank God . . . she's alive!"

McManus slapped his shoulder. "There you are. Some jolly good news."

"So what now? We're going in?"

McManus nodded. "Of course we'll go in. This is the kind of thing my men are used to doing—house-to-house, urban fighting. Not for the faint-hearted. It's combat up close and not very pretty, I'm afraid."

He shook his head. "Of course, if the Confederate army had the gumption to go in and clean up this mess earlier instead of ignoring the problem, we wouldn't have so many eugenics to deal with now." He puffed his lips. "*Pfft*. Useless lot. Nothing more than poorly trained farmhands, fools, and felons."

"So, when?"

McManus turned to Liam. "When are we going in?"

Liam nodded.

"I shall call in the regimental carrier first. A few things my chaps are going to need." He turned away from Liam toward the rest of the mounted platoon, pulling down the communicator from his helmet.

"Summon the Sky God," said White Bear, grinning.

"Excuse me?"

"Big Bird in the sky. It comes and makes much snow. *Dah?*"

"Oh, right. You like the snow, do you?"

White Bear nodded vigorously.

Liam turned to look at the silent city, once upon a time a city called Baltimore. From this distance it didn't look dead—just peaceful. He could see tall buildings toward the middle of it, the chimneys of factories, the steeples of churches farther out, and the ordered rows of brick houses in the suburbs. A quiet city slumbering in the midday sun.

He heard the thud of heavy feet approaching and turned to see Bob. "Anything?"

"Negative," Bob rumbled. He'd gone to climb a nearby water tower in the hope that would give him a better chance of sniffing something out. But still no messages from Maddy; not even a partial message, not even a single tachyon particle. Which could only mean one thing: she had her own problems to deal with.

Same thing, different day. When *weren't* they desperately fighting their own separate fires?

Chapter 48

2001, New York

"I presume you are referring to our divisional communications hub?" said Wainwright.

Becks nodded. "Colonel Devereau has explained that the hub services communications between this section of your front line and your High Command back in Fredericksburg, Virginia."

He cocked an eyebrow at Devereau. "It appears you have spies at work over here, Bill."

"We know where it is. Have for some time. Just south of what used to be Times Square. We've seen the dish and the antennae. If our sky force was worth spit in a barrel, we'd have bombed it to rubble years ago."

Wainwright got up and walked toward one wall of his office. A huge map all but covered the entire wall: pinheads protruded, notes were tacked to it, and pen marks and scribbles identified troop deployments and defense concentrations all along the east side of Manhattan. In a war with some movement to it, that information would have been critical military intelligence. But for Devereau, most of the information on the map was old news, showing bunkers, pillboxes, and trenches built many decades ago, when both he and Wainwright were boys in shorts. Devereau knew as much about the deployment of Wainwright's men as he did his own.

The Southern colonel tapped the map with a finger. "Here it is; as you say, just below what used to be called Times Square. Not so very far away from here."

"So?" said Maddy. "Let's go get it."

"Not so far away—but the communications bunker is garrisoned by a detachment of British troops." He shrugged. "They don't trust regular Confederate troops to guard it—they see us as just a bunch of dumb ol' corn-seed hicks."

He looked at the map for a moment, then turned back to them. "That would mean taking it by force—*attacking* it." He let those words ring off the hard walls of the room. Eventually he shook his head and sighed. "I'm sorry. That is the only communications equipment we have along this section of the line. Is there no other way to fix your machine?"

"Negative," said Becks.

Wainwright looked at them, at the magazines open on the table, at the small glowing screen of the device the girl had called an "iPhone." The evidence of another world was there. He was more than certain the North didn't have this kind of technology, or the knowledge, the imagination, the ability to produce the images in those magazines. And he was doubly certain they could never have constructed such a device.

"What you're asking . . . is for me to carry out an act of treason."

"Being here, talking to you now, James, I too am guilty of treason," said Devereau. "We are both already guilty enough to face a firing squad."

Wainwright nodded, accepting the point. "But this—taking that bunker, exchanging fire with British soldiers"—he bit his lip—"you do understand what that means?"

"An act of mutiny . . . yes."

The words had a sobering effect on both officers.

Maddy picked up on that. "Look—maybe there's another way."

"Negative," said Becks again. "A radio communication transmission dish is the component we require. Modification would have to be made to—"

Maddy raised her hand to hush her. "You guys will never face a firing squad, because as soon as we're done fixing your dish to our technology, we can change this world back."

Devereau turned to her. "But, should this plan fail for whatever reason, then the consequences for our men as well as ourselves would be . . . dire, to say the least."

Wainwright sat down at his table. "Colonel Devereau and I being guilty of treason is one thing. We would both face our firing squads. But a *mutiny* . . . ?" He poured himself the dregs of cooling coffee from the chipped jug between them. "Every man of the regiment would be punished whether they took part or not."

Devereau nodded slowly.

"I can't ask my men to do that."

"We could show them all what we just showed you," said Maddy.

"No." He shook his head. "No. I fear not many of them would fully understand. And, not understanding, they would not dare risk facing charges of mutiny."

There was a knock on the door to the room.

"Enter."

A young man's face with a gray forage cap perched on a thatch of ginger-colored hair looked around the door. "Sir?"

"Yes, Corporal."

"You asked me to warn you when the British were coming. Well, they are, sir."

"Thank you, Lawrence. Instruct the men to prepare for an inspection."

"Yes, sir."

The door closed behind him.

"You'll need to leave immediately," said Wainwright. "It should take them ten minutes to make their way down here. Best you be long gone by then."

"Please!" said Maddy. "Please—think about it!"

"Here, ma'am; you should take your things with you," he said, gathering up her magazines.

Becks grabbed the magazines and the iPhone and placed them in a shoulder bag.

"Well, just think about it. We have to fix this history!" begged Maddy. "You think this war is bad enough? . . . *It could get worse!*"

Wainwright stiffened, ignoring her pleas. "Colonel Devereau, will you please take these ladies with you back to your lines?"

Devereau nodded. "Of course." He offered Wainwright a salute, which the Southern officer returned crisply. He turned on a boot heel, opened the door, and stepped out into the concrete corridor outside.

"Come on, Miss Carter," he said, grasping Maddy's arm, "we have to leave right now."

"But . . ." She gripped the edge of the table to stop him from ushering her out. "But he's our only freakin' hope! We have to—"

"Sergeant Freeman!"

Freeman's head appeared in the doorway.

"A little help here, please!"

Becks, surprisingly, agreed with the colonel. "It is advisable to leave now, Madelaine. We should recalculate our options back at the archway."

Five minutes later they were on the launch and chugging sluggishly back across the East River. Maddy stared at the slowly approaching rubble-and-ruin landscape of Brooklyn and wondered if their only hope was to try to convince Colonel Devereau and his men to launch their own attack to capture the communications bunker.

Looking at him, looking at Sergeant Freeman and the other soldiers, old and young alike, sitting in their threadbare uniforms with the same patient look of defeat etched on each face, she realized they weren't fighting men. They were draftees—men serving whatever time they were required to serve, counting away the days until they might one day see their homes again.

Unless there was some other option, some other course of action, they were well and truly stuck in this mess. Forget helping Liam and Sal; forget worrying about handwritten warnings from the future. She and Becks were nothing more than two civilians stuck in the ruined and contested wasteland of an eternal war.

Chapter 49

2001, outside Dead City

Liam gazed out of the forward observation windows of the carrier's bridge, a long horseshoe array of glass panels that allowed the late summer sun to flood in and bathe the place in warmth and light. Passing beneath them was a patchwork of fields that had seemed so much larger on the ground, while just ahead the fields faded into the outskirts of the Dead City. Ordered rows of suburban homes with yards long ago gone to seed gave way to smaller, more tightly packed homes, then those gave way in turn to drab brick tenement buildings. Farther ahead, the apartment buildings grew taller and shared standing room with factories and warehouses and offices. All as dead and still as gravestones in a cemetery.

"We'll be landing shortly," said Captain McManus. He nodded at a thickset man in his forties, with silver-gray hair and muttonchop sideburns that flared out generously. "Colonel Donohue is sending us in with three companies of men and some of our experimentals."

"Experimentals? Please explain," said Bob.

McManus smiled. "You'll see soon enough."

The drone of the carrier's engines changed in tone, and the vessel began a gentle descent. Liam saw tendrils of mist waft up beside the bridge windows and remembered the bizarre sight of the sky suddenly filling with a blizzard.

"What's with all the snow?"

"The carrier uses lighter-than-air gases and vacuum voids to create lift. But it's still not quite enough to make a ship this size entirely buoyant. So from the bottom of her hull we vent a cloud of nitrogen that chills the air, causing it to become more dense—which, of course, provides us with additional lift. We are, in effect, creating a bed of thicker air on which we sit—and we just carry that bed along with us."

"But the snow?"

"Well, if the air's humid, then the moisture in the air becomes snow, you see?"

"Captain McManus?" called out the colonel.

"Yes, sir?"

"Ready your men for disembarking."

"Right you are, sir." He tapped Liam's arm. "This way."

McManus led them out of the bridge onto the quarterdeck outside and down a ladder to the spar deck below. As he descended the steep steps, Liam made the mistake of looking out past the brass handrail at the slowly looming cityscape below.

"Oh Jay-zus," he said queasily. "I didn't want to do that."

"Vertigo. Some of my men suffer from it," said McManus, grinning. "Just don't look down."

Liam and Bob joined him on the deck at the bottom, and then, to Liam's relief, they were led inside again, past several soldiers who politely stepped aside for them as they descended another ladder into a large equipment hangar.

He stopped at the bottom of the steps. "My God," he whispered.

The hangar looked to be between fifty and seventy-five feet wide and three or four times that in length, roughly the size of two football fields. The space was filled with three hundred men forming up into ranks, checking each other's backpacks and webbing, and several dozen huffaloes corralled in one corner. It was cold, the air chilled by the artificial arctic mist being generated outside the hull. Plumes of visible breath streamed from every man.

Despite his wretched, churning concern for Sal's perilous circumstances—his hope that somewhere in the city below she was still alive—Liam experienced a moment of wonder at the bustling activity before him.

Across the hangar deck he saw several dozen doglike animals. But not dogs, not like any dogs he'd ever seen: larger, almost as big as lions, but lithe and thin like grayhounds. They had oddly humanlike heads—baboon-like, in fact, with keen human eyes that seemed to convey intelligence.

"What are those?"

"Hunter-seekers. Eugenics, of course. We used them to great effect in Afghanistan and northern India. They're very good at sniffing out insurgents, squeezing their way into caves and tunnels and what-have-you, and then calling in their position and describing the troop strength."

"'Calling in'? You mean they can . . ."

"Talk? Yes, of course. Be useless to us otherwise." He raised an eyebrow and chuckled at Liam's wide-eyed stare. "Oh, I wouldn't expect anything too deep and profound to come out of their mouths. You won't get *Hamlet* out of them, I'm afraid. They're really no smarter than small children."

"What? Seriously, did you just say 'small children'?"

"An intelligence designed to be equivalent to that of a five-year-old child," McManus replied. "We made our mistakes with earlier classes of eugenics; designed some to be far too intelligent for their own good. That's the trick, you see? Engineer them to be clever enough to carry out the tasks they're designed for and no more. If they're kept simple-minded, it's easier to keep them happy."

Liam was busy digesting the fact that in this insane world there were baboon-dogs that could talk. Meanwhile, McManus wandered off to locate his junior officers and NCOs.

He turned to look at Bob, who shrugged and smiled at him.

"This is getting to be far too weird a reality for me," whispered Liam.

Bob nodded. "We must find them soon. Before another wave arrives."

Chapter 50

2001, Dead City

Food. There was food, of sorts. Sal watched the eugenic creatures hungrily devouring the scraps they'd scavenged on their raid. She could see several old, rusted cans being passed around, the labels that indicated their contents long ago faded or torn off. Rats, plenty of rats, caught and skinned and cooked over a small fire. Cobs of corn being stripped out of their husks.

She saw Samuel among the muttering cluster of creatures, organizing them, ensuring every creature in his pack had something to eat.

Pack.

That's the term she'd used for them earlier. But now—now that she knew that at least some of these things could talk just like humans, and the others, well, they might not be able to talk, but they behaved with a clear intelligence—"pack" felt like the wrong word to use.

Samuel came over to her and Lincoln with a handful of food items cradled in his thin arms.

"You musht eat shomething or you will shtarve."

He held out a rat carcass on a stick. It was still sizzling from the fire. "It'sh very good!"

Sal shook her head. "I can't."

"God's teeth," said Lincoln. "I can't eat a rat!"

Samuel shrugged. "I will have it, then. How about shomething elshe? Corn?"

Sal nodded. It was raw, but then she realized she was starving. "Please."

Lincoln nodded. "I have eaten corn raw before."

Samuel handed them each a cob in its husk and then squatted down on his haunches to consume the rat.

The building's cellar echoed with the sounds of eating, slurping, chewing, the grunting satisfaction of hunger being sated.

"Samuel . . . ," said Sal quietly, "why . . . why are we here?"

The eugenic looked up from his carcass. "You are both our prishonersh."

"Did you say prisoners?" asked Lincoln.

"Yesh."

Sal peeled the last of the husk away and hungrily nibbled some of the kernels of corn off the cob. "But why?"

"Sholdiersh will be coming here shoon."

"Soldiers?"

"One of the other bandsh, they killed shome people. Very shtoopid." Samuel looked at them. "Killed humansh, like you. That will make the sholdiersh come here. I know thish." He shook his head and casually slapped his forehead. "That wash *very* shtoopid."

Shadd-yah . . . *how human a gesture was that?* It was just the sort of thing Maddy would do, exasperated and stressed out over something.

"We are to be hostages?" asked Lincoln.

Samuel cocked his head. "Hosh-tagesh? What doesh that mean?"

"You will use our lives to bargain for yours."

"Perhapsh." He nodded slowly, ideas forming and reforming behind his big eyes. "If we give you back, shafe and shound . . . maybe they leave ush all alone?" He hunched his narrow shoulders. "We don't normally kill humansh. It meansh trouble. Shomething bad musht have happened." He tore another chunk from the cooked rat.

Sal saw how carefully he chewed. Careful to keep the loose, irregular flaps of his lips free of his teeth. She dared herself to ask.

"What happened to your mouth?"

Samuel shook his head. "I wash *birthed* with a normal mouth. Jush like yoursh, Shaleena. I wash deshigned to work on machinery."

"Designed?"

"Yesh—made by shmart men in a faraway town called Oxford. They grow ush genicsh over there in big vatsh—"

"Genics?" Sal frowned. "Do you mean you're genetically engineered . . . *things*?"

"You say you worked on machinery," said Lincoln.

He nodded. "Mechanic," he said with a hint of pride. "A mechanic genic. Very clever, I am. My genic type fixesh broken machinery in factoriesh. Makesh them work very shmooth again. But . . . me and my big mouth . . ."

Sal figured he was grinning, but it was hard to tell.

"I got in shome big, *big* trouble."

Lincoln pulled corn from between his teeth. "Trouble?"

"Yesh. One of the big worker genicsh got crushed and killed by one of the factory machinesh. I shaw what happened. It wash a humansh fault. The machine wash shet up all wrong. And I shaid sho. But the humansh wouldn't lishen to me." He shrugged casually. "Sho I told all the manual-worker eugenicsh they should put down their toolsh and shtop working until they fixshed the machine and shet it up right. Otherwishe, there'd be another one killed, and another, and another."

"What happened?"

"They shewed my mouth up with a needle and thread. Shaid I wash a troublemaker. Shee, they don't like it when a genic talksh back to them! That, and when they shearched my bunk room they dishcovered I had booksh. They didn't like that at all. Didn't like how I taught myshelf to read. Very dangeroush. Givesh all the other eugenicsh big . . ." Samuel struggled to say the next word carefully. He just about managed to say it without a lisp.

". . . ideas."

He took another careful bite. "They shtopped making the shmart type like me yearsh ago. Too much trouble with all the talking back!"

"I still do not understand how they *make* you," said Lincoln.

"At firsht, a century ago, it wash breeding one animal with another to make new animalsh. 'Shelective breeding,' they call it. But now they know how to make a creature from *nothing*. I heard shomeone shay the shmart men in Oxford can play with the 'code of nature.' Shome might even shay it'sh the code of God. The proper term for thish technique, though, ish 'eugenology.'"

Samuel finished his rat and discarded the wooden skewer with nothing more than the rodent's blackened bones and a few rags of sinewy meat left on it.

"They write thish code, and then they grow ush, jush like tomato plansh, in a big factory farm."

"*Grow* . . . like plants?"

"Yesh . . . in large tub of shtinky, gunky shtuff they call protein growth sholution."

"*Shadd-yah,*" whispered Sal. "Just like Bob!"

One of the other eugenics called out Samuel's name. "Uh-oh, shomeone needsh me." He looked at their uneaten corn. "Eat it. You will need your shtrength for later." He got up and padded across the cellar on his knuckles and flat feet, leaving Sal and Lincoln alone.

"Good God, his story is remarkable," said Lincoln. He looked at Sal. "Grown, just like a field of beans? Unless he is making fools of us . . ."

Sal shook her head, biting into the corn cob again. "He's talking about genetics; it's a pretty big technology in my time. Everything's genetically modified. Just like Bob."

"Bob? Your big friend?"

"Uh-huh; he was designed just like these things, then grown in a large tube of gunk."

Chapter 51

2001, New York

"Colonel James Wainwright?"

He refused to stand to attention and salute the British officer. The man had rudely, arrogantly, strode into his room without even the courtesy of knocking. Wainwright did, however, bother to look up from signing the stack of requisition forms in front of him.

The officer looked to be about half Wainwright's age, barely into his twenties, and yet had achieved a rank above his.

"Yes, what is it?"

The officer bristled at Wainwright's dismissive tone. "It is customary to salute a senior officer."

Wainwright sat back in his chair casually and splayed his hands. "Well? What do you want?"

He didn't recognize the young man's face. He must be a relatively newly commissioned officer. The collar and chest insignia denoted he was from SSID—Signals, Security, and Intelligence Division—the group of officers carrying out the inspection along this section of the front line.

The young man stepped forward, pulled a chair out from the desk, and sat down. "Colonel Wainwright," he said quietly, "acting commander of the 38th Virginia Regiment."

"I know who I am, thank you."

"Let's dispense with formality, if you wish. You can call me Rupert."

Wainwright said nothing. He studied the young officer with barely concealed contempt.

"How long have you been in command here, Colonel Wainwright, roughly?"

"In command? Nine years, three months, and seven days, if you must know. But I've been staring across this infernal piece of river at the enemy for nearly twenty years."

Rupert steepled his fingers thoughtfully. "A long time."

"Far too long."

"Well"—the young man lowered his voice a little—"it should come as a relief, then."

Wainwright looked sharply at him. "Relief?"

"You know . . . things are in motion. The Powers That Be have a feeling this stalemate, this *cold* war, has run its course, served its purpose, and now they'd like to be finished with it."

That caught Wainwright's attention. He sat forward. "Good God, a truce! Is that what you're talking about?"

Rupert chuckled at that. "No, of course not. A *push*, colonel. A final push. And we're going to make that push into the Northern heartland through what's left of this pile of rubble." He shrugged apologetically. "Sorry, did I say 'rubble'? I meant through what's left of *New York*."

"That's madness! They're dug in as deep as ticks on a dog's back. Any infantry landing on the far side would be mowed down—"

"Oh, I wouldn't worry too much about that, old chap. Between the sky navy's pounding and the experimentals we'll be sending in alongside your boys, I think we'll—"

"Experimentals?"

Rupert smiled coolly. "Yes. Eugenics."

"You're mixing *eugenics* with my men?"

"Don't panic, colonel. These aren't like the old varieties. Far more reliable."

Wainwright stood up, leaning over his desk toward the young man. "We had a promise from High Command! A cast-iron promise! No more military-purpose eugenics. No more of those . . . those *monsters!*"

"Tsk, tsk. They're not *monsters*, colonel. They're just tools for a specific job. Just tools from our tool box."

"A *tool*, boy, doesn't turn on its owner. A *tool* doesn't rip the enemy to shreds, then turn on its handler and rip him to shreds—and then, when there's nothing left to kill, rip *itself* to shreds."

"Oh please, you're referring to that Preston incident, aren't you? That happened nearly twenty years ago. We have much more reliable behavior inhibitors in our eugenics now."

"The men won't tolerate this," said Wainwright. "My men won't fight alongside them!"

"Tolerate, did you say?" Rupert stared at the Southern colonel coolly. Then eventually his face softened.

"Well now, strictly speaking, Wainwright, they won't be alongside them anyway; your men will be in the first wave ashore. Creating a bridgehead for the attack. Then"—he smiled—"we'll ship our *monsters*, as you call them, over and let them loose on the enemy."

"This is insane! I . . . I'm . . . I'll protest this through—"

"Well, here's the thing. You can protest all you like, colonel. And you can do it from your cell in Camp Elizabeth."

"What did you say?" The mere mention of the military internment camp silenced Wainwright—a long pause in which his mind raced to determine what this Rupert might know about him.

"That's right. I'm actually here to relieve you of duty . . . and I suspect you'll face a relatively prompt court martial."

"Why? What's the charge?"

The young man raised an eyebrow. "I think you know why. Or would you like me to clarify that for you?"

Wainwright nodded. "I think you'd better!"

"Well, you see, I have a file on you. Jolly fat one, actually. It's been open for a couple of years now. Too many rumors floating around that you've gone soft on the enemy. We know you've had unauthorized meetings with officers from the other side on several separate occasions. We know that several years ago you ordered the release of Northern prisoners of war to return—"

"They were deserters! They weren't fit to fight anyone. They just wanted to return home!"

"Even this morning, a little bird told me you received a visit from across the river. I'm afraid this really won't do. What with the build-up for the offensive, we really can't afford to have a front-line commander who's in the habit of taking tea with the enemy."

Wainwright stared at him. "You are relieving me of my command?"

"With immediate effect, I'm afraid." The young officer offered him an insincere shrug of sympathy. "Now, there are two ways we can do this. I can summon a squad of my chaps to drag you out, kicking and screaming. Not very dignified. I'm sure you wouldn't want your boys seeing you leaving like that. Or we can do this like proper gentlemen. You'll assign a temporary regimental commander to cover, then gather whatever personal effects you want . . . and we shall leave together." He smiled. "It would be far better for you and your men that way, I think."

Wainwright glanced at the open door. He could see the hallway outside, the pooling of light from an overhead bulb, and the shadow of a soldier standing to attention.

His or mine?

The young man stretched a white-gloved hand across the desk toward him. "I shall need your sidearm, colonel, if you don't mind."

Wainwright unsnapped the holster, feeling the firm grip of the revolver in his hand. "Please!" he whispered. "I'll come without a fuss—but, listen to me, you can't send in eugenics alongside my men. It'll be a massacre!"

"We need proper regiments on the front line now, Wainwright, men prepared to fight. Not traitors like you, or cowards, or these semi-literate peasants that you call 'soldiers.' There will be British troops in the vanguard once we have a toehold. But your peasant militia will be the ones going in first—"

The gun was suddenly in his hand and the room already booming with the fading echo of a single shot fired before he had a conscious thought of what he'd just done. Through the cloud of dissipating blue-gray smoke he saw the young man staring back at him, a third eye in the middle of his forehead, puckered and red and spilling a small dark trickle of almost black blood down his surprised young face.

His mouth flapped open with a gurgle. "You . . . you . . . ," was all he managed to say before his eyes rolled upward, showing just the whites, and he toppled over onto the floor. One booted foot began to kick, post mortem, against the leg of his desk.

Wainwright aimed the gun at the doorway as the shadow outside jerked and moved. A head suddenly appeared around the door, that of his ginger-haired adjutant. He stared wide-eyed at the gun, then at the still-twitching young man.

"You . . . just . . . shot . . . a *British* officer?"

"Yes, Lawrence, I do seem to have done that." Wainwright pursed his lips thoughtfully for a moment. "How many men did he bring?"

"Twelve."

"Where are they?"

"Canteen, sir."

"Arrest them."

"Arrest them?"

"You heard me. Confiscate their weapons, strip them of any radio equipment, and lock them up in the stores bunker. Then . . . then"—he balled his fists, tapping them against his desk insistently, urging his racing mind to focus—"then I want you to double the guards on our command bunkers and gun emplacements. Nobody comes in, nobody goes out."

"Sir." The lieutenant turned to go.

"And, Lawrence?"

"Yes, sir?"

"Pull all the cables in the radio room linking us to the communications hub."

"All of them?"

"Every last one!"

He was sure the British were going to miss their officer soon enough, and word would find its way back that there was trouble brewing; but the longer it took for that news to travel, the better.

The young lieutenant looked pale. "What's going to happen to us, sir?"

"Nothing good, I'm afraid. I must talk to the men."

"Shall I have them assembled?"

"No . . . no, not yet. I need to go see someone first." He looked up at Lawrence. "Not a word to anyone about this yet, do you understand?"

He nodded.

"And lock this room up. I'll be back as quickly as I can."

"Where are you going, sir?"

"To meet the enemy."

Chapter 52

2001, Dead City

"God's teeth! 'Tis a freak show," whispered Lincoln.

Sal found herself nodding. She estimated there were about a hundred and fifty of them in the abandoned Albion Theater. Rows of stained and faded burgundy velvet seats, sprouting tufts of stuffing through ripped seams, faced a stage made of damp and rotting wooden boards beneath a partially collapsed roof. Moisture dripped from above with a steady *tap-tap-tap,* and the waning afternoon sun cast slanted rose-tinted rays down into the gloom of the auditorium.

Samuel, it appeared, was one of the leaders of this odd assortment of unnatural creations, along with two others: a leadership committee of sorts. One of them was even thinner than the type she thought of as salamander-like; she wondered where the creature managed to store its internal organs. Its arms and legs were like sticks, bulging unpleasantly at the joints. Its head, instead of being loaf-shaped like many of the other types, was tall and tapered like a traffic cone. Samuel had told them every eugenic's shape was designed specifically for a purpose. Sal could only imagine that this one was designed to slither through pipes, or at least wriggle through some very tight places. It looked like a flesh-colored cigar with limbs.

". . . have ignored us . . . this long, because we . . . just a nuisance . . . not a danger!"

Its chest was so slim and its lungs must have been so tiny that it was forced to pant like a dog on a hot day, its words broken up into garbled bites between each rapid breath.

"I say that we . . . stay hidden here." It shuffled on thin, trembling legs to a stool at the side of the stage and perched on the edge of it.

Another of the leaders spoke. This one looked like an even bulkier version of the ape-type. It swayed, top-heavy with muscles that flexed and wobbled with a life of their own. Its head looked like an apple, nestling—almost lost—between two watermelons for shoulders. And on top of its head was perched an old-fashioned top hat. Sal realized that even though its head looked no bigger than an apple, compared to its body it had to be the same size as an adult human's for the hat to fit so snugly.

It's huge.

The rest of the eugenic was oddly out of proportion; its waist tapered in, and the legs, short and fat, seemed almost like an afterthought.

"If them humans come . . . ," it said in a voice so deep Sal felt something vibrate in her own chest. It stabbed a finger as big as a canteloupe at her and Lincoln. "If them come, maybe we kill these both . . . show them soldiers their heads. Them be frightened off! Not bother us no more!" The ape's deep voice made Bob's rumble sound like the whine of a mosquito.

Samuel put the shotgun he'd been cradling in his skinny arms down on the stage and scooted forward. "No, that'sh shtoopid! We need them alive! If we kill them, they will take bloody revenge on *all* of ush!"

"I'm sure no . . . humans will come . . . Samuel," whispered the cigar-like one. "They have . . . left us alone . . . this long—"

"But that wash before shome shtoopid genicsh killed shome of them!" Samuel scuttled across the stage and looked up at the ape's tiny apple head. "It wash one of your group lasht week, washn't it?"

The ape shrugged guiltily. "Maybe."

"You idiot!" snapped Samuel. "We're all going to be dead thanksh to you!"

"They won't enter . . . the city, Samuel," panted the cigar. "They still fear . . . all the poisons and . . . the diseases."

Sal noticed his thin legs were shaking again under the stress of standing. He may have been designed to squeeze into tight places, but clearly those legs weren't created to hold his weight for long. Once again the cigar sat on the edge of the stool. "Why did you . . . steal some humans . . . anyway?"

"Becaushe, Henry, I heard about thish fool'sh shtupid raid! I heard about the humansh being killed—women and children—and I knew we better have *shomething* to bargain with when they come for ush here!"

The ape stooped over Samuel, his looming shadow filling half the stage. "Call me *fool* again, Sam . . . I squash you!"

Samuel looked up at him, his ragged lips flapping. Sal wondered whether that was out of fear or frustration. The audience stared in silence, and the *tap-tap-tap* of rainwater continued in the background.

Sal watched the frozen tableau. For a moment she wondered whether somehow she'd been sucked down a rabbit hole and was stuck in some bizarre postapocalyptic version of Alice's Wonderland.

"Gimme them humans," said the ape. "I kill them, go take 'em heads and throw at them redcoats if them come. That scare them away! If not"—he grinned at the shotgun lying on the stage—"then we now got nice big gun!"

Samuel shook his head. "They have bigger gunsh, you big dumb mump! And many more of them, too. We wouldn't lasht a minute fighting them, Jerry!"

The ape—Jerry—smacked a three-digit fist down onto the old floorboards. The entire stage rattled. "I want fight them—not running like . . ." He scratched his head, struggling for an example.

Samuel waited until it was clear Jerry wasn't going to come up with anything. "Truth ish, Jerry, you killing humansh wash a big mishtake."

"Didn't mean to, Sam! Them got in the way, an'. . . an'. . . just happened. Real quick."

"Well, we can't un-happen it now. It'sh done." Samuel shrugged his bony shoulders. "Perhapsh my taking shome human prishonersh wash a mishtake too." He lowered his big head. "We've pushed our luck too far thish time. I shay we musht all leave. Find a new place to hide."

"Where will . . . we go . . . Samuel?" wheezed Henry.

Samuel put a finger to his ragged lips, thoughtful for a moment. "We could try north."

There was whispering and muttering from the audience.

"Shome of you know I can read, right? Well, I ushed to read thingsh that are called booksh."

"*Books?*" The ape's apple-head frowned. "What them?"

"Marksh on paper, you big mump. Wordsh. Knowledge."

"Call me a mump again and I smash you!"

Samuel casually waved away Jerry's outburst. "Shush; let me finish. I ushed to read booksh about the world. How it ushed to be. They call booksh about that short of thing 'hishtory booksh.'"

The audience of genics muttered the phrase, trying it out on their own varied lips.

"There ushed to be humansh treated jusht like ush. They called them 'Shlavesh.' They looked different. They had dark shkin, were treated like complete mumps. But shome of the pale humansh felt shorry for them, and they figured they wash jusht ash normal ash other humansh."

"So . . . Samuel, what is . . . your point?" said Henry. His thin, wheezy voice whistled asthmatically.

"You know about the human war, right? There'sh one shide called the 'Northies.' And then there'sh our bunch. Maybe if we go north and find the Northies, they might treat ush different."

"Them Northies," rumbled the ape. "You say them human too?"

"Yesh, of courshe they are."

"Them will treat us just same. *All* humans bad."

"Not *all* humansh. Shome of them—

"All humans BAD! I kill them what come in our city!"

Some of the audience of eugenics roared support for that.

Samuel sighed. He turned to look up at the big ape, then pointed to the top hat rammed tightly on his head. "Then why, Jerry, if you hate humansh sho much, do you try to look more like one of them? Hmm? And why did you pick a human name?"

Jerry's face frowned at that: anger and confusion in equal measures. The theater was silent for a moment. Samuel let that question hang in the air for the giant to ponder.

Eventually a big fist reached up and pulled the top hat off. Jerry tossed it across the stage. "Stoopid hat anyway," he rumbled.

"Jerry, Henry, *all of you*, lishen to me! I shay we musht leave here tomorrow. I *know* the humansh are coming—I can feel it in my bonesh—and they will kill ush all, if we shtay. I'm sure of it!"

Jerry shook his head defiantly. "Them come here? We gonna smash them up!"

There were more roars of approval from the seats.

"Well, that'sh up to you. Me? I'm leaving tomorrow, and I'm taking those two prishonersh with me," he said, pointing toward Sal and Lincoln.

"Them stay here!"

Sam waddled up to Jerry to stand toe to toe with the ape and glowered up at him. "They're *mine*. I found them! You want them, you gotta take 'em off me."

Jerry's tiny black eyes returned the challenge; his huge fists clenched and flexed as they glared at each other for a dozen silent seconds.

"You gonna shmash me up, then?"

Jerry said nothing.

"Well?"

Finally Jerry looked down, shame-faced, at the stage boards between his big feet. "No, Sam," he muttered.

"That'sh right . . . you're not." He shook his head. "Becaushe without me to figure out the complicated thingsh for you, you'd be losht." He looked out at the bizarre menagerie sitting among the rows of thread-bare seats. "All of you would be!"

Their noises—chirps, mutterings, howlings—dwindled to silence.

"We have to leave. The army men will come because humansh were killed. We should leave tomorrow morning and head north to find a new home." He glanced at Sal and Lincoln. "Not all humansh hate our gutsh. These two sheem different to me. Maybe the Northy people think different too." He shrugged. "Maybe not, but I know we can't shtay here, not anymore. We knew thish day wash gonna happen eventually, anyway."

Ancient weather-worn timber creaked to fill the long silence.

"Sam's right . . . I think," panted Henry. "We have . . . to go."

Jerry looked at him, sensing wiser minds than his had reached a consensus he couldn't begin to argue against.

He sighed. "Maybe you right."

"Of courshe I am."

"Sorry, Sam," he said finally.

"Don't worry about it." Sam reached out and patted one of his bulging knuckles. "You big ol' mump, you gotta jusht trusht me. All right? We'd be real dumb to shtay put and fight the sholdiersh. Real dumb."

Sam waddled toward the edge of the stage and looked out at the dark rows of seats. "And we ain't no dummiesh, are we?"

Chapter 53

2001, Dead City

Sal stared up at the stars through the shutters of their coal cellar. *Oddly calming*, she thought. In a world turned upside-down, where everything was wrong, bizarre, you could at least look up at the sky and see normality: stars that shined regardless of who won a civil war, or who should or should not be president. Their light was billions of years old. They didn't care that a girl from 2026, stuck in the year 2001, in a world that should never have been, was watching them.

Funny.

Across from her she could see Samuel on a nest of worn blankets, twitching in his sleep, his ragged lips rustling like tent flaps with every shallow breath. Around him other genics of all the standard types she'd seen were curled up and fast asleep, producing a chorus of breathing—different sounds, different rhythms, soft whimperings, half-spoken muttered words. Feet and hands jerking and curling. She realized these manufactured creatures dreamed in their sleep just like humans. Twitched and flexed like babies in a womb.

Babies. Children. Yes, just like frightened children. Even the smart ones, like Sam and that strange thin one, Henry. Even that giant ape—ferocious though he might look, he was like a little baby inside that miniature head. And wasn't it so childlike, their futile efforts to look more human? The items of clothing they each tried their best to wear properly, the names they chose for themselves. They had every reason to despise humans for the way they'd been treated, yet they did all they could to be more like them.

After the gathering at the deserted theater, the various packs had returned to their dens to settle in for the night. She and Lincoln had spoken with Sam for a while, softly, as the other creatures began to fall asleep. She'd asked him about his life, what it was like to be "made." He'd told her about the growth farms in the English countryside—enormous factories of iron struts and grimy glass where almost full-grown genics were birthed from giant copper vats, then cleaned, clothed, and numbered. And about living from day one in schoolhouses: long huts stacked with hard bunk beds and straw mattresses. Living there to be taught the basics they needed for their lifelong roles, taught by other genics designed specifically to teach. His description of the growth farms had reminded her of the enormous internment camps back in 2026 along India's northern border with Pakistan; the lives of refugees lived entirely within chain-link compounds, one day like any other.

Then, with no warning at all, he'd been crated up like so much freight and shipped to a far corner of the British Empire.

Sam had told them that at first he'd worked in a very hot place where the humans were of Sal's color, mostly darker. There he'd maintained field harvesters, stripping them and cleaning the engines alongside human workers who lived only marginally better lives than the genics did. It had been one of them who had taught him how to read.

Then, again without warning, he'd been packaged and shipped to another country, then another. Eventually he learned from the scraps of books and pamphlets he picked up and squirreled away the names of all these strange places: New Rhodesia, Great Albany, the British Central District, Cape Georgia, and finally ending up in a place called America.

Sam said he could read most things. Only occasionally did he find language too difficult for him to understand. But his one big regret was that he could only write in a child's untidy scrawl. His hands, designed to hold sockets and wrenches, lacked the dexterity to handle something as straightforward as a pencil.

If he could have written things, he said he would have liked to have written "singsong stories." Sal had no idea what those were. Perhaps he meant poems.

On that note, he'd said he needed his rest, and was fast asleep within seconds. She wondered if that was a deliberately designed ability, to be able to flip a switch inside and be instantly unconscious. Or whether it was a lifetime's habit, learning to get rest when it was available.

"Abraham?" she whispered in the dark.

There was no reply.

"Lincoln?" she tried again. Nothing.

She was going to ask him what he thought of an idea she had. To see if they could slip out of the cellar unheard, escape the city, and try to intercept these soldiers the genics were certain were coming their way. Perhaps, seeing them free and unharmed, the soldiers might let the creatures go, and be redeployed to do something more useful elsewhere. Or, if not, then perhaps she and Lincoln might be able to send them off in the wrong direction on a wild-goose chase. Give these things a chance to escape and find a new home somewhere else. But the deep voice of a genic grunted irritably out of the darkness.

"Shut up . . . resting now."

So much for that idea, then.

Chapter 54

2001, outside Dead City

Liam watched the night sky. He was looking at the very same stars as Sal. In front of them was the outline of the dark city suburbs.

McManus prodded the dying fire with a stick. "We shall wait till first light, Liam. Then we'll send in the hounds."

Another delay of hours. Liam did his best to contain the frustration behind his gritted teeth.

"They should find those runaways easily enough—and your sister and friend, too."

Liam glanced across the trampled field, lit by several campfires. The "hounds" that McManus referred to were those large baboon-headed dogs. He could see them clustered around one of the fires, eating rations of food out of a trough. He saw flashes of long teeth as they periodically raised their heads and chewed hungrily on what appeared to be dry protein nuggets.

"They look pretty ferocious, so they do. Are you sure my sister's going to be safe from them?"

"Indeed. Those hunter-seekers won't harm them. They've been instructed."

"How will they know who it is they're not to hurt, though?"

"White Bear has had them all get a taste of the tracks left by the genics. They know the smell of your sister and have orders to follow the scent, locate her and your friend, and then report in."

Liam looked at him skeptically. "'Instructed,' you said? You make them sound almost human."

McManus grinned. He put his fingers in his mouth and whistled. One of the hunter-seekers looked up from his feeding trough. "Yes, that's right, you over there! Pack-Alpha—come here!"

The creature obediently got up off its haunches and trotted across the camp toward them.

Liam shared a look with Bob. "I've never seen a dog so well trained."

"Well, first, remember these things *aren't* dogs," said McManus.

The hunter-seeker came to a halt in front of them. It was waist high, almost as big as a Great Dane.

"You may sit, Pack-Alpha."

"Thanks, guv," it grunted, settling its slim hindquarters on the dusty ground.

"This civilian is Mr. Liam O'Connor. And the big chap is Mr. Bob O'Connor. It's their sister and friend who've been taken by the runaways. Now, for their peace of mind, would you please tell them what your orders are."

It turned intelligent baboon-eyes to Liam; a pink tongue protruded from its long, furry muzzle and moistened its thin, dark, leathery lips. "Follow smell-trail. Find humans."

"And what will you do when you find them?"

It cocked its head, and Liam could have sworn the thing rolled its eyes as if that was the most stupid question a person could ask. "Call home."

McManus pointed to a leather strap around the creature's neck. Beneath its jaw was a small brass box with a simple toggle switch on it. "They flip that switch and it turns on a short-range radio beacon, which we can then follow in. It also opens the microphone so they can tell us exactly what they're seeing. They make excellent reconnaissance units."

He turned back to the genic and squatted down to inspect an identity number on its collar. "Ahh, you're Pack-Alpha-Two. Sorry, didn't recognize you there . . . George, isn't it?"

Liam choked a surprised laugh. "*George?*"

"Ahh, yes. We let them pick their own informal names. They like to do it. Makes them feel a part of the regiment. Doesn't it, old chap?"

The creature nodded. "Good name, George. Just like King."

"That's right, just like our King George." McManus patted the top of George's small round head. "George is one of our best. Did some really excellent work rooting out the bad chaps from the mountains in Afghanistan, didn't you?"

"Bad men. I kill."

"You did jolly well, George. Very well indeed."

George turned his baboon-head to look back at his pack and the trough, a worried frown rolling along the protruding brow above his eyes. "Go eat now, guv?"

"Ah, yes—better get off before those greedy beggars in your squad finish all the chow. Dismissed."

The hunter-seeker turned and trotted back across the makeshift camp.

Liam shook his head at the bizarre conversation he'd just witnessed.

"Yes; they're a very helpful eugenic product," said McManus. "Far more efficient at tracking than any human can be, better even, dare I say, than White Bear."

"Why did you not use those hunter creatures earlier, then?" asked Bob. "When we were following the trail from the farmhouse?"

Bob nodded.

"Tracking's not just following a scent or footprints. It's thinking, assessing how you personally would attempt to hide your trail. It's like playing chess—predicting an opponent's move. George and his chums can't do anything sophisticated like that. They're jolly good, though, at following a scent. Tracking and following a scent; two very different things."

"The names . . . ," said Liam. "Why do they pick names like that? Human names?"

McManus shrugged. "Eugenics . . . that's the odd thing—they *all* want in some way to be more human. After all, I suppose they must think of us as . . . as, I suppose, their *parents*, in a way. They are just children really, though. Simple-minded children."

High up in the sky the regimental carrier slowly maneuvered in a wide turning arc, a searchlight periodically lancing out into the darkness and combing the ground around the camp. McManus poked and prodded their campfire with a stick, stirring the glowing embers to life.

"Sometimes they even run away, seeking a chance to live a normal life away from this war."

"Like black slaves used to do?"

McManus stopped midstride. "'Black slaves'?" He glared at Liam. "Good grief! You're talking about *human* slavery?"

Liam nodded. "Yes."

"Barbaric!" he spat. "An abhorrent, savage practice. I thank God we live in modern, more enlightened times."

"So . . . your side, the South—"

"Anglo-Confederacy," he corrected Liam. "'North' and 'South' are old names from bygone times."

"The *Anglo-Confederacy*, then—it doesn't keep human slaves anymore, does it?"

"Good God, Mr. O'Connor! Are you actually *trying* to be offensive this evening?"

Liam winced. "No, I . . . I'm sorry. I just wondered . . ."

"Do you honestly think His Majesty's government, our armed forces, this prestigious regiment, would fight alongside any nation that actually kept *humans* as slaves? We put an end to that in this country nearly a century and a half ago!" McManus shook his head disapprovingly. "Good Lord! Look around you, why don't you, Mr. O'Connor.

We're not barbarians in the British army!" He got up and strode off, leaving Liam and Bob behind.

Liam looked at Bob. "What? I just asked a question, that's all!"

"I believe you may have angered Captain McManus," said Bob.

Liam nodded. "I think you're right." He looked around, just as McManus had suggested, at the men sitting beside campfires in their woollen undershirts and suspenders, the junior officers around their brazier warming their hands. He'd been so distracted by their desperate mission to rescue Sal and Lincoln, distracted by the bizarre technology of this world and the strange talking creatures it had spawned, that he'd failed to note that at least a third of these men and officers in crimson tunics and pith helmets were dark-skinned. Professional soldiers recruited from every corner of the British Empire.

"Oh . . . I see." He pressed his lips, realizing now why his clumsy question might have caused McManus to snap angrily at him. "I guess I probably need to go and apologize."

Chapter 55

2001, New York

Devereau watched his Southern counterpart jump down off the prow of the launch and wade through the lapping tide up the shingle toward him.

Wainwright stopped a yard away and offered him a crisp salute. "Colonel."

"Twice in one day." Devereau returned the salute. "We make poor enemies, don't we?"

Wainwright nodded politely at Maddy and Becks standing a little behind Devereau. "William, we must talk quickly."

"What's the matter?"

"The British are preparing an offensive in this sector."

"Another?"

Every two or three years, it seemed, the Anglo-Confederacy probed somewhere along the front line with a halfhearted assault. Thousands of men dead or injured for a front line that might have shifted a quarter-mile in one direction or the other. It made headlines in newspapers. It gave the generals on either side a chance to earn campaign medals. But it achieved nothing useful.

"No, William, this one's for good. They want a significant victory this time."

"Oh?"

"They want to take New York." Wainwright stepped a little closer and lowered his voice. "And they're sending in experimentals."

Eugenics. Devereau felt the hairs on the back of his neck rise. He fought to keep a calm expression on his face. "James, are you certain of this?"

"Certain?" Wainwright laughed bitterly. "I have just committed an act of treason. Of course I'm certain! They're coming your way, William, and they're going to throw every little monster in their box of tricks right at you."

"God help us," whispered Devereau. He glanced over his shoulder at Maddy and Becks, then back at Wainwright. "James, perhaps you'll reconsider your position on the discussion we had this morning."

"That's why I'm here, old friend. These two young women, do you . . . ?"

"Do I believe their story?" Devereau considered his answer for a moment. "You've seen their pictures, their small device . . . I'm no technician, but I swear that thing is beyond even the capability of the British."

Wainwright nodded.

"And there's more to see in their bunker if you want to come and—"

Wainwright raised a hand. "There's little time. I *believe*—I have little choice but to believe them. I have nothing left but hope that they can change all of this."

Devereau turned and beckoned Maddy and Becks to join them.

Maddy smiled. "Colonel," she said politely.

"Miss Carter. I have agreed to join my efforts with Colonel Devereau and help you fix your time machine."

"Really? Oh, that's—"

"William, Miss Madelaine, Miss Becks . . ." Wainwright drew a deep breath. "I have committed an act of treason and mutiny. As soon as it is discovered, the British will be swarming all over my sector. If there are parts you need to take from the communications hub, then we will need to move quickly."

"If we can retrieve what you need from there," said Devereau, "how long will it take you to fix your time machine?"

Maddy turned to Becks. "Becks?"

"I am unable to give a precise estimate. Connecting and configuring a radio communications dish may take"—her eyelids flickered for a moment—"thirteen hours."

"*What?*" gasped Wainwright. "That is far too long!"

"In addition, we need to establish a source of power. Our generator utilizes petroleum-derived diesel. Do you have this fuel type?"

The colonels looked at each other. Wainwright shook his head. "I have not heard of it. Southern engines run on a liquid-form fuel we call maizolene. I believe it is a mixture of corn-based alcohol and Texas oil."

"As I suspected," said Becks. "A variety of hybrid ethanol. Then we would need to adapt the generator to run on this fuel. This may not be possible. In which case we would need to acquire one of your engines and use that as the motorized device to turn the generator's dynamo to produce electrical power."

Maddy sucked her teeth. "That sounds like a *lot* of work."

"Correct." Becks's eyes blinked again. "Approximately thirty hours of work." She turned to Maddy. "But I am making several significant assumptions in this calculation. It could take much longer."

"Good God, there is no time for this! The British will be here before we can—"

"Unless we buy her the time she needs," said Devereau. The others looked at him. "James," he continued, "you and I have said this before, have we not? This war is not the war it started out as. It's not *our* war."

Wainwright nodded. "This is a war no *American* would want." The colonels eyed each other silently, long enough so that Maddy felt the need to say something. "What? What the hell are you guys thinking?"

"James . . . I think . . . no, I *know* my men would join me. What about yours?"

The Confederate colonel turned to look back across the East River. "I believe they might." He glanced at Devereau. "Particularly if they learn what the British are planning to do."

"What?" Maddy looked from one to the other. "What are you two talking about?"

"An uprising," said Devereau.

"A mutiny," added Wainwright.

Both men smiled at the thought of it. "It could spread," said Devereau. "Really, it could spread right along the front line. If someone somewhere dared to start it."

"Word would need to get out. You and I, William, we'd need to make absolutely sure the news got out."

Wainwright grinned suddenly. "There is not a regiment, old friend, not a single Confederate regiment, that would not celebrate an end to this damned war!"

"Oh my God! Is that your plan, then?" asked Maddy. "A popular uprising?"

"If news spreads among the men," said Devereau, "that the British plan to deploy eugenic military units again on American soil . . . yes, good Lord, this could . . . this could truly take hold. The soldiers on both sides and the general public would be terrified of another Preston Peak massacre!"

"And if it comes to it," added Wainwright, "our men, I'm sure, would fight side by side."

Maddy thought she saw tears in Devereau's eyes. "My God, James! This could be it, a *tinderbox* issue Americans can unite on! Military-use eugenics being deployed over here again!"

"That's what needs to be said, old friend. Loud and clear. So everyone can hear it." His grin widened. "This is the match to the fuse."

"Indeed."

Maddy looked from one colonel to the other. "So is this what we're doing, then? Starting a revolution?"

They both nodded. "And not a moment too soon," said Devereau.

Maddy squared her shoulders. "Okay. So, do you guys need to shake on it or something?"

Wainwright offered his hand and Devereau grasped it. "We have much to do, James, and very quickly."

"Indeed. I will go back and present this to my men."

"As shall I," said Devereau.

Chapter 56

2001, outside Dead City

The British troops were up and gathering at dawn with the noisy clatter of equipment and belt buckles, the thudding of boots on pressed soil, the shouting of sergeants. Liam watched with guarded fascination as they scrambled quickly to assemble into ranks by platoon, by company, until he was looking at three hundred soldiers, rows of red tunics and crisscrossing leather belts shifting gently as chests heaved for breath. White pith helmets in endless ranks, their pointed peaks shading the eyes of hardened faces that looked like they'd seen plenty of action.

Liam was impressed by their discipline and efficiency. If they fought half as well as they mustered, he wondered how a war anywhere in this world could last long in the face of such an impressive machine as the British army.

McManus had confided in them last night that this regiment, the Black Watch, was actually considered one of the finest in the British army: an elite regiment that had experienced combat on every continent in the world—and had been chosen to field-test the newest generation of experimental eugenic units.

Speaking of which, he watched the hunter-seekers moving out of the camp at a trot as the last of the tents and camp equipment were being rolled up and stowed in the large saddlebags of the pack huffaloes.

The hunter-seeker that had chatted briefly with McManus last night—"George"—exchanged a polite nod with the captain as his pack, the last to leave, moved out. They broke from a trot into a loping gallop as they spread out in a loose line across the weed-strewn field and, several minutes later, disappeared a quarter of a mile away into the dead and overgrown outskirts of the suburban edge of Baltimore. Liam could just make out a line of backyards, bordered with rotting and leaning picket fences; deserted shanties; abandoned carts; and rusting automobiles of an old-fashioned coach design, their spoked wheels tied to the ground by thick brambles and briars.

McManus issued orders to the junior officers and NCOs before joining Liam and Bob. "They should locate the eugenics soon enough. Did you see how quickly they set off? I believe they already have the scent."

Liam nodded. "Are you sure, captain, they won't descend into some sort of, well . . . some sort of *bloodlust* when they find them?"

He shook his head. "They may be eugenics, but they are also members of the British army. They'll behave." He pulled down the brass mouthpiece from the earpad at the side of his helmet.

"Captain McManus here; we've just sent in the hounds. And we're now moving out toward the city." He gave a crisp nod at the response over the earphone. "Yes, sir."

High above them, Liam could see the carrier slowly circling, catching the first dawn rays along its shimmering copper hull. It was seeing the sun a good hour before they were going to feel the warmth of it on their own faces.

"Right, then," said McManus. "We'll get our men moving in so we'll have less ground to cover once they've pinpointed a location." He smiled. "We'll find them this morning, don't you two worry."

Liam nodded. Given how quickly those baboon-dogs had crossed the hardscrabble field, he actually felt very confident they were going to find them. It was whether they were going to find them in one piece that was worrying him.

The walrus-mustached sergeant bellowed for the troops to move out, and section by section they peeled out of their rows to join the back of the lengthening column moving down the broken pavement of what was once the main road leading into the city.

"You chaps want to walk or ride?"

"We'll walk," said Liam.

"Jolly good," McManus said, tightening the strap of his helmet. "Well, no point hanging around, then. It's only beggars and desk clerks you'll find at the *rear* of a column!"

Chapter 57

2001, Dead City

Sal felt a hand on her shoulder, tugging her insistently. "Wake! Now!"
She looked up to see one of Samuel's pack, one of the "apes." She recognized it as the one who had carried her here the night before last.

"What's the matter?"

"*Them* come!"

Sal sat up on her bed, a loosely gathered pile of grubby coal sacks, to see the entire pack awake and hastily scrambling to gather their few possessions. She saw Lincoln sitting up beside her, just as confused and groggy from being so rudely awoken.

"What the devil's happening *now*?" he growled.

Samuel padded over. "They're here already! Sholdiersh! They coming! We musht leave!" He reached down for Sal's hand.

"Please!" She refused to get up. "Why don't you just run! Abraham and I will go to the soldiers; we'll tell them we're okay!"

Samuel looked for the briefest moment like he was considering that suggestion. But then he reached for her hand again. "No—you come with me!"

She snatched her hand back. "No!"

The eugenic muttered a curse under his breath. He turned to the ape standing beside him. "Get them up!" He turned to address the others. "Let'sh go!"

Samuel led the way out of the coal cellar. The ape yanked Sal and Lincoln to their feet. "You come!" he rumbled, pushing them both in front of him.

They climbed a flight of stone steps out of the cellar and crossed the creaking wooden floor of what was once a lounge. From the meager daylight seeping in through shuttered windows, Sal saw old high-backed armchairs draped with dust covers and a wall lined with books quietly moldering away.

They were in a hallway illuminated by morning light streaming in through an open front door. Then they were stumbling down porch steps, through an overgrown front yard, and out past a rusting gate onto a wide, weed-choked avenue flanked on either side by tall three-story townhouses, with proud verandas and porticoes.

She caught a glimpse of wooden boards nailed over windows and front doors, the faded red lettering of plague and infection warnings hurriedly spray-painted on them decades ago.

Ahead she could see Samuel scooting along the avenue with a strange shambling gait—hunched over like a primate, his disproportionately short legs working so very hard to keep him ahead of his pack of "apes," slender "salamanders," and several other eugenic types.

She noticed several miniature ones, no more than a foot and a half tall, with bodies like meerkats, but bald and pale like all the others, and with similarly loaf-shaped skulls. They were all wearing the same miniature striped overalls, and she suspected they must have been some sort of work team. She wondered what sort of mundane job they'd been designed for. Every now and then, to keep up, they used their arms, running like monkeys. She heard their frightened babbling, their twittering voices using pidgin English words.

Behind them, some way down the avenue and around a corner, Sal could hear the echoing crack of gunshots and the high-pitched death rattle of something brought down. A eugenic from one of the other packs, she guessed.

They're close!

They scrambled together along the avenue until they came to an intersection. In front of them Sal saw a grand old redbrick building with marble columns supporting a large portico. A clock tower stretched proudly from its roof. She guessed it might once have been a courthouse, or a library, or some building with a public purpose. Before it, decorative flower beds had gone truly wild and native. They were fronted by a low stone wall that still boasted patches of blistering and peeling white paint. On it she saw a faded sign on a rusted plaque:

ROBERT E. LEE UNIVERSITY

Samuel was frantically waving his spindly arms to the left. "Thish way!" he screamed. "Thish way! Hurry!"

Other packs emerged from side streets and spilled out of the open doorways of abandoned homes to join them.

They were on a much wider avenue now, but it was cluttered with abandoned carts and old automobiles. Panic had swept through this city long ago, the streets and avenues congested with civilians desperate to leave. Carts laden with suitcases, valuable heirlooms, and gilt-framed family portraits had been left to rot, weather, and fade in the open air.

They charged past a sign reading NORTH CHARLES STREET. Now a graveyard of vehicles, and, yes, here and there Sal could see bleached bones, the dark leather of desiccated skin, and tufts of hair in among rusting chassis and the iron spokes of cartwheels.

They'd just begun to pick their way through the jam of long-dead vehicles when they heard the echo of gunfire again. It sounded closer than last time. Sal wrenched her hand free of the ape that had been clasping it.

"NO!" she shouted. "Please! Just let us go!"

The ape grappled with her, hoisted her up, and held her under one arm.

Samuel led the way through the barricade of vehicles and finally stopped. The clutter was slowing them down too much. He turned off the broad avenue into a smaller alleyway, the others following. He stopped and slumped against a brick wall, gasping and wheezing, exhausted from the last few minutes of running. Such a small body, with lungs and a heart not designed for this kind of exertion. The other eugenics crowded around his panting form, waiting for him to recover, waiting for further instructions.

"GO!" he gasped. "GO! There'sh no time to wait for me. Go! GO!"

"But which way, Sam?" asked one of them.

"Go north!"

"Which way izzat 'north'?" asked one of the salamanders.

"North!" He pointed up at the strip of sky above the alleyway. "Keep the shun, the shun up there! In the shky—keep it on your right!" he said, slapping his right shoulder for those in his group that didn't know their left from their right. "Keep the shun . . . on that shide of you!" he gasped. "Now GO!"

Several of the eugenics did as they were told and shambled off reluctantly down the alleyway toward a smaller intersection at the far end, looking over their shoulders unhappily, hoping Samuel was following close behind.

The ape holding Sal and dragging Lincoln by the arm hesitated to leave Samuel, and some of the others waivered uncertainly, shuffling from one foot to the other.

"Sam? You come too?"

Samuel waved his hands. "Go . . . all of you . . . jusht go!"

Sal wriggled. "Let me go! Please!"

The ape's voice growled. "Sam . . . you come too?"

"I . . . can't . . . keep . . . up . . . anymore."

From farther down North Charles Street came more gunshots and the screams of eugenics brought down. It seemed the whole city was beginning to stir to life, with creatures emerging from their hiding places in blind panic, like rats leaving a sinking ship. Sal suspected the city had been home to far more than the hundred fifty or so eugenics they'd seen at the theater meeting.

The gunshots seemed to be echoing from different ends of the avenue. The soldiers were coming from all directions, tightening a noose around them.

Sal looked up at the ape's face. "Put me down! Let us go, and pick Sam up instead!"

The ape nodded, loosening his hold on Sal and turning to Samuel. "I carry *you!*"

The small eugenic shook his oversized head. "No . . . but . . . do ash she shaid. Let 'em both go."

The ape placed Sal on the ground and released Lincoln's wrist. Lincoln snarled with relief and rubbed his arm where the brute's hand had been wrapped around it.

Sam sighed. "You go to thoshe sholdiersh if you want."

Sal remained where she was. She knelt down in front of Sam. "Sam, you've got to run now!" she said. "Abraham and I, we'll stop them, stall them somehow. Buy you some time! But you've got to leave now!"

His brow creased. Confused. "You want me to eshcape?" he wheezed.

"Yes!" She looked at Lincoln. "Yes, we do, don't we?"

He nodded. "Odd creature though you are, I see in you"—he searched for the right words—"I see in you *admirable qualities*, sir. A good soul." He knelt down beside Sal. "Better than quite a few I've met."

Sam looked up at him, wide eyed. "Never been called 'shir' before."

They heard gunfire and shrieking from the far end of the alley. Sal turned to see the eugenics who'd headed down that way doubling back to rejoin them. Beyond their shambling forms at the far intersection she saw a row of four-legged creatures, like hunting dogs, but not quite. Behind them was a line of uniformed men with guns. The far end of the alley was blocked off.

"*Shadd-yah!*" Sal shared a glance with Lincoln.

What do we do?

The alleyway lay in the dark shadow between two old brick tenement buildings. Most of the windows and doors were boarded up, but some of the boards had worked loose and fallen away. The creatures could lose themselves inside those buildings and hide in the gloomy labyrinth of rooms and hallways, but only for a while. They'd be trapped in there.

She heard noises from North Charles Street: soldiers pulling the cluster of vehicles roughly aside, the splintering crack of old cartwheel spokes, the groan of stressed, rusting metal being dragged to the curb. They were busy clearing a way through the traffic jam.

And then she felt it: a cold tickle on her cheek. She felt it again. Moisture.

I'm not crying, am I?

She felt a tingle on the back of her hand and looked at Lincoln. A snowflake was fluttering lazily between them, seesawing down.

"Snowing?" grunted Lincoln.

It was. More dancing flakes of snow descended around them. She looked up at the narrow strip of daylight above and saw nothing but blue sky. For a moment her mind instinctively queried why, how, it could snow on a sunny September morning; then a dark form obscured the sky. The alleyway dimmed as the blue vanished and was replaced with the smooth, dark copper hull of some gigantic vessel.

"They here now," said the ape, looking up, his small eyes wide as pennies.

Chapter 58

2001, Dead City

Captain McManus nodded at the message coming in over his earpad. "Right you are, we're on our way over."

He turned to Liam. "Good news, Mr. O'Connor. We've got a report of a handful of the runaways boxed up in a small alleyway; couple of guests along with them. One girl; one man, quite tall. Sound like your two?"

Liam exhaled a sigh of relief. "Are they all right?"

"Apparently. They've both been seen on their feet. That's obviously a good sign." McManus opened up a map of the city. "They were spotted near the old university on North Charles Street." He looked up from his map to the streets around them, taking a moment to get his bearings.

"Ah . . . yes, very close indeed." He pointed up at the carrier hovering over the city a block away. "Just over there, in fact. Right underneath her." He toggled a switch on his mouthpiece. "All units in the vicinity of the carrier, this is Captain McManus. We have a group of eugenics and their human prisoners bottled up in an alleyway. Nobody is to engage them. Repeat: no firing. Just hold your positions, chaps, until further orders."

He tapped the switch on the mouthpiece to turn it off. "Well, now, gents—shall we?"

A look of belated relief stretched across Liam's face. "Aye."

"We go hide," said the ape anxiously, pointing up at the fire escapes and the dark, open windows of the tenement blocks.

"No!" said Sal. "No—if you run from them, if you hide in those buildings, they'll come after you! They'll kill you all!"

A mewling whimper of fear rippled through the creatures huddled around Samuel.

"What we do, Sam?" asked one of them. "What we do?"

Sal craned her neck to look out the end of the alleyway into the wide avenue. She could see dozens of red tunics hunkered down with guns trained on them. The soldiers had dragged several vehicles and carts aside to create a narrow passageway up and down North Charles Street. She turned to look down the far end of their alley. The soldiers and their dogs were settled there, patiently waiting. Above, the sky was still blocked by the air vessel, a searchlight occasionally blinking on and combing up and down the alley.

"I'll go out there," she said, pointing to the soldiers. "Let me talk to them! Let me explain you're not dangerous, that you haven't hurt anyone. That you'll come out peacefully."

"They kill us!" one of them gasped.

"You have to trust me!" she said. "I think they must've come to rescue me and Abraham. If we go out and show them we're not hurt, they'll—"

"*Sodjers* kill others. Me saw it!" said a eugenic from another group. "Wuz all hands up . . . and they does the bangs bangs!"

"If you try to run, I'm *sure* they'll shoot you down!" snapped Sal. She turned to Samuel. "Please, Sam—let me go out and talk to them!"

He scratched his chin, his fingers trembling. His eyes darted nervously from one end of the alley to the other. "You think sho? You can make it shafe?"

"You're not monsters . . . you're not dangerous. I can tell them that."

He pressed his ragged lips together. "You tell 'em, then. Tell 'em we're not bad. We didn't hurt anyone."

She nodded. "I will."

Samuel smiled. "I trust."

"Okay," Sal smiled. She got to her feet.

"A moment, young lady!" said Lincoln. He tore the bottom half of the sleeve off his dirty shirt. "A white flag . . . well, truth be told, it's brown, but they shall understand it as a flag of truce," he said, tying it around a strip of wood. "Allow me." He got up and walked cautiously to the mouth of the avenue. "COMING OUT!" he bellowed loudly. "PLEASE DO NOT SHOOT YOUR GUNS!" He waved his makeshift flag up and down several times to be sure it was seen.

"I AM STEPPING OUT!" Lincoln's voice boomed again, and then slowly he emerged into the morning sunlight streaming down the broad avenue, both arms raised. "I am Abraham Lincoln! I bear no arms!"

"Step out into the road, if you don't mind, sir, so we can see you nice and clear!"

"I have a girl with me! She wishes to parley!"

There was no response to that. Lincoln turned slowly and nodded at Sal to step out beside him. She emerged into the sun, shading her eyes with her raised hands. "Please! Don't shoot!" she called out.

"Stand beside the gentleman," a voice replied. "There's a good girl!"

She did as she was told. "There are some eugenic creatures with us in the alley! They also want to come out and join us peacefully!"

There was no answer. The morning was still and silent except for the soft hum of idling motors up in the sky. From far away came an echoing crack of gunfire.

"Sal? . . . Is that you?"

Chapter 59

2001, Dead City

The voice came from farther up the avenue. She couldn't see anything with the glare of the sun in her eyes, but she recognized the voice. "Liam?"

"Aye! Jay-zus!" His voice echoed back down the avenue. She heard the slap of his feet on asphalt, and finally he emerged in front of the soldiers and stood before her. "Well, look at you . . ." He checked her over. "Look a state, so you do."

She felt a rush of relief so intense her legs felt unsteady beneath her. She noted the bandage on his head. "You got hurt?"

"Knocked out, Sal. Stupid, I should've ducked. That's why I—"

"So, this is your *sister*, is it?" called out another voice, crisp and commanding.

Sister? She glanced up at him. He nodded slightly. She realized Liam must have told them that for a reason. Out of the bloom of sunlight, she saw a tall, wide shape emerging—unmistakably Bob. Beside him was another man, slim, wearing a white pith helmet.

"This fella here," said Liam as they approached, "is Captain McManus. It's really all thanks to him we found you, so."

Beneath the helmet's peak she saw the taut face of a young army officer. "Sister?" He frowned, confused. "But you're white and she's . . ."

"My *step*sister, so she is," cut in Liam. "Closest family I got, so help me."

McManus cocked his head and shrugged. "Well, then"—he extended a white-gloved hand—"really rather pleased we found you in one piece, young lady."

She reached out and shook it lightly. "Thank you."

"And you, sir?"

Lincoln shook his hand. "Abraham Lincoln."

"Jolly good to have retrieved you unharmed, Mr. Lincoln." McManus nodded politely. "Now; we've got a few of these runaways back in the alley, have we?"

Sal nodded. "Look—please don't hurt them!"

He frowned at her. "Don't hurt them?"

"Please! They're harmless!"

He tapped his finger pensively against his chin. "How many of them are there in that side street there?"

She shrugged. "A couple dozen, I think."

"These creatures, Captain—they did not kill any people. It was other creatures. Nor have they hurt us," said Lincoln.

"They treated us really well," added Sal. "Gave us food and water. They didn't hurt us."

"Really?" McManus looked bemused. "That's untypical behavior for these things. They're feral animals. You can't predict how they'll behave from one moment to the next."

"You sure they didn't hurt you?" said Liam. "I mean they were . . . well, they seemed pretty ferocious back in that farmhouse."

"They were scared, Liam! They're like frightened children."

"Frightened, perhaps, but still exceedingly dangerous. They need to be apprehended. And then we can decide what's to be done with them. I can't promise clemency if we discover any of them were directly involved in the recent killings—you understand that?"

Sal nodded. "Honestly, it wasn't any of them."

He glanced over her shoulder at the deserted brick tenement. "Do we need to flush them out of there as well?"

She shook her head. "No—I told them not to go inside and hide. That it would just make things worse."

"Very sensible advice."

"They're all waiting back in the alley. They just want to come out like we did. Just come out with their hands up."

He shrugged. "Good." He cupped his hands around his mouth. "YOU RUNAWAYS HIDING IN THE ALLEY . . . BEST YOU COME OUT NOW!"

Nothing emerged from the alleyway. For a moment Sal had a sinking feeling that fear had gotten the better of them and they had quietly slipped away into the tenement buildings on either side. But then they heard a soft, frightened whimper emerge from the gloom.

Too frightened to budge.

"Let me try," she said to McManus.

"If you wish."

"SAMUEL!" she called out. "It's okay! They're not going to hurt any of you! Do as he said, all of you! Just like I did—slowly, with your hands nice and high!"

Silence. Not a murmur. She was about to cup her mouth and try again, but then the first pale figure slowly emerged, blinking, into the sunlight.

Samuel. He was doing as she'd instructed: his thin, child's arms raised above his oversized head. From twenty yards away, she could see he was trembling. The ape emerged behind, towering above him, huge muscular arms raised.

"No shoot!" it cried in a deep voice.

Sal nodded encouragement. "That's right! No one's going to shoot you. Come on!"

The others began to emerge one by one. "That's it . . . come on. It's okay!"

Captain McManus studied the creatures as they stepped into the daylight. "By the shape of the heads I'd say these are mostly Watson-Rutherford class eugenics. Manufactured fifteen . . . some of them *twenty* years ago," he mused. "Hmm, all old stock, in very poor condition by the looks of them, largely malnourished."

He ordered some of his men over to herd the group together.

Liam stepped beside Sal. He put an arm around her shoulders and hugged her. "It's a relief to see you again," he whispered, squeezing her tight. "I let you down, Sal. God, I'm so sorry! When I came to . . . I was . . . you were already gone—"

She put a hand to his mouth. "I'm okay. Honest."

"But if—"

"We're both fine, Liam." She smiled. "Hungry—*very* hungry, but fine."

"Closer together, Corporal!" barked McManus. "Don't want any of these devils sneaking off!"

"Mr. Lincoln? You're not hurt?" asked Liam.

"As this young lady said, we are both fine, Mr. O'Connor. But I could eat a whole barn full of horses!"

"Liam?" Sal stepped back. "Heard anything yet from Maddy?"

He shook his head and lowered his voice. "Nothing."

McManus was busy issuing orders and appraising the condition of the eugenics. "Not a thing," Liam added. "She must have problems of her own to deal with."

"And those of you wearing clothes," called out McManus, "let's have those removed, if you please—you're *not* human!"

Sal turned to look up at Bob and smiled. "Good to see you too, coconut head."

"I am glad you are both unharmed," he replied.

She punched his flank gently. "You know, one or two of these genics have got even bigger muscles than you!"

He scowled. "Muscle-tissue *density*, not size, is the determining factor."

She tipped her head back at the creatures. "See the big one back there? Hmm? Jealous?"

He looked puzzled. "That is not a human emotion I have managed to generate files on yet."

"Not jealous? Yeah, right." She turned around to point out the ape and stopped dead. "Hold on! Hey! . . . What's going on?"

The others turned to see Captain McManus unsnapping the flap of his gun holster. The creatures were huddled tightly together in the middle of the avenue, their items of clothing—hats, scarves, aprons— discarded on the ground. The soldiers had formed a loose circle around them, a cautious dozen yards between them and the eugenics, rifles raised to their shoulders and aimed.

"Excuse me!" called out Sal. "What are you doing?"

McManus ignored her. "Mark your targets, men!"

"Jay-zus!" Liam jogged over toward him. Sal followed. "Captain McManus! Stop! You're not planning on *shooting* them, are you?"

He turned to Liam. "What? Yes, of course we are."

Sal saw Samuel at the front of the huddle, his eyes picking her out. His ragged lips moved. A whispered, unheard question.

Sal? You told us . . . ?

"Clearly they're not a danger to anyone now!" said Liam. "Can you not see? They have no weapons! Look at them, they're—"

"They are faulty, Mr. O'Connor. Faulty eugenic units. Which makes them unreliable. As I said, unpredictable."

Sal looked at him. "*Faulty?*"

"Quite faulty, yes." He nodded casually. "They can't be reconditioned. Honestly, they're in an appalling condition anyway. And we certainly can't leave these things running around on the loose." He turned back to his men. "Ready!"

"Stop!" she shrieked. "Please! Stop!" She grasped his gun hand.

"Excuse me! Would you mind letting go?"

"Look! Captain," said Liam, "I don't think this is right either! You can't just shoot them like this!"

Lincoln had joined them now. "My friends are quite correct, sir! These poor wretches should not be treated in this way!"

McManus looked at them all, bewildered by their concern. "You *do* understand these are not"—he gestured to the shivering huddle of ash-white eugenics—"that these are not—*people*? Good grief, they're not even animals. They're eugenic products! Blood and bone factory machines; that really is all they are."

"No!" cried Sal. "*Jahulla!* No! They're more than that! They . . . they . . . they're just like us! They're intelligent! They can talk and—"

"Of course they can talk. Some of them were designed that way. Good God, some of the smartest ones can almost be convincing. But listen, young lady," he said softly, almost sympathetically, "don't ever make the mistake of thinking one of these things can be your *friend*."

He twisted his hand out of her grasp. "Understand, they are products. That's all! Machines. More importantly, they are broken machines—and that makes them unreliable. Unpredictable." He raised his gun. "Dangerous."

"Please!" cried Sal. "Stop!" She saw Samuel, his scrawny arms folded in front of his face. McManus released the safety catch on his sidearm and filled his lungs with breath.

"TAKE AIM!"

The ape standing behind Samuel quickly moved a thick arm down and wrapped it around Samuel's small torso protectively, as if the bulk of his muscle would to be enough to shield him.

"FIRE!"

Chapter 60

2001, New York

Colonel Wainwright regarded his men, gathered together in the rough ground between their main command bunker and the trench facing out across the East River. Just short of three hundred men left in his regiment. The last time the 38th Virginia had been at its full strength of six hundred was many decades ago, long before his time.

It seemed the Southern command was adopting the Northern habit of letting regiments run down until their numbers hit a critical minimum and then completely disbanding them. He shook his head. Foolish; a regiment's fighting spirit lay in its history. The 38th had been raised back in 1861, had been commanded by General Lee, had fought under Pickett and charged the Union troops at Gettysburg. They'd taken Cemetery Ridge and sent Meade's men packing. That kind of a legacy bonded men, made them commit that little bit more to the esprit de corps.

They stood watching him now with uncertain faces. He knew rumors were already spreading among the men. They knew something serious had happened in the command bunker earlier today. They knew a dozen British soldiers had been arrested, disarmed, and locked up. Tongues were wagging with increasingly persistent talk that something big was imminent. The news the British officer had brought that a new offensive was about to be launched was hardly a surprise to

Wainwright. He, along with every man in the trenches, knew the British had been pulling in units from all over the empire. Talk of that and other half truths and whispered rumors had managed to filter its way along the entire length of the Sheridan line.

That young officer had merely confirmed the truth of it.

"The British are massing their resources for an offensive, men. And the spearhead of that offensive will be none other than this very sector."

The men stirred; a wave of unease rippled across them.

"The 38th Virginia will be in the first wave." The men shook their heads incredulously. They all knew what that meant. Appalling losses. As the landing boats spilled them out onto the far shore, the enemy would be pouring a withering wall of gunfire on them from their entrenched positions. Flanking fire on the right from the shattered end of the Williamsburg Bridge, on the left from the ruins of the factories. It would be a massacre.

He could see they were all making the same silent assessment. Wholesale slaughter.

But that isn't the worst of it, boys.

"The second wave . . . ," said Wainwright. He paused, waiting for the men's murmuring to die down. They needed to hear this, and hear this *clearly.*

"The second wave . . . will include eugenics."

His voice was drowned out by the roar of the men. Nearly three hundred voices raised in alarm, disbelief, anger, and, mostly, fear. He raised his arms to hush them. Despite the fact that these men trusted, obeyed, and respected their colonel, the noise continued unabated.

He pulled his sidearm out of its holster and fired a shot for the second time in as many days.

The men's voices quieted until all that could be heard was the uneasy shuffling of feet on gravel.

"I believe . . . ," he began. *Make this good, James; make this very good.* "For a long time . . . for many years now, I have believed that we are no longer fighting for a *Confederate* cause. That we have become no more than cannon-fodder; meat for the grinder, in service of *British interests*."

This time the men roared in unison. A roar of support for someone who had dared to say what every man privately thought. Dared to say a thing that would guarantee an undignified traitor's execution against a brick wall.

"There!" Wainwright stroked his chin. "It is said; and for that, I am now a dead man!"

Across the river, Devereau's men filled the bottom floor of the factory and half of the bomb-damaged one above, rows of booted legs dangling over the rough edge where the floor had collapsed long ago.

". . . they will not allow us to retreat," he continued. He and the men gathered here knew exactly what that meant. Directly behind the front line, units of the French Foreign Legion patrolled. Federal troops falling back without approval from High Command would be considered deserters and shot on sight.

Still, many of them must be considering that option, he mused. Far better to run and hope to evade the execution squads than stay and face those eugenic monsters from the South.

The factory echoed with the men's response, clamoring voices that bounced around the empty pockmarked walls of the building.

"I . . ." His voice was lost in the noise. "I do not believe . . ." He stopped. The men weren't going to hear him.

"SILENCE FOR THE COLONEL!" bellowed Sergeant Freeman.

The effect was almost instantaneous, if not complete. Freeman glared at the few men still muttering to each other. They hushed quickly under his withering gaze.

Devereau tried again. "I do not believe we should fight in this war anymore!"

Now the factory was silent.

"No; I do not believe in it anymore." He shook his head slowly. "I do not have faith in our generals, and I no longer have faith in the government of the Union of Northern American States."

A lone voice toward the back of the factory let out a whoop.

"Say it, Colonel!" shouted another.

"Our hometowns . . . our cities . . . our states . . . our *nation* is a nation under foreign occupation. Make no mistake, men, we are *already* a conquered people. Conquered not by the Anglo-Confederacy but by France and her allies: Austria, Prussia, Switzerland, and a dozen other nations that I'm sure many of you have never even heard of!"

He laughed a hollow laugh. "We weren't beaten on some battlefield. We didn't fight the good fight and lose . . . no. We did far worse: we *invited* our conquerors in!"

The factory echoed with angry voices. Devereau hushed them again by raising his hands.

"This is the time, men . . . I believe this is the real fight. Not brother against brother. Not American against American. But men of America against the British and . . ." Devereau paused. There was going to be no un-saying this. He glanced at Maddy, standing back and to one side of him, giving him the space on the small podium of ammo crates. She nodded slightly. She knew what he was going to say. ". . . and men of America against the French."

The men stirred uneasily. Whispered.

"We once shared a nation with those boys on the other side of the river. We could fight for that nation again . . ."

Chapter 61

2001, New York

Wainwright nodded. "That's what I said, gentlemen! A joining of forces! An uprising! Dammit!" He balled his fist and punched his own thigh angrily. "I'll call this exactly what it damn well is! . . . A *mutiny*!"

The word hung heavily in the open air; it bounced off the far wall of a collapsed building, ricocheting like a gunshot.

"Mutiny!" he said again. "And it starts here with the 38th Virginia."

The men roared support for that.

"More than that, boys . . . more than that, we're not going to stand alone. We shall be joined by others! The 11th Alabama to the north will join us and next to them, the 7th Maryland . . . and every other regiment along the Sheridan!"

The men roared jubilantly. Several forage caps catapulted into the air out of the huddled mass of shabby gray uniforms.

Wainwright smiled triumphantly, punching the air with his men. Of course, only he knew that was a lie. He'd made no contact with their fellow regiments up the line. Not yet, at least. He was counting on their support. Banking on it, in fact. Surely they were going to follow the example set by the 38th?

"But hear this, men!" He raised his gun again to fire, to quiet them down, but they hushed on their own. "Hear this, men! We will be supported by regiments on the far side of the East River . . . by federal troops from the Union of Northern American States!"

A mixed response from the men. Perhaps that announcement was a step too far for some of them to take. After all, for every man standing in front of him, the men across the river—the North—had always been The Enemy.

Wainwright realized he was committed now. He had to rally these men, make them see they needed each other, needed those boys in the 54th Massachusetts.

"They're men no different to you or I. Americans . . . no different from us. You know, we shared a dream once! A language! A heritage! A belief—in a land of the free!"

He saw some heads nodding. He heard voices raised in ones and twos.

"Once, a hundred forty years back, we foolishly chose separate destinies. But now, do you see? Do you see? We can share a common goal once more! We can have one American nation again . . . be masters of our own destiny!"

He stopped, and realized his words bouncing back at him from the far wall were doing so across a somber, heavy, *expectant* silence.

My God, maybe I misjudged the mood of my men.

"Who's with me?"

The ground between the command bunker and trench suddenly erupted with a deafening roar of whooping, ragged voices he was sure must have been heard by Devereau's men all the way on the far side of the river.

He fired his sidearm into the sky, again and again, until the magazine was empty and its click was lost in the deafening cacophony. All the while as he grinned and cheered, he desperately hoped he could make good on his promise that the Alabama boys of the 11th at the north end of Manhattan and the 7th Maryland beyond were already signed up to the idea of this rebellion and ready to stand together with them.

Whether they were or not, though, he realized there was no turning back now.

Devereau nodded. Smiled. The men's cheering voices reverberated through the ruins of the factory. He hadn't been certain his men were ready to take such a drastic step as this—to extend a hand of kinship across the river to the Confederates. He had only suspected, perhaps even hoped, that they might feel the same way as him.

But looking at them now, at their jubilant faces, every man roaring a huzzah of support, he thought: *We could actually do this.*

He turned to look at Maddy and Becks. Maddy was grinning and giving him a big thumbs-up.

Really . . . we could actually do this.

Perhaps this mutiny could achieve so much more than merely buy time for these two mysterious young time travelers to fix their machine. Devereau was still not entirely sure he could believe what they'd told him. Despite all the images and gadgets they'd shown him, it felt too unreal. Too much like a wish or a dream that would vanish the moment you reached out for it. Regardless, the wheel was turning. The die was cast. Time travel and alternative histories, whether all that really existed or not, here was a very real chance for everything to be changed.

Perhaps this rebellion might truly spread along the entire length of the front line like a virus: tens—no, *hundreds* of thousands of soldiers, North and South, turning around and confronting their foreign puppet masters. Even if Miss Carter's assurance that she could rewrite this unhappy history came to nothing, the mutiny by itself might just bring this eternal war to an end.

Devereau found himself joining in. A cry roared from his throat in unison with his men. The noise filled his ears, made them ring. And what a wonderful, deafening, roaring noise it was; it sounded like a cascade of water, a dam crumbling beneath the weight of millions of tons, pure energy unleashed. A runaway train approaching . . . a storm front descending. It sounded like walls tumbling, liberty bells chiming, government buildings being stormed.

It sounded like a revolution.

It sounded like hope.

Chapter 62

2001, New York

"Ma'am, you're a lady! My men are perfectly capable of attacking and taking that communications bunker."

"Negative," cut in Becks. "The communications bunker will contain sensitive equipment that could be damaged by a conventional assault. We cannot allow that risk. I suggest an alternate strategy."

Wainwright was a bit taken aback by the young lady's forthright manner.

"What, then?"

"How many British troops garrison the structure?" she asked.

Wainwright shrugged. "Usually two sections: twenty or thirty men, no more."

Becks turned to Maddy. "That is acceptable."

The pair of them had just crossed the river on Devereau's launch. Off the back of the boat, a couple of Northern soldiers had been unspooling a big roll of insulated communications cable, and, as they stood now just outside Wainwright's command bunker, communications officers from each side were debating how best to feed the cable inside and wire it up to create a direct line between the colonels. As Maddy had been quick to say, their uprising was going to live or die on the strength of how effectively the two of them communicated.

"You think you can take it on your own?" asked Maddy.

"Affirmative. I calculate a higher probability of success without significant equipment damage than"—she cast a glance at the half-strength company of soldiers Wainwright had assembled for the job— "than these—"

Maddy waved her silent before she blurted anything that might sound rude.

"Becks is very *special*," said Maddy quickly. "She's not just a pretty face."

Wainwright frowned. "Ma'am, I appreciate that you come from a very different time to ours, but the arithmetic of the situation is still the same: twenty-four armed and well-trained British soldiers are in there, and you expect one young lady to—"

"Becks is a combat unit."

Wainwright looked at her, frowning, stroking his chin. "A what?"

"She's a genetically engineered human with a silicon-wafer processor for a brain. She's extremely tough, extremely strong, and extremely fast. In short, she's a bit of a killing machine."

The colonel eyed her up and down. "Are you telling me this young lady is not—"

"Not human." Maddy shrugged. "Not really."

His eyes suddenly widened. "My God!" he gasped. "Do you mean to say she's a . . . a *eugenic*?"

Maddy shook her head. "I'm not really sure what those are, but I guess the best way to think of her is as an organic robot."

"'Robot'? I have not heard that word. What do you mean, ma'am?"

"Robot—like, say, like a machine."

"Machine!" He looked at her again. "But she is not constructed of metal and wires!"

"No . . . no, she isn't," Maddy shrugged. "But she might as well be."

Wainwright's eyes narrowed suspiciously. "You are not making sense, ma'am."

"Look—we're wasting time here," said Maddy. "We need the communications hub, and we need it *intact*. Trust me." She smiled. "Becks can handle that."

"I will need guns," said Becks casually.

"Of course you do," replied Maddy, patting her shoulder. "And I'm sure Colonel Wainwright here will give you all the guns you'll need. Won't you, Colonel?"

Wainwright looked at his men standing in several rows across the rubble-strewn assembly area. "You say . . . she *alone* can do this?"

"Yup. Look, if she can punch out a dinosaur, I think she can manage a few soldiers."

Wainwright stared at her for a moment. "Excuse me? Ma'am, I must have misheard you. I thought you just said—"

"Your men, colonel," cut in Becks, "could provide useful backup. A perimeter should be established around the bunker to ensure no additional British troops are able to reinforce the garrison. What occurs *inside* the perimeter and inside the bunker"—she smiled coolly—"is best left to me."

Maddy nodded. "Trust me. She's right!"

Wainwright studied them both, not quite sure what to make of them. For sure, they were from some other world—their manner, their dress, the words they used—but this one girl taking a bunker on her own?

"You look unconvinced, colonel," said Maddy.

He looked over her shoulder at his men waiting patiently just out of earshot. "My men, myself—we have signed our death warrants. As of this moment, we are all dead men walking, unless, as my friend, Colonel Devereau, assures me, you truly have this machine that can replace our world with a better one." He cocked a thick eyebrow. "This is something I have to take on trust, since I have not seen this device. Nor, for that matter, has Colonel Devereau witnessed it working."

"It works," said Maddy. "Otherwise Becks and I wouldn't be standing here."

He shrugged. "My point, ma'am, is that I have entrusted the lives of my men to the truth of your story. And now you ask that I trust that this young woman can make a successful assault on a defended position *entirely on her own?*"

"Affirmative," said Becks.

"Look," said Maddy, "we don't want to trash this place, right? So an extended gunfight is probably not a good thing. Becks is the alternative; you have to trust me. And look, if she fails"—Maddy shrugged a shoulder casually—"then you send your boys in. How about that?"

Wainwright turned to Becks. "You believe you can do this on your own?"

Becks trained her cool gray eyes on the Confederate colonel. "We should proceed directly. We are wasting valuable time."

Chapter 63

2001, New York

Private Sutter stared across the rubble from his guard position, a short section of trench leading down four steps to the entrance to Defense Structure 76—the official name for the communications bunker. He and the other men on garrison duty were not officially supposed to know it was a radio-signal hub for this section of the front line. Which was stupid, seeing as how the dish and antenna array were completely visible far above them, perched on the partially caved-in roof of the tall building beside the bunker. A twisted trunk of wires snaked down the open front of the building, from exposed floor to exposed floor, all the way down to the ground and into the bunker.

No, they weren't supposed to know what this place was, and it was drilled into them to refer to it only as Defense Structure 76. Should he ever be captured and interrogated by the enemy, Defense Structure 76 could mean anything: a turret, a machine-gun emplacement, an artillery station.

Sutter shook his head. Not that those useless peasants in blue across the river were ever going to do much more than shake in their boots and hunker down in their entrenched positions like cockroaches hiding in a dirty kitchen.

And perhaps they were right to be afraid, Private Sutter mused. He'd heard from Lance Corporal Davies, who'd heard whispers from someone working in regimental equipment procurement, that "something big" was most definitely afoot. An offensive of some kind? Had to be.

All sorts of rumors were beginning to surface, and the men in his platoon were itching for a fight to get themselves sent into. Pretending to be security guards for a small concrete box that did little more than broadcast propaganda messages across this part of the line . . . well, that wasn't the kind of soldiering Sutter had signed up for.

He leaned against the sandbags, bored, gazing down a track of cleared rubble—a track just about wide enough for a single vehicle and flanked on either side by banks of brick and debris and dust.

It had been an important road once. On the corner of the building beside him, he could make out a faded sign spotted with rust: 7TH AVENUE. Used to be one of New York's main streets, he recalled someone telling him.

Doesn't look like much now.

Through the open door of the bunker he could hear the muted clank of a kettle going on the stove, the click and clatter of dominoes being dealt, the laugh of someone telling a dirty joke they'd probably all heard a dozen times or more.

He sighed. Bored senseless and missing afternoon tea as well. Marvelous. He was halfway through wondering whether one of the boys might actually think to bring him a mug of tea when he saw someone walking down the cleared track ahead.

A lone figure, it seemed. Yes. Just one—and, a little closer now, he could see it was a woman.

A woman? Private Sutter hadn't seen a woman since he and the men had replaced the last poor bunch of bored-stupid guards three months ago. She was walking purposefully toward him.

Sutter grinned; a little female company. That'd be nice for a change.

He picked up his white helmet and put it on, tightened the strap beneath his chin, and then took a step up the ladder and out of the trench so that he could be seen more clearly.

"Halt!" he called to the woman, his rifle in his hands but aimed at the ground. She was hardly a threat, after all.

The woman kept walking toward him, oblivious to his challenge. Closer now, he could see she was wearing a Confederate-gray officer's cape. More than that, he could see she was beautiful—the face of an angel, pale and smooth, long dark hair cascading down her shoulders.

"Miss!" he called out again, and then, almost apologetically: "I'm going to have to ask you to stop where you are!"

Her stride remained unbroken, and now she was off the track and clambering up the bank of rubble toward him.

"Miss! Please!" He found himself reluctantly raising his carbine. "I need you to stop right where you are, love!"

Closer now, only a dozen yards away, climbing steadily up skittering rubble toward him. She was smiling.

Sutter wondered whether this was a setup. Or perhaps a test. He knew this area of the line was being inspected for battle-readiness. If so, he'd already let this young lady get far too close. He was going to get a sharp rebuke if this was indeed a test.

"Halt or I shall fire!" he challenged, angry with himself.

This time she did finally stop. Another few yards uphill, four or five more strides, and she'd have been right beside him.

"Identify yourself!" Sutter barked.

Her smile widened. "My name is Becks."

Her cape flapped. He thought a breeze had caught it, lifted it. It was only as something glinted in the air between them that he understood it was the movement of her arms that had stirred the cape.

Sutter felt a punch in his throat that left him winded, gasping for air. He dropped the rifle, his hands reaching up to determine why his open mouth didn't seem to be letting in a breath. Then he felt something odd sticking out. He looked down to see the hilt of a bayonet protruding from beneath his chin.

Right, I see . . . His foggy mind finally understood that he had a knife lodged in his throat.

He found himself sliding forward, light-headed, and slumping onto the sandbag in front of him. He looked up at the woman as she stepped carefully over him. She really was very beautiful. She dropped down into the trench beside him and yanked the protruding blade from his throat.

Sutter gushed dark blood all over the sandbag.

Beautiful. She really is. Like an angel. His mouth flapped open, blood spilling over his lips and down his chin as he tried to ask her if that's what she was.

She smiled at him. "Please die quietly now," she said in an almost motherly way as she covered his mouth with her hand.

Chapter 64

2001, HMS Defiant

All she could see, staring up at the bunk above her, *all* she could see, were fleeting images of the bodies, large and small, lined up head to toe at the side of the street. Just like bags of garbage. Sal realized she couldn't really find a word to describe how she felt right now. Empty? Hollow?

Is this shock *I'm feeling? Am I in a state of shock?*

The bunk creaked as Lincoln stirred on the mattress above. One booted foot hung over the side; he was far too long in the leg for these cramped bunks. She could hear the gentle thrum of far-off engines vibrating through the carrier's hull, the quiet murmur of men along a passageway. The faint clang of pots and pans in a galley.

About thirty-six hours . . . That's all she remembered Liam saying as she and Lincoln were taken aboard the carrier for an army doctor to quickly inspect them.

About thirty-six hours; he'd said something about the carrier picking up troops, and then heading north, and they were getting a lift part of the way . . . and then she was here, stretched out on this bunk in the vessel's sickbay, and she suddenly realized how completely exhausted she felt. As if the mattress beneath her had somehow drained her of life; sucked the very blood from her veins to leave a withered husk lying on top of it.

She saw their bodies: glassy eyed, dead animal-human faces gazing up at the blue sky.

Samuel, his small ragged mouth hanging open, frozen in an uneven "O" of terror.

She watched them being tossed onto the back of a vehicle like so many sacks of oatmeal. She heard one of the men say the bodies were to be "processed" and fed to the huffaloes. Then she saw some other creatures, new types of eugenics: large, shaggy bull-like animals with vaguely horselike heads and slender hindquarters, and doglike creatures with heads that reminded her of baboons. Both types seemed to have the dull eyes of dim-witted beasts. Faces that lacked emotion or expression.

Not like Samuel and his fellow runaways. New breeds—less intelligent, less inquisitive, less likely to question their lot.

Controllable.

She closed her eyes reluctantly, too tired to keep them open, but knowing that against the smooth, dark canvas of her eyelids she was going to see Samuel's blood-spattered face once again.

"Several stops, actually," said Captain McManus. "We're collecting the rest of the regiment."

"The rest?" Liam frowned. "There's *more* of you on this . . . ship?"

"Eight hundred thirty-six, if my memory serves me. Six hundred twenty-seven men and officers of the regiment. Twenty-four hunter-seekers and fifty huffaloes; and, of course, the carrier's crew and support personnel—one hundred twenty-three in total." He sipped his tea. "But we have three companies of men spread out across the Virginia countryside on various maneuvers—patrols, peacekeeping." He smiled.

Peacekeeping?

The term didn't sit well with what Liam had witnessed earlier this morning.

"When we've got them all aboard, we'll head north and set down outside New Wellington, New Jersey. It's at the mouth of lower New York Bay," said Captain McManus. "There's a carrier dock there. We'll be stopping to resupply the regiment and refuel the carrier before heading north again. You and your friends can get off there if you wish."

Liam nodded. He'd noticed there was a buzz of activity aboard the ship: junior officers scurrying to and fro with clipboards under their arms. "Is there something happening?"

McManus looked up from his teacup. The officers' mess was small, little more than a space for three bench tables with stools to either side. The walls were decorated with regimental trophies and grainy sepia photographs of groups of smiling young men in formal dress uniforms. Overhead, a glass chandelier swung gently from the low ceiling, tinkling softly from the vibration of the carrier's engines. They had the place to themselves.

"A little situation appears to be developing up north that needs to be dealt with." McManus shrugged. "Nothing my men can't handle." It was obvious to Liam the officer wasn't going to give him any more than that.

Liam stirred a teaspoon in his cup absently, while Bob looked down at his tea, studying a pattern of leaves floating on the surface.

"My ordering the disposal of those eugenics . . . ," said McManus. "That's troubling you, isn't it?"

"To be honest . . . yes." Liam picked up a hardtack biscuit from a plate between them and turned it over and over. Not really hungry. Not really sure why he'd picked it up. Something for his hands to do. "Yes, it is."

"They were older genics. Ones designed and grown a while back. Some of them were twenty, even thirty years old. They were unreliable, Liam. Dangerous." He sighed. "Back in the 1970s, they produced tens of thousands of them for all sorts of different roles." McManus shook his head. "Good grief, even as household workers—cooks, butlers, would you believe? And for those sorts of tasks they needed to be intelligent enough." He sipped his tea. "We've learned a lot about eugenology since then. How it's far easier to design the shape and musculature of a creature than it is to design how it will behave, what it will think. These days we know better. The eugenics are crafted with far simpler minds." McManus shook his head. "It was madness, looking back now with hindsight, *madness* to have created eugenics intelligent enough to, for example, read and write. To hope we could grow creatures who would be our engineers, technicians, doctors . . . and assume they could be controlled like pets."

"Those creatures . . . ?" Liam looked up at him. "Are you saying those creatures were smart enough to read and write?"

McManus shrugged. "Most of them were the old-class manual laborers. More intelligent than the heavy-lifter genics we produce now, but not by much."

He studied Liam's troubled frown. "Look, Liam . . . I think you're making the mistake of thinking of these creatures as some form of *natural life*. They are not. They are organic products, bone and muscle machines—nothing more. And when a machine starts to be unreliable, then it is time for it to be dismantled. Otherwise, people get hurt."

Bob muttered. Something was going through his head. Liam glanced across the table at him. He looked troubled as well. Liam wondered whether his support unit felt some sort of kinship with the eugenics. After all, from what he could guess, they'd sprung from the same science.

"They were machines that had gone bad. Very dangerous." He leaned forward across the small table. "I shall be honest with you, Liam. I wasn't quite sure whether we would find your stepsister and friend in one piece. They are really very lucky to be alive."

"I s'pose."

"Lord knows how many more of those things are still out there. Most of the old-generation genics have been rounded up and processed, but I think there are still a few hundred scattered among the Confederate states: runaways living in derelict dwellings, or running wild in woods and mountains. It is a problem that needs to be addressed; and one day, I suppose, we shall have to track down the last of them. But it's not something we can do right now."

"Why not?"

McManus looked like he was going to ignore Liam's question, but then spoke. "Let's just say the British army is being kept very busy at the moment." He changed the subject. "You and the others, what are your plans once we have dropped you off? A return to the safety of Ireland, may I suggest?"

Liam shrugged. "We *were* going to visit New York—"

"You know, it really is as if you have arrived from another world entirely." McManus studied him intently. "Did you really not know that New York has been a war zone for nearly seventy years?"

Liam nodded. "Huh? Yes, of course. Maybe me an' Bob and the others'll go explore the west instead."

McManus nodded. "It would be a much safer excursion for you. I believe it is still an unspoiled wilderness if you head to the far western mountain states like New Wessex and New Albany. I have heard from White Bear that there are still tribes of Indians living in that wilderness."

"Eight hundred twenty-four," said Bob.

The other two looked at him.

"Huh?"

"Eight hundred twenty-four personnel," said Bob. "You have itemized that number of personnel, but initially you said there was a total of eight hundred thirty-six personnel. That leaves twelve unaccounted for."

McManus made a face. "Ah, well, I am no mathematician . . ."

A klaxon sounded softly.

McManus looked up. "We shall be descending shortly for a pickup. If you'll excuse me?"

Chapter 65

2001, New York

"Well? Can we use it?"

Becks crouched beside the antenna array, a motorized rotating platform two foot in diameter topped with a dozen aerials like bristles from a hairbrush, and above them, a flared, cone-shaped dish of fine aluminium mesh.

Maddy shivered as a fresh breeze whipped across the rooftop. From where they stood on top of one of the tallest buildings still standing, she could make out most of the shattered remains of New York. A scarred landscape of jagged, broken buildings like the stumps of rotting teeth. A panorama of crumbling concrete gray with a dash of green here and there where nature had decided to get an early start on reclaiming the land for itself.

Down below, following the twisted trunk of cables over the lip of the roof, was the familiar outline of Times Square—although she'd discovered from Devereau that it had been renamed Place du Libertaire the last time the French-run North had held the city this side of the East River. She felt dizzy looking down. She stepped back from the edge and turned to Becks, who was quietly studying the antenna array. "So? What do you think?"

The support unit nodded thoughtfully. "The dish can be used to project tachyon particles. The antenna platform may also be useful."

"Hmmm." Maddy pushed her glasses up. "I guess I can figure out how to hook up the platform to our computer system. It's just an electric motor. Yeah, we should just take the whole thing."

"Affirmative."

She left Becks inspecting the bottom of the platform and crossed the rooftop toward where Wainwright stood with a couple of his men.

"We *can* make use of it," she said. "We just need to get it down in one piece."

Wainwright nodded. "Good. I shall have my men help your . . . uh . . . your . . ." His gaze wandered over her shoulder to the crouching form of Becks. His voice trailed to nothing.

Maddy had the distinct impression he was going to say *your eugenic*.

"My men are telling me she killed every last man inside. The entire garrison."

Maddy nodded. She'd arrived in time to see the last of the bodies being carried out of the bunker and Becks standing outside the entrance, her pale face splashed with ribbons and dots of drying blood and a friendly *Did I do okay?* smile stretched across her lips.

It had actually made her shudder.

"Not a single prisoner taken," said Wainwright quietly. "What on earth is she?"

"Her mission priority was capturing the antenna intact. Not, I'm afraid, to take any prisoners."

She decided it would be too difficult to explain to Wainwright that the lives she'd just taken with her bare hands were some that never should have been lived anyway. The bloody corpses lying outside the bunker were men who would be living very different lives once history had been corrected.

But her imagination flashed images of the short and brutal struggle that must have gone on inside. It made her shiver at the thought that she, Sal, and Liam shared the archway with two creatures, Bob and Becks, who could tear the three of them to ragged shreds if the notion popped into their heads—if a line of computer code decided it was a "mission priority."

"To answer your question, Colonel . . . you ask what is she?" She turned to look at Becks, now lying on her back to inspect the space beneath the array platform disconnect the power cables.

"She's a killing machine; a combat unit from the future, I suppose. You could think of her as an advanced type of one of your eugenics."

"Good God!" His eyes widened. "I would prefer *not* to think of her . . . *it* . . . as that," he muttered.

"Becks is a *she*, not an *it*. You'd hurt her feelings if she heard you say that." She forced a chuckle. The laugh died in her throat.

"And you, Miss Carter? What about you?" His eyes narrowed. "Are you some artificial construct? Some sort of superwarrior in disguise? A eugenic?"

"Once upon a time I was a computer-game programmer. Someone good at sitting down and tapping away at a keyboard. That's me." She shrugged. "I'm no one special, I'm afraid."

A breeze tugged at them, sending dust devils skipping across the rooftop.

"Have you sent your message, Colonel?"

Wainwright nodded. He'd broadcast a rallying call to the regiments up the line before they dismantled the array. They could only hope his stirring speech would do its job and other Confederate troops farther along would signal their intent to join the mutiny. But there had been nothing so far.

"We shall hear from them soon." He smiled. "I'm sure."

"Then we should get started dismantling this thing," said Maddy. She looked up at the blue sky, then southwest toward the horizon, where a distant bank of clouds promised them an overcast day later on. "Who knows how long we've got until the British come for us."

Wainwright followed her gaze. "Indeed."

Chapter 66

2001, New Wellington

Liam and the others stood on the gun deck just in front of the forward turret: a dome of plated metal ten feet high and two dozen in diameter, lined with knuckle-sized rivets. Two long artillery barrels protruded from gunnery slits, for the moment covered with a protective tarp.

They watched as the carrier slowly descended toward New Wellington through a ghostly sky of thinly combed clouds. To their left, the east coast of America; to the right, the surly gray Atlantic Ocean. Ahead of them he could see a grid-like blanket spread beneath the prow of the carrier: roads, streets, avenues cutting the city into a chessboard of housing, industrial, and business districts.

"Look," said Liam, pointing toward the coast.

The misty sky above New Wellington was haunted by the spectral silhouettes of a dozen elongated sky ships, several of them similar in profile to the carrier on which they were standing.

"I see . . . eleven," said Lincoln. "No—twelve, if I'm not mistaken."

Sal squinted as she spotted faint dark slivers farther out above the sea. "And more coming in." She looked at the other two. "Do you think every one of them is full of soldiers?"

"I guess those are other British regiments." Liam tugged at his borrowed peacoat and turned up the collar against the fresh wind. "Something big is underway, that's for sure."

Closer to them, close enough to see the detailing of decks and gun turrets and the large segmented central gas-ballast tanks, a carrier almost identical to theirs was settling into a dockside berth. With the echoing of a horn like a distant whale's song and a faint roar of compressed gas, it blasted the open ground beneath it—a space the size of at least two football fields laid end to end—with a blizzard of snow and nitrogen gas. It seemed to settle on its own cloud, a white cushion that slowly billowed outward and finally faded, revealing the acres of asphalt dusted with snow.

Liam could see four other similar landing strips, each one towered over by a pair of docking cranes hundreds of feet high. As they watched, the freshly landed ship was embraced fore and aft by the cranes, swinging around until they locked snugly onto the vessel, cradling it like a baby.

As the last of the nitrogen cloud cleared, the bottom of the ship's hull began to open and loading ramps emerged. They watched the peppercorn dots of tiny figures disembarking and slowly forming into orderly ranks on the landing strip.

Liam and Sal looked at each other, a wordless exchange that Liam knew meant she was thinking the same thing. *Yet another sight, another amazing sight, that was never meant to be.*

He leaned his elbows on the brass rail and looked out again at the vision, another moment in time that he knew he was never going to forget. Like the inland sea of Cretaceous Texas and that sweeping plain dotted with herds of dinosaurs; or the glistening wall of chain mail and armor of Richard the Lionheart's advancing army, a horizon of fluttering pennants and waving pikes, the sturdy frames of trebuchets in the distance. Moments etched into his memory as permanently as letters carved into marble.

He realized that, if by chance he died tomorrow, in his short life he'd already seen more things—heard, tasted, smelled, *experienced* more of history—than any person, any historian could ever dream of.

"Now that's something, eh, Sal?"

She nodded, silently picking out her own details to remember.

Lincoln stared in turn, wide eyed and ashen faced. "And this? This is but a *portion* of the might of the British army?" he said.

Liam nodded. "Aye. More where this lot came from, I'd say."

"God . . ." His courtroom bawl was robbed of its power, left little more than a fluttering whisper. "God's teeth."

Six hours after arriving over New Wellington, after waiting their turn in a line of leviathans floating in the sky—enormous, dark, and brooding like anvil clouds—their carrier finally landed amid its own blizzard of snow, and the first companies of the Black Watch disembarked.

Captain McManus was busy, along with every other officer, organizing his companies on the landing pad. The men were going to need billeting in the camps around the docks for the duration of the layover, supplies had to be ordered and secured, shore-leave rotations needed to be arranged, damages needed to be repaired, and shortfalls requisitioned. A million and one things for him and every other junior officer to attend to. So his farewell was necessarily brief.

"I should return home to Ireland, if I were you, Liam O'Connor. There's much afoot—and it'll all be happening *north* of here."

Liam knew better than to question him further. McManus was already saying far too much. The young officer studied him and then Sal, who returned his gaze with a cold glare.

"I suspect you think of me as a cold-blooded murderer, perhaps?"

She said nothing.

He took her silence as agreement. "I have seen what these creatures can do. Not just the runaways, but our very own trained eugenics. If it were my choice, there would be none of these aberrations in this world.

Man has no business rewriting Nature's work." He tugged the chin strap of his helmet tight. "But there it is—the genie is out of the bottle. We are where we are."

He offered them a crisp salute and a warm smile. "I am just relieved you were both unharmed." He regarded them one after the other. "A rather strange 'family' you make, if I may say so."

He offered Liam his hand. "And you, sir . . . strangest of the lot. If I believed in such things, I would say you had dropped out of the sky from an entirely different century."

"Ah, well." Liam grinned. "I've always been a bit behind the times, so."

McManus let his hand go, tipped a nod at them all, and turned to head back to his men waiting patiently in the shadow of the carrier's hull. The time travelers watched the captain go, the afternoon thick with the noise of boots and harnesses, sergeants barking orders like trained Rottweilers, and the clank and clatter of supply wagons rolling down the ramps.

"What now?" said Sal.

"North," said Liam. He looked at the others. "New York. We've got to find a way back home, right? Unless we hear otherwise from Maddy, that is."

Bob nodded. "Affirmative."

"She's in trouble," said Sal. It was stating the obvious. "She needs our help."

Liam nodded. "We need to get there as quickly as we can." He glanced up at the sky; another half dozen carriers still hung there like storm clouds, waiting to descend and disgorge their troops. "Before this lot head north and flatten what's left of New York."

Chapter 67

2001, New York

Maddy shaded her eyes as she looked upward. Becks and a technician from Wainwright's regiment, Second Lieutenant Jefferson, were busy attaching the antenna array's motorized platform to the top of their archway's mound of brick. It needed to be securely fixed, not wobbling in any way. It would have been steadier on the ground beside their crumbling home, but then it would have been too low, obscured by the crater's lip.

Jefferson had suggested mounting it on the top of the overshadowing stump of the Williamsburg Bridge support. But that would have meant running out a lot of cable—cable that could easily be snagged and severed by the dense nest of twisted, sharp-edged metal above them. And more than that, Maddy felt insecure not having the array right beside them.

From the bottom of the platform a trunk of cables looped down the side of the bricks, through a hole in the roof, and down into the back room. There it snaked across the grit-covered floor and through the sliding door into the main archway, past the computer desk, over the small crater in the floor to the metal rack holding the displacement machine.

Maddy had spent most of yesterday spitting curses as she fiddled around with the components in the back of the rack; she suspected it had taken aback Sergeant Freeman, who had been looking on curiously.

Half guessing, half consulting the schematics diagram she'd made a while back, she hooked up the data and power cables through the computer system so computer-Bob could control and fine-tune the orientation of the dish. Of course, computer-Bob wasn't aware of any of that just yet. The networked computers were offline right now, and would remain so until they got the generator turning over—yet another job on the To Do list.

Their generator was absolutely kaput. More precisely, the motor was. The fuel tank had ruptured when a part of the ceiling collapsed; all they had left was the dregs sitting in the bottom of the tank. The rest had spilled out and filled the back room with the stink of diesel.

However, the alternator and the voltage regulator were undamaged, and only required an alternative source of mechanical input—another motor—to generate a usable electrical charge. The answer to that problem was straightforward in theory, if not in practice. They needed to jury-rig a motorized vehicle of some sort.

Devereau's regiment, being infantry, didn't have a single truck, jeep, or tank to offer. The only two possibilities the colonel could offer to Maddy were to cannibalize their solitary launch for its feeble outboard engine, or to try to disassemble and relocate the army's aging generator, buried deep in their defense bunkers.

Wainwright had something more promising to offer: one of their older tanks, slowly rusting in the compound between their bunkers. "One of the Mark IV Georgian models," he'd said, and Devereau seemed to know what he was talking about.

"Southern Chicken Friers."

"Chicken friers?" Maddy looked at them both.

Wainwright nodded. "Thin armor plating and bad design. Heat transferred from the engine through the whole vehicle makes it like sitting in an oven."

"But also, the fuel tank is poorly positioned and exposed," added Devereau. "One could aim gunfire to damage the fuel tank, knowing the fuel would flood down into the vehicle, and . . ."

"Indeed." Wainwright nodded. "Not called the 'frier' for nothing."

As she watched, Becks and Jefferson finished securing the mounting. On the far side of the East River a swarm of men in blue and gray were already busy with welding torches, working industriously on the makeshift raft that was going to float the old Mark IV tank across to them.

Colonel Devereau was busy overseeing the repairing of the abandoned trench system. Both he and Wainwright had agreed that to defend the far side of the river, the Confederate side, would be a pointless exercise, as the defenses were all aimed the wrong way: northward toward the river. The British would be arriving from the south. So it was to be here, on this side, that both regiments were going to hold the ground together.

The abandoned trenches held a commanding position over the flattened ruins that sloped gently down to the river. If the British really were planning an amphibious assault, this would be where it would land. A kill zone, if they could make proper use of the trenches.

Maddy had asked why they'd do that—attempt an amphibious landing. Why didn't they just parachute their men down behind the line from one of those big sky-navy ships?

She got two blank stares.

"Para-shoot?" Devereau frowned. "What the devil is that?"

"Never mind."

He followed her gaze toward the sparks on the far side of the river. "A heartening sight, is it not? Our men working alongside each other."

"Yes. I just hope we have enough time."

Devereau nodded. A warrant for his own arrest had arrived this morning, delivered by an officer wearing the dark blue, almost black, uniform of the Union Intelligence Division, accompanied by a patrol of Foreign Legionnaires. Word had inevitably found its way up his chain of command already.

He'd been hoping to hear news that the men of the 5th Maine farther up toward the east end of the Sheridan-Saint Germain line were going to be the first to follow suit and join them. But so far he'd heard nothing.

He looked to his right, down along the sweeping curve of the river. Among the jagged, far-off spikes of ruined buildings, he imagined his fellow Northern officers must be curiously watching the flurry of activity over here, wondering how long "Devereau's Foolish Mutiny" was going to last.

It would last a great deal longer if you had the guts to make a stand alongside us!

Matters were no better for Colonel Wainwright. A warrant had arrived from Richmond for his arrest on a charge of mutiny.

He and Wainwright had spoken briefly this morning on their temporary phone line. The news he'd been hoping for from that side of the river hadn't materialized. Wainwright's broadcast inviting the other Confederate regiments up the line to join them had either not been received, or, as he suspected, they lacked the will or the courage to join their fellows.

The last detachment of men from the 38th was due to cross the river later today and dig in on this side. Just under six hundred men and officers in all. Not much with which to withstand the might of the British army, and quite possibly a regiment or two of the elite French Foreign Legion too.

He suspected discreet meetings had already occurred between generals at the very top of both sides, agreements made to temporarily work together to quickly crush this little mutiny.

He looked at the lines of trenches being dug deeper and reinforced with sandbags and wooden struts. They ran parallel to the river, extending from the support stump of the Williamsburg Bridge toward the cracked and grimy ruins of the Bryson Glue factories as Brooklyn followed the East River up and merged with Queens. Men would be positioned in the factories with perfect flaking-fire positions looking down on the shingle and the approach.

It was here, though, in this open space, these five hundred yards of bombed-out rubble and craters, flat ground that sloped down to the river—it was here, where there was space for dozens of landing craft to drop their ramps simultaneously, that they were going to have to hit them the hardest.

And it was dangerously close to the frail dome of bricks in which the supposed time machine was located.

Their first line of defense was "the borderline," a long, straight trench running from the bridge support to the glue factory. The second line was "the horseshoe," a hastily dug trench that followed the perimeter of the large bomb crater at the bottom of which the brick mound nestled.

Finally, if and when the horseshoe was overrun, there was "the fort." The entrance to the archway had been reinforced with a small nest of sandbags and support bars, and topped with a roof of more bags and shoveled dirt. It was a bunker in which three Gatling-gun teams would be stationed, firing out through gunnery slits.

Where we'll make our last stand . . . if it comes to that.

He buried that thought beneath a reassuring smile. "We shall hold this ground long enough for you to activate your machine and write us a brand-new history, Miss Carter. I am certain of that. This is a good piece of ground to defend."

Chapter 68

2001, New Wellington

New Wellington's streets were clogged with vehicles, both motorized and horse drawn, refugees all attempting to head south to avoid the coming fight. Word was already spreading. Right now, the port city's main street was a motionless logjam, a deafening turmoil of angry voices, snorting, unsettled horses, and rattling combustion engines.

The sidewalks on either side were filled with pedestrians carrying possessions on their shoulders and backs. Liam and the others found themselves standing in front of a hardware store, watching the tide of foot traffic traipsing past them.

"It's like *everyone's* leaving!" said Liam.

"What's going on?" asked Sal. "Did McManus tell you?" She spat his name out like bad-tasting phlegm.

"There's something going on in New York," said Liam. "He said something about a new offensive."

"More war, is it?" grumbled Lincoln. "Has this corrupted world not had enough of it already?"

"But if the fighting's going to happen up in New York, why is everyone here running away? This is far enough from the fight, isn't it?"

"Not really far enough," answered a gruff voice behind them.

They turned to see an old man in the store behind them.

He'd opened his door without their hearing. "You not heard the rumors, then?"

"Rumors?" Liam shrugged. "Aye—the British are attacking."

The old man waved his hand like that was old news. "That much *everyone* knows, boy. No, there's talk this time they gonna be fightin' with *experimentals* once again." He nodded at the people streaming past them. "News was in the morning papers. Some dockworkers down at them landing bays caught sight of a bunch of new-type tube-breeds."

Liam looked at Sal and the others, unsure whether the old man was referring to the hunter-seekers or the huffaloes.

"Stupid fools! They don't give half a cent about the things they unleash on us over here! Crazy-minded monsters bred to kill? It's only America, right?" He shook his head angrily. "Bad enough we got tube-breeds all over the country in every farm, every factory—*but crazy ones bred and trained just to kill?* It's no wonder it's got everyone a-jitter now. They're scared there's gonna be another Preston Peak!"

He nodded out at the congested street. "Twenty-four hours from now, this place is gonna be a ghost town. An' I guess I'll have to board up my store an' mebbe head south myself until they're sure they've gathered up all their monsters and got 'em back in their cages again. God knows I don't want to be the only fool in town if they gonna lose control of 'em all over again."

"Right," said Liam, nodding.

"Anyways . . ." The old man frowned. "You an' your friends comin' in to buy some stuff?"

"Ah, no, we were just . . . sort of getting out of the way of the—"

"Well, this ain't a darned hotel!" The man glanced at Bob's hulking form, hunched over to fit his bristly head beneath the awning on the store's porch. "You're blockin' me up from proper customers! You better scoot off my boards—that or buy somethin'!"

Liam sighed. "All right, all right, we're going."

He led the way down three steps onto the sidewalk and into the bustling crowd, moving against the flow. All manner of people—rich and poor, bowlers to flat caps, lace bonnets to threadbare shawls—a tide of anxious city people, all grumbling curses and muttering rebukes as Liam waded against the trudging tide.

An hour later they were standing on the side of a road heading northeast out of New Wellington, still choked with vehicles and carts heading south; they made painfully slow progress, but were moving at least.

"Seems like everyone north of here is leaving," said Liam.

He wondered why so many civilians would have bothered living so close to the front line anyway. After all, according to McManus the war was an ongoing struggle, a constant ebbing and flowing of the front line, which stretched westward across New York State, Pennsylvania, Ohio, and Illinois, with minor skirmishes here and there every summer that shifted the line half a mile one way, then the other.

But it was a stalemate war, wasn't it? A war people had grown used to living with. Grown used to it rumbling on quietly in the background like a thunderstorm passing by.

People manage; that's what they do.

Except, of course, not now. Not with rumors of a big push going around. Not with rumors of killer eugenics being deployed not too far away from them.

"It's silly," said Sal. "The eugenics weren't dangerous—not the ones that took us, anyway. Were they?" She looked up at Lincoln.

"Pitiful beings," he said. "If truth be told, they were quite sad creatures."

Liam couldn't help wondering what to make of the eugenics. Looking at the flood of people going past, he could understand their fear. Back in that farmhouse, the attack had seemed ferocious, truly terrifying at the time. And yet now he realized those creatures had just been a band of runaway workers, frightened for themselves, just doing their best to scavenge and survive.

But if they'd been a frightening sight, he couldn't begin to imagine what *military* eugenic creatures must be like. Although, he'd already met some, right? The hunter-seekers. They hadn't seemed so bad.

He shuddered at the thought of something.

There must be other types we've not yet seen.

"We should get going. The road looks like it's clearing up a bit. We should make better time now that we're out of town. How far is New York from here, Bob?"

"Information: one hundred eleven miles."

"Ahh, well, that's all right." Liam smiled. "That's not so far to go, then. Shall we?"

Chapter 69

2001, New York

"Oh my God!" cried Maddy. She turned to Becks, standing beside her in front of the computer desk. "It's actually working!"

She could see the softly glowing amber standby light of the surge protector. "We've got enough amplitude coming in!"

"Affirmative."

Maddy ducked down and punched the power switch of the nearest of the networked PCs beneath the desk. One of the monitors winked on. She switched on the next one and the next, until all nine computers were busy whirring, at different stages of booting up.

Maddy wanted both of the colonels to see this. Although she knew they more than half believed her story, it would do no harm for them to see this machinery stir to life. She trotted across the floor, skidding on loose grit and skipping over the thick coil of power cables running out through the raised shutter door. It snaked around the low entrance to the "fort" and turned left along a freshly dug trench for twenty yards before rising up over the rear trench wall and across several yards of wasteland toward the opened rear engine hatches of Wainwright's Mark IV tank. The engine casing, bulky and pitted with rust, shuddered unnervingly like a feral cat trapped in a hatbox. It was spewing a thick cloud of smoke from an exhaust pipe at the top of its box-shaped iron turret.

The tank's laboring engine was spinning a flywheel. Around the wheel was a cam-belt—a loop of thick leather—taken off the vehicle's driveshaft and leading to their battered and sorry-looking generator. They'd hauled it out earlier and set it up beside the tank. The belt was turning the generator's internal rotor and armature.

Down the slope toward the river she could see Wainwright and Devereau standing above the borderline. Devereau squatted down and talked to someone in the trench, while Wainwright smoked his pipe and looked out across the river.

"Hey! You two! Colonels!" she shouted above the rumble of the tank's bad-tempered engine.

They both looked her way, and she waved them over. "It's working! We got power!"

She waited for them to jog over, and then led them back down into the trench, following the cable past the fort and ducking inside the archway across the floor to where the row of computer monitors were all now showing the same desktop wallpaper she'd put on several days ago, an image of Homer Simpson.

"Good grief!" gasped Devereau, unsure what to make of the wall of grinning faces.

Maddy pulled out a seat and sat down at the desk. "Computer-Bob? You there?"

"This . . . this yellow face," said Wainwright, ". . . is the face of your computer?"

"Huh?" She looked at the monitors. "Oh, no, he's just a . . . a . . ." She wrinkled her nose. "Doesn't really matter."

A dialog box appeared on the monitor in front of her.

> Hello, Madelaine. It appears a significant malfunction has occurred.

He was seeing the wreckage of the archway behind her. That, or he was registering internal problems with one or more of the networked computers.

> I also detect unauthorized personnel in the archway.

"That's okay, Bob—that's okay. They have my authorization to be here."

> Affirmative.

Wainwright's jaw hung open. "You have a *machine* that can *talk* to you?"

"Oh, yeah—Bob, he's . . . well, *computer-Bob*. Not, of course, to be confused with *Bob*, who's a . . . well, sort of a guy-shaped computer and a copy of computer-Bob—and some of Becks, actually, who by the way is also a copy of computer-Bob . . ." She looked up at the colonels and realized she was losing them. "Just think of Becks and this computer system here as *family* . . . sort of."

"Family?" said Wainwright, looking at Devereau, not really any the wiser.

"Bob, we got hit by a time wave, a big one."

> This is apparent.

"The wave was caused by Lincoln being here in 2001 and not back where he should be."

> That is the most likely conclusion. What is Lincoln's location now?

"We do not have that information," said Becks.

> Hello, Becks.

"Hello, computer-Bob."

Maddy wrapped her knuckles impatiently on the desk. "Save the love-in for later, you two. We need to send them a message right now!"

"Their last known location," said Becks, "was the window opened near the FBI training academy in Quantico, Virginia. That was five days ago."

> Correct. I have those coordinates in my event log.

"They'll have been making their way to us," said Maddy. "How far is it?"

"Information: two hundred twenty-six miles."

"They should've made it back by now, then, right?" She pursed her lips. "Unless they decided to stay put and wait for me to open a window right where we dropped them off?"

> **This is an equally likely possibility.**

Maddy balled her fist and cursed. Both colonels exchanged a bemused look at her colorful choice of words.

"Hang on!" She held a finger up. "I can give them all the time they need—say, a whole month if that's what they need to—"

"We cannot hold the British for a whole—!"

Maddy shook her head. "Relax . . . relax. This is time displacement. We can open the portal up as soon as the machine's charged up enough, in about twelve hours' time. But I could set the time-stamp to open a space one month from now. You see, with time displacement, all time—past, present, and future—is effectively *now*, as long as you've got enough energy to reach it. Easy peasy."

A cursor flashed across the dialog box.

> **Negative.**

"What?"

> **Diagnostic on the displacement machine indicates the tertiary downstream phase analysis module has failed. We cannot at this time open a window in the future.**

She banged her fist on the desk. "Why is it always so freakin'. . . ? Arghhh!" She shook her head.

"Does this mean your machine cannot operate?" asked Devereau.

Maddy sighed. "No . . . no, it just means we have to wait this out in real-time." She shrugged. "Stupid me; I was hoping for the easy option."

She settled back in her chair. "All right . . . all right, plan B, then. We pick a place roughly halfway between New York and Quantico, and give them, what? Two days—no, three days; time enough to make sure they can get there."

"From now?" asked Devereau.

She nodded, then noticed the look of concern on both men's faces.

"We can hold on here that long, can't we?" Her eyes went from one to the other. "Right? I mean . . . you know, if they attacked, say, right now? Your men could hold this ground for three days?"

The officers' eyes met. It was Wainwright who broke the long silence. "It will depend on what force they throw at us; and, of course, how quickly they have decided to respond to news of this mutiny."

"And how well our men fight," added Devereau.

Wainwright nodded. "The officers in my regiment I know will fight to the death. As men of rank, we all would face firing squads if we were to surrender. The enlisted men? They would be sent to a British military prison."

Devereau nodded grimly. "A similar fate awaits our officers. But I think my men will fight well, because there can be no retreat if the British attack. The Legionnaires will be lined up behind us ready to shoot anyone caught retreating."

"So?" She was still waiting for an answer. "Three days, then?"

Wainwright stroked his chin. "To be certain . . . you can promise us this new history?"

"If I can pick them up and drop them back in 1831, yes."

And if Lincoln is still alive.

She suspected Bob and Liam were probably fine; so far they seemed to have been able to weather anything. And Sal would probably be fine with them looking after her. But Lincoln . . . the guy was a loose cannon. A big-mouth. A hothead. Anything could have happened to him over the last week.

"Then our men will give you your three days," said Wainwright. "What do you say, William?"

Devereau nodded. "This is a good defensive position."

Maddy turned back to face the webcam on the desk. "Okay, computer-Bob. Three days rendezvous from now; we just need to pick some place halfway between here and Quantico. Somewhere relatively quiet and peaceful, if possible."

> **Affirmative.**

"We got enough charge to send a broad-range signal?"

> **Affirmative. Information: my diagnostic has also picked up calibration errors on the transmission array.**

"Affirmative," said Becks. "A replacement component—a conventional radio communication dish—has been connected. I can run the recalibration with you, Bob."

"Well, you two take care of that now." Maddy turned to Wainwright and Devereau. "Either of you got any relatively up-to-date maps we can look at? We need to pick a place for our guys to get to."

Chapter 70

2001, New Wellington

Sparks danced up into the night sky from their campfire, one of several dozen they could see up and down the side of the roadway. Refugees heading south on foot, stopping at the side of the road for the night to rest, eat, and perhaps sleep.

They were cooking cobs of corn they'd plucked from a field earlier this evening over the fire. Somewhere on the other side of the road, someone was roasting coffee beans, and someone else was frying bacon.

"It's cooler tonight," said Liam.

Sal, snuggled beside him, nodded.

"You all right, Sal?" he said.

She nodded again, her eyes on the fire, glistening.

"I know," he started. "Look, I know what happened was hard—"

"Hard?" she whispered. "Hard" was a lazy, careless word to use for what they'd witnessed. "I . . . I keep seeing it, Liam. You know?" She looked up at him. "I see Samuel looking at me, looking right at me when they shot him. He was . . ." Her voice faded to nothing. Together they stared at the fire in silence, watching the cobs slowly blacken on the edge of the coals.

"I feel . . ." She chewed on a fingernail. "I feel strange. Like I'm . . . like I'm not who I used to be. Not the same Saleena I used to be."

Liam nodded. "We've both seen a lot, you and me."

"It's like my old life—my parents, my home, my school friends—that's all become someone else's life, not mine anymore. Do you know what I mean?"

"Aye," he said softly. "Me too."

"It feels like you, me, and Maddy have been together for years." Although she knew exactly how long it had been: one hundred fifty-five days—seventy-five bubble-time cycles, plus five days.

"For me it has," said Liam. "Six months in 1956; another six months in the twelfth century. And another in dinosaur times." He looked at her, quizzical. "You know what? I've lived a whole year longer than you since we were recruited."

"I know." She looked up at him, tilting her head to look at the lock of gray hair by his temple. "You do look older."

"Well, I'd be seventeen now, I suppose." Mock serious. "I went an' missed me birthday!"

She smiled and punched his arm lightly. "Happy birthday, then."

He reached out and prodded one of the charred cobs with a stick. Still too hard to eat yet. On the other side of the fire Lincoln was muttering something to Bob about his childhood, something to do with skinning hares.

"You're right, though," Liam said after a while.

"About what bit?"

"That we're different people now. You, me, and Maddy. I've seen things, done things, that I think have changed me."

"Like what?"

"Well . . . I killed a man, so I did."

"Really?"

He nodded. "The fight for Nottingham. Killed a soldier with me sword. He looked at me—was staring at me as I did it to him. Like . . . I don't know, Sal, it was like he wanted me to *know him*, in his final moment, like he wanted to make sure I remembered him forever." Liam shook his head. "And it worked. I see him every night in my dreams. That same fella. The same face."

"Do you ever dream of the moment when Foster recruited you?"

Liam closed his eyes. Not recently. Since Nottingham it had been this man over and over, haunting his sleep. "I used to."

"I do," she said. "Almost every night. I remember every little detail. I see it all every night like a holo-movie."

She'd told him once about how she'd been recruited. "The fire?" he asked.

Sal nodded. "Every morning I wake up and want to cry, because it's like I've just left my parents—my *mathaji*, my *baba*—all over again."

"I can barely remember my parents," he said. He tried to remember them and struggled to conjure their smiles, their frowns in his mind. Only one memory successfully gave him their faces, a fleeting recollection of holding in his hands a badly faded photograph of them in an old tin frame. He shook his head. How could that be the only decent enough memory he'd managed to hang on to?

"But there's this thing, Liam, this odd thing . . ."

He gave up fishing for another mental image of Ma and Da. They were gone. People from someone else's life now. "What? What odd thing?"

"My memory of Foster saving me from that burning tower. There's this moment, when the building finally begins to collapse. It's horrible." She shook her head and winced at the sensation of the floor collapsing beneath her feet, of falling . . . and the fire beneath, waiting for her to drop into it as if she was falling into hell itself.

"I'm falling, Liam—but beneath me, spinning beneath me, there's this stuffed animal. A teddy bear. A blue teddy bear. It belonged to one of my neighbors, Mrs. Chaudhry's little boy. I used to babysit him."

He shrugged. "What's so odd about that?"

"Because I've seen it, Liam. The same bear—the *exact same* bear—in that antique shop near us."

Chapter 71

2001, New Wellington

On the other side of the fire, Lincoln grimaced, confused and frustrated. "How can a world be made so very different from the absence of one man?" he muttered. "It seems a highly illogical notion. A man such as myself, even." He scratched at his dark beard. "I had hopes of making some mark, but to cause an entire new world to come into being from my *not* being there? I still struggle to make sense of this."

"Since all time—past, present, and future—exists at the same time, it is logical to say the future has already happened," said Bob. His eyes warily scanned the night around them as he spoke. "Therefore, all events are predetermined to happen a certain way. Every event, every human is a part of that sequence of events." He looked at Lincoln. "The predetermined sequence—you would call this 'history'—can tolerate the absence or alteration of minor events. Your influence on the outcome of the Civil War was a significant event."

"Surely it is important that you tell me more about the life ahead of me, then? For me to make all the correct decisions in my life in which I end up as this wartime president of the North?"

"Negative. You do not need to know. The events of history, the circumstances of your life, and what is in your own nature will conspire to direct you correctly."

"But there must surely come many moments in my life ahead where my destiny might hang on the outcome of"—Lincoln shook his head, trying to think of an example—"of the simple toss of a coin, or even the distracting smile of a pretty woman."

"If the course of your life was dependent on such marginal variables, you would be a minor sequential event, and your absence would not have caused this time wave." Bob cocked his head as he fished for an appropriate saying from his database. "Destiny has a plan for you."

Lincoln gazed at the flames as though in their flickering, momentary shapes hidden answers lay waiting to be discovered. "In other words . . . you are saying I must trust my instincts?"

"All that you will be already exists in you," said Bob. "The human mind is a store of data . . . memories. The memories plus the behavioral template you inherit genetically define you."

Lincoln nodded. He thought he understood the gist of that. He'd once had a conversation very similar to this one with his father. A simple, uneducated man, but wise beyond the grime on his farmer's hands.

We are all that we see and what our forefathers have seen.

And in the last few days he had seen some very questionable things—those creatures for instance. Creatures capable of intelligent thoughts and speech—*reading and writing, for God's sake!*—treated like possessions. Like objects, things to be dispensed with or recycled when broken. To know a creature has humanlike intelligence and yet still treat it like a yard dog—or worse, treat it like cattle?

He nodded. "I believe you may have a point there, Bob. My father once—"

"Just a moment." Bob cocked his head and started blinking.

Lincoln scowled at him. "What the devil is the matter with you?"

Liam had stopped talking with Sal. Both looked across the campfire at Bob.

"Bob? Are you—?"

"Affirmative, Liam. I am detecting tachyon particles."

"At last!" said Sal. "What's Maddy saying to you?"

Bob's head remained cocked, like a dog listening for his master's whistle. "Just a moment . . . I am compiling the message."

Lincoln looked at the three of them, one to the other, as if they were all crazy. "Are you saying he is *hearing* Miss Carter's voice?"

Liam shrugged. "In a manner of speaking."

Soon Bob nodded, straightened up, and looked at Liam. "We have a rendezvous data-stamp."

"Where?" asked Sal.

"More to the point, *when*?" added Liam.

"Seventy-one hours, fifty-nine minutes, three seconds."

"Three days, to you and me," said Liam to Lincoln.

"Location is thirty-one miles due west of our present location. A location known as New Chelmsford."

"Thirty-one miles!" Sal looked at Liam. "*Jahulla!* That's . . . that's quite a trek for us. Isn't it?"

Liam thumbed his chin as he looked out across the night. The direction in which they needed to go was going to take them away from the north–south road they'd been walking along. Across countryside, away from roads clogged with refugees. Away from New York.

Quite deliberately. She's found us somewhere safe to head toward.

"It's a walk, so it is . . . but it's not so hard. We'll make an early start tomorrow."

Chapter 72

2001, New York

Wainwright sipped his coffee and smacked his lips approvingly. "And this is called 'instant' coffee?"

Maddy looked at the jar on the side table beside their kettle. "That's right. We're sort of lazy in our time. Coffee's as easy as boiling water and spooning granules into your cup." She laughed. "None of this roasting-and-grinding-your-own-beans nonsense."

It was a reassuring feeling having the power back on in the archway, seeing the soft glow of computer-Bob's monitors and the hum of the displacement machine slowly recharging. Outside, out of sight but still chugging, the tank engine was turning over, giving out a mechanized bad-tempered mutter that sounded like it was ready to throw in the towel at the first hint of criticism.

The men were embedded in the trenches now; both Confederate and Union soldiers merged into one full-strength regiment between them. Dark blue and gray tunics side by side, staring out at the broad, moonlit East River and the broken skyline of Manhattan beyond.

"The British rarely launch nighttime assaults," said Wainwright, returning to a discussion of their preparations. He snorted a laugh. "Something to do with being 'jolly unsporting.'" He sipped his coffee. "Of course, that doesn't mean they won't try one this time."

They had a small team of men over on the far side of the East River, watching for the first signs of the British approaching. The telephone cable was still running across the span of water. At first sight they'd make the call, give a rough estimate of the size of the force, and then hasten back over the river in the launch.

"I think, however, tonight we can afford to savor our coffee." Wainwright pulled a small, dented flask out of his pocket. "Colonel Devereau? A little mule-kick to go with your 'instant' coffee?"

Devereau smiled and raised his mug for the Confederate to pour a measure of whiskey into his coffee. "Just a little; not enough to keep your mother up."

"Indeed." Wainwright tapped his mug against Devereau's and they both slurped a mouthful.

"Miss Carter?" said Devereau. "Tell me more about time travel. The idea of it I find wholly fascinating, if a little confusing."

"What do you want to know?"

Devereau looked stumped. "Well . . . to begin with, what is it like to actually travel in time?"

She closed her eyes, thinking. "It's . . . it's very weird. Ghostly white. You're in this space, sort of between space. In another dimension. Because that's what you're doing, leaving conventional space-time and reentering it at another place, earlier or later."

"What's the phrase you just used?" asked Wainwright. "'Another dimension'?"

"That's it. You understand the three dimensions, right? Up and down, left and right, forward and back?"

"Ah! You mean axis of motion, Miss Carter?" said Wainwright. "You are talking of those things?"

"Yup. 'Spatial dimensions'—that's what we call them. Well, in my timeline, physicists talk about something like eleven spatial dimensions. Eleven axis of movement."

"That makes no sense!" said Devereau. "Once you have up and

down, left and right, and forward and back, what *other* direction is there?"

"Well, that's just it. We humans can't visualize dimensions beyond three, because that's the space in which we live. But those other dimensions *do* exist, whether we believe in them or not—whether we can experience them or not. Look, imagine a two-dimensional world." Maddy pulled a sheet of lined paper off a pad on the kitchen table and laid it down between the colonels. She grabbed a Sharpie and drew a stick figure on the page. "Here's Fred living in this two-dimensional world. Now, Fred can see and move around in four directions: up and down, left and right. Okay?"

They both nodded.

She scrawled another stick figure, this time with a skirt and pouty lips. "And this is Loretta. Now, if Fred looks at Loretta, he won't know if she's a boy or a girl. Why do you think that is?"

Both colonels stroked their beards thoughtfully.

"What do you think Fred sees when he looks at her?"

"A badly drawn stick lady?" said Wainwright.

"No. He sees nothing but a flat line. He can only look along the surface of the paper. And, if you put your head right down on the paper yourself, you can almost kinda see things from his perspective. Loretta *is* just a line. He'll never see her luscious lips or girly skirt. He'll only ever see a line, because he can't look *down on*, or, more precisely, *into* this page. He won't know she's a lady, and so they'll never fall in love."

Devereau frowned. "But can Fred look up? Could he see us?"

"No. Even though we're right here leaning over him, because he can't comprehend 'into' or 'out of' this piece-of-paper world, he can never be aware of us." She sat back in her armchair. "That's how, as natives of a three-dimensional universe, we can't see or make sense of further spatial dimensions. But just because we can't see them doesn't mean they're not there."

"I see." She wondered if he did.

"So, traveling in time," she continued, "for Fred would be like floating him off this piece of paper and dropping him down again in the other corner."

"That, I imagine, would be an unsettling experience for Fred," said Wainwright.

"I'm not too excited about it when I do it," Maddy replied. "It feels like falling."

They were quiet for a while. Outside of the archway, somewhere in the night around a campfire, some of the men roared with laughter.

"If you are successful, and this Abraham Linford—"

"Lincoln."

"Abraham *Lincoln* is returned to his correct time, you say history will attempt to rewrite itself?"

"That's right."

"Tell me," said Devereau, "what will that be like for us? For me, for James here, for our men? What would we be aware of? Would we know it is happening?"

She nodded. "You'll see it coming. It's quite a thing to see."

"Would you describe what we'd see, Miss Carter?" asked Wainwright.

"Well"—she looked at Becks, who offered her no inspiration, just a calm, passive gaze—"Well, it's . . . it's a wall of reality, like the front edge of a tidal wave. A wave that starts as a ripple and travels through days, months, years, decades, even centuries, getting bigger and bigger. And when it finally arrives . . ." She shook her head and closed her eyes. Goose bumps teased the skin on her forearms. "It's like looking at—I don't know . . . Like the crust of the Earth has split and one edge is swallowing the other. It's as big as a mountain range, but it's all twisty and churning like liquid. And it comes fast, guys . . . really fast. You can't outrun it."

She opened her eyes.

Devereau looked pale. "It sounds truly terrifying."

"First time you see it"—she shrugged—"I suppose it is."

"And when this wave reaches us, Miss Carter . . ." Wainwright splayed his hands. "What then?"

"You change. The world changes."

"Change? Would this be felt in any way? Would it hurt? Be unpleasant?"

"No. You just cease to be and another version of you appears. Simple."

The men exchanged a glance. Wainwright's eyes narrowed. "It sounds to me as if . . . as if I will be *destroyed* by this wave. *Vaporized.*"

Maddy bit her lip. He was actually right.

"This wave would mean the end of me?" said Wainwright. "The man I have become, a lifetime of memories sweet and bad, my family back in Richmond, all gone? Destroyed?"

She wondered whether she should spin the truth a little, make it sound a little more acceptable, palatable, for the Southern colonel. Instead she decided to be honest with him. "Yes—it does sort of mean the end of you. But . . . ," she added quickly, "but also a new you."

"Another me?" Wainwright frowned. "*Another me?* Surely that would merely be another man who just shares my name and my likeness?" He looked at Devereau. "William, is this not us sacrificing our lives so that other men, who look just like us, can enjoy a better life?"

"Perhaps." Devereau nodded slowly. "But, James—are we not dead men anyway?"

The Confederate colonel's uneasy frown deepened.

"Our mutiny will be a short-lived one," Devereau continued. "I'd hoped the flames of rebellion would have spread further, but, well . . . it appears now that we are in this alone. There we are—that's the way it is." He sat forward, the armchair's old springs creaking. "But, Colonel, I put this to you . . ."

"What?"

"If by dying on a battlefield or being destroyed by this 'wave,' you could end this war, banish both the French and the British from our shores, *and* unite our separate northern and southern states once and for all—and be able to achieve all of this in one instant—is that not a good way to go?"

Wainwright studied his colleague for a long while. Eventually his frown gave way to a grin that spread beneath his mustache.

"Putting it like that, Colonel Devereau . . ." He raised his mug and clanked it against his friend's. "To foolish men who wish to change history."

Chapter 73

2001, New York

Sergeant Freeman squinted his bleary eyes at the hazy sky. Beyond the strip of Manhattan, beyond the broad and sedate Hudson River, was New Jersey.

"The South."

Freeman realized that where he and young Ray were huddled, near the top of a tall building he guessed must have once been a bank or something—right here was the closest he'd been to actually even *seeing* the South. From where they were sitting on dust-covered stools, looking out a cracked window frame, it looked no different to the crumbling ruins in which he'd been living for more years than he cared to remember. The rising sun coming up behind them picked out the skeletons of dockside cranes, twisted and contorted; the rusting hull of an old Sherman Ironside, a navy ship scuttled nearly seventy years ago when the South made their second assault on New York.

He shuddered as a fresh breeze sent dust devils spinning across the open floor. The wall to the east was completely gone, exposing a cross section of the building's many floors. He turned to look at all the old office things—typewriters, filing cabinets, desks, chairs—all of them coated in a thick layer of plaster dust and pigeon droppings.

The sun was filling this floor, streaming in where the wall should be. He shaded his eyes from the glare. If he squinted a little, he could just about imagine how this office must once have looked. Busy with activity. Busy with well-dressed young men moving purposefully, making money. And the big-framed windows looking down on New York, on all that promise and wealth and hopefulness. A doleful smile slowly spread across his leathery face.

"Helluva view folks musta had from up here," he muttered.

"'Sup, sir?"

Freeman shook his head. "Ain't nothing, Ray. Just an old man's nonsense."

"It's darned cold."

"Sunrise'll warm us up shortly, son."

He rubbed his hands together. The young man was right. It *was* cold up here. Wind chill an' all. He should've asked the colonel if they could have taken a brazier up here with them. At the very least, several flasks of hot water or some such.

Ray was looking up the long west side of Manhattan Island. Thin tendrils of smoke in the distance signaled the cooking fires of other Southern regiments. "You reckon them other regiments upriver gonna join us too, sir?"

"In due course . . . I'm sure. We just gotta make a show of things for a while." He glanced back at the hazy labyrinth of bomb-ravaged Brooklyn. "Our boys and them Southern boys, we just gotta make us a stand. Show them others upriver that we all are serious 'bout this rebellion. That we're finally finished with this war."

Freeman doubted it was going to be that simple. More than that, he sensed that same doubt in their colonel.

Bed's all made up now. Nothing left to do but sleep in it.

"Sir?"

Freeman turned back to Ray. "What is it, son?"

"What's that?" The boy was pointing. Freeman followed the direction of his finger and squinted once again to make better use of his old eyes. It looked like thunderclouds on the horizon. Made sense. They were due rain sometime soon.

A row of heavily stacked clouds.

"Pass me them binoculars, Ray."

The young man fished them out of a pouch and passed them to the sergeant.

"Now then," he said, fumbling with the focus dial. "Let me just get a . . ."

The bell grabbed Maddy and hauled her out of a troubled dream. She opened her eyes and found herself staring at the springs of Sal's bunk above. For a moment, with the gentle glow of the lightbulb above casting a patchwork of shadows from its wire grille and the hum of the computers, she thought all was well once more. That the idea of a civil war still being fought across the rubble of New York had been nothing but her sleeping mind's amusement.

But then the long clattering trill of a bell came again.

She turned her head and saw Colonel Devereau jerking awake in one of the armchairs. He reached out and picked up the phone from its cradle on the table.

"Yes?"

Maddy swung her legs onto the floor as Wainwright stirred and Becks ducked under the shutter and entered the archway.

Devereau nodded solemnly as he listened, then said: "Good man. Come back immediately." He put the phone back on its cradle.

"They're coming."

A moment later they were all emerging from the arch, stepping out into the glare of morning. She followed the colonels along the trench past grim-faced men already organizing, checking their packs, their ammo pouches, their rifles, buttoning their tunics, and replacing forage caps with hard helmets. Up a short stepladder and out of the horseshoe-shaped trench, she joined the colonels on the open ground sloping down toward the borderline and the river.

A launch was steaming across the glass-smooth water toward them, leaving a rippling "V" in its wake.

Becks stood beside her. "They are here."

Looming low in the sky above Manhattan like an archipelago of floating islands, a fleet of giant sky carriers had arrived.

Chapter 74

2001, en route to New Chelmsford

Liam wiped sweat from his face. The morning had started out so chilly. Now, at midday, with the sky a rich blue and the sun hanging high, it was a summer's day come late.

Traipsing across field after field, punctuated by the occasional meadow, and now finally in an apple orchard that seemed endless, they were exhausted.

"Five minutes," gasped Liam. "I've got a stitch in me side." He slumped against the trunk of an apple tree. "Five minutes' rest here, then we'll carry on."

Lincoln slid down beside him, equally spent and grumbling about blisters on his feet.

Sal didn't want to sit. She knew if she did, she wouldn't want to get up again. Anyway, there were more pressing matters.

"I need to, uh . . . to go and . . ."

Liam waved her off. "Don't wander too far."

"Okay."

She turned away and ducked down under the low-hanging branches of the nearest tree. She could still see them, which meant they could see her. She walked a little farther from them, between rows of trees, through grass tall enough to tickle her fingers. She ducked down again,

under another cluster of apple-laden branches, and found herself on
the edge of a clearing.

A glance backward. She couldn't see them anymore, although she
could hear the gentle rumble of Bob's voice.

Good enough for modesty.

She turned back and was about to step around the tree trunk beside
her and into the clearing when she spotted it, almost yelping with
shock as she immediately ducked down into the long grass.

A eugenic.

It was sitting on the edge of the clearing. Huge. One of the apelike
ones, with a tiny head emerging as little more than a lump from its
huge shoulders. She froze where she was, petrified that if she moved
again she might attract its attention.

She peered more closely at it. It looked a size larger than the apes—
half as big again, even more top-heavy with muscle mass. But it was
the creature's face that struck her.

No mouth. Or, rather, where a mouth should have been, a short
length of pipe emerged, sealed at the end. The creature also appeared
to be wearing a skullcap of some kind. She watched it for a good minute
before suspecting it was dead.

Liam squatted down in front of it and peered closely at its small face.
Its eyes were open, dilated and glazed. They could hear it breathing,
hear air rustling in through the slits of its nose and wheezing out like
a blacksmith's bellows.

"Well, it's not dead; I can tell that much."

"The creature is in a stupor," said Lincoln.

Sal reached out and touched its apelike face, its pale skin as smooth
and hairless as a baby's. The cap she thought it had been wearing, a
leather one, seemed to be attached—fixed in place to a band around its
forehead by a pair of clips. She looked at Liam. "It comes off, maybe?"

He nodded. "Go on; I don't think this brute's going to mind."

Carefully, she undid one clip and then the other, and gently eased the cap up off the band.

"Oh, that's just gross!"

Beneath a scuffed glass cover, they could see its skull had been scooped empty of brain. In the cranial cavity, through the scratched glass, they could see something gray and ribbed, the size, shape, and texture of a walnut. It was penetrated by half a dozen small brass rods and linked by wires to a control box that blinked an amber light.

"Information," said Bob. "Electronic impulses sent through the rods to the organic tissue stimulate brain activity. A much simpler version of the silicon-organic interface in my head."

Liam blew out a queasy breath. "McManus said they were controlling their creatures much better now. So this is how: they scoop the poor thing's brains out and shove in whatever *that* is instead."

"It *is* a brain, isn't it?" said Sal.

"Aye . . . but a tiny one. Like a rat's or something."

Sal made a face.

"Or maybe they grow these things without brains now," said Liam. That somehow seemed a more palatable idea. Better than growing smart creatures and then lobotomizing them like this.

They heard a distant whistle sounding.

"What was that?" asked Lincoln.

Men's voices echoed through the orchard. They heard the clatter of machinery firing up.

Liam shrugged. "Maybe that was the end of a lunch break."

The light on the box suddenly changed from amber to green.

Sal tilted her head. "Does that mean it's just turned itself 'on'?"

Liam looked at the others. "Uhh . . . who thinks we better go?"

Sal nodded. She popped the leather cap back on and managed to snap one of the clips in place before the eugenic stirred. Its small eyes twitched and flickered, and then focused on Sal for a moment.

"Oh Jay-zus!" whispered Liam. "It's woken up!" Liam pulled Sal back and stood in front of her. "Easy there, big fella . . ." His voice trembled.

The creature slowly pulled itself to its feet and stood erect for a moment, easily two foot taller than Bob. Its all-black eyes, small and glistening like a spider's, seemed to be studying them without the tiniest hint of curiosity. Then, without any warning, it turned around and pushed its way through the gap between the nearest two apple trees.

Liam ducked down low under the branches and peered after it to see the creature push through another row of trees into an area of the orchard that was busy being harvested. He saw a dozen others like it, leviathan-sized eugenics assembling around one end of what appeared to be some sort of combine-harvester.

In the sky half a mile away, he saw a sky vessel slowly approaching, descending. Just like the farming operation they'd seen in action a week ago.

He looked back at the enormous eugenic workers. The sheer size of this particular type . . . they made Bob look pitifully small. "We haven't seen this kind before," said Liam.

"We should proceed," said Bob, hunkering down beside Liam. "We have twenty-one miles to the rendezvous location."

Liam nodded. "You're right."

Chapter 75

2001, New York

Maddy spat grit out of her mouth. "Oh my God, that was close!"

The artillery barrage began several hours after the British had arrived, just as Colonel Devereau had said it would. With every percussive thump of a shell landing on this side of the river, the archway seemed to shower more dust and particles of brick on them. They were partly protected from a direct hit by the mangled remains of the bridge above—but the way their roof seemed to be shedding pieces, she had no doubt a near enough miss would do as good a job as a direct hit.

She picked up the computer keyboard in front of her and turned it over, pouring dust and grit out from between the keys and onto the desk.

"Jeeez . . . I'm surprised anything's still working in here!"

Her words were lost beneath another nearby thump that unleashed a second shower of debris from above. Ten minutes of this bombardment so far, and already Maddy's nerves were jangling.

One hit—just one—and I'm going to be entombed beneath an avalanche of bricks.

She had half a mind to leave the archway and stand outside in the trenches. At least she wouldn't die by being crushed. Becks was sitting beside the displacement machine, protecting the rack of circuit boards from falling fragments. The computer keyboard in front of her might still work with nuggets of brick lodged inside it, thought Maddy, but she doubted the fragile circuits of the displacement machine would be quite so forgiving.

And what about the antenna array outside? If it got knocked, they'd have to reset it—go outside, stand on the crumbling roof, and recalibrate it, or God knows how off-target their window was going to be.

Worse still, what about a hit on that old rust-bucket tank outside, still loyally chugging away? No tank, no power. They'd be dead in the water.

"Becks!"

"Yes, Maddy?"

"There's no way we're going to survive two days of this!" Another heavy thump deposited a shower of debris on Maddy's scalp. She spat out grit and shook her head, sending another smaller shower of dust out of her hair and onto her lap.

"We need to open the window *now!*"

"We can't do that, Maddy. They may not be at the rendezvous coordinates yet."

Becks—Queen of the Freakin' Obvious.

"I know that, I know that, but . . . we've got to do something before we get hit!"

Both Becks and Bob had a local wireless range, but neither of them could transmit a message to each other across more than a mile or two at best.

"Information: the chances of a direct artillery hit are relatively low, Maddy. Equipment failure is far more likely to occur as a result of the cumulative impact vibrations."

"Well, there you go! We need to do something—soon!"

Becks had nothing to offer. Another thud sent the monitors blinking out. A moment later they all flickered back on.

"Oh, this is totally not good, Becks. We've got to do *something!*"

She looked around her desk for inspiration.

Come on . . . come on. What do I do?

They should send a message to Bob and the others. Let them know they needed to speed things up, open the window much sooner than arranged. At this rate, in two days' time, there wasn't going to be an archway left—nor trenches, nor troops, just a pockmarked wasteland of brand-new craters.

"Computer-Bob!"

The dialog box appeared in front of her.

> **Yes, Maddy?**

"New message for Bob."

> **Proceed.**

"Archway under attack; need to open window at stated coordinates much sooner." She bit her lip.

How much more of this can the equipment take? Another few minutes, hours?

But that question was balanced by another equally important one: how far away were Liam and the others from the extraction point? There was simply no knowing. It's quite possible they were very close; after all, she'd picked a place roughly two-thirds of the way up from Quantico to New York, and a dozen miles westward off the main highways. Somewhere quiet. They *might* have been very close when they got the message . . . they just might. And that message was sent about eighteen hours ago.

They could be right there, twiddling their thumbs, waiting impatiently for the window to open. On the other hand, they might be fifty or a hundred miles away, struggling desperately to make it there in time.

"Window to open in ten minutes' time!" said Maddy. "End of message."

> **Affirmative. Compiling message packet.**

"Maddy," called Becks. "If we open a window in ten minutes' time, then it will take approximately another twelve hours to recharge the machine for a second attempt."

Maddy winced and cursed. She knew that anyway. Becks was right.

They couldn't afford to panic and blow their accumulated charge. She glanced across at the rack and saw all twelve green LEDs lit up. A full charge, and that had taken them the whole night and most of today with that poor old tank rattling away.

"Computer-Bob, cancel that. New message!"

> Message canceled. I am ready for your new message, Maddy.

"All right . . . Okay, the message is this: *Archway is under attack. Proceed to coordinates as fast as you freakin' well can! Will watch for you with pinhole probe. Will open as soon as we see you.* End of message."

> Affirmative. Compiling message packet.

She turned to Becks. "We'll open a pinhole window now and grab an image, and if they're not there, we'll do it again in another, say, half an hour's time. And again, and again . . ."

"This will drain the power."

"So sue me!" she snapped, then grimaced guiltily; Becks was only doing her job. "This way, we'll at least get in a few free looks, right? Before we've used up enough of the charge that we can't open a proper window?"

"Correct."

"Then that's what we're gonna do. Until we absolutely need to conserve what's left."

Computer-Bob had been listening.

> Maddy, shall I send this message? Please confirm.

"Yes! Confirm sending the message. Do it!"

Chapter 76

2001, New York

Devereau looked at the men huddled in the bottom of the borderline. An artillery bombardment like this on a defensive position was more successful at draining morale than it was at whittling down the enemy's numbers. The shells were mostly pitting the sloping wasteland with new craters. One or two shells had gotten lucky and caved in a section of the trench; nothing that couldn't be hastily dug out and repaired before a landing arrived.

No—it was the way it sapped the fighting spirit of the men that the bombardment's damage was done. Left them feeling helpless, impotent, as the enemy pounded them from afar.

Down the trench he could see Sergeant Freeman bellowing encouragement to the men around him, a mixture of men from his own regiment and Wainwright's Virginians. Devereau grinned; it was NCOs like Freeman who were the backbone of a regiment. Grim-faced veterans with a lifetime of scars and battlefield voices that carried over even the percussive thump of landing artillery shells. Men followed their generals and colonels, but it was the sergeants and corporals they turned to for a reassuring nod in the heat of battle.

He was about to glance over to the horseshoe to check whether the tank was still running when he suddenly found himself lying on his back at the bottom of the trench, watching a small avalanche of dark soil rain down on him. Instinctively he covered his face and closed his mouth as dirt began to cover him. Devereau tried to flail to get himself up, but his arms and legs felt leaden.

And it was all of a sudden so silent. The only noise was his heart thudding rhythmically. The rumble of the artillery bombardment sounded like it was going on a thousand miles away, a summer thunderstorm in another county.

He felt hands on him, digging him out of the dirt, pulling him up out of his temporary shallow grave. A face right above him—one of Wainwright's Confederates—all beard and dirt-smeared skin beneath the brim of his helmet. The man was shouting something, but Devereau couldn't hear what he was saying. All he could hear was his pumping heart and that distant rumble.

"I am all right!" he shouted back at the man. Not that he could hear himself. Not sure if he'd shouted it or whispered it. The man helped him to his feet, and Devereau quickly patted himself down to make sure he hadn't been nicked by shrapnel.

The arterial thumping in his ears had become a shrill ringing that he imagined would drive him very quickly insane if it was a permanent condition. He picked his forage cap out of the dark soil between his boots and put it back on. Straightening the peak, he saw a dozen faces down the trench looking warily at him.

They're watching you—show them some bravado.

He pulled his saber—more a ceremonial addition to his uniform than a practical one—from its scabbard and held the blade close to his face, using the polished surface as a mirror as he adjusted his cap and straightened his collar. He gave himself an approving nod before tucking the saber back, knowing there'd be a ripple of grins among the men to either side.

The ringing in his ears was beginning to diminish, and this time he could just about hear the Confederate soldier's voice.

". . . ir, the . . . arrage . . . opped!"

"What?" He cupped his ear.

The man nodded over the lip of the trench. "Stopped, sir! Barrage has stopped!"

Devereau took a step up onto an ammo box to give him a clear view ahead.

Stopped . . . yes, they have! He could feel that the sporadic vibrations of impact and shockwave had ceased. And now the cratered slope in front of them was bathed in a swirling mist of white smoke.

"Smoke," he whispered. The last volley of artillery fire had established a smoke screen. He turned to the Confederate beside him. "They're coming!"

After the relentless noise of the bombardment, the sudden calm was unsettling. His ears, the ringing diminished now to a background hiss, struggled to pick out the noise of the approaching British. In that cloud of smoke, somewhere, they'd be crossing the East River now— God knows how many landing boats sputtering across the water.

"Ready yourselves, men!" he shouted across the silence. "Check your weapons, check that you have ammo supplies to hand! It goes far too quickly, gentlemen!"

He looked out again at the featureless wall of white drifting on the breeze. He cursed that today of all days the weather was so still. Any other time, a stiff Atlantic breeze would have already whisked away much of the smoke screen.

"Sergeant Freeman!"

"Sir!" his voice returned from farther up the trench.

"Are you ready for a scrap?"

"Ready, sir? Been ready all mornin', colonel. Now ah'm just gettin' downright annoyed they takin' so long."

He heard a ripple of nervous battlefield laughter make its way along the men.

Devereau smiled. *Good man, Freeman.*

Then he heard it: the faint, droning *put-put-put* of a chorus of engines coming from somewhere out there on the river. He reached for his revolver, unsnapping the holster and wrapping his gloved hand around the pistol's grip. He pulled it out a little too quickly. It caught, and he nearly dropped it on the ground. But he didn't.

The Confederate next to him made a face. He'd spotted the fumble and offered Devereau an understanding nod. Luckily none of the other men had seen.

He sighed. The last thing his men needed to witness was just how scared their colonel felt.

He could hear the engines more clearly, and made out now, amid the swirling smoke screen, the faintest outline of a dozen flat-topped landing rafts approaching. He'd seen the South use these before: huge rafts with raised side panels that dropped down as they beached. Each of these landing rafts was capable of transporting an entire company of men.

Good God . . . twelve hundred men, two whole regiments, in the very first wave?

He found himself momentarily robbed of breath.

Steady yourself, colonel.

He filled his lungs. "Wait until they drop the ramps, men!" he bellowed. "Then we'll give 'em hell!"

A defiant cheer rippled down the trench.

He could now make out detail on the landing rafts, the fluttering of company colors above, the outline of an officer standing beside the helmsman at the back of each craft. He heard the pitch of the engines drop, and then, finally, a clatter and hiss as one after the other of the dozen landing rafts rode up the shingle and out of the water, grinding to a halt.

He could hear the muffled voices of British officers barking orders behind their raised metal panels, readying their men for disembarking. Several nervous shots were fired from the trench, sending sparks flying off the panels.

"Hold your *damned* fire!" roared Sergeant Freeman.

Devereau's mouth was dry.

Any second now.

He could hear the chorused voices of men down the slope. They *huzzah*ed at something being said to them, a roar of confidence. The roar of veterans certain that this little skirmish was going to be over before the last of the swirling smoke screen had blown away.

Then he heard a bugle blowing.

Simultaneously, all twelve landing rafts dropped their panels. They swung down heavily and crunched onto the shingle, forming ramps. Devereau found himself transfixed at the sight of so many of them—swarms of bloodred tunics and white helmets—surging down off their rafts.

"FIRE!!!!"

Chapter 77

2001, en route to New Chelmsford

They passed through a small town—East Farnham, another rural town, with one main street lined with shops selling farming supplies, hardware, and tools. One town hall and a church, and clapboard homes with picket fences.

They were getting used to the occasional sideways glances from beneath the brims of felt hats and lace bonnets, curious looks at their grubby and unfamiliar clothes and at Bob in particular. Liam wondered whether they thought he was some prototype design of eugenic.

Speaking of which, he spotted a couple more of the lobotomized leviathans, hefting bales of animal fodder off the back of a delivery wagon. Their lumbering movement was almost robotic, like poorly operated machinery. Again he marveled at their size: ten or eleven feet tall, and perhaps eight feet from one rounded mass of shoulder across to the other.

"Could we not stop for the night in this town?" grumbled Lincoln. "My feet feel like they've been pulled through a knothole backward!"

Liam nodded sympathetically. He felt every bit as exhausted. Fifteen miles on firm asphalt was enough of a hike, but to do it across ploughed fields of thick, freshly turned soil, meadows of tall knotted grass, through woods deep with spongy leaves hiding gnarly roots ready to trip you up . . . he was just as spent.

They had about another sixteen miles to go. That's what Bob had said the last time he'd pestered the support unit for an estimate.

"Aye, I suppose we could do that. We've got another whole day and a bit to get us there. And that's not so far for us to do tomorrow."

They had no money to pay for lodgings, not that he could see anyplace that looked like an inn or a hotel. But a barn, a shed, even an outhouse would be more appealing for a night's sleep than some open field.

He turned around to tell Bob they were going to find somewhere on the edge of this town to stop for the day. Even though it was still only midafternoon, they all needed a rest, and there was more than enough time for one.

But Bob had stopped in his tracks. He was a dozen yards behind them, frozen like a statue and staring listlessly up at the clear blue sky.

"Uh . . . Bob? You all right?"

"I think he's *receiving*," said Sal.

Liam looked around. *Could have picked a better bleedin' place.* His odd behavior was attracting even more curious stares from the townsfolk crossing the narrow main street. He sauntered casually back and tugged on Bob's sleeve.

"Hey, big fella . . . you're spookin' the locals, so you are."

Bob ignored him, busy catching and collating the tachyon particles winking invisibly into subatomic existence in the air around them.

"Your friend all right there, young man?" asked a lady, clutching a basket. She stopped midstride and peered out from her bonnet, shading her eyes from the afternoon sun.

"Oh, he's fine," said Liam. "Just a little tired, ma'am."

She nodded and passed by, casting one more curious glance back at them before crossing the street.

"Uh, Bob . . . ? How about we just walk a little while you're doing the message thing? You're attracting attention."

Bob remained rooted to the spot.

"Bob?"

Finally he blinked awareness back into his glazed eyes and looked down at Liam.

"Liam," he said. "I have just received a message from Madelaine."

Liam's eyes widened. "Well?"

Bob frowned at his flippancy. "Negative. The message does not indicate she is well."

The other two joined them now. "Was it Maddy?" asked Sal.

"Affirmative. A partial message. The signal has been corrupted slightly. Message content is as follows: *Archway is un . . . tack . . . roceed to coordinates as fast as . . . freakin' well can. Will watch for . . . with p . . . hole probe. Will ope . . . oon as . . . ee you.*"

Liam looked at the others. "She sounds stressed. That's never a good sign."

"Un . . . Tack . . . ?" Sal frowned. "Well, that's 'under attack,' clearly." She looked around at the others. "Right?"

Liam cursed.

"Recommendation: we should—"

"I know, I know," cut in Liam. "We can forget about a rest!" He looked around, up and down the main street. He could see a couple of horses tethered to a rail outside one of the stores. Farther along, a flatbed wagon pulled by a pair of huffaloes was slowly rolling up along dusty tracks carved into the street.

Too slow.

They were not following any road map to get to the rendezvous point; they were merely going as the crow flies, making a beeline over fields and hedges, through woods and streams. They needed something that didn't require a road. He looked the other way up the street.

He saw the delivery vehicle still laden with bales of cattle feed: a long flatbed hooked up to a motorized tractor. Above a small driver's cabin a chimney pot was impatiently puffing clouds of exhaust into the sky.

"You, sir . . . are thinking of stealing that vehicle?" asked Lincoln.

Liam nodded. "It may not be the fastest thing on the road, but it's faster than walking, right?"

Sal and Lincoln nodded.

"All right, then," said Liam, "I suppose we better go and, uh, *borrow* it."

Chapter 78

2001, New York

Devereau counted thirty seconds of almost continuous fire from his men before the crackle of gunshots began to wane as empty ammo clips were expelled with the telltale *ping* of their rifles' ejector springs.

A new bank of gunpowder smoke was slowly drifting down the slope from their trench. As it thinned and cleared, he could see that the shingle and the shallow water around the ramps were littered with the bodies of the dead and wounded—a devastating opening salvo that at first appeared to have decimated the British. But they were now starting to return fire, and he could see that a lot of the crimson tunics lying half in and half out of the lapping water were men who had instinctively ducked to the ground and were now picking themselves up and leveling their carbines.

Divots of soil began to erupt along the top of the trench. Devereau found himself ducking down like his men as the British organized their covering fire.

His men were now firing independently as they replaced their clips, taking opportunistic shots in singles and doubles over the sandbags.

Devereau chanced another long glance, his head foolishly above the line of sandbags for another half a minute. He quickly counted forty, maybe fifty British casualties. Not bad for their opening salvo. But that was the best chance they were ever going to get to even the numbers. Now the British were dispersed across the shingle, making use of the new craters and the grooves and dents of old building foundations and exposed basements, of the ruined humps of corner walls, little more than resilient piles of old masonry still managing to hold together after so many decades of punishment.

A shot whistled past his left ear. He cursed and ducked back down again. Devereau reloaded his revolver, struggling with shaking hands to slide each bullet successfully into its chamber.

Their best—their *only*—tactic would be to hold the British there on the slope, keep them from organizing a cohesive advance on the trench. And try to whittle them down one lucky shot at a time.

Pick out the officers first. He knew the British soldiers would be doing exactly the same—targeting the sergeants, corporals, captains, lieutenants—in an attempt to leave their opponents leaderless.

He chanced his head above the sandbags again and quickly aimed his revolver, firing all six rounds at the bull-shouldered figure of a bearded sergeant gesturing frantically at his men. The ground spat six clouds of dust, and the sergeant ducked lower in the dirt, most probably thanking his lucky stars for Devereau's poor aim.

He stepped back down again into the trench and reloaded his revolver, this time with a steadier hand.

"Sir!"

Freeman's voice.

"What is it, Sergeant?"

"They're groupin' up for a push! Thirty yards left of the stack, sir!"

There was an old smokestack midway along the landing area, the last remnant of a brick factory that had been here half a century ago, now little more than a ring of shoulder-high bricks. Devereau peeked over the top. Freeman was right. He could see the tops of white pith helmets coalescing behind the stack, waiting for the command.

And the command would be answered by an eager roar from the

men getting to their feet, and the percussive rattle of covering fire from farther along the shingle.

With one hasty assessment he could see this first attempt at storming the borderline was probably going to be successful. Some of them were likely to make it into the trench, and then it was going to be down to hand-to-hand fighting.

"Fix bayonets!" he shouted. The Confederate soldier standing next to him nodded and passed the order on as he fumbled his bayonet out of its scabbard.

"Aim your fire at the officers as they come up!" he added. "Pass it on!"

He tucked his revolver back into its holster and pulled out his ceremonial saber.

This is how this war was fought in the beginning, he told himself. *Muskets and sabers and nerves of steel.*

"Ready for it, sir?" asked the Confederate.

Devereau stroked his chin and nodded. "How about you?"

The man slotted the bayonet home beneath the muzzle of his rifle. "Figure I see 'em like you do, now we on the same side, sir."

He heard a chorus of voices from downhill: the British troops mustering up their adrenaline. The chanting of three *huzzah*s, each louder than the last, the third ending with a roar that peeled along the entire length of the landing area.

Here they come.

"Fire at will!" screamed Devereau.

Southern and Northern soldiers stepped up together as one, their rifles thudding down on the sandbags—a ragged line of several hundred wavering muzzles tipped with glinting bayonets. A wall of flash and smoke erupted as they lay down a withering barrage of fire at the British as they sprinted up the slope.

Chapter 79

2001, en route to New Chelmsford

"What in the name of the Lord are you doing, sir?" cried Lincoln.

"I'm trying to steer the bleedin' thing!"

Liam had two control sticks to work with. After zigzagging back and forth across the narrow main street, spilling giant bales of feed from the trailer behind them, Liam had the gist of how the control sticks worked—almost. The left stick controlled the large wheel on the left, and the right stick, the right wheel. To turn right, for example, he realized he had to pull back on the right and forward on the left. To go straight forward, both sticks forward.

By the time he'd finally figured this out, the small town of East Farnham was behind them, littered with the chaos, damage, and debris of Liam's learning curve. The tractor rolled down the dirt road out of the town, flanked on either side by orchards of plum trees.

"Jay-zus, we did it!" gasped Liam.

Lincoln and Sal clung uncomfortably to the bucket seat inside the driver's cabin. Bob was standing outside on the now-empty flatbed. Liam thrashed the tractor as fast as it would go—little more than the speed of an asthmatic jogger—for a half mile before finally pulling over to one side of the dirt track.

Five minutes later they were on the move again, a great deal faster now that they'd detached the trailer.

"So, which way?" Liam shouted above the din of the rattling engine.

Bob pointed off the dirt track they were running along, across a pasture full of what looked like eugenically modified draft horses. "That way."

"Hold on!" said Liam, pulling the left stick back a little. The tractor's gigantic wheels rolled effortlessly over a wooden picket fence and across the pasture, scattering horses that seemed to stand almost as tall at the shoulder as Indian elephants.

"Information: fifteen miles, one hundred seventy-six yards in this direction."

"Right," said Liam, gripping both control sticks with white-knuckled concentration. "Okay . . . fifteen miles."

The tractor was romping along now, bouncing alarmingly on the uneven ground, swerving every now and then to avoid the unpredictable, panicked movements of the draft horses flocking alongside it.

"Whoa!" Sal pointed through the cabin's mud-spattered windshield. "Watch out for the—" The tractor rolled over a long wooden feeding trough, sending splinters of wood and cobs of corn into the air.

"Never mind," said Sal.

Liam crashed out of the far side of the pasture and swerved right to avoid running into an open barn. A moment later they were rolling across a yard crisscrossed with laundry lines.

"Watch out, look—kids!"

Several children playing amid fluttering bedsheets scattered in panic before them.

"Oh Jay-zus! I'm sorry! I'm sorry!" Liam bellowed through the open side window as they rumbled out the far side of the yard, across some-one's vegetable garden, and over a cheerfully colored wooden playhouse.

They were rolling across a vineyard a moment later, flattening row after row of budding grapevines. Sal pointed out a long line of greenhouses nestled between the rows of vines. She noted the look of shock on an old man's face as he stood in the doorway, watering can in one hand and pruning shears in the other. The tractor's huge wheels churned a lane of soil mere inches away from him and the fragile framework of timber and glass.

"Hey, Liam—you actually managed to *miss* something."

His face was rigid with desperate concentration. "I've never driven anything before in me life!"

Branches of a vine thrashed against the windshield, smearing it with grape juice.

"Liam!" said Sal.

He was squinting through the slime of juice and grime on the glass, too focused on seeing through it all to take heed of Sal.

"LIAM!"

"*WHAT?*"

Sal squeezed his shoulder gently. "Maybe someone else should be driving instead? Huh?"

"Good God, yes!" barked Lincoln, holding his head where he'd whacked it against the cabin's low roof.

Liam nodded. "Uh . . . Okay, yeah. That's . . . probably a good idea."

He eased both throttle sticks back slowly, evenly, to prevent the tractor lurching one way or the other. Finally it came to a stop, the tractor's idling engine grumbling irritably at the way it had just been treated.

Bob leaned over Liam's shoulder. "Recommendation: I should drive this vehicle."

Liam nodded eagerly, slowly easing his viselike grip on the throttle sticks. "Uh, yeah . . . I think that might be best."

Chapter 80

2001, New York

Devereau looked around him, for the moment not facing an adversary. The floor of the trench was already a squirming carpet of bodies, the dying and the dead, red, gray, and blue tunics tangled with each other.

More British were dropping down into the trench, swinging the balance of numbers against Devereau's men, a hundred different one-on-one duels becoming two-on-one.

We're going to lose this trench . . . quickly.

Down the trench he could see Sergeant Freeman parrying and lunging with calm, machinelike certainty. Behind the man a British soldier was getting ready to spike Freeman in the back. Devereau reached for his revolver, raised, aimed, and fired it empty. Through the drifting smoke he saw the soldier drop and Freeman turn to see the fate he'd just narrowly escaped.

Devereau waved for Freeman to join him, and the sergeant began to pick his way over the bodies, roughly shoving a couple of struggling men to one side before finally joining him. "Sir?"

"This trench is lost. We need to sound a retreat to the horseshoe!"

Freeman nodded; his opinion as well, it seemed. "Yes, sir." The sergeant was reaching for the signal whistle on a chain tucked into his breast pocket when Devereau caught sight of new movement. The rearmost lip of the trench was suddenly lined with figures aiming guns down at them. He heard a voice give a command, and at once the air was thick with clouds of gunsmoke and the deafening rattle of gunfire. Amid the elongated scrum of struggling men down the entire length of the borderline trench, men in red tunics were flung back against the muddy wall, clutching ragged wounds.

Those British soldiers still standing once the gunfire started to falter and empty ammo clips pinged into the air began to disengage from their hand-to-hand duels and scramble back over the lip of the trench to beat a retreat down the slope.

Colonel Wainwright dropped down beside him. With an adrenaline-fueled roar he scrambled up the far side, firing his revolver wildly at the withdrawing British troops.

Reckless fool.

"James! Get down!"

Volley fire from farther down the slope brought Wainwright to his senses as plumes of dirt erupted beside him. He dropped back down with a whoop of excitement.

The rest of the men in the trench carried his whooping cry and turned it into a regiment-wide jeer at the beaten redcoats, regrouping down on the shingle, taking cover in the relative safety of the craters or behind the ruined stumps of wall by the riverside.

Freeman spat the whistle out of his mouth and grinned at Devereau. "Hell, sir—we showed 'em some fight! Didn't we, sir?"

"Yes, we did that, sergeant."

He looked at Wainwright moving down among the men, swinging his saber in the air triumphantly. "See to our wounded, sergeant." He squeezed past Freeman and a dozen other men lofting their helmets above them on the tips of their bayonets.

"Helmets back on, you fools!" he shouted.

Finally, standing beside Wainwright, he said, "Colonel! I thought the plan was for you to remain in the horseshoe! What happened here?"

Wainwright shrugged guiltily. "True, but it would have been a shame to lose a trench so early in the battle, would it not, William?"

Devereau's scowl eased. *It would at that.*

"Well . . . it seems you came down at just the right moment." They watched the British troops rallying down on the shore. Regimental sharpshooters fired off sporadic rounds up at the borderline to keep them from daring to press their attack down on the British.

"Fact is, they have a toehold on this side now," he added.

Wainwright nodded. "We could charge them. They are still disorganized; we have the height and the element of surprise."

"But not the numbers. There are over a thousand men down there, and we have just under six hundred. Not enough. Our best bet is digging in and holding fast like ticks on a dog's back."

Both men watched the British over the top of the sandbags. Engineers were hastily detaching the landing-raft side panels and assembling them on the shingle, creating rudimentary fortifications for them to huddle behind; their wounded were being dragged to the relative safety of covered positions to be treated by a field physician. Devereau marveled at their discipline under fire, so quickly and efficiently turning a complete rout into entrenchment, temporary defeat into consolidation.

"Good God; it's no wonder half of this world is under the Union Jack." He stepped back down into the mud and turned to see Wainwright squatting and inspecting the collar insignia on the uniform of a dead redcoat.

"And they're just a regular line regiment, William. Not even *elite* troops."

Devereau nodded. There was worse yet to come, then—perhaps one of the notorious regiments: the Black Watch, the Grenadier Guards, the King's Guard.

"You did it!" Both colonels looked up to see Maddy and Becks standing on the lip of the trench.

"Better get down here, ma'am!" said Wainwright. "They have sharpshooters."

As he spoke, a single shot whistled close by. Maddy scrambled down into the trench. "Oh my God! Was that . . . ?"

"Aimed at you?" Devereau nodded sternly. "Yes."

Becks dropped down beside her.

Maddy looked around at the bodies splayed along the bottom of the trench, some still stirring, moaning. She glimpsed ragged wounds, puckered pink flesh, dark blood leaking, spurting. She could smell the acrid odor of cordite in the air, and, beneath that, the other smells of battle: sweat, vomit. And she heard the murmur of the pitiful voices of dying men.

She felt ill—light-headed and queasy.

Wainwright noticed. "How quickly we forget what war actually looks like."

Maddy swallowed, pale-faced, choking back her own urge to vomit. "I, uh . . . I came to find you." She took a few deep breaths. "I sent another message through. To make the rendezvous sooner."

"How soon?"

"I can't say, but we have a way of knowing when they're there. And the moment they arrive, we can pick them up."

"When?" asked Devereau.

"It could be anytime," she replied.

A grin flashed across his face. Wainwright shared it. "Then the longer the British fool around down there on the beach, the better it is for us."

"Indeed." Devereau turned to Maddy. He lowered his voice. "And the moment you send your colleagues back to . . . What year was it?"

"1831."

"1831 . . . this world will change?"

"Pretty soon after, yeah. Sometimes immediately. Sometimes a few hours."

"It is impossible to accurately predict the arrival time of a reality wave after a timeline event alteration," added Becks.

"But it would be *soon*," Maddy reassured them. She glanced around quickly at the shifting carpet of bodies. "Soon enough that, you know, you could stop this fighting once I've sent them back."

"You mean, surrender?" Wainwright and Devereau shared a look. "I wonder . . . would this time wave arrive soon enough for us to both escape the firing squad?"

Maddy shook her head. "I . . . I can't say when. It might even be a day or so—"

"Then I think we are in agreement, Colonel Wainwright, that we would rather fight on until the moment this wave arrives?"

Wainwright nodded. "Complete agreement, Colonel Devereau."

Maddy sighed. "All right, but . . ." She turned and pointed up the slope toward the horseshoe trench, and beyond that to the very top of the hump of bricks in the shadow of the overhanging ruins of the Williamsburg Bridge. "The antenna array has *got* to be protected, whatever happens. Do you understand? If it gets damaged, then this is all over."

"Then we shall keep the fight down there for as long as we can," said Wainwright. "What of my tank? Is its engine still running?"

"Yeah, it's running; we've got power. And the displacement machine is charged up and ready to use. So that's good."

"So we wait, then," said Devereau.

Maddy nodded. "I find I do a lot of that in this business, you know? Waiting." She half smiled. "Kinda sucks."

Chapter 81

2001, New York

Captain Ewan McManus looked up at the sky. The low, combed-out clouds above New York were a beautiful salmon pink from the late-afternoon sun. Another couple of hours and it was going to be dark.

Colonel Donohue had his officers gathered around him: company captains, lieutenants, sergeants. "We're up next, gentlemen. Word is the Lancashire Rifles have wet their toes and got a firm foothold for us over there. As you can see"—he turned around and gestured past the sappers putting the final pieces of their landing rafts together to the far side of the East River—"the . . . uh, *mutineers* have two lines of defense: a set of trenches running parallel to the river, from those factory buildings there on the left all the way along to the remnants of that bridge on the right; and behind that, they have a bow-shaped trench, which seems to curve beneath the bridge. I imagine they will be treating that as a secondary defense position."

McManus craned his neck along with all the other officers to get a better look.

"Beyond those two lines, we're into the old Northern defense line. As I'm sure you're already aware, a Confederate regiment, Virginians I believe, the chaps that up until recently were holding the ground we're standing on right now, have mutinied along with a Northern regiment. So . . . we find ourselves in the rather unusual position of having a temporary understanding with the French High Command."

"Understanding, sir?"

Colonel Donohue nodded. "Neither side really wants this nonsense to spread. So the French are prepared to let us go in on their behalf and sterilize the wound, so to speak."

"That's very trusting of them!" called out someone. A ripple of good-natured laughter spread among them.

"Quite so." He smiled. "And the more fools they."

Heads nodded. Although it was still officially supposed to be top secret, every officer in every participating regiment was well aware that this little uprising was a convenient opportunity for the British to launch their final push against the North. In fact, this futile act of rebellion couldn't have come at a better time for them. The French were prepared to hold back while the British stepped in and crushed it, not knowing their intention was to continue pushing on, punching through the North's front line and rolling up their east-coast flank.

"Captain McManus?"

"Sir?"

"I think this might just be a splendid opportunity to field-test our Dreadnoughts before the real fighting begins, don't you?"

"Yes, sir."

"Take your company ashore as support for them—but I'd really like to see how well our experimentals perform on their own, all right?"

"Support only, yes, sir."

"The rest of you can follow in the second flotilla. Best not have too many of our chaps nearby when those monsters get a sniff of the enemy."

Colonel Donohue turned around again to look at the landing area on the far side of the river. A low mist of gunsmoke hung above it like a membrane, and every now and then a distant crackle of gunfire was accompanied by another faint plume of blue-gray smoke winking into existence.

"And God help those poor souls when that happens."

Chapter 82

2001, near New Chelmsford

"Bob? How much farther now?"

Bob eased back on the throttle sticks as the tractor's big ridged wheels rolled down into a shallow river and splashed arcs of spray to either side of them.

"Information: two miles, one hundred seven yards from this location."

The tractor emerged from the river on the far side, leaving two deep ridges carved in the wet mud of the riverbank.

"Two miles?"

"Affirmative."

"Then stop right here."

Bob did as instructed, easing the throttles down to an idle, disengaging the gears, and pulling a brake lever. He looked at Liam. "Why?"

Sal nodded. "Yeah—we're nearly there!"

"That's exactly why," said Liam. He turned and pointed out the mud-spattered rear window of the cabin. "We've left a trail a blind man could follow. If there were any policemen or militia called to find this tractor, it won't be difficult for them."

It was approaching dusk. The sun was casting a rose-hued glow and long, cool shadows across the pastoral landscape around them. Far away to the right, a small village nestled among sycamore trees, and chimneys leaked threads of smoke into a peach sky.

"If we drive all the way to the rendezvous point," he continued, "we could be leading a posse of coppers or soldiers right to the window. It's two miles from here; if we get running, we could be there in, what, twenty minutes or so?"

Bob nodded. "This is a sensible tactical decision."

Lincoln groaned and pointed at his old boots; one of them was flapping open at the front where a seam in the leather had split. Long hairy toes waggled through a threadbare sock. "My feet are as spent as a pauper's purse."

"Oh *shadd-yah*! You lazybones."

Liam opened the cabin door and jumped out onto the riverbank. "Come on! It's not far now!"

Bob dropped down heavily beside him. "Correct; not far."

Sal pushed Lincoln out in front of her. "We'll be there soon enough."

Chapter 83

2001, New York

Maddy looked at the monitor in front of her. Another fuzzy, low-resolution, blocky image of what appeared to be a muddy field full of long wooden sheds. She could see a few trees, and a sky growing dark.

Computer-Bob was sending a narrow-thread signal to the rendezvous location, briefly checking every ten minutes for any density fluctuations and grabbing a pinhole image of the location at the same time. It was slowly eating into the full charge they'd had on the displacement machine; of the twelve green LEDs, three of them were dark now.

Another dozen glimpses and they were going to be eating into the energy they'd need to get Liam and the others back to 1831 and then bring them home.

Come on, Liam! Where the hell are you?

🕓

He could make out six more landing rafts slowly chugging their way across the river. Devereau watched with growing unease as the soldiers still holding their position on the shingle behind their panel-barriers began to edge away from the middle of the landing area, toward which the six boats seemed to be heading.

"James . . . ," he said in the gathering gloom. Wainwright was somewhere nearby. "Wainwright!"

He heard Wainwright make his way along the trench, a hasty word of encouragement and a pat on the shoulder for each man he passed. Soon he was beside Devereau.

"What is it?"

Devereau pointed and handed him his binoculars. "Reinforcements coming."

Wainwright squinted into the lenses, adjusting the focus as he panned up along the boxlike hull of one of the rafts. The protective panels were up, hiding whatever troops were inside. He thought he caught the bobbing of a head over the top, some sort of movement from within. He trained the binoculars on the flag fluttering lifelessly at the back of the craft, beside the helmsman's position.

"If I could just see the regimental banner . . . I could tell . . ." His words faded.

"What? What is it?"

Wainwright lowered the glasses. "Black Watch."

Devereau knew them: one of the British army's very best regiments. He blew out a puff of air and forced a smile. "Well, then, we shall have a more even-handed fight this time around."

Wainwright shook his head warily. "No . . . William," he said, his voice lowered to a whisper for Devereau's ears alone. "This isn't good. The Black Watch are the regiment they have been testing experimental units with."

"Experimental units?"

The haunted look on Wainwright's face told Devereau more than he wanted to hear. "Good God . . . you don't mean . . . ?"

"Eugenics . . . yes."

Devereau turned to look back at the river. The six panel-sided rafts were nearly all the way across, the sound of their motors chugging and spitting in the stillness that had settled over this contested patch of cratered and weed-strewn wasteland.

He stroked his beard absently. "Then . . . we must be sure to concentrate all our fire on those rafts. On whatever monsters are inside."

Wainwright nodded.

Because whatever creatures are in there . . . if they get into the trench . . .

"The men should know this," he added.

"Agreed."

Devereau cupped hands around his mouth. "Listen . . . men!"

The soft murmur of voices along the trench, a hundred different whispered conversations, ceased.

"The rafts approaching . . . those vessels out there contain eugenic units!"

He'd expected a roar of panic, perhaps even the clatter of weapons dropping and the first of his men clambering out of the trench and making a run for it. Instead he was met with absolute silence and several hundred grime-encrusted faces along the line of the trench turned his way, faces absorbing the meaning of what he'd just said.

"Understand, we CANNOT afford to let these monsters reach us! Is this clear?"

Frozen faces, frozen expressions, mouths hanging open—yet silence still.

"Is this CLEAR?"

Sergeant Freeman took the lead. "Yes, sir."

"Whatever creatures step down from those rafts, we will kill every last one of them! We will gun them down before they even step foot on the shingle!"

Some of the men cheered unconvincingly.

"Check your weapons, check your ammo! And make ready!" He turned to look back down at the river.

Of the six landing rafts he'd spotted approaching, the two on the left and two on the right had pulled slightly ahead, beaching themselves in the spaces between the first wave of vessels. The middle two were holding back.

What are they up to?

The panels dropped on the four flanking rafts, and British troops wasted no time spilling down the ramps into the water. Some of his men began firing uncertainly.

The middle two . . . whatever monsters they have for us are in those.

"HOLD YOUR FIRE!"

Freeman and several other NCOs carried the order up the line, and the firing ceased. The last thing they needed to be doing as the panels dropped on the last two rafts was swapping out empty cartridges.

The Black Watch waded quickly ashore and took up the covered positions on the shingle that had been vacated by the first wave of men. Devereau found himself getting impatient, cursing at the panels to drop, anxious to see what horrors the eugenologists back in Britain had conjured out of the coded chemistry of nature.

He heard a British officer barking an order. And then, a moment later, he saw several dozen small, round grenades tossed onto the shingle. They began to hiss as they spewed thick mustard-colored columns of smoke. His first thought was that it was poison gas, but he realized the men down there were not wearing gas masks, and surely they would have tossed their grenades up the slope toward the trench had they been poison.

Wainwright cursed. "Another wretched smoke screen."

"HOLD YOUR AIM!" shouted Devereau.

We'll hear the splash.

"FIRE ON MY COMMAND!"

Several moments passed in a prolonged, agonizing silence as the yellow mist thickened and spread along the shore, effectively shrouding the middle two rafts, and beginning to hide the other rafts as well.

Then he heard it—the *clank* of latches being released in unison somewhere in the smoke and the splashes of ramps landing in the water.

"FIRE!"

The entire length of the trench was edged with a ribbon of gray-blue cordite smoke as rifles rapidly fired one shot after another and several machine guns spit muzzle flash and stuttered out a steady stream of bullets into the yellow mist.

Above the cacophany of gunfire he could hear the rattle and clang of rounds impacting on metal and the splash of something heavy landing in the water.

Something big.

The yellow mist was slowly thinning and spreading, drifting up the slope toward them, hiding what was in there for longer than was fair.

He squinted into the yellow, managing to just about pick out the stump of the brick smokestack; the head and shoulders of a soldier holding aloft a regimental flag, too foolishly confident to keep down while the volley was still going on; the edge of the left-most raft; and looming above the battlefield, the ghostly outline of the bridge.

Then something darker, much closer than anything else, becoming more defined as it scrambled uphill toward them.

"God help us," he whispered as it emerged out of the last curling skeins of the rolling mist.

Chapter 84

2001, New York

It was humanlike, in that it had two arms and two legs, but that was the end of any anthropomorphic resemblance. It towered over them, almost as tall as a double-decker bus, almost as wide as a house. As it emerged from the smoke, Devereau noted that it seemed to have no head; there seemed to be nothing but the slightest bump on a ridge of muscle and bone that linked one shoulder to the other, with pinhole dots for eyes and a tube where a mouth might have been.

As it charged up the last dozen yards of the gentle slope, Devereau could see that the creature looked more like some sort of machine, a mechanical automaton covered in linked plates of thick metal that clanked together noisily as it lumbered forward.

He realized that, like him, his men had stopped firing. They were frozen in a state of horrified fascination.

"FIRE!" he screamed.

The sparks of impacting bullets showered the ground around it as the giant's loping run faltered and finally ceased. Its enormous arms flailed angrily, and Devereau saw, beneath the overlapping plates of metal, glimpses of pale gray flesh spattered with dark droplets of blood.

The leviathan stumbled one final step forward before finally collapsing heavily down onto its knees, and then, still shedding a shower of sparks from the gunfire concentrated on it, it slowly keeled over like a felled tree lying across the trench, one thick arm flopping into the trench and crushing a man.

My God . . . it took our entire regiment to bring it down.

Out of the smoke emerged eleven more. This time only half the men managed to concentrate fire on them; the other half already had to eject and replace empty cartridges. The giants were on them in mere seconds, standing over the borderline, one or two of them even standing astride it, swinging their huge metal-plated arms down into the trench.

Their fists—the size of beer kegs—were enclosed in a variety of different experimental attachments. Some of them had iron cages from which foot-long spikes protruded. A couple of them had blades that looked like Devereau's saber, welded to iron bands around their three fingers, like impossibly long claws. One of them even had a rotating saw blade powered by a chugging engine strapped to the creature's upper arm.

The men standing beneath them stood no chance.

Gunfire from farther along the line resumed; one of the Confederate machine-gun teams managed to bring another of the creatures down, concentrating their stuttering fire on its chest. As it collapsed, Devereau got a closer glimpse of the small head almost completely recessed into the chest: two dark pinhole eyes, a mere gash for a nose, and a pipe emerging from where the mouth should be, curling around under the left-shoulder armor plate to a pair of cylinders strapped to its back.

Ten of these things still—*ten*! Sweeping their spiked and bladed fists into the trench, dismembering, crushing, eviscerating every poor soul within easy reach.

"They're killing us!"

Wainwright nodded. "We should fall back!"

He was right; remaining here within range of their brutal arms was utter insanity. The trench was already lost. At least with more open ground to cross to reach the horseshoe trench, there was a chance the men deployed there could bring down a few more of them.

"Fall back!" Devereau cried, his voice lost amid the cacophony of screams, the shriek of metal on metal, the clatter of guns, and the clanging of bullets sparking off iron plates.

He tried again, cupping his mouth. "FALL BACK!"

"THE HORSESHOE!" added Wainwright.

A bugle sounded the retreat, and those men still alive, still with arms and legs, began to scramble out of the trench like startled crows from a field.

🕐

"What's happening out there, Becks?"

"I will observe," she said, heading toward the shutter door.

From the distant noises Maddy could hear, it sounded like the British were trying their luck again on that first trench. But this time around the nature of the battle sounded different: less gunfire, more voices. She'd heard the regiment's bugler sound some signal. She had no clue what that meant, but could guess it probably wasn't good news.

"Oh God . . . they're coming!" she said. She realized her whole body was trembling. She hated the sound of her voice, shrill and warbling, like a little girl, like a child.

Why am I such a freakin' dork?

She envied the colonels, both of them cut from the same cloth— leather-faced veterans with a dignified calm about them, a gentlemanly formality. What the British called "a stiff upper lip."

And here I am trembling like some pampered chihuahua on a park bench.

"Bob? Do another probe."

> Maddy, the last one was only seven minutes ago.

"I know! I know! Do it anyway!"

> Information: if we increase the number of times we check for them, we will drain the stored energy more quickly.

"Jesus! I know that already! Just do it!"

> Affirmative. Activating density probe.

Becks squeezed past the entrance to the machine-gun bunker and into the horseshoe trench that looped around the archway.

The men lining the dirt wall, reinforced with sandbags and slats of wood, waiting for the battle to reach them, looked at her with bemusement.

"It ain't safe out here, miss," said one of them. "Better get back inside."

"I will be fine," said Becks, shrugging off the comment. "Thank you for your concern." She found a space between two soldiers and stepped up onto an ammo crate to get a look over the rim of the trench.

The rubble-strewn ground sloping down to the borderline was thick with men staggering uphill toward them, many of them bloody. Beyond them she could see a pall of thinning yellow mist over the front trench and other men spilling out of it. She could see several large silhouettes looming over the trench. She counted nine of them.

"What are those?" she asked the man beside her.

"M-monsters! Called up from hell itself by them British."

"They genics, ma'am," said the other. "Grown from blood an' body parts." The man shook his head at the other. "Ain't no devils or demons from no hell. Tha's all jus' voodoo crock." He sighed. "Worse than that, anyhow—it's nature all messed up in a way it shouldn't be."

She nodded, guessing what the soldier was saying.

Genetically engineered units.

The first of the retreating men flopped down into the horseshoe farther along, wide-eyed and gasping for breath. "Jesus! You can't . . . y-you can't do nothin'! Can't do . . . nothin' to stop . . . them!"

Others collapsed over the edge and rolled down into the mud beside him. "Genics! Damn British is usin' genics on us again!"

She could recognize fear spreading among the men, spreading like flames across a summer-dry field of wheat.

These soldiers are exhibiting extreme stress reactions.

She calculated that their ability to fight was severely impaired. In fact, she was almost certain, by the looks on their faces, that this defensive position was in danger of being abandoned.

"ATTENTION!" she barked loudly.

Faces, pale and blood-spattered, turned toward her.

"Information: the large units ahead of us are genetically engineered combat units. They are designed to withstand significant damage—but they *can* be terminated!"

"They're demons! We can't beat what the devil sends!"

"No, dammit! She . . . she's right!" shouted one of the bloodied men. "We got us two of 'em! I saw two of 'em go down!"

"Concentrate your fire specifically on vulnerable locations!" said Becks. "The circulatory system, the nervous system. Chest and head." She looked down at them sternly. "Is this clear?"

The men eyed her silently.

"A single correctly targeted projectile will kill these units! You will concentrate your fire on their heads and chests!"

She turned to look down the slope and saw Devereau and Wainwright staggering toward them. She pointed at them. "Look! Your commanding officers! They will confirm what I have just said!"

They huffed up to the horseshoe, gasping and wheezing, among the last of the men making their way back from the borderline. Devereau spotted her standing out in the open. "What the hell are you doing, woman? Get down!"

She ignored his outburst as both men clambered over the sandbags and flopped to the ground beside her. Devereau stood up, panting, almost doubling over to get his breath.

"I am fine," she said to him. "You must sit down and recover now." She reached out for him and Wainwright and pushed them down until they were squatting on the floor, wheezing for air. She knelt down beside them. "Rest. Your soldiers will need you to be combat-ready."

Wainwright, slumped beside Devereau against the dirt wall, looked up. "Did you say . . . 'combat-ready'?" he wheezed.

"Affirmative."

He turned to look at Devereau and managed a grin. "What a"—he huffed and panted—"what a remarkable young lady this one is, huh?"

Devereau nodded. "A real trooper."

Chapter 85

2001, New Chelmsford

"Information: the rendezvous location is two hundred fifty-seven yards ahead of us."

Liam stared over the wooden fence at the muddy field beyond. "You're joking! . . . Maddy chose a pig farm?"

Bob shook his head. "I am not making a joke at this time."

"She must really hate us." Sal was almost retching from the overpowering odor of pig manure. "They are filthy animals."

"It's just mud and some pigs. Come on."

Liam pulled himself over the fence and landed with a glutinous splat on the other side. "Ah . . . now, it's a bit deeper than I thought."

The others clambered over one by one and joined him, Sal last, muttering under her breath with each sinking step through the foul-smelling mud. By the failing light of dusk they could see that the pigs in the field seemed to be congregated in a far corner—feeding time, presumably. Or perhaps it was some porcine social event going on.

"Which direction, Bob?"

Bob pointed a finger toward a space between two long, low pig huts.

Liam led the way, squelching, until they hit some drier, firmer ground.

"I am detecting particles," said Bob.

"She's probing for us," said Liam. "Hurry! She needs to know we're here!" He sprinted forward into the gloom toward the space between the huts. Finally there, he jumped up and down and flapped his arms. "This it?" he called back to Bob. "Am I in the right place?"

"Affirmative."

"What on earth is the fool doing now?" asked Lincoln, shaking his foot free of slop.

"Motion," said Sal. "He's trying to register on their density probe."

They joined him between the huts a moment later as the last rays of the sun's waning light faded beyond a horizon of gently rolling hills.

"Hey! Yoo-hoo! We're here, Maddy!" Liam hopped around excitedly. "Come get us!"

Bob cocked an eyebrow. "You are aware she cannot hear us, Liam?"

"I know; I'm just . . ." He grinned sheepishly. "I'm just ready to go home, is all."

Lincoln sat down on the edge of a water trough, undid the laces of his boots, and took them off. He picked up one and began shaking out the gunk that had gotten inside it. "So, we shall be returning to the year 1831?"

Sal nodded. "Taking you back home, Mr. Lincoln."

"I see," he grunted. There seemed to be a shade of disappointment in that. "It will be an odd thing, returning to New Orleans. Returning to work as a flatboat crewman."

She picked up his other boot and with a stalk of hay began digging at and flicking out the mud. "But that's not what you're going back to, is it?" She offered him a friendly smile. "Not anymore, right?"

He looked up at her. "You are talking about this destiny you say I have?"

"Yes."

"I was a poorly educated woodsman with no money before this . . . this misadventure. When I return, I shall still be a poorly educated woodsman with no money, but one who now smells of pigs."

"No"—she grasped his hand—"no, Abraham; you have seen what I have seen. Right?"

Their eyes met for a moment.

"This is all wrong," she whispered. "This world and . . . and those poor creatures, intelligent creatures, treated like objects, machines, tools. Your country, fighting itself for over a century? For what? For other countries' goals? You—*you* are the reason all of this has happened."

"And only I can change that?"

She nodded.

"What am I," he sighed, "but a penniless vagrant? How am I to find my way from *that* to president?"

"You managed to do it," said Sal. She frowned. "Or *will* manage to do it. After all, you are very stubborn, aren't you?"

"And quite rude, so you are," added Liam. "That's always a help."

"And," she said, squeezing his hand, "you know what the right thing to do is. The right course to take with your life; no one normally has the luxury of knowing which way their life *should* go."

"You have acquired privileged knowledge of your future," said Bob. "This is a tactical advantage that you will be able to use to—" He stopped talking and held an arm out. "Liam, you should step back. I am detecting particles."

Liam sat down on the trough beside Lincoln. "And not everyone gets to see all that you've seen, Mr. Lincoln, and still go back to live their lives." He shrugged sadly. "Sal and I don't have that."

She nodded. "This is what we do now. This is what we'll *always* do, I suppose."

In front of them, a portion of the darkening blue sky, dotted with the first early stars, began to tremble and squirm.

"Oh, look," said Liam, brightening, "here's our lift home."

Chapter 86

2001, New York

Maddy could hear that the fighting had resumed; this time the crack of gunfire was much closer.

She was worried that something, or someone, would damage the antenna array above. It would take just one stray bullet, that's all, *just one*—then this effort, this sacrifice, the bodies she'd seen lying side by side like sardines in a can, all of this would have been for nothing.

Becks was outside fighting alongside the men. She could imagine the support unit felt quite at home, content, covered in blood and mud, doing what she did best.

She heard someone bellowing orders—Devereau, she guessed—followed by the deep, throbbing *burr* of one of their heavy machine guns. She turned to look out the entrance. She could see boots and drooping belts of ammo beneath the shutter: the machine-gun teams emerging from the fort and redeploying along the horseshoe.

It's getting real close.

Both colonels had insisted the three machine-gun teams would be the last line of defense, that the fort would be their Alamo.

Clearly these plans were now fluid.

Oh crud . . . Get a move on, Liam, for God's—

> **Maddy?**

"What?"

> **The density probe has just picked up some movement.**

"Repetitive—not random?"

> **Correct.**

"Grab an image!"

> **Affirmative.**

She saw the light-meter on the displacement machine flicker as energy was discharged and dispatched along the heavy-duty insulated cables up through the jagged hole in the roof to be targeted by the array outside: space-time being discreetly teased open, an unfathomable spatial dimension punctured with a pin hole.

She watched the monitor on the right as a blocky, low-resolution image appeared. The same image as last time: a muddy field, some sort of low hut, a darkening sky. But this time she could just about make out the blurred silhouette of some stupid fool caught doing jumping jacks in midair.

Liam.

"That's them!"

> **Affirmative. Activate the window?**

"Yes! Do it!"

The light-meter, bars of LEDs like a graphic equalizer, fluttered excitedly with the sudden expenditure of accrued energy. Two remote windows were being opened simultaneously: one a hundred miles south of here, another in New Orleans in 1831. That was going to drain their charge completely. The rest was going to be up to them.

She listened to the displacement machine's circuitry hum and saw the green charge display silently wink to red, one light after the other.

And the rest was going to be just waiting. And hoping.

Yet again.

Another of the leviathans slowly collapsed to its knees, the thick armor plating over its chest misshapen and twisted under the battering of a steady stream of high-caliber rounds. Blood was pouring down its front from numerous ragged wounds. It flailed its huge, blade-tipped fists pitifully, angrily.

"Got us another one!" roared Sergeant Freeman, punching the air.

"Come along! Here! This is good. Right here!" Wainwright waved the other machine-gun teams into position against the trench wall. "Fire on those eugenics! Upper chest area—there are gaps in the armor! Do you see?"

Devereau was studying the slope below, illuminated now by crimson flares being shot into the night sky from the British landing rafts that bathed the whole mud-churned and cratered battlefield with a flickering bloodred light. Beyond the six remaining eugenics clanking slowly uphill, bearing the weight of their armor—several tons of it each, he guessed—British soldiers were amassing in the borderline. He could see officers moving among knots of men, poised to step over the top and support the eugenics with a charge. And there, sitting astride sandbags, a British officer calmly observing the events taking place uphill from him through a pair of binoculars.

Chapter 87

2001, New York

Becks watched the brutal ruthlessness of the enormous beasts with detached fascination. Their arms swung tirelessly, scooping out of the trench and into the air bloody parts of men and divots of dirt alike. There were no moments of hesitation, no doubts, no confusion of morals or ethics; as much thought was devoted to the process of killing as an electric band saw might give to a plank of wood.

She could identify with that: a world simplified down to the barest essentials, to mission parameters. And that's where her empathy, her sense of kindred-spirit, with these curious monsters ended. She had her *own* mission parameters to fulfil.

One of the machine-gun teams lay in tatters just beyond the nearest leviathan, the thick barrel of the gun still smoking and aimed skyward on its tripod legs. She ducked down low, scrambling over the writhing bodies of the wounded, between the giant's thick legs. At the same time that the genic sensed her movement below it, she reached the machine gun, pulled it off its mount, and swung its barrel up.

With no armor plating beneath it, the monster's soft flesh was exposed to the high-caliber bullets. The genic flailed, enraged, the feed-pipe that protruded from its small face whipping from side to side. She heard a deep moan coming from its chest, its throat; a cry of rage and agony locked behind a sealed mouth.

The gun's stuttering fire ceased as the overheated barrel choked on the ammunition belt. But Becks had done enough damage. Blood rained down on her as the leviathan took several staggering steps, finally flopping onto the downhill side of the trench. She felt the ground vibrate with the impact of several tons of iron and flesh.

As another fresh flare exploded above the trench, bathing them in an artificial crimson dawn, she took in the state of the battle with one snapshot blink of her eyes. Two eugenics remained, the last of the twelve, wreaking havoc farther along the horseshoe. She saw arcs of dirt and glistening wet viscera spinning up into the night sky. The few men not maimed, dismembered, or dying were beginning to break and scramble out of the trench and run for their lives. And two hundred yards downhill from all this, the British soldiers were now advancing in three ordered and steady lines on the rebel position.

Colonel Devereau was up and out of the trench, attempting to rally the fleeing men. Wainwright was busy firing a rifle down the slope at the advancing British.

Their bunker of sandbags and piled dirt—the fort—their last line of defense outside the archway, was sitting empty. A mistake.

"Devereau!" she yelled. Her voice—she chose a slightly deeper register than a normal human female, almost masculine, though not quite— carried across the noise of battle. Devereau looked her way. She pointed toward the fort and tossed the machine gun out of the trench at him.

"You must redeploy this in your final defensive position!" she bellowed.

Devereau nodded. A last stand from the fort; perhaps that was already his intention with the half a dozen men he'd managed to stop from fleeing. The heavy machine gun and the several yards of belted ammunition lying on the ground would help.

There were a few other men still alive in the trench, gathered around another silently smoking machine gun, trapped between the two leviathans, cowering from the sweeping arc of gore-covered spikes and the growling, spinning blade of the motorized circular saw.

[Assessment: heavy machine gun—tactical value = HIGH]

Acquiring a second heavy machine gun to fire out from their final position was worth the calculated risk. She pulled a saber from the hands of one of the dead. She vaguely recognized the man's dark face; the gray flecks of coiled hair, the beard. His glazed, sightless eyes gave her permission to take the sword and make good use of it.

Becks pulled herself up out of the trench and began to make her way toward the last two leviathans, skipping along the stacked sandbags like they were stepping stones across a babbling brook. Finally within striking range of the nearest of them, she pulled the saber back and, using every fiber of muscle in her body to execute a low, sweeping, roundhouse blow, swung the blade around to bite through the coarse skin and the muscle and bone of the creature's shin, as thick as a human torso. The bare foot, a yard long with flexing toes as big as apples, flopped into the trench like a side of beef. The genic, missing everything beneath the cut, lost its balance and fell over, the thick plates of iron armor scraping and clanking as if a dump truck had emptied a full load of salvaged metal onto a scrapheap.

Already exhausted under the burden of its armor, the leviathan struggled like an elephant with a broken spine, desperate to right itself once more.

Becks appeared over its small head, looking down at the two beady black eyes, moist and glistening in the light of the descending flare above them. Its eyes, without whites, looked as expressionless and void as the eyes of some giant insect—and yet, the glistening moisture around them . . .

Tears?

She processed that observation in the few nanoseconds of a single computer cycle. Tears of anger, she wondered—or was it *relief*?

The spider-eyes slowly closed as if knowing, *accepting* even, what was coming. She thrust the sword down into the soft flesh beneath its feed-pipe, and the genic lurched, giant ribbons of muscle all over its body flexing one last time, then sagged down dead.

She turned in time to see the last leviathan collapse, finally sufficiently weakened from the blood loss of dozens of gunshot wounds.

Again, she eye-snapped an overall appraisal of the battlefield. The British were only a hundred yards downhill. She estimated no more than a couple dozen men left alive in the horseshoe trench, some of them firing sporadic, opportunistic shots down the slope, most frozen in shock.

And behind them, out of the trench, rushing past the still-chugging tank, fifty or sixty men fleeing, limping, scrambling for the distant safety of the ruins of Brooklyn. Devereau seemed to have gathered a kernel of a dozen men, most looking too badly wounded to make a run for it anyway. They had the heavy machine gun, at least.

Wainwright joined her and nodded at Devereau, herding the men toward the fort. "We must buy them enough time to set up the gun in there!" he cried.

"Affirmative." She pointed to the few other men along the trench. "I will delay the enemy. Order these men to redeploy in the fort and the archway. This must be protected for as long as possible!"

Wainwright nodded. He picked his way along the trench and started tapping the remaining few men on their shoulders, gesturing toward the archway.

Becks stepped forward, reached down for the still-smoking heavy machine gun, and hefted it casually up off its tripod to rest it on her hip.

She aimed it downhill at the British, now only fifty yards from her, and began to fire.

Chapter 88

1831, New Orleans

Abraham Lincoln stared at the street in front of him. Early evening. It was busy with dockworkers finishing for the day and trappers and traders stowing bales of beaver pelts and Indian-friendly trade goods aboard their flatboats. Raucous voices exchanged greetings and farewells in pidgin English and French, the street clattering with the sound of metal-rimmed cartwheels and shoed horses.

Across the rutted dirt thoroughfare was the inn, the very same inn where he'd squandered the last of his money drowning his woes in the bottom of a glass. It seemed to him to be more than a lifetime ago that he'd staggered out onto that porch.

"I am where you first found me," he said.

Sal nodded. "And this is where you have to be."

"New Orleans." He smiled. "It seems to me to be a much smaller place now."

"I guess so." She looked up at him. "After all that you and I have seen, I suppose it must."

He laughed. "And what *incredible* things. I shall, I'm sure, be the victim of sleepless nights until my dying day."

"It must remain secret. All of it," she said. "You know you can't tell anyone about any of those things that happened, right?"

"If I am to one day be president, young lady, I would be a fool to talk of flying ships and animals that speak and machines that transport a person through time. I would never stand a chance of being elected. The people in this new country would not tolerate a deranged lunatic for a leader."

Sal shrugged. "Well . . ."

Lincoln scratched at his dark beard. "But I shall caution any man who will listen to me that this country will not prosper unless it is a united one." He looked at her. "That, at least, is something I am permitted to say?"

She looked at Liam. He was talking quietly with Bob a few yards away. She turned back to Lincoln and shrugged. "I think you were always destined to say something like that anyway. At least now you know *why* America can't go splitting itself into pieces, right?"

"I believe there is much in this time to put right," muttered Lincoln, "before we can be the nation our forefathers dreamed of."

It was then that they heard the first sound of thundering hooves approaching. Cries of warning rang out from farther up the street, followed by the crash of barrels of whiskey and ale rolling off the back of the runaway cart and thudding onto the hard dirt strip, and the spray of yeast-excited foam through split kegs.

Liam and Bob joined them, standing back from the thoroughfare as the cart approached. Six wild-eyed horses careened in a manic zigzag toward them. They roared past, shedding more barrels from the back of the cart in their wake. They watched the horses and cart weave crazily through the congestion ahead until, finally, the cart rocked over and shed the last of its load. One of the cartwheels collapsed under the burden. Splinters of wood and shattered spokes arced into the sky; a twisted metal wheel rim spun off on its own tangent. They watched the cart being dragged along on its axle by the panicked horses until it was lost from sight.

"The cart that killed you," said Liam. He cheerfully patted Lincoln's back. "Well, not this time, anyway, Mr. Lincoln."

Bob nudged Liam. "Remember the secondary objective," his voice rumbled quietly.

Liam nodded. He offered Lincoln his hand. "Been a pleasure to meet a future president, so it has."

Lincoln nodded and grasped his hand firmly. "I shall . . . endeavor to do my best, Mr. O'Connor. Good Lord willing."

"You'll do your country proud." Liam smiled. "I know you will."

Bob leaned forward. "Secondary objective?"

"Right, right." He looked at Sal. "We have to go. Something else we need to take a look at." He shook Lincoln's hand and smiled. "Look after yourself, Mr. Lincoln."

"I will that, sir."

"Sal"—Liam gestured up the street—"we need to check that out, *right now.*"

She nodded. "I'll catch up."

After a final farewell from Liam and a terse nod from Bob, they strode swiftly up Powder Street, following the trail of chaos to find its cause.

Sal and Lincoln looked at each other. "It's been a funny week, hasn't it?" she said.

The tall young man's laugh sounded like a growl. "To say the very least, ma'am."

"You know . . . ," she started, knowing it was wrong to say much more to him—certainly wrong to warn him of the grim fate that awaited him only days after the North's victory. "Never mind."

Lincoln raised an eyebrow, curious. "What? You were about to tell me something."

She shrugged. "Just that . . . that your face ends up on the five-dollar bill." She smiled. "How cool is that?"

"The five-dollar bill?" Lincoln looked surprised. "They'll have paper money of such value?" He shook his head, amused by that.

Sal glanced up the street. She could still see Liam and Bob. She didn't want to lose them, though. "I have to go now," she said. "So should you."

"Indeed."

She reached out, grasped his hand, and squeezed. "Good luck. I'll look you up on the Internet and read all about you when we get back home."

She offered him a little wave, then turned away and jogged up the street toward the other two. Lincoln watched the three of them go until they finally disappeared among the growing crowd of people filling the street, curious to see what had caused all the commotion.

Well then, Mr. Lincoln, what now?

He looked down at his mud-spattered trousers and flapping boots, and decided that whatever his future—his destiny—was, he stood a better chance of realizing it if he did *not* smell of pig manure. He strode toward the quayside and the sedate Mississippi River, a glistening, mirror-smooth surface that reflected the setting sun.

Chapter 89

2001, New York

Captain McManus walked slowly down the curved trench, stepping as often as he could on dirt and not on the limbs, torsos, or faces of dead men. These chaps, even though mutineers, deserved better.

He held the white flag above him, a handkerchief tied to the tip of a bayonet. In his other hand he carried a lantern to be sure that the men huddled inside the bunker at the end of this long, curved trench could clearly see his approach.

The bunker was little more than a mound of piled dirt and sandbags over a framework of wooden beams, something clearly erected in haste. It stood in the looming shadow of an enormous bridge support, alongside something else, another hump, like an Eskimo's igloo but made of shoddy bricks instead of blocks of ice.

Why here? Why a last stand out here in this godforsaken wasteland? It would have made far more sense to set up a defensive position in among the ruins of the factory buildings on the far side. Fighting passage by passage, room by room, his men would have taken heavy losses to reclaim the ruins from them.

Instead they chose this open ground? It made no sense.

He stepped past a thick cluster of bodies, many of them British. He stopped for a moment to study the body in the middle.

A woman.

He shook his head. Through his binoculars he had seen her earlier. The young woman had held the entire regiment at bay for the better part of five minutes. Handling an Armitage & Burton Gatling gun on her own. Firing from her hip, no less. Firing until the thing had eventually overheated and jammed, then fighting with her bare hands until, finally, she too had gone down.

Good God.

He wanted to crouch down and get a closer look at her. That could wait. A matter to resolve first.

"I'm approaching under a white flag!" he called out. "You chaps in the bunker, can you see it?"

"Stop right where you are!" a voice replied. "We can hear you well enough from there!"

McManus nodded and planted the bayonet in the dirt beside him, then placed the lantern beside it. "Right, then. I'm sure you know why I'm here. Shall we call it a day, gentlemen?"

🕐

Devereau turned to Wainwright. He was slumped on the dirt floor between two other wounded men, clutching his side. A shot had winged him as he'd tried to provide some covering fire for Becks. One side of his gray tunic was black with blood.

"They're asking for terms, James."

Wainwright laughed wearily. "Tell him we're not in the mood to take prisoners."

Devereau grinned. He was about to turn around and repeat that for the British officer's benefit, but he caught sight of the silhouette of Maddy, crouching in the entrance to the archway. The faint glow of light coming from the row of computer monitors spilled across the concrete floor, littered with the wounded and dying.

She glanced to her left at the British officer, thirty or forty feet along the trench, then quickly scooted across the gap between the archway and the low entrance to the fort. She crouched to scramble inside and joined Devereau, looking out through the firing slit at the British officer and his white flag.

"You should surrender," she whispered. "It's done!"

He looked at her. "Your machine? It has returned this Lincoln to his correct time?"

"Yes!"

"There's really no need for any more bloodshed tonight!" called out the British officer.

"And when will this reality change?" whispered Devereau.

Maddy shook her head. "Soon. I can't say exactly when, but soon."

"Do you have wounded men in there?" said the officer. "I can assure you, your wounded will be taken care of! Your enlisted men, junior officers, NCOs . . . all will be treated humanely as prisoners of war. You have my word!"

"For God's sake, what are you waiting for?" asked Maddy.

Wainwright moaned softly. "William . . . we should let our boys go."

Devereau cupped his hands around his mouth. "Will the Confederate men be treated the same as the Northerners?"

A pause. "I offer you my guarantee: none of the enlisted men—no junior officer—will face a court-martial. They will *all* be treated as prisoners of war!"

Devereau turned to Wainwright. "You hear that?"

Wainwright nodded and smiled. "Then it seems just you and I will face the firing squad."

"That's better than we'd expected." He nodded, accepting that gratefully.

"But . . ." Maddy looked at both men, from one to the other. "But that'll take days or weeks, right? A hearing? A court-martial? That stuff takes time to organize. Look, the new reality is coming, I *promise* you. It could come any time now. In five minutes, five hours . . ."

The soldiers in the small machine-gun nest looked on in confusion at the exchange.

"Or, perhaps, *never*?" Devereau shrugged. "That is a possibility, isn't it?"

She shook her head. "No—I promise you, this will all change!"

"Come along, gentlemen!" called the officer. "I'll offer these terms one last time!"

"Surrender!" she pleaded. "Please—just do it. Surrender! It's okay now, things will be fixed, I promise you!"

"Let me ask you something, Miss Carter."

"What?"

"If I had died in this fight, would this new reality still create a new me?"

"Yes, of course!"

Devereau glanced at Wainwright; both men shared a smile, a silent agreement. He turned back to the firing slit, cupping his hands again.

"All right. You have it. My men are coming out. We are surrendering!"

Chapter 90

2001, New York

Dammit!

Maddy glanced back over her shoulder at the hump of the archway.
I need to be there! I need to be back inside!

She trudged along the bottom of the muddy trench with the other soldiers, her arms on her head as instructed. British soldiers stood on top of the sandbags to either side, looking down at the defeated defenders. She kept her eyes on the back of the man in front of her, not daring to look up at them, not daring to meet any soldier's eyes. She did, though, glance once more over her shoulder.

I need to be inside when it comes!

If and when the time wave came, if she was out here beyond the protective reach of the archway's force field, she would almost certainly find herself . . . *merged* with the re-formed ground or welded in a ghastly and fatal way to a brick wall or a trash can or something.

Thirty yards along the trench, where some sandbags had collapsed into a small mound, was an easy step up and out. Physicians and orderlies from the British regiment offered a helping hand to the wounded, and Maddy accepted a hand that pulled her up over the lip of the trench. She muttered a muted "thank you."

Above her the sky was filled with the giant airships she'd seen earlier today offloading troops over Manhattan. Their spotlights flickered across the wasteland, bathing it in dancing pools of brilliant white.

She could hear the rhythmic chugging of that old, rusted tank *still* going, reliable old thing, faintly coughing and spluttering across the deathly still battlefield.

The cratered wasteland was littered with bodies, many of them stirring slightly. The orderlies were moving among them, looking for survivors to treat. Every now and then a solitary shot rang out; battlefield mercy for those too far gone to save.

She hadn't seen Becks for a while. Not since the density probe had picked up on Liam and the others. How long ago was that? Ten minutes? Half an hour? She realized her mind was dulled with shock, her perception rendered unreliable. As if she was stepping sluggishly through a dream.

"Becks," she whispered to herself. Saying her name aloud triggered something she never thought she'd actually feel for a support unit. Concern. She had always laughed at Liam's fondness for both Bob and Becks . . . and now here she was. Actually worried she might come across her corpse on the ground.

Captain McManus regarded both American officers, slumped beside each other against the earthworks and sandbags inside their bunker. He squatted just outside the low entrance.

He nodded slowly. "All right, then," he said finally. "If that's what you gentlemen want."

The Northern colonel offered him a grim smile. "It is, captain."

McManus pursed his lips, nodded once more, and stood up. They were quite right, of course. Neither of these two gentlemen were going to escape a firing squad for this act of rebellion. Examples would need to be made of them. This way, the way they wanted it, would save them the misery of a few hours of waiting, agonizing, and the dishonor of being stripped of their rank insignia before being marched out into a courtyard at daybreak.

He saluted them both, then stepped away from the entrance to give them a little privacy. He turned to look at the soft, pale-blue light leaking out from beneath a half-lowered metal shutter to his right. He wandered over toward the shutter door and ducked down to look under it.

He could see a cracked and uneven concrete floor littered with badly wounded men. Many of them, it was obvious, weren't going to survive long. A lot of them were already dead. He decided he should get an orderly in here as soon as there was a spare one.

He sighed at the appalling mess and ruin battle made of such frail things as human bodies. Particularly the damage done by those experimentals. The injuries spread out in front of him were quite horrific. He was actually relieved the entire test batch of twelve had been killed. They'd looked like they were out of control. His own men would most probably have had to gun them down.

His eyes drifted up to the source of the soft blue light. A row of rectangular screens that flickered with blurred images and bright colors.

He squinted curiously.

Now, what the devil is all this?

🕐

"So"—Devereau flipped open his holster and pulled out his revolver—"that went well, I thought."

Wainwright chuckled, burbling blood from his mouth. "Indeed."

He watched Devereau absently stroke the handle of his gun. "Tell me, William, do you really believe there are other *possible* worlds out there? Or have we been led on a wild-goose chase by this girl?"

"I can't say. You saw as much as I. All those pictures . . ." He smiled. "I think I do believe her."

Wainwright nodded. "It would be something if it's true."

"Maybe you and I will wake up in that world?"

"After we leave this one? Perhaps." Wainwright reached for his own sidearm, groaning with the effort of moving. He laughed.

"What's so amusing?"

"Five years ago, I think it was . . . one of my sharpshooters called in to say he had a clear shot on you. Had a clear head-shot and wanted to take it."

"And what did you tell him?"

"I said no, obviously."

"Why?"

Wainwright wheezed a sigh. "Wish I could remember. I . . . don't know. It felt unsporting."

Devereau shook his head. "Unsporting?" He laughed at that.

Wainwright joined him, groaning with pain as his body shook. "You know, Bill, I have a feeling our broadcast signal, our call-to-arms to the other regiments, was blocked somehow." He winced, then took a deep breath. "I do believe our mutiny would have spread if only word had gotten out. I can't believe it was only us—only our two regiments—who wanted an end to this ridiculous war."

"Nor can I." Devereau buttoned up his collar carefully and straightened the peak of his forage cap. "Ah, well . . . we gave it a darned good try, did we not, Colonel Wainwright?"

"That we most certainly did."

Chapter 91

1831, New Orleans

The trail of chaos led a quarter of a mile up Powder Street, with battered and split wooden kegs spilling liquor onto the ground and penniless vagrants clustered around each one, eagerly filling their cupped hands.

They passed a woman with a broken leg howling for a physician, an overturned baker's wagon that had spilled loaves across the track, and a trapper's bundle of beaver pelts and deer hides scattered across the way, ruined and torn by hooves and wheel rims, before finally finding themselves looking into the gated courtyard and stables of the brewery.

"The cart came from here," said Bob.

A crowd of brewery workers had been drawn out to the courtyard from inside the two-story brick building and had gathered around something. They could see workers turning away ashen-faced, doubling over and retching. A woman screamed and ran from the courtyard past them.

"Excuse me? Miss? What just happened?" asked Sal.

The woman shook her head and babbled something about "the devil's work." Then she was gone, hurrying away as fast as her feet could carry her.

"This is the contamination event," said Bob.

"Aye. Come on, we should go have a look."

They crossed the courtyard, heading toward brick stables. They could hear the distressed horses inside, the clattering of restless hooves, snorting and lowing behind the stable doors.

The crowd of people had gathered around something on the ground. Among the babble of frightened voices, Sal could hear snippets of whispered words:

". . . witchcraft . . ."

". . . work of the devil . . ."

A man with a loud voice was busy castigating the brewery workers about the evils of drink . . . and that *this* was God's warning to them, *this* was God's punishment.

They pushed their way through the crowd to get a better look; not difficult, since the gathered crowd was reluctant to draw any closer to what it was on the ground that had first attracted them.

Finally Liam, Bob, and Sal could see for themselves what it was—the cause of the disturbance, the cause of the runaway brewery cart. Liam stopped where he stood, queasily covering his mouth with a hand.

"Jay-zus-Mary-'n'-Joseph . . ."

Sal took another step closer and squatted down beside it.

"Don't touch it!" screamed one of the crowd of people. "It is a creation of evil! A demon!"

She ignored the warning and reached one hand out carefully toward it—the monstrosity. If she could believe in things supernatural, then "a creation of evil" sounded like the perfect description for this pitiful ruin of a creature lying on the ground amid its own blood, steaming offal, and twisted sinews.

"Is that a *person* or something?" she whispered.

It was as if a slaughterhouse had dumped a day's worth of refuse into the courtyard. Amid the glistening, bloody gristle she could see the hindquarters of a horse, still flexing weakly, kicking spasmodically. But worse still—the stuff that she was sure would fuel a lifetime of future nightmares for her—the blood-spattered head, shoulders, and upper torso of a man welded to the flanks of the same horse, or perhaps it was a second horse. As if God had decided to construct a centaur, and in a moment of frustration and irritation had given up and hurled the failed mess down to Earth.

Her hand gently touched the dead man's head.

His eyes flickered open.

Chapter 92

2001, New York

Maddy and the other prisoners were seated on the ground fifty yards away from the horseshoe trench, guarded by only a handful of British soldiers. It was clear to them that there was no fight left in the small, ragged huddle of Union and Confederate soldiers.

She watched them processing the bodies of their own dead first. Checking for signs of life before pulling regimental collar tags from their necks and carrying the corpses down to the river's edge, where they were being loaded aboard the landing rafts.

She noticed nearby a particularly dense mound of bodies with crimson tunics, busy with orderlies squatting among them feeling for signs of life. And there—as a body was disentangled and carried away by a couple of them—she saw Becks.

She got to her feet and started to pick her way across the battlefield.

"Hey! Miss! Sit back down!" shouted one of the British soldiers guarding them.

Maddy ignored him, drawn to the pale face staring up through its nest of bodies. She pushed her way past an orderly and squatted down on the ground beside Becks's cold, still face. Dark blood caked the right side of her head, trickling down from a gunshot wound to her temple.

"Becks?"

The orderly, a young man with freckles and jutting ears, looked at her sympathetically. "You know this woman, miss?"

She said nothing.

"By the look of it, whoever she was, she put up one hell of a fight."

His voice sounded far away. She barely heard it. Instead she gazed curiously at the spatter of a tear on Becks's left cheek, for a moment wondering whether a support unit could actually cry. Then she realized the tear was one of her own. She wiped her eyes beneath her glasses and sniffed.

I'm crying for a freakin' meat robot. She scowled, angry with herself for being so pathetic and weak. *It's a machine—a tool. That's all, you moron!*

"Becks?" she whispered. "Becks . . . I'm so sorry."

Sorry for what? Sorry that I never bothered to get to know you like Liam did?

Maybe. Maybe she was sorry about that. But then again, wasn't it better not to treat these things as human, as *friends*?

"I'm sorry," she whispered again, stroking one of Becks's dark eyebrows. The one she'd made a habit of raising every time she had a question she wanted to ask.

She was vaguely aware that the orderly was remonstrating with the guard who'd come after her, to give her some space, that she wasn't about to run anywhere, to escape.

"Becks, I'm sorry that we never just . . . you know, never just *talked*."

Like Liam did, like Sal did. Both of them were quite comfortable with the idea of hanging out with Bob and Becks as if they were just like them—human.

She traced a line down Becks's cold cheek. Dead. Beneath the bodies lying across her were injuries Maddy didn't need to see—didn't *want* to see. Obviously too much catastrophic damage at once for her body's self-repair system to cope with.

The raised voices in the background were a million miles away.

Muted. Some other place. This moment was hers alone. A chance to say good-bye. Her own time and space.

But the voices increased in number, and raised in pitch and urgency. Voices all around her.

"Good God!"

"What is THAT?"

She looked up at the orderly and the soldier, both now silently staring into the sky. The other orderlies stared too, gazing open-mouthed at the night sky above Manhattan. Curious, she turned to look in the same direction.

And saw a horizon that twisted, undulated—a liquid reality of impossible possibilities.

The time wave.

Everyone—every soldier, every officer, every prisoner—was now frozen in place, looking at the roiling sky, bewildered, transfixed, frightened, and dumb-struck.

Maddy—you've got to move! You have to be inside! *You have to be protected!*

She looked toward the archway. She could see orderlies stepping out of the shutter entrance to see what the commotion was all about.

Run! Maddy, run!

She was about to get to her feet when she suddenly realized she couldn't leave Becks's body there. That message, locked away inside the support unit's mind . . . There was a way to retrieve it and the memories that would preserve who she was. A way to do it; Liam once did it for Bob.

Her chip.

She looked around and found a rifle with a bayonet fixed to the end. She reached for it, expecting the guard or the orderly to bark a warning at her. Instead their eyes and everyone else's were locked on the sky.

Panicking, fumbling, she tried to get the bayonet off, tugging at it with a growing frustration.

How does it come off?

She tried twisting it, and the mount unlocked with a dull scrape. She wrenched it off the barrel, dropped the rifle, and looked down at Becks.

Do it!

She would have to thrust the tip of the blade into her skull and dig around inside for that silicon wafer, not much bigger than a memory stick, a sim card.

She pressed the bayonet's tip against Becks's forehead, just above her brow line.

Do it! Now!

She tried to push down, but couldn't.

If you can't do it, then take the head—take the whole head!

She moved the tip down to the soft flesh beneath Becks's jawline.

Cut! Cut! CUT!

"I can't . . . I can't!" she whimpered under her breath. She looked up. The time wave had rolled in from the Atlantic and was now twisting and contorting Manhattan, like clay on a potter's wheel, molded and remolded, like molten wax in a lava lamp.

And now it was crossing the East River.

Maddy closed her eyes, gritted her teeth, and did what needed to be done. Then she got to her feet and started to run. Her feet slapped the ground noisily as she pushed her way past men staring listlessly up at the approaching wave.

So quiet!

So perfectly still.

Just the sound of her panting breath, her feet on rubble, and a deep, deep rumble that sounded like the Earth itself was preparing to split open.

She dropped down into the trench, slipping and falling in the blood-soaked dirt onto her hands and knees. She scrambled to her feet, pounding down the last dozen yards past a young British officer who barely seemed to notice her, his eyes glazed with wonder.

"Good Lord, so beautiful," she heard him whisper as she brushed past him, then past a pair of orderlies carrying a loaded stretcher between them, standing, like everyone else, utterly motionless, transfixed, their task for the moment completely forgotten.

Maddy reached the crumbling archway and cast a quick glance back at the sky. The front of the reality wave was across the East River, taking the armada of landing rafts and turning them into a million different things: Viking longboats, Roman triremes, Spanish galleons, sea monsters . . .

She ducked under the shutter. The floor was still littered with bodies, a few of them barely alive and moaning deliriously from gunshot and bayonet wounds. Hands reached up to her, pleading for water.

Across the archway she could see the computer system was still up and running, that tank—that beautiful old reliable Mark IV rust bucket from a previous era of this endless war—was *still* running, still feeding the archway with power.

"Bob!" she screamed as she picked her way over the splayed limbs of the dead and wounded men.

She saw a dialog box appear on one of the screens, although she was too far away to read the response.

"It's Maddy!" she gasped. "Activate a field! NOW!"

She collapsed against the computer desk, gasping, wheezing, close enough now to read computer-Bob's response.

> **Information: insufficient power to include the entire field office.**

"Then . . . then do it just around me!"

The cursor began to shift across the dialog box.

> **Caution: there will be obstructions within the radius.**

Of course, the archway had dropped by several feet. "In the air, Bob. A portal midair! I need to jump into it as the time wave arrives!"

For a full second, perhaps two, the cursor blinked without a response, then finally began to jitter to the right.

> Affirmative.

Outside the shutter she saw loose dirt being scooped up by the air pressure just ahead of the wave. She reached out for Becks's head, cradling it in her arms. Maddy climbed up onto the computer desk. "NOW, BOB . . . DO IT NOW!"

In front of her a portal shimmered open, suspended three feet above the floor. There was no knowing if that was high enough, whether she was going to emerge into the unchanged archway lodged up to her waist in the concrete floor. Undoubtedly fatal. Horribly fatal.

She jumped for the portal just as the wave arrived and tore the archway into a million different possibilities.

Chapter 93

11:31 p.m. September 11, 2001

Police Precinct 5, New York

The police sergeant lurched violently in his seat, the squad car rocking on its suspension.

"Whoa! Hey! Bill! You nearly spilled my darned coffee!"

Sergeant Bill Devereau turned to look at his partner. "Huh? Sorry. Must've nodded off for a moment there."

His partner nodded. "You can say that again; you were muttering like some juiced-up crackpot."

Bill Devereau shook his head, wide awake now. "I . . . Crazy, I just had the weirdest dream."

"Yeah?"

Devereau narrowed his eyes, stroked his chin thoughtfully. The memory of it was fading fast, blurring; the definition of it vanishing, like cream stirred into coffee. "A war . . . or somethin' like that. New York was all just ruins . . . like, I don't know, like Stalingrad."

Sergeant Wainwright sighed. "I'm sure you ain't the only one havin' nightmares, buddy." Their precinct had lost some men earlier today when the Twin Towers came down, good men. And they'd be lucky to find anything of them in those smoldering ruins. They were going to be burying empty coffins for weeks to come.

Devereau stopped stroking his clean-shaven chin. "It was weird . . . In the dream, I had a beard, would you believe? Big bushy thing."

Sergeant Wainwright turned to look at him. "A *beard?*" His face cracked with a cavalier grin. "Beard? You kiddin' me? You'd look a total idiot with a beard."

Devereau nodded. He checked his face in the side mirror. Yes, he probably would.

"You're gettin' too old to be on the beat, Bill, seriously, if you got to be catchin' sleep like that on duty."

"Was up late last night, that's all."

Wainwright nodded thoughtfully. His gaze rested on a bundle of newspapers dropped off outside a corner store. Tomorrow's papers. Tomorrow's headlines.

There was only going to be one story in every paper tomorrow.

"Guess there's gonna be a lot more sleepless nights for everyone."

Devereau nodded. The dream had gone, blown away like morning mist along a riverbank. All that was left was a nagging sense of trouble lying ahead. A storm coming.

"You got that right, partner."

Chapter 94

2001, New York

Maddy opened her eyes. She must have blacked out for a moment there. Her glasses were askew on her forehead and there was drool on her chin. She adjusted her spectacles, wiped her mouth, and sat back down in the office chair.

"Sheesh," she whispered.

The corner of the desk she'd been standing on was still covered in a thick coat of rust-colored brick dust, but it ended suddenly, sharply. A curve of dust, then none. Beyond that, her desk looked normal. Dr Pepper cans, pizza boxes, scraps of paper and pens, candy wrappers and magazines. But none of the debris that had cascaded from above during the artillery bombardment earlier.

She looked down at the floor, now no longer a crazy paving of fractured concrete, littered with the broken bodies of dead and dying men. It was restored to how it had been a week ago. The archway was no longer a crumbling ruin.

She looked down at Becks's still face, her hair matted with drying blood. There was a job still to do, but not now. Not yet. She gently placed the head on the cabinet beside the desk, turning Becks's pale face away from her so she didn't have to look at it.

The monitors were all on, several of them playing live news feeds.

"Bob? You there?"

> **Hello, Maddy. Just a moment . . .**

She heard the hard drives on each of the linked PCs begin to whir and click.

> **I am detecting multiple timeline continuity errors.**

Yes, of course; Bob had extended a preservation field around her alone. The rest of the archway, including computer-Bob, had not experienced the trauma of the last week.

> **Information: external date is registering as September 18. We appear to be seven days outside our time envelope.**

"Right," she said. "Yeah, a bunch of stuff happened, Bob. You recall Abraham Lincoln running out on us?"

> **Of course. According to my internal clock, we sent Liam and the others to retrieve Abraham Lincoln two hours and sixteen minutes ago.**

"Yeah . . . well, you're now out of sync. We need to reset the archway field and go back to our normal deployment time. You need to do that now."

> **Affirmative, Maddy.**

"Then we've got to open a window for Liam and the others to bring them back."

> **I do not have a reliable time stamp for them. My last data stamp is . . .**

"They're not down in Quantico, Virginia, anymore. We'll need to use the data stamp before that one. You should still have that sitting in your memory cache."

> **New Orleans, 1831? This does not make sense. How did they get there?**

She smiled wearily at the webcam. "It's a long story, Bob. I'll talk you through it later, okay?"

Chapter 95

1831, New Orleans

The man's bloodshot eyes focused on Sal.

"My . . . my God! It's . . . it's . . . *you!*" he gasped. His mouth flapped open and closed. A thick rivulet of blood oozed out from between his lips.

Sal leaned close to him, grabbed one of his hands, and held it tightly. "You . . . you're going to be fine!"

No, he wasn't. Of course he wasn't. She looked at the awful inside-out remains of two horses and one man. One of the horses was still kicking; the other was already dead. And so would this poor man be, very soon. He was so very far from fine.

Bob knelt down beside her. "This was a density overlap error. This man will not last . . ."

"I know!" she hissed, glaring at Bob to shut up.

Liam's face looked gray, like he was going to throw up, but he somehow managed to hold the churning contents of his guts in check as he hunkered down beside them. "I've seen this before. It's a time-window mistake!" He shot a glance at the dying man's face. "Maybe he's a . . ." His eyes widened. "Jay-zus! Maybe he's a TimeRider? One of us?"

"Listen . . . listen to me," gasped the man as he struggled to find his breath between mouthfuls of blood. "I . . . I . . . tried . . . warn . . . you . . ."

"Warn us? What do you mean?"

"P-Pandora . . . it . . . was me . . ."

Pandora? Liam looked at Sal, then back at the man. "You left that note? In San Francisco? That was you?"

"Y-yes . . . I . . . my name . . . J-Joseph . . ." The man's eyes started to glaze, to roll. He was going into shock.

"What is Pandora?" asked Sal.

His mouth gushed blood. His hand began to spasm, flexing and squeezing hers.

"Pandora! What is it? Please!"

His gaze focused back on her. ". . . W-Waldstein . . . the . . . end . . . he knows . . ." His voice was little more than a rustling whisper.

Sal leaned in closer till she could feel the tickle of his dying breath against her cheek. "You'll be okay," she whispered to him pointlessly, squeezing his hand again, as if that was going to help. "You're going to be fine."

"*You! . . . S-Sal . . . Saleena . . .*"

She looked at him, their faces inches apart, intimately close. "You *know* me?" she whispered.

"*You . . . y-you are . . .*" His hand began to spasm again, gripping hers tightly, painfully. ". . . *are . . . n-not . . . who you th-think . . . y-you . . . are . . .*"

His eyes rolled until only the whites were showing, his hand crushing hers. Then suddenly he released her hand with a lurch. Out of his nose came a fine spray of blood.

"I . . . know . . . a-about . . . the . . . th-the . . ." His mouth gushed blood onto his chin. He sighed. Not so much a death rattle, just a simple and protracted sigh of relief at escaping the agony.

But it came with words, two very faint words. She could have sworn that's what she heard him mutter as the poor man died; it wasn't her mishearing him. It wasn't a random contortion of mouth and tongue. She was almost certain she'd heard two distinct words. A message for her alone.

The bear.

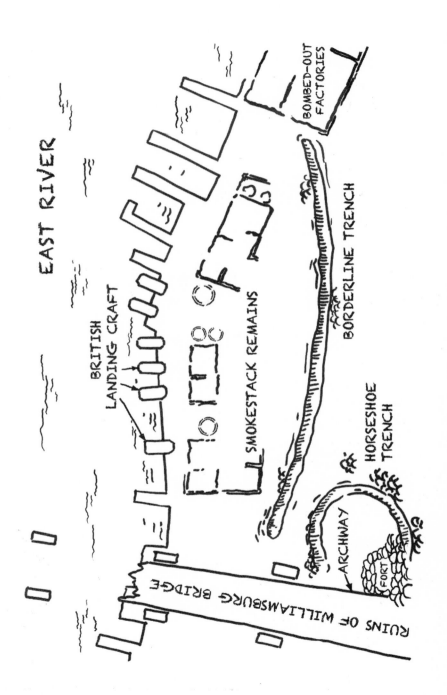

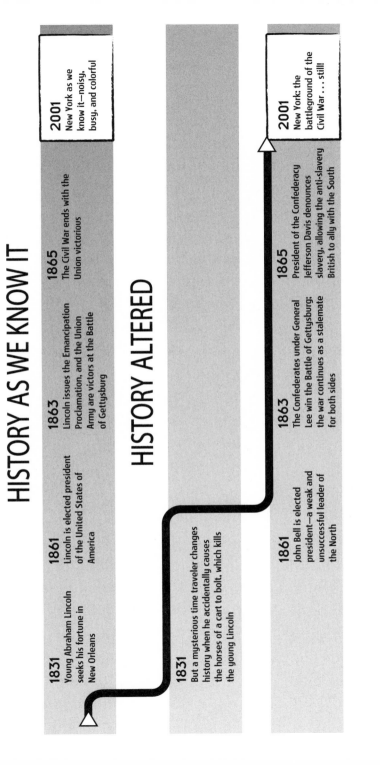

HISTORY AS WE KNOW IT

1831
Young Abraham Lincoln seeks his fortune in New Orleans

1861
Lincoln is elected president of the United States of America

1863
Lincoln issues the Emancipation Proclamation, and the Union Army are victors at the Battle of Gettysburg

1865
The Civil War ends with the Union victorious

2001
New York as we know it—noisy, busy, and colorful

HISTORY ALTERED

1831
But a mysterious time traveler changes history when he accidentally causes the horses of a cart to bolt, which kills the young Lincoln

1861
John Bell is elected president—a weak and unsuccessful leader of the North

1863
The Confederates under General Lee win the Battle of Gettysburg; the war continues as a stalemate for both sides

1865
President of the Confederacy Jefferson Davis denounces slavery, allowing the anti-slavery British to ally with the South

2001
New York: the battleground of the Civil War . . . still!